HIDDEN IN SNOW

ALSO BY VIVECA STEN

Still Waters

Closed Circles

Guiltless

Tonight You're Dead

In the Heat of the Moment

In Harm's Way

In the Shadow of Power

In the Name of Truth

In Bad Company

Buried in Secret

HIDDEN IN SNOW

TRANSLATED BY
MARLAINE DELARGY

VIVECA STEN

This is a work of fiction. Names, characters, organizations, places, events, and incidents are either products of the author's imagination or are used fictitiously. Any resemblance to actual persons, living or dead, or actual events is purely coincidental.

Previously published as *Offermakaren* by Forum in Sweden in 2020. Translated from Swedish by Marlaine Delargy. First published in English by Amazon Crossing in 2022.

Published by Amazon Crossing, Seattle

www.apub.com

ISBN-13: 9781542037495 (paperback)
ISBN-13: 9781542037501 (digital)

Cover design by Ploy Siripant

Cover images: © Cosmic_Design / Shutterstock; © Szabo Ervin-Edward / EyeEm / Getty; © Kitthanes / Shutterstock

Printed in the United States of America

To Nicole and Pierre
Without you we would never have ended up in Åre!

PROLOGUE

The snow forms a hard, solid covering as Sebbe Granlund turns into the staff parking lot at VM6, the chairlift at the midpoint of the ski resort where he is working for the season.

The temperature is minus twenty, but it feels colder. The treetops are thick with rime frost, and the mountain known as Åreskutan is barely visible through the snow mist. The harsh electric lighting creates a black-and-white landscape with long shadows against white snow.

The winter season in Åre has just begun.

It is only a short walk to VM6, but the warmth of the car is gone in seconds. The air freezes the hairs in Sebbe's nostrils as he unlocks the station. It is just after nine; the resort opens at nine thirty, so everything must be ready by then. As usual the lifts started operating at the beginning of December, but there are few skiers on the slopes so far.

He presses the green button to set the machinery in motion. A loud noise slices through the silence; then VM6 begins to move. It is one of the older lifts, with seating for six people at a time. One chair after another passes before his eyes.

Sebbe takes out his phone to check Snapchat. The seats are covered in snow from last night's fall; he ought to go out and clear them, but the cold keeps him indoors. It won't really matter for the first half hour. The sun won't rise until nine forty-five, and there won't be many people around before then.

He glances up. A shadow has caught his eye, an unexpected figure on one of the chairs, almost as if someone has come down from the top.

He cranes his neck, tries to see, but it is still dark out there.

The chair is approaching the boarding platform. It does actually look as if a person is half-lying at the far corner, but there's something weird; the posture is contorted, slumped.

The dark silhouette doesn't move, even though the chair has almost arrived.

Sebbe acts instinctively, presses the stop button, and hurries outside. The chair comes to a sudden halt, dangling a few yards away. The abrupt movement makes the figure slide down even farther.

Sebbe remains where he is as his brain processes what he is seeing.

It looks like a mannequin—and yet it doesn't. The human features are there, but every sign of life has been obliterated. The eyebrows and eyelashes are thick with snow crystals, the face has stiffened in an icy grimace.

The skin is blue white, the lips shrunken from the cold.

The chair sways, and the body slides off and lands on the snow at Sebbe's feet.

He stares openmouthed at the frozen corpse.

"Shit," he whispers. "Not you."

MONDAY, DECEMBER 9, 2019

1

Hanna Ahlander fails to avoid the slush on the sidewalks as she plods from the subway to her apartment in Solna. The dampness finds its way through her sneakers to her socks, and she swears quietly.

The strap of her purse is cutting into her shoulder, and she swaps it to the other side.

She is trying to stop thinking about this afternoon's conversation with her boss, Manfred Lidwall, but his words continue to echo inside her head: *difficulty in working with others, insubordination, lack of discipline.*

Manfred can't stand her. He made that very clear.

If she doesn't voluntarily seek a post elsewhere, he will do everything in his power to terminate her employment. She has been sent home to think things over. He doesn't want to see her until January, after the Christmas and New Year holidays.

Her throat constricts at the thought of leaving her job with the Stockholm City Police, a job she loves in spite of everything that's happened.

The rain-soaked asphalt seems to absorb the light; the world is painted in shades of black and gray. In a couple of weeks, it will be Christmas Eve. There should be snow and freezing temperatures, soft snowflakes gently drifting down.

Instead, the sky is weeping.

Not that it matters; Christmas atmosphere is the last thing on Hanna's mind. She hasn't given a thought to gingerbread cookies or Advent candle bridges over the past few weeks.

The heavy raindrops plaster her hair to her forehead. She bends her neck to try to protect her face, but the rain drips down the collar of her jacket, making her shiver. She increases her speed, desperate to get home, and wobbles as she takes a misstep. She's spent the last few hours knocking back vodka shots in a bar, with the same thoughts whirling around in her mind.

Why couldn't she keep her mouth shut? Why couldn't she do what everyone else did, and toe the line?

She should have dropped the issue of the botched investigation, poor Josefin, who was beaten to death by her husband.

Who just happened to be a police officer.

If only she'd turned a blind eye, minded her own business, she wouldn't have ended up in this situation.

Her colleagues have closed ranks, and she is no longer a part of the community.

She is almost there. She shares a three-room apartment on the fourth floor with Christian. The light is on in the window, which means he's home.

She longs for him to hold her in his arms but doesn't know if she can tell him what's happened—that the City Police and her boss want to be rid of her at any price.

How is she ever going to be able to say it out loud?

Shame floods her body.

Manfred said he couldn't even bear to look at her.

There is a great deal she hasn't been able to share with Christian over the past six months, and she still can't face it. Not tonight. Some other time.

Right now she just wants to get indoors, pour herself another vodka, and sink into a hot bath. Shut out the world, stop thinking about everything that's gone wrong.

Her eyes fill with tears, but she angrily blinks them away.

She's going to pretend that things are perfectly normal, at least for a little while until she's managed to digest the situation. She can consider the future tomorrow.

With a sigh she pushes open the main door and stomps up the stairs. She hesitates outside her front door, quickly wipes away a tear that has broken through.

Puts her key in the lock and turns it.

2

When Hanna walks in, the first thing she sees is a wheeled black suitcase in the hallway.

She drops her purse on the rug, takes off her wet jacket. She wonders if they have visitors, then realizes it's Christian's, the one he uses when he's going away for a few days.

"Hello?" she calls out. "I'm home."

She kicks off her shoes, moves into the open-plan kitchen and living room.

Every surface is spotlessly clean as usual. They have just finished renovating, and Christian has put a lot of time and effort into the choice of colors and materials. It was his idea; Hanna could easily have lived with the previous decor for a while longer. However, she has to admit that it looks good. The gray granite countertops blend perfectly with the kitchen cupboards, and the eye-wateringly expensive wooden flooring provides that extra-special finish.

Except that it feels as if her realtor partner has styled their home ready for one of his viewings.

Hanna searches for something to drink. They don't have any vodka, but she finds a bottle of red wine and pours herself a large glass. The tears are scalding her throat, but she swallows and swallows. She doesn't want to cry anymore about her job. She can't change anything now.

Then she catches sight of her reflection in the glass door of the oven. She looks terrible. Her wet hair lies completely flat against her head; her mascara has run. She doesn't normally wear much makeup, but today she wishes she'd at least used a little gloss on her cracked lips.

She takes her wine into the bathroom and rinses her face, then turns the faucet to run herself a hot bath. A deep breath, then she heads into the bedroom to say hi to Christian.

All she wants is a hug.

He is lying on top of the lilac bedspread, fully dressed, busy with his phone. He looks up as she walks in. Even though they've been together for five years, she can't help reacting to how good looking he is.

She feels a tingle in her belly, as she always does.

Christian fulfills every masculine norm. He has a strong jawline, thick light-brown hair, and a boyish charm that he knows exactly how to exploit. He is a top-class realtor who loves his job and revels in every new sale. His long-term ambition is to open his own office. His lust for life is infectious; when Hanna is with him, the future always seems brighter.

Although she doesn't want to talk about her terrible day, she longs for the solace he can give her. She would love to crawl into his arms and sob, feel the warmth of his body, hear him say that everything will sort itself out.

That everything is going to be all right.

Christian gets up from the bed, still holding his phone, but he doesn't touch her. He doesn't hug her, doesn't reach out to stroke her cheek. Nor does he say a word about her red, swollen eyes, or the fact that she looks like a drowned rat.

Something is wrong.

She realizes that Christian is nervous. His jaw is clenched; he seems to be steeling himself before he opens his mouth.

"We need to talk," he says bluntly. "This isn't working."

It takes a moment for the words to sink in. She doesn't understand. She tries to interpret his expression, but his face is closed, impossible to read.

"What do you mean?"

"Us. It's not working."

There isn't a sensible thought in her head. Her tongue feels thick and shapeless; it refuses to cooperate. She stares blankly at the glass in her hand as panic fills her chest like a sticky dough.

"What are you saying?" she eventually manages to stammer.

"You and I—we can't be together anymore."

"Why not?"

Stupid question.

"Because you're impossible to live with," he informs her.

Hanna is still struggling to take in what he's saying. She has to concede that things haven't been great between them for a while, but all couples fight sometimes, that's just the way it is. Surely, he must realize that?

Admittedly the demands of her work have taken their toll recently, and she knows she's brought home her anger at the unfair way she's been treated. She's been sullen and contrary in the evenings, or simply gone straight to bed, but she hasn't been that bad.

Or has she?

"I'm impossible to live with?"

"We make each other unhappy," he says, walking past her into the hallway.

Hanna stumbles after him.

"This is for the best," he goes on. His voice is weary, but at least that's better than the icy sharpness at the beginning of the conversation. He reaches for his suitcase. Suddenly Hanna hates that case.

"What do you mean, 'this is for the best'?" It's as if she's incapable of formulating a sentence independently. Is she really standing here saying this crap?

Christian sighs. "All we do these days is argue. We haven't had sex in months. There's no point in going on. You're unhappy, and so am I.

We'll be better off without each other. It's sad, but that's just the way it is."

Hanna is overwhelmed by a strong sense of unreality. The apartment looks the same as it always does. Their outdoor clothes are hanging up; their shoes are in a neat line. Just as they were when she left home this morning, before everything came crashing down at work.

Is her personal life being smashed to pieces as well? On the same day?

She watches Christian run his hand through his light-brown hair, the hair she's stroked so many times after they've made love. They belong together—he must know that.

If he leaves, she has no one. She'll be all alone.

Don't go! she screams inside her head. *I can change!*

"I love you," she whispers.

Christian freezes. A shadow passes over his face, an almost microscopic movement, but Hanna sees it. She understands, even though he hasn't said a word.

"You've met someone else."

He hesitates, then nods without looking at her.

He might as well have punched her in the face. During their five years together, Christian has often said that anything can be forgiven—except infidelity. They would never be the kind of people who went behind each other's backs. Their love was strong and honest.

"I'm going to stay with a friend for a week—that will give you time to move out," he says, pulling up the handle of the case.

"Move out?"

Hanna slowly looks around, her gaze falling on the attractive leather sofa that Christian acquired from a show home. The velvet-covered armchair by the wide window with a view over Lake Råsunda. That's where she likes to sit, with her legs tucked underneath her. The wool throw draped over the armrest was a Christmas present.

She blinks, realizing that Christian owns the apartment. He'd just bought it when they met. She'd been living in a scruffy sublet studio apartment ever since she qualified as a police officer.

The choice to move in with him had been very simple.

This has been *their* home, but now he's intending to throw her out on the street, just like that.

Hanna straightens her shoulders.

"You can't do that to me." Her voice trembles; she hates the fact that she can't control herself. "Where am I going to live?"

At least Christian has the decency to look embarrassed.

"Don't make a fuss, Hanna," he mutters. "This is my apartment. I'm the one who's paid almost all the bills."

Yes, because you were earning a lot more than me. She knows it would be pointless to say anything, even though they both agreed on the arrangement.

A police officer's salary doesn't go far.

Christian's phone rings. He rejects the call, but not before Hanna sees the name on the display.

Valérie. She doesn't know anyone called Valérie. What kind of a name is that anyway?

Suddenly she understands.

"You're going to her place. That's where you'll be staying while I move out."

Christian hesitates just a fraction too long. "Yes," he snaps, turning away.

Turning his back on her. It's the final straw.

Christian is leaving, before they've finished talking. He's just dropped a bombshell, and he can't spare five fucking minutes to listen to her.

"Look at me!" Hanna yells. "The least you can do is look at me!"

When Christian turns to face her, Hanna's right arm moves of its own accord.

She throws the red wine right in his face. A cascade of blood-red droplets runs down his forehead and cheeks. Big, dark patches appear on his clothes.

She gazes at him openmouthed. What has she done?

"You're fucking crazy!" Christian snarls. He wipes his face with one hand, which doesn't help at all.

"Make sure you're out by Sunday at the latest. I want the keys back!"

He slams the door, and Hanna drops to her knees. She's so shocked that she can't even cry. She's finding it hard to breathe.

Then she hears water splashing as the bathtub overflows.

TUESDAY, DECEMBER 10

3

As Detective Inspector Daniel Lindskog gets ready for the day, both Ida and the baby are fast asleep beneath the mint-green coverlet on the double bed. Ida is lying on her side, her long, tousled dark hair spread across the pillow. Alice is on her back, snoring gently with her mouth half-open.

Daniel pauses by the bed, gazing down at his daughter. His love for Alice has opened a space in his heart that he hadn't even known existed. When he touches her tiny fingers, something happens. He becomes a different person, a man who would face any peril for his child.

For thirty-six years he has lived without understanding what unconditional love means. There is nothing he wouldn't do for her.

However, he can't deny that her deep slumber this morning is a relief. Alice has woken many times during the night, and even though they live in a spacious three-room apartment, it isn't possible to escape the despairing crying of a baby with colic. After the first few months, they are all exhausted.

Daniel feels as if he has grit in his eyes and lead in his body as he steps into the shower. The scalding-hot water isn't enough to get him moving; only the shock of turning the faucet to ice cold wakes him completely.

He pulls on his jeans, opts for a thick dark-blue woolen sweater over his shirt. As an inspector he isn't required to wear a uniform, but warm clothes are a must at this time of year. You never know when you might need to go out in the cold. That's why he's had a beard for several years; it protects his chin. It also looks pretty good, although he would never say so out loud.

He skips breakfast to avoid disturbing Alice. He can get a cup of coffee at the police station, and he's never been particularly hungry in the mornings. It's better to let Alice sleep, because that means Ida can sleep too. She's still finding the readjustment difficult. Becoming a mother was overwhelming, and she's a little insecure in the role. The fact that Daniel isn't around during the day doesn't help matters.

Even though they never used to fight, they've recently had several massive arguments about seemingly minor issues.

Daniel often feels guilty. They hadn't planned on having a baby, at least not when they'd been together for only six months. When Alice came along, they'd barely gotten to know each other properly.

Ida had talked about having an abortion, but Daniel had been filled with joy at the thought of being a father. This was what he'd wanted for years.

Ida is ten years younger. She was a cool ski instructor, at a completely different stage of her life, when they met one Saturday at Bygget, Åre's most popular night club. The memory still makes him go weak at the knees. She was so full of life, so pretty that he couldn't take his eyes off her. They danced all night, and he went home with her.

It was love at first sight, stronger than anything he'd ever experienced before.

Ida livened him up, talked him into crazy excursions on the snowmobile, mountain picnics. She grew up in the area and knew virtually everyone. He'd already lived in Åre for two years, but with Ida he finally started to feel at home.

A child with her would be fantastic—that was his first reaction when she showed him the pregnancy test with the two blue lines. He wanted it so much and painted their future together in bright colors.

Now, when she is permanently exhausted, the guilt comes creeping in.

Daniel silently slips out of the apartment and runs down the stairs to the main door. He scrapes the car windows meticulously; the windshield is covered in a thick layer of ice crystals, and there's a good four inches of snow on the roof. He spends almost ten minutes clearing it all off, working up a sweat.

He actually lives within walking distance of the station—in the summer it takes no more than fifteen minutes to get there, but today the temperature is minus nineteen degrees Celsius, and it's pitch dark. He's due to meet a colleague, Anton Lundgren, shortly; they are going to the Duved school to give a talk. Providing information and encouraging cooperation is an important part of police work in rural areas. He often works with Anton, a cheerful and straightforward local guy. When Daniel hurries home to Ida and Alice in the evening, Anton usually heads off for one of his countless weight-training sessions.

Åre has a small police station, with only three investigators and seven uniformed officers when the place is fully staffed. Daniel officially belongs to Östersund, but spends three days a week in Åre.

He starts the car, wondering if there's been much activity in the village overnight. Probably not. Thursday will be worse, the night before the feast of Saint Lucia, when the schoolkids like to party. As long as it's only the local teenagers, there isn't usually a problem; it's the tourists who keep his colleagues busy. The season hasn't started yet, but soon there will be fistfights in bars, disputes in the cab line, people looking for trouble in the hamburger restaurant. Drunk-driving offenses and the odd theft of ski equipment are also part of everyday life.

The snow is falling heavily as Daniel drives off shortly before seven, heading for Åre police station.

4

A persistent, penetrating sound wakes Hanna.

It takes a few seconds for her to realize that the terrible noise is coming from her phone. She gropes for it on her bedside table, the effort making flashes of white lightning shoot through her brain.

Vague recollections of large quantities of alcohol come to mind, crawling into bed with a bottle and drinking until she passed out.

At long last the noise stops, and Hanna sinks back on the pillows. Then it starts again. She reaches out and finally manages to locate the phone.

"Hello," she croaks.

"Did I wake you?" her big sister, Lydia, asks cheerfully.

Lydia is ten years older. She is a successful lawyer with two unbelievably well-mannered children and is happily married to an equally successful man who works in finance and earns a disgusting amount of money.

Hanna loves her sister but can't really handle being around her. Lydia is a constant reminder of everything their parents expected from their children. The kind of expectations that Hanna will never be able to live up to.

"Do you know what time it is?" Lydia goes on. She gets up early every morning in her great big house on the island of Lidingö. Hanna peers at the display. Eleven o'clock. It doesn't matter. She has no job to go to.

Christian has left her.

The shock hits her again, and her stomach contracts.

Everything hurts.

"I'm coming down with something," she manages to say.

It's true—she *is* sick, in a way. There's a huge, aching void where her heart ought to be.

She can't suppress a sob.

Lydia might be energetic and successful, but she is neither deaf nor insensitive. She immediately realizes that something is wrong.

"What's happened?"

"Nothing."

Hanna hadn't intended to tell anyone. She's used to standing on her own two feet, and in any case her situation is nothing compared to the abused and vulnerable women she meets in the course of her work.

But she's so upset. She feels wretched, as if she's a complete failure. If she tells her sister the truth, it will make it real.

"What's happened?" Lydia says again.

Hanna bursts into tears.

"Hanna?"

"Christian's left me," she manages eventually. "And I've lost my job. My boss yelled at me yesterday, told me to find something else to do."

It all comes pouring out. Snot is dripping onto the pale-blue duvet cover. She screws up her eyes, but the tears keep falling.

"I have to move out of the apartment by Sunday."

She tries to dry her eyes with a corner of the bedsheet, but it doesn't help much.

Lydia inhales sharply. "Where's Christian?"

"With his new girlfriend. Valérie."

For once, even Lydia is lost for words.

"Wow," she says at last. "Bastard."

Hanna cries even harder.

"It'll sort itself out," Lydia reassures her after a little while. Her voice has softened; she sounds more like the big sister who read to Hanna when they were children and less like the powerful woman who is interviewed in business magazines. "You'll be okay, sweetheart. I know you will," she adds.

"What am I going to do?" Hanna whispers. "How am I going to earn a living?"

There is a knock on the door at the other end of the line, and a deep male voice murmurs a few words.

"Sorry, I have a meeting," Lydia informs Hanna. The usual efficient, slightly stressed tone is back. "I'll call you later. Let me give the matter some thought."

"Don't tell Mom," Hanna begs. "Promise."

The roles in their family were carved out long ago. Lydia is the hardworking, successful daughter that her parents boast about to their friends in Spain, while Hanna is the late arrival they prefer not to mention. She has always disappointed them. Her bohemian lifestyle and her eventual choice of career made her ultrabourgeois mother and father choke on their red wine.

The only thing her mother really approved of was Hanna's relationship with Christian.

And now it's over.

Hanna puts down her phone and pulls the covers over her head. Christian's betrayal is incomprehensible. How can he do this to her? After five years together?

The knowledge that he's staying with his new girlfriend right now makes it even worse. Yesterday Hanna and Christian woke up in the same bed. Now he's gone for good.

Plus she has nowhere to live. Stockholm's housing market is a jungle. There are no rental properties available, only apartments to buy that cost millions. Money she doesn't have, and never will have.

She can't borrow from her parents. The very thought of calling them and telling them what's happened is unbearable.

They call her "our little mistake." She's never been able to do anything right.

She couldn't hold on to Christian, and at the age of thirty-four, she can't afford a place of her own.

What is she going to do? Where is she going to go?

5

Lydia calls an hour later, just as she promised.

Hanna is still in bed. She's finally stopped crying and is staring apathetically at the ceiling. She ought to have a shower, take a painkiller for her headache, try to eat something.

She is incapable of moving a muscle.

"Okay, so this is what we're going to do," Lydia says gently, as if she were talking to a child. "You go to our house in Åre and rest for a few weeks."

"Åre?" Hanna mumbles.

She and her sister spent every winter break there with their parents, but Hanna hasn't been back since she left high school, even though she's always loved skiing.

Certain memories still hurt.

Lydia continues briskly: "Meanwhile I'll look into your legal position in relation to the apartment. Christian can't just throw you out—I won't allow it. There's a government document on cohabitees and their joint homes. I'm also going to have a word with your employer."

Lydia makes everything sound so simple.

"We were up in Åre last weekend, but we're off on that cruise I mentioned on the twenty-sixth. The house will be empty until at least the end of January."

Lydia and her husband, Richard, built a large house outside Åre a couple of years ago, in an area known as Sadeln. Hanna has never been there, but Lydia has proudly shown her pictures of the elegant decor. The sofa alone probably cost more than Hanna earns in three months.

"It'll be perfect," Lydia says firmly.

Hanna doubts that, but she has no other options. She has nowhere to go, and no job. Nor does she have very much money.

"I've booked you a plane ticket."

Lydia doesn't wait for Hanna's response.

"The flight leaves at three thirty this afternoon. You also have a seat on the transfer bus from Östersund Airport, which stops in Åre Björnen. It's a ten-minute walk from there to the house, or you can take a cab."

Her sister's dynamism makes Hanna feel even more helpless. How can she go away when she can't even bring herself to have a shower and get dressed, let alone get on a plane to Åre?

She doesn't even have the energy to be grateful. It's an effort just to hold on to her phone; her hand is trembling, even though she is lying down.

"Speaking of which, a cab will pick you up at a quarter to two. You're already checked in."

"I can't afford a cab to Arlanda," Hanna objects.

Lydia is like a steamroller once she gets moving. Her attitude—that everything is fixable—is overwhelming. It's as if she has a mental list and simply ticks off one point after another. As if *doing* something always helps.

"It's prepaid, don't worry about that." She gives a little sigh of satisfaction. "So there you go—the situation is under control."

Nothing is under control, but Hanna has neither the strength nor the ability to explain why. Nor is she capable of resisting Lydia.

"Thank you," she whispers wearily.

"There's plenty of food in the freezer, help yourself to whatever you want. You're welcome to use our ski equipment too—we've got so much spare gear that we could open our own rental shop." Lydia gives a little laugh at her own joke. "Call me when you get there so that I know you're okay. I have to go—I'm meeting an important client at his office, and I can't be late. Christmas—everything has to be ready before the holiday. You know how it is."

They end the call, and Hanna tries to digest what's just happened.

Lydia is sending her to Åre to lick her wounds. It's all organized—Hanna just has to get dressed and pack a bag. The cab will be here soon.

Åre.

She sees Åreskutan before her, as clearly as if she were standing at the foot of the majestic mountain. Lydia hadn't considered building her dream holiday home anywhere but the mountains of Jämtland. Hanna has always loved the place as well, but it reminds her too much of her childhood, particularly the years when she was alone with her parents after Lydia left home.

Now she has no choice. If she doesn't go to Åre, she has nowhere to go. She doesn't want to call her friends and ask for help; they're all busy with their own lives, especially just before Christmas. She is too embarrassed; she can't cope with explaining what's gone on.

She curls up in the fetal position. Her intense longing for Christian makes her feel like she's falling apart.

Waking up with him in the mornings. The security of living with another person.

Being part of a couple.

She can still smell him on the pillow next to her.

If only she could turn back time, make everything all right again.

6

The door of the room where Amanda Halvorssen is due to have her review session with the class adviser, Lasse Sandahl, is closed. Lasse is the head of economics at Jämtland High School, where Amanda is in her final year.

He must be delayed; they were supposed to meet at four. She hopes he won't be long. The school is in Järpen, and the bus home to Åre leaves at twenty to five.

Amanda turned eighteen in September, so there is no requirement to have a parent present. It's the first time, and it feels good. Mom is hard work, with her constant comments on Amanda's progress. She pokes her nose into most things, always wanting to know where Amanda's going, who she's hanging out with. It's as if she can't understand that her daughter has come of age and is able to make her own decisions.

That's why Amanda hasn't told her about Viktor.

She knows exactly what her mother would say if she found out about Amanda's new boyfriend. Viktor, with his bad reputation, definitely wouldn't be appreciated at home.

Amanda sits down on a bench by the wall in the white-painted corridor and takes out her phone. She checks her appearance in the blank screen. Her newly dyed, shoulder-length black hair looks good. As always she has used plenty of black eyeliner and a dark-red lipstick that she bought a few days ago; it was a bit too expensive, but she doesn't care.

She opens Snapchat and idly scrolls through. Ebba, her best friend, has sent several snaps and a message, even though they saw each other less than a quarter of an hour ago.

Where the hell is Lasse?

She is alone in the corridor; the majority of the almost four hundred students have left for the day. Amanda is hungry and wants to go home. Plus she's freezing; it's cold indoors at this time of year. When the temperature drops below minus twenty, it's hard to keep the large school building warm.

She hears footsteps on the stairs; then Lasse appears. He wears jeans and a sweatshirt, even though he's at least thirty-five.

"Sorry I'm late," he says breathlessly. "I got stuck in the principal's office."

"No problem," Amanda mutters.

Lasse unlocks the door and leads the way into the room with moss-green curtains. There is a round table in the center, surrounded by three chairs upholstered in black. Amanda sits down opposite Lasse, not too close.

"So, Amanda," he begins. "How do you think things have gone this semester? You'll be taking your final exams in the spring—soon you won't have to put up with me and the other teachers every day."

He gives her an exaggerated smile, and once again Amanda is struck by how yellow his teeth are. She smiles back to keep him in a good mood.

"Okay, I guess," she replies with a shrug.

Her grades are all right; she can't be bothered to study in the evenings, although she knows she should.

Lasse rummages around in his shabby briefcase and pulls out a sheaf of papers.

"How do you think you did in the national English assessment on Friday?" he asks.

Amanda picks at the dark nail polish that has begun to chip on one thumb. She found it difficult to concentrate on the questions, even though she knew it was important. She'd lain awake for hours the night before, wondering what to do.

Her thoughts tumbled around and around, but she couldn't find an answer. She knows she ought to talk to an adult about what's happened, but it's all so complicated.

"Amanda?" Lasse's voice brings her back to reality.

"Sorry?"

"You've lacked focus recently. Is there anything you'd like to share?"

The irony in the question stuns Amanda.

He is the last person she would confide in.

Before she has time to react, Lasse moves his chair a fraction closer. He reaches out and places his hand over hers.

"I'm here to help."

The hand lingers for a little too long. She feels his sweaty palm on her skin before she pulls away.

"I'm fine," she assures him. "I think I've just been working too many hours instead of studying." She makes a discreet attempt to lean back, increasing the distance between them. "To earn money to buy Christmas presents," she adds.

"I understand," Lasse says, leafing through his notes. "But your absences are also a cause for concern. That's not dope."

Lasse would very much like to be seen as a friend despite his age. He uses expressions that sound stupid coming out of his mouth.

"And I've had a cold," Amanda lies. "One cold after another, in fact. I'm sure things will be better next term."

Lasse goes through what her various teachers have said, while Amanda tries to look as if she's listening, and as if she cares.

At the beginning, when Lasse became their class adviser, she thought he was good looking and cool. A lot of her fellow students liked his slightly flirtatious style, the way he made each person feel kind of special. He wasn't like the other teachers.

She continues to pick at her thumb; there's hardly any polish left now.

Finally, they're done. It's just after four thirty; she's going to have to run to catch the bus.

When they get to their feet, Lasse moves toward her and puts his arm around her shoulders. She can't shake it off without making a big thing of it.

"I hope you'll come to me if you need to talk," he says. "I'd be very disappointed if you didn't."

She can't work out if it's a simple invitation or something else, something that might cost her.

The smell of stale cigarettes and coffee on his breath fills the space between them.

Amanda nods, smiles stiffly, and glances at the door. There are no windows; no one can see in.

She just wants to get away as quickly as possible.

7

It is six fifteen when the airport transfer bus drops off Hanna in the center of Björnen.

In Stockholm the ground was clear; up here it's deepest winter.

Everything is white.

Hanna has traveled to Åre like a zombie, concentrating on putting one foot in front of the other and not saying a word unless it was essential. And yet she feels exhausted, as if she's run a marathon. Her chest aches with sorrow, and she hates herself for making such a mess of her life.

The GPS on her phone leads her away from the compact town center with its apartment buildings, chairlifts, and ski rental shops. She crosses a bridge, passes the cross-country skiing arena, and heads for the new development known as Sadeln.

The snow crunches beneath her feet; otherwise the silence feels somehow unreal. The falling snow muffles any sound, and the world is wrapped in a white blanket. The cold numbs her fingers and toes.

After ten minutes she reaches the entrance to the complex. Slate walls line both sides of the road, and she sees the word *Sadeln* displayed in shining copper letters.

It feels both expensive and inaccessible. As if only those with legitimate business there are welcome; anyone else needn't bother.

She trudges up a steep hill and takes a deep breath when she reaches the top.

It's impressive and so . . . big.

The houses are spread out over wide slopes, the forest seems to go on forever. In spite of the darkness, Hanna can see the modern vernacular architecture, broad turf roofs, generous balconies, and huge picture windows. The plots and buildings are much larger than in Björnen; there is space here, endless views.

Down below, Lake Åre rests in frozen hibernation.

It feels a bit like a ghost town, although it will soon wake up when the season starts in earnest. The silence is almost tangible, the houses dark and empty, with the curtains drawn. The odd Advent candle bridge and the exterior lighting can't chase away the desolation of this place, where there isn't a soul in sight.

Hanna plods on with her backpack and suitcase. Lydia said ten minutes, but she must have been walking for at least fifteen by now. She should have taken a cab, but didn't want to spend any more money than necessary. Not when the future is so uncertain.

When her boss, Manfred Lidwall, called her into his office yesterday and made a point of closing the door, she knew what was coming.

She'd been angry and disappointed for so long, she'd protested and been as obstructive as possible, because no one was doing anything. However, she still didn't want to believe that she was the one who was going to be punished. She'd kept on hoping that someone in the higher echelons would reopen the investigation, make sure their colleague Niklas Konradsson paid for what he'd done. He'd beaten a woman to death. Her name was Josefin, but no one cares about her. They have all closed ranks around Niklas.

And now Hanna was in the firing line, accused of insubordination and a lack of team spirit.

Manfred didn't even ask her to sit down. He simply stood there with a hostile expression on his face, arms folded. His tone was icy when he told her to seek a post away from the City Police; otherwise he would make sure she was relocated to a place where her career would effectively be over.

He brought up several things. How tired he was of her blatant disrespect, the fact that she was *this* close to being charged with professional misconduct. None of her colleagues wanted to work with her any longer. Her outburst the previous week, when she'd accused him of being both incompetent and corrupt, had been the final straw.

Hanna didn't think a superior officer was allowed to express himself as Manfred had done. He probably wouldn't have dared if they hadn't been alone in the room, but with just the two of them there, he allowed himself the luxury of a personal attack.

Hanna tried to tell herself that he was a complete shit, but there was no escaping the sense of shame and embarrassment.

They didn't want her anymore.

She had more or less been kicked out.

She continues along the road, where the snow is hard packed. There are no sidewalks, only piles of snow on either side. She stops to get her bearings, and realizes that Lydia's house must be the one about a hundred yards up ahead.

Her jaw almost drops.

It's enormous, a massive, tall wooden building with two wings. It's at the top of the hill, with no neighbors who can see inside. Colossal, beautifully mullioned windows make the most of the views, while the lighting on the facade itself creates a kind of halo that enhances the impression of exclusivity.

Lydia wasn't joking when she said they'd spared no expense.

Somehow Hanna had imagined an ordinary cabin, but this combination of glass and dark wood has little in common with the norm in the Swedish mountains. It's more reminiscent of a mountain lodge in Aspen, Colorado, or a grand chalet in the Swiss Alps.

In Sweden people are expected to keep a low profile rather than show off their money and possessions, but Lydia's place does exactly the opposite.

The roar of an engine breaks the silence.

Hanna only just spots the beam of the headlights before a dark SUV comes racing around the bend of the narrow road. She vaguely remembers a twenty-miles-per-hour sign back at the entrance, but this vehicle is certainly not sticking to the speed limit.

For a second she stands there, frozen to the spot. The driver is traveling way too fast, the high hood looms up in front of her, ominously close.

It's going to hit her.

Instinct kicks in and she hurls herself at the nearest pile of snow. Fortunately, it is soft enough to give way, and she tumbles off the road in a cloud of snow.

The car sweeps past, only inches away. It's sheer luck that she manages to move her feet before the rear wheels thunder past.

Hanna lies there on her back, her heart pounding. She's afraid to check whether she can move all her limbs; has she escaped uninjured?

Tentatively she sits up. She doesn't seem to have broken anything, although she banged her hip when she threw herself sideways.

She gazes after the SUV, which has already disappeared. The driver must have seen her, yet he didn't stop to check if she was okay.

Idiot.

Was it a man behind the wheel? Hard to say, everything happened so fast. She didn't register either the model or the number plate, just that it was as black as the darkness that now surrounds her once more.

He was definitely crazy; he almost ran her down.

She could have died.

She's so shocked that her immediate impulse is to stay exactly where she is. She could go to sleep here on the ground; at least then she wouldn't have to deal with everything that's happened.

It's all too much. She's covered in snow, and it's even found its way inside her jacket and started melting. She has no feeling in her toes.

Christian would be sorry if she was found here in the morning.

She shakes her head, drags herself to her feet. She brushes off the worst of the snow, picks up her case, and staggers the last few yards up to the house.

The main door is at the back, past the separate ski entrance, presumably to avoid spoiling the view.

She fumbles with the code to the ultramodern lock. She is shivering so violently that she can hardly stand still.

She has never felt so small, so abandoned. The realization that Christian has left her is hammering away in the back of her mind.

At last, she manages to open the door. The smell of the wooden house envelops her immediately, a reminder of something comforting from her childhood, a crackling fire, hot chocolate with whipped cream. Sitting on her big sister's knee while Lydia reads her a story.

The relief of coming into the warmth almost makes her burst into tears.

WEDNESDAY, DECEMBER 11

8

It has turned twelve by the time Hanna gets out of bed and shuffles into the kitchen in her scruffy old pajamas.

There is nothing wrong with Lydia's guest rooms. There are four on the lower ground floor, three with generous double beds. Hanna has chosen the one in the eastern corner, decorated in burnt tones of red, brown, and orange, with an amazing view over the lake.

In spite of the comfortable accommodation, she slept badly, waking several times to find she'd been crying in her sleep.

She pads over to the Nespresso machine and presses the button for extra-strong coffee. In the freezer she finds bread and lots of other food. It is packed with meat, fish, and vegetables; there are even homemade cinnamon buns. The fridge provides marmalade, Kalles caviar, and other spreads with use-by dates well in the future. There is a box of eggs on the top shelf. Of course there are eggs, even though the house was supposed to be empty.

Lydia said the place was well equipped. Hanna has to smile at her super-organized sister.

She makes herself two sandwiches, then flops down at the table and puts on the TV to dispel the silence. She stares out of the floor-to-ceiling windows. The sky is overcast, and snow is falling gently. Up above Renfjället a barely visible corona of light reveals where the sun has hidden itself. Lake Åre lies down in the valley, linking the mountain slopes.

She follows the lake with her gaze until it curves west toward Duved. Beyond the mountains is Norway, less than forty miles away.

She forces down one sandwich and throws the other in the trash. She drinks her coffee, but it does nothing to diminish her headache. The bottle of red wine she'd liberated from Lydia's cellar when she arrived yesterday evening is standing empty on the countertop. Hanna knows enough about wine to make an educated guess at the price; it must have cost at least two hundred kronor.

She makes another cup of coffee, then takes out her phone and starts scrolling through old photographs of Christian. After a while she reaches the ones she took last summer, when they went to visit her parents in Guadalmina in Spain. They've had a house there for decades.

She took a lot of pictures during their stay, mainly on the patio where they would enjoy a drink in the afternoons. Christian wore a white shirt with the sleeves rolled up almost every day. The Mediterranean behind him was as blue as his eyes, and the sun turned his light-brown hair gold.

Dad and Christian played a round of golf every morning, and Hanna suspected that Christian sometimes let him win.

Her parents' obvious delight in their "son-in-law" almost made her ignore the fact that they preferred to ask about him rather than her. None of her previous boyfriends had managed to evoke that satisfied expression on her mother's face.

Nor had she, to be honest.

Christian represents everything that her mother and father adore. He grew up in one of Stockholm's more prestigious suburbs; he has a degree and parents who still live in a beautiful house. The similarities with her own upbringing are ridiculous.

Except that Hanna has never felt at home in that environment. She has always been out of place.

She never fit in, unlike pretty, popular Lydia, who always achieved high grades and had a stream of well-brought-up boyfriends politely calling round to see her.

It wasn't until she met Christian that Hanna felt special. She also loved her parents' reaction when she finally arrived home with a man who met their demands.

It was so nice to be . . . good enough in their eyes. For once.

She sees a hare come hopping across the garden, all by itself. Its clear footprints break the snow cover, its big hind feet perfectly placed in front of the forefeet.

It seems to be as lonely and abandoned as she is.

9

Amanda and Ebba are sitting outside the school, smoking. The sky is gray, and it's freezing cold. Ebba is doing her best to enjoy her cigarette, even though the bench they're sitting on is turning her thighs to lumps of ice.

She feels the nicotine spreading through her body.

The air is filled with featherlight snowflakes.

"It's so fucking wrong," Amanda says after a deep drag. "How the fuck can they do this to someone our age?"

Ebba glances at her friend. This isn't the first time they've talked about it. Amanda has said that she's thinking of exposing the whole story. Telling it like it is so that everyone will know the truth.

Her eyes are burning beneath her red hat, the one that matches the scarves they bought together.

Ebba has never seen Amanda so stressed, which worries her. She realizes it's not right to keep quiet, but she can't help being afraid of the consequences.

What will happen if everything comes out?

"Don't you think you ought to speak to your mother?" she suggests.

"She'd be furious. I know exactly what she'd say."

Amanda throws down the cigarette butt and stamps on it. Hard, so that only brown fragments remain on the snow.

"What about your dad?" Ebba ventures.

Amanda snorts. "You know exactly what he's like. If there's the slightest risk that it might affect his political career, he'll do whatever it takes to keep it quiet."

When Amanda gets wound up, it's hard to reason with her. She has a much more fiery temperament than Ebba; she's always the one who reacts to injustices or contradicts the teachers. Amanda doesn't care what people think. She does things that Ebba would never dare to do, and she's capable of saying just about anything.

Amanda doesn't lie awake at night worrying, as Ebba does.

"They're not going to get away with this," Amanda says, making a sweeping gesture with one hand.

Ebba feels the anger emanating from her friend.

"We need to go in," she says. "We've got math in three minutes."

She jerks her head toward the entrance of the pale-yellow school building. The sign above the door says **JÄMTLANDS GYMNASIUM!** (Jämtland High School!) Ebba has always wondered about that exclamation mark.

She gets to her feet with a hard knot in her stomach. She is concerned about her parents' reaction if they find out what she and Amanda have been up to.

She wishes she'd never gotten involved; she should have said no right from the start.

"What are you going to do?" she asks.

Amanda doesn't answer.

10

The water is at exactly the right temperature as Daniel cautiously lowers Alice into the bath.

She wriggles a little as she always does at first, before she contentedly relaxes, with his left hand supporting her back.

He is on his knees on the white floor, with the pink baby bath placed in the middle of the shower. This is their precious time. He always tries to get home early enough to bathe his daughter.

One of the big advantages of his placement up here is the regular hours. There are few major criminal investigations. He occasionally longs for a faster pace, but he doesn't miss his old job with the narcotics squad in Gothenburg, the dispiriting attempts to deal with far too many parallel cases. The feeling that every crime they solve is immediately followed by two more. The endless gang wars and shootings.

He is from Norrland after all; he grew up in Sundsvall. The atmosphere in Åre is a welcome reminder of his origins. He was lured down south by the big-city vibe of Gothenburg, but he soon realized there was a downside.

He soaps Alice, who gurgles happily. Her soft, fair hair feels like silk against his palm as he rinses her little head. He finishes up by cleaning her navel with the tip of his index finger.

He wishes his mother, Francesca, had gotten the chance to meet Alice. Ten years have passed since the car accident, and he has learned to live with the loss. Before Alice was born, days or even weeks could pass without him thinking about his mother.

Now she is in his thoughts almost every day.

He was only twenty-six when she died. She was still living in Sundsvall, and an ordinary walk to buy some milk became the last thing she ever did. The driver fled from the scene. The case is still unsolved, a wound that won't heal. Daniel had already moved to Gothenburg and traveled home in a daze to organize the funeral.

He didn't bother informing his father. Why should he care that Francesca was dead, since he'd shown virtually no interest in her while she was alive? He'd persuaded her to move to Sweden from Italy, then left after only a few years, when Daniel was little. Francesca was too ashamed to return to Italy as an unmarried mother, so she stayed in Sweden.

Daniel has no relationship with the Italian side of his family, and contact with his Swedish father is minimal. He's married to someone else now and lives in Umeå. He had two more children, a girl and a boy. Daniel has met them only a couple of times during rare visits that gradually petered out altogether when he was about ten years old.

The sense of being let down is still with him, a deep, infected wound. He has always sworn that he will be a different kind of father.

He will never abandon Alice, whatever happens.

Nor will she ever need to be afraid of him, as his own mother was afraid of her father, the bad-tempered grandfather Daniel has never met.

He grew up with stories of his grandfather's outbursts of rage. Francesca used to tell him about how her father would explode, and the rest of the family would have to take cover until he calmed down. Her tone was lighthearted, but it must have been a considerable strain. Growing up with a man who ruled the roost with his temper can't have been much fun.

Daniel has promised himself that he will never take out his own fiery temperament, which he sometimes struggles to control, on Alice.

"How was work today?"

Ida is standing in the doorway, her hair freshly blow dried. She seems happy. Daniel slipped away early and was home by four, which gave her time to have a nap, then put up some Christmas decorations in the kitchen.

She looks like her old self again, the attractive ski instructor he met at Bygget just over a year ago, rather than an exhausted new mom.

He shrugs.

"Okay. We had a couple of online briefings with Umeå. Tomorrow it's Östersund as usual."

Technically speaking he's with the serious-crimes squad in Östersund, but his boss is happy for him to work from Åre three days a week. It means he spends a lot of time in the car, but the arrangement suits him very well. It gives him the chance to put down roots in Åre; this is where he belongs now, with Ida and Alice.

His girls.

He picks up his daughter and wraps her in the big towel Ida is holding.

"How about lasagna for dinner?" he says. "With homemade tomato sauce?"

Daniel enjoys cooking; he's always liked spending time in the kitchen. He often jokes about his Italian heritage, his passion for pasta and Parmesan cheese.

"Sounds good," Ida says with a smile, reaching out to take Alice. "Come to Mommy, sweetheart," she coos.

Daniel gives her a kiss on the forehead.

At this moment, with Alice giving them her best toothless smile, he can hardly remember why there have been so many arguments between them recently.

THURSDAY, DECEMBER 12

11

Amanda is standing in front of the mirror in Ebba's bedroom, trying to make a decision.

Should she wear the ribbed yellow top from H&M or the red one she bought online? It's the evening before Lucia, and red fits better with the Christmas theme, but the yellow one makes her breasts look better.

She examines herself critically from every angle, frowns at her bottom, and eventually settles on yellow.

Ebba is already in the bathroom, doing her makeup. Avicii's last album is playing in the background. A man's voice sings "SOS," and Amanda does a little dance, smiling at her reflection. Not bad. It's party time, and she's really been looking forward to tonight.

She thinks about Viktor, and her smile broadens.

They've been seeing each other for a while, but secretly. He's never going to hit anyone again, especially her. Viktor has been open about his past; he swears the whole thing was an accident, and Amanda believes him.

Plus he's a fantastic kisser; he takes her mind off everything else. She needs him now. She can't keep brooding about what happened last week. She's promised herself that she will let it go, at least for a few hours. She still feels dirty, wishes she'd never accepted the money.

If she could afford it, she'd pay back every single krona.

Her good mood is beginning to fade. Amanda resolutely adjusts her top, chases away the dark thoughts, and joins Ebba in the bathroom.

Her friend is busy applying mascara, with a large gin and tonic next to the washbasin.

Amanda picks up the glass and takes several gulps. The darkness recedes as warmth spreads through her body. *That's better.*

Tonight is all about having fun. She has another drink.

Ebba's parents and her younger brother have gone to a birthday celebration in Stockholm; they're away all weekend. Amanda wonders if they know about the party. Probably not, but that's not her problem.

Ebba nods at the glass. "Leave some for me. The others will be here soon."

They'll all be graduating from high school in the spring; this is their last Lucia Eve together. Amanda is sick and tired of studying, but she likes her friends. They're the ones who've kept her in school this year; without them she would almost certainly have dropped out, in spite of her mother's insistence that she go on to higher education.

"Make room for me," she says with a smile, squeezing in next to Ebba in front of the mirror.

She sweeps back her crow-black hair and takes out an equally black eyeliner, which she applies with great care.

"Wille texted to say he's bringing plenty of booze," Ebba says as she checks her eyeshadow, then dabs on a little more at the corner of one eye.

"Nice."

They've been in the same class as Wille since primary school. All three of them grew up in the village. Wille is the one who has the best contacts. Not that it's difficult to get hold of booze, but he always finds the stuff that tastes good and is relatively cheap. Mackan is bringing beer and cigarettes, and so is Viktor. They both have older siblings who are happy to buy more or less anything for a small fee.

Amanda feels a little tingle in her tummy when she thinks of Viktor.

Ebba's phone pings. She holds it up so that Amanda can read the message:

We've arrived! Love Mom x

PS—No partying while we're away!

"Won't she be furious when she finds out you've had people over?" Amanda asks, continuing to apply her makeup.

Ebba grins and pulls down her black top. It's meant to be off the shoulder, but keeps riding up.

"It's fine," she says. "They won't be back until Sunday night—that gives me plenty of time to clean up."

She finishes off the gin and tonic and winks at Amanda.

It's pitch dark outside the window. It's been snowing all afternoon.

Amanda adds yet another coat of mascara.

Tonight they're going to have such a good time. She refuses to worry or be afraid; that can wait until tomorrow.

Right now she is going to *PARTY*!

12

Hanna is lying on the sofa in the living room. It's almost seven thirty in the evening. She has crawled there with yet another bottle of wine; she's done very little except drink and doze since yesterday afternoon, torturing herself with thoughts of what she should have said or done to make Christian stay with her.

When she got home on Monday, she thought the disaster at work was the worst thing that could happen to her.

The sound of her phone ringing makes her jump.

For a heartbeat she hopes it's Christian, that he's changed his mind, realized she's the one he loves. They could turn back the clock, pretend the last week didn't exist.

Then she remembers how she left the apartment.

She checks the display and sees her mother's name. She doesn't want to talk to anyone, especially not her mother. Has Lydia told her about Christian, even though she promised not to?

"Hello?" she says in a croaky voice.

"Darling," Ulla says in the tone that means Hanna has messed up again. Hanna immediately feels guilty as she searches her memory. What has she forgotten this time?

"When are the two of you arriving for New Year?" her mother asks. "You promised to email me your flight details."

Hanna had totally forgotten that she and Christian were meant to be flying down on the thirtieth to celebrate New Year in Guadalmina.

Over the years she has tried to avoid Spain as much as possible; the only thing that made it bearable was when Christian started coming with her. His charm made her mother and father drop their constant nagging about how she ought to leave the police, get herself a better-paid job with higher academic status—something they could boast about to their friends, whose children are lawyers, auditors, or doctors.

"What time do you land?" her mother goes on. "I assume you'll be renting a car—Dad and I can't be expected to chauffeur you around."

She laughs, as if to take the sting out of her words. Hanna can hear cicadas in the background. Presumably Ulla is sitting on the patio, where they've planted lemon trees in big terracotta pots.

"You've no idea how many invitations we've had for the next few weeks—I love all these Christmas festivities!" She lowers her voice a fraction, as if she has something extraordinary to impart. She always sounds a little breathless, almost girlish, in a way that everyone except Hanna seems to find delightful. She continues with obvious pride: "Can you imagine—we've been invited to the mayor's Christmas party on the twenty-third. Everyone will be there—I'm going to have to buy a new dress!"

Hanna feels slightly sick. She doesn't know which will be worse—telling her mother that Christian has left her or going to Spain without him as a protective barrier.

She can't possibly admit that she's been "encouraged" to leave her job in Stockholm. Her only consolation is that Lydia doesn't seem to have said anything.

"I'm working," she lies, trying to sound sober. "I'll speak to you tomorrow."

Ignoring Ulla's protests, she ends the call.

The familiar lump is there in her throat. She doesn't want to be transported back to her childhood memories, but it happens anyway.

Her mother was forty-one and her father fifty-two when she was born. They'd never wanted more than one child, and Lydia had fulfilled all their expectations. They were the perfect family trio until Hanna ruined the idyll ten years later.

Hanna grew up with the story of her mother's difficult pregnancy; she heard it over and over again during her childhood. How her mother put on so much weight and almost died during labor. How Hanna did nothing but scream for the first few months, leaving everyone exhausted.

After Lydia's birth, Ulla regained her figure with ease. The second time it was a different matter.

Hanna can still remember her mother stepping onto the bathroom scale every morning and evening. She can still hear the endless questions: *Do I look slimmer in this dress? Which color makes me look thinner? Does my tummy stick out in this new skirt?*

Hanna constantly assured her that she was the most beautiful mommy in the whole wide world, but it didn't help. She spent her childhood consoling and admiring her mother in order to compensate for the damage she thought she'd caused.

It was her fault that Mommy had lost her beauty.

Hanna doesn't even own a scale; she swore she'd never buy one. She doesn't want to think about her weight—she prefers to dress in baggy sweaters and loose-fitting clothes, even though she's naturally slender.

She buries her face in the pillow and closes her eyes. All she ever wanted to do was to make her mother happy. And for her mother to love her as much as she loved Lydia.

Her sister has told Hanna that she can stay in Åre for at least a month. She's going to have to come up with an excuse for not flying down to Spain. She can't possibly travel there alone. There's no way she'd be able to handle her parents' disappointment over the breakup with Christian.

The last time they were in Guadalmina, her mother had raised the subject of marriage, making one comment after another, reminding Hanna that she was thirty-four—best not to wait too long before having children. She'd always refused to help out Hanna financially, but she was happy to pay for a huge wedding.

Christian would be a fantastic father!

Her mother repeated this several times, in a way that was supposed to be funny. Instead it sliced through Hanna like a razor blade.

The memory brings tears to her eyes.

Ulla was absolutely right. Christian will be a wonderful father—but not to Hanna's children.

13

The music is pounding in every room, the party is in full swing. Amanda is sitting on the sofa, smoking a cigarette. She wonders how Ebba is going to explain all this to her parents when they get back. She would never dare to invite her friends over if her mom and dad were away. Mom would go crazy, even if there was no damage.

She hears a burst of laughter from the kitchen. It sounds like Viktor. She gets up and heads that way; she feels like dancing and making out.

Viktor and Wille are leaning against the sink. They must have really gone for it in the past hour; they can hardly stand up. They gaze at her with unfocused eyes, making drunken jokes. There are several crumpled beer cans on the table, and the floor is sticky with spilled booze.

The boys are caught up in their own conversation; they're not interested in her. Amanda is furious. She's about to walk away when Viktor reaches out to stop her.

Amanda shakes off his hand. She's drunk too, but not enough to want to get close to him when he's behaving like this.

She frowns as she sees him grab hold of a chair to stop himself from falling over.

"For fuck's sake, you're so drunk!" she snaps, tugging down the yellow top, which has ridden up over her stomach.

"Fuck's shake you're sho drunk," he mimics her, although he's slurring his words so badly he can barely finish the sentence. He seizes her arm, pulls her close. He's surprisingly strong, in spite of the state he's in. "What's wrong?"

Amanda twists away as Viktor tries to kiss her.

"Come on—I really like you."

He thinks he sounds romantic; he doesn't realize he's yelling. She turns her head away, but that doesn't stop him; he keeps attempting to plant a sloppy kiss on her ear.

His grip is too tight, her cheek is pressed against his chest, she can hardly breathe.

She tries to shake off his hands, but he won't let go. He squeezes harder, one hand groping for her ass.

"Stop it!" Amanda struggles to free herself. "I mean it, Viktor!"

"She's not interested," Wille says before belching loudly.

At last Viktor lets go.

"Sorry," he says with a shrug, as if nothing has happened.

Amanda gives him a withering look, then goes back to the living room to find someone else to talk to.

Viktor is a fucking idiot. If he's going to behave like that, she doesn't want to be with him anymore.

14

The party is getting out of hand. It's well past midnight. There's a burn mark on the sofa, and the entire house stinks of smoke. A couple is doing God knows what at one end of the sofa.

Amanda is sitting on the stairs by herself. This wasn't how she'd imagined the evening. Ebba has disappeared, and she doesn't give a shit about Viktor. If he wants to behave like an idiot, then he has only himself to blame. She has no intention of running after him, begging to be with him.

She goes upstairs to look for Ebba. Loud groans can be heard from the main bedroom—Ebba's parents' room.

It sounds like Mackan, the coolest boy in the class. Amanda guesses that Emily is the chosen one this evening. She's been after him all term, and she was pretty drunk earlier on.

Amanda checks out Ebba's room. It's empty, as is her brother's. She moves on to the bathroom and finds Ebba on the floor with her back to the blue-tiled wall, her head resting on her knees. Her brown hair has fallen forward and is hiding her face.

There is a strong smell of vomit and a nasty reddish-brown mark on the toilet seat.

Poor Ebba.

"Are you okay?" she says, kneeling down beside her friend.

"No," Ebba whispers. "I'm drunk." She hurls herself at the toilet again. When she throws up, bits of vomit get stuck in her hair, but she doesn't seem to notice. She sinks down onto the floor, whimpering.

"Don't you think you should go and lie down?" Amanda suggests, stroking Ebba's back.

"In a minute. I just need to rest for a while."

The tears begin to flow.

"Mackan's with Emily," she mutters. "I hate him."

Amanda sighs. How can Ebba have fallen for Mackan when he's such an asshole? He knows he can have anyone he wants, and he makes the most of it. At least half the girls in their class are desperate to be with him.

Right on cue, loud noises emanate from the bedroom.

Suddenly Amanda has had enough.

She ought to stay and console Ebba, help her to bed, and make a start on cleaning up the mess. Instead she gets to her feet. She is tired of drunken classmates and the smell of beer and vomit. She'd so looked forward to this evening, but nothing has turned out the way it was supposed to.

She can't help brooding, just as she's done all week since she realized what was going on, how terrible it was. Her drunken classmates suddenly seem childish and naive; they have no idea.

She can't keep the dark thoughts at bay, and the situation is made worse by the fact that her fear is now mixed with anger at Viktor. Why did he have to be so vile, tonight of all nights?

She wants to go home and sleep in her own bed, try to work out a solution to the whole horrible mess.

She'd really like to tell her mother everything. Get a big hug, hear her mom say that everything will be all right. Then again, she knows exactly what Mom would say if she found out the truth.

Found out what Amanda has been up to with Ebba.

"Listen, I'm going now," she says. "I'll help you clean up over the weekend. By the way, I've had enough of Viktor. He's completely wasted tonight."

Ebba gives a slight nod.

"Mmm," she mumbles, eyes fixed on the floor.

"See you tomorrow," Amanda says.

That's a bit of an exaggeration; it's almost one o'clock in the morning. In six and a half hours, they have to be in school for the Lucia procession. Both Ebba and Amanda are taking part. She hopes that Ebba will manage to sober up before it starts; otherwise the music teacher will go crazy. They've been practicing Christmas songs and carols since October.

Amanda goes down to the hall, rummages for her jacket among the pile of garments on the floor. She pulls on her hat and boots—it's freezing outside.

She lingers for a moment with her hand resting on the door handle. It's snowing now, big white flakes whirling in the wind. The buses don't run at this hour, and it will take her forty minutes to walk home.

The quickest route is via the E14, but it's not really safe; the cars drive so fast along there.

Should she change her mind and stay over?

She glances toward the kitchen. She can just see Wille through the doorway, but there's no sign of Viktor. The music is just as loud as before, even though nobody's dancing anymore. The cigarette smoke mingles with the smell of something else, something sweeter.

Viktor appears, staggering past on his way to the downstairs bathroom. He's in such a hurry that he doesn't bother closing the door. Amanda can hear the stream of urine hitting the bowl, no doubt splashing on the floor.

Waste of fucking space.

She makes a face and turns away.

She hears Viktor emerge, but ignores him. She doesn't even want to look at him.

"Are you leaving?" he shouts.

Amanda doesn't answer.

Suddenly he's in front of her, blocking the door.

"Come on, Amanda . . ."

He tries to kiss her, but this time she's ready for him.

"Don't touch me!"

He's had several hours to fix things between them, but instead he chose to hang out with Wille, drinking. Although to be fair he does seem slightly more sober now.

"What's wrong with you tonight?" Viktor looks irritated as she turns away. "Why are you so miserable?"

"Seriously?" Amanda snaps.

He makes another attempt to put his arms around her, and she pushes him away. She doesn't mean to use so much force, but she's stronger than he thinks—and Viktor is drunk and unprepared. He loses his balance and crashes into the wall. He lands heavily on the stone floor and swears out loud.

Amanda stares at him. He looks furious; his face is distorted with rage. She doesn't know whether to say *Sorry* or *You only have yourself to blame.*

Her mouth goes dry with stress.

Viktor scrambles to his feet, narrowing his eyes.

"What the fuck do you think you're doing? Bitch!"

His tone frightens her. Viktor has never spoken to her like that. For the first time she wonders whether what he did to that girl in Umeå really was an accident.

Whether he's capable of doing it again . . .

When he comes toward her, she doesn't know if he's going to hit her or kiss her.

Amanda yanks open the front door and races out into the night. Viktor calls out after her, but she keeps on running.

FRIDAY, DECEMBER 13

15

The bedroom is in darkness when Lena Halvorssen is woken by her alarm.

She gropes around on the bedside table, switches it off. It's six o'clock on the morning of Lucia. It's hard to get her body moving, but the kids have to go to school, and her first patient is due at eight fifteen.

Harald is still asleep. She gives him a little push, but he merely grunts. His stubble is more gray than black these days, and his double chin is clearly visible, resting on the covers.

Lena sighs and swings her legs over the side of the bed. Ludde is there in a second, wagging his tail. She bends down and strokes the black retriever before she pulls on her dressing gown. It's time to wake the twins. Mimi and Kalle are still sharing a room even though they're nine years old. The plan is for one of them to take over Amanda's room when she leaves home. She'll graduate from high school in the spring, and given how much she and Lena have argued over the past year, it can't come soon enough.

Lena lingers in the doorway of the twins' room. They're so sweet, rosy cheeked and fast asleep. Their beds are arranged in an L-shape, tousled blond hair sticking up on each pillow. Kalle is the calm one; he's shy and cautious, a little thinker. Mimi is bolder; she speaks first and thinks second. She comes up with mischief; Kalle tags along.

Lena wishes she could keep them at this age. She doesn't want them to grow up and turn into moaning teenagers. She was only twenty-three when Amanda was born, not an experienced mother, and it hasn't been easy. How is she going to cope with two pubescent kids at the same time, hormones exploding in all directions?

She glances toward Amanda's room. Her eldest daughter always takes forever in the bathroom. Should she wake her first? No, she can't face that particular battle until she's had a cup of coffee. It's going to be a struggle to get her up after Ebba's party. Lena didn't hear her come in, but it must have been late. She's probably had only a few hours' sleep; it's doubtful if she's even managed to sober up.

Lena is under no illusion that the Lucia party was alcohol-free.

In spite of a quick shower, it's six thirty by the time Lena is ready. She shakes Mimi and Kalle awake. Harald ought to get up too, but he's still lying in bed like a corpse. The council meeting must have gone on until late yesterday evening; she didn't hear him come home either.

She takes a deep breath before opening Amanda's door. She pushes down the handle and peeps in, calls out, "Amanda," in her softest voice. When there is no reaction, she pushes the door wide open.

The room is empty, the bed untouched.

She feels an immediate spurt of anger. *For goodness' sake.* If she's going to sleep over at a friend's, she has to send a text; that's the deal. She's not allowed to spend the night somewhere else—not even at Ebba's—without letting them know.

Lena goes back to their bedroom to wake Harald.

"Amanda isn't home," she says without any attempt to hide the irritation in her voice.

"What?"

Harald stares blankly at her, still half-asleep. He props himself up on one elbow, and the striped duvet slips down, revealing the mat of gray hair on his chest.

"Amanda," Lena repeats. "She must have stayed over at Ebba's without telling us. She drives me crazy when she does this."

She perches on the edge of the bed and picks up her phone to send an angry message to her daughter.

Harald gently pats her hand. He is the peacemaker in the family, but he's also the one who lets Lena deal with any issues when the kids step out of line.

Ludde has padded after her and is looking longingly at the bed. He is strictly forbidden from jumping up.

"Calm down," Harald says. "It's Lucia, you know what happens. She probably fell asleep at Ebba's before she had time to text. I'm sure she'll go straight to school."

Harald's words help to ease Lena's frustration. He's good at that, calming those around him. That's why he's an effective chair of the council, in spite of a fragile political coalition.

He makes people feel safe.

"I expect you're right," she says, sending a nicer message than she'd intended:

Did you stay over at Ebba's? Don't forget the Lucia procession 🙂

Harald pulls her close, and she rests her head on his shoulder. His skin is still warm from sleep; his body smells good even though he hasn't showered yet.

"She's only eighteen," he says. "Don't you remember what we were like at that age?"

Indeed she does. She and Harald were in the same class at high school; they've known each other forever; although they didn't get together until the spring when they graduated.

She gives him a reluctant smile; Harald has that effect on her. He's almost always in a good mood. She's overreacted, as usual. That's why she and Amanda argue so much. Sometimes she doesn't understand what drives her; she just can't help it. Things are different with the twins. She has much more patience with them, even though she loves all three of her children equally.

"Up you get," she says. "There's coffee and Lucia buns in the kitchen. And gingerbread cookies."

Harald's face lights up. He loves cakes and cookies, especially her homemade ones.

Lena puts down her phone. She'll try and give Amanda a call later in the morning, between patients.

Why does she always have to worry so much?

16

Lena has just finished treating a person's bad back in dire need of naprapathic therapy. She has a fifteen-minute window before her next patient, which is enough to freshen up her consulting room, wipe down the bed with disinfectant, and drink a cup of black coffee. At least if she's quick.

Instead she takes out her phone to see if Amanda's been in touch.

Nothing. No new messages.

She stares at the blank screen. It's lunchtime. The Lucia celebration in school should have been over long ago. Even if Amanda has classes, she's had plenty of opportunity to respond.

Lena keys in another message:

Just wanted to check that everything's okay? Love Mom

She presses send.

The constant mom anxiety that never really goes away is gnawing at her. It makes Harald smile. *Amanda's eighteen—she's officially an adult. She can do what she likes,* he says.

It's time for Lena to let go.

Not while she's living at home, she always replies.

As long as Amanda is living under her roof, Lena wants to know where her daughter is.

She stands there with her phone in her hand, unable to explain why she's so uneasy. Åre is a safe place, a good place to grow up in. The most common crimes are driving offenses and drunken tourists getting into a fight when they've partied too hard.

But things can go wrong. Car accidents happen everywhere, even in quiet places. With all the snow that fell last night, visibility would have been poor. If Amanda was walking home late, she could have been hit by a vehicle.

The image of an unconscious body in a ditch flickers through Lena's mind.

"Stop it," she murmurs to herself.

Should she call Harald, see if Amanda's contacted him instead? She does that sometimes when she knows Lena will be on the warpath. She selects his number, but it goes straight to voicemail. No doubt he's in a meeting as usual.

She hadn't intended to call Amanda but does it anyway, although her daughter hates Lena trying to reach her during the school day. The phone rings and rings, but there is no answer.

She must be in class. Or maybe she didn't bother going in at all; she might still be fast asleep at Ebba's. There's a simple explanation.

Lena hears a knock, and a woman pokes her head around the door. It is Cia, one of her regular patients, who has a bad shoulder, which benefits from ultrasound treatment.

"Is it okay to come in?" Cia asks.

"Of course." Lena puts down her phone. "Good to see you."

Her body is crawling with anxiety, but she forces herself to smile.

Everything is fine. It has to be.

17

Harald Halvorssen closes his notebook with a little bang. He is sitting behind his desk; the head of finance has just left the room after a budget review.

It wasn't good news. There are far too many gaps and not enough money to go round. The political coalition of four parties comprises strong-willed individuals all pulling in their own direction.

The situation isn't new in Åre. The last few terms of office have seen various forms of political upheaval. Traditionally his own Center Party has dominated, with occasional interruptions by a red-green majority. Now he's dependent on the latest upstart party, For the Good of Western Jämtland, which promotes local issues and holds the balance of power.

Somehow he's going to have to make everyone understand that further cuts will need to be made. Åre is growing like few other rural communities, but the tax rate is already high.

He leans back on his chair and links his hands behind his neck. His belly sticks out. Work takes up so much of his time that he doesn't get around to exercising as much as he used to. These days he would never complete the Vasaloppet cross-country ski race in six hours as he used to.

His gaze falls on the framed photograph on his desk: the whole family up on Åreskutan. It was taken last Easter, with the sun shining brightly as it often does in April. They'd taken a packed lunch. The twins were excited and could hardly stand still; even Amanda was smiling at the camera.

Harald sighs. He doesn't understand why she and Lena fight so much. Lena typically speaks her mind when she gets annoyed, and Amanda reacts by slamming doors and yelling. He tries to mediate as best he can, but sometimes it's like a minefield; whatever he does, he upsets somebody. It's easier to handle the opposition in the council chamber than to get his wife and daughter to agree.

His phone buzzes; a message from Lena.

Can't get hold of Amanda, has she contacted you?

Harald glances at his watch. Quarter to five. Where has the day gone?

He quickly replies:

No.

Another message arrives in seconds.

She hasn't been in touch! Do you think something could have happened?

Harald sighs again. Lena gets worked up too easily. This isn't the first time Amanda has ignored her mother's texts. Secretly he sympathizes to a certain extent; Lena can be too controlling. She always wants to know exactly where he and the kids are; otherwise she becomes stressed and starts catastrophizing.

He's about to respond with some reassuring words when there's a knock on the door.

Mira Bergfors is his right-hand woman. Her long black hair shines in the glow of the overhead light, framing her finely chiseled features.

Harald feels fortunate to have such a beautiful PA. She's thirty-one, married with a three-year-old daughter named Leah.

"You're a free man," she informs him with a smile. "Your next meeting has been postponed, so you can go home."

Harald rarely gets away from the office before six thirty or seven; this is a rare luxury. It's Friday and Lucia, but he had a meeting booked at five.

"Excellent," he says, returning Mira's smile.

"I was thinking of leaving too." She turns away, and Harald can't resist admiring her well-shaped backside in the black jeans that fit like a second skin.

He knows what it's like to caress that soft body.

He suddenly realizes they're at work. He quickly adopts a neutral expression and raises a hand in farewell. "Have a nice weekend," he says.

He starts a message to Lena, then changes his mind and calls her instead. She answers right away, sounding agitated.

"I still haven't heard from Amanda! I've texted her and called her several times!"

"Have you spoken to Ebba? Maybe she went back there after school," Harald ventures, trying to calm her down.

"I tried earlier, but she didn't pick up."

Harald looks out of the window. It's stopped snowing, and a pale crescent moon shimmers against the dark sky.

"I'll stop by Ebba's house on the way home and check," he says. "I was about to leave anyway."

"Okay." Lena sounds a little better.

"Listen, don't worry so much."

"But what if something's happened to her?" Lena says. "Something bad?"

18

It's beginning to feel like the weekend at Åre police station. Daniel is in the staff room with the two local officers, Anton and Raffe. They don't really hang out together, but they get along well. It's become a habit to have a cup of coffee on a Friday before it's time to go home.

It's been a quiet week; they can tell the season isn't yet in full swing. However, Daniel is still looking forward to a few days off. He's wondering if Alice is old enough to take on a trip. They could ski to Fröå mine with her safely tucked up in a sled and have lunch in the café.

Anton is in full flow, telling them all about a new alto saxophone he's hoping to buy; he plays in a jazz band in his free time. He's interrupted by the district communication center, which is based in Umeå.

Anton takes the call while Raffe flicks through a magazine that has been left on the table. His full name is Rafael Herrera; his family came over from Chile as refugees in the seventies. He grew up in Strömsund and is a keen snowboarder. He even competed at the national level on the junior team.

Both he and Anton have been stationed in Åre for considerably longer than Daniel, although Daniel is the only one who actually lives in the village. Anton has an apartment in Duved, while Raffe is in the church village of Kall, because that's where his girlfriend comes from.

Anton hangs up and turns to his colleagues.

"A girl from Åre seems to have been missing since yesterday evening. She went to a Lucia party, but hasn't been heard of since. She didn't show up in school today."

"How old is she?" Raffe asks, scratching his ear.

Just like Daniel he has a short beard, but Raffe's is almost black while Daniel's is paler, tending toward ginger.

"She turned eighteen in September. Her mother called it in."

"What's her name?" Daniel asks.

Anton checks his notes. "Amanda Halvorssen. She's at the high school in Järpen and lives on Pilgrimsvägen in Åre."

"And where did this party take place?"

"Five minutes from here—Trollvägen."

"She's probably at a friend's," Raffe says, yawning. "And she's forgotten to call her mom."

Raffe is probably right, Daniel thinks. Most teenagers who are reported missing have simply ended up at a friend's place. At that age they don't think, their impulse control is poor, the frontal lobe not fully developed. The ability to analyze consequences is lacking in every way.

He remembers what he was like back in the day in Sundsvall, the parties where he got too drunk and passed out on someone's floor. His single mom was sitting at home, worrying herself sick, but that didn't stop him.

He takes a gingerbread cookie from the tin in the middle of the table. The lid shines in the glow of the red Advent candle bridge on the windowsill.

"Her parents have called everyone they know," Anton informs them. "No one's seen her since last night."

Daniel glances over at the window. The sun went down several hours ago, and it's at least minus twenty out there.

The forces of nature shouldn't be underestimated.

"Apparently her mother sounded very worried," Anton adds.

Daniel frowns. In the city, they wouldn't investigate after such a short period of time, unless there was a reason to suspect that a crime had been committed. The norm is to wait at least twenty-four hours, but he doesn't like what he's just heard.

Partying kids and minus twenty degrees isn't a good combination.

He finishes his coffee and gets to his feet.

"I think we should go and have a chat with the family," he says. "Just to be on the safe side."

Anton also stands up. "I'll come with you."

Anton grew up in Åre, and he knows all about the dangers of the weather. How small a human being is in relation to nature's bitter winds and icy temperatures.

Around here a teenager who isn't warmly dressed can freeze to death in a few hours.

19

The latest message from Lydia lights up the screen of the phone in Hanna's hand.

How are you feeling now?

Hanna is sitting on the generous pale-brown velvet-covered sofa in the living room, with a blanket over her knees. She is still in her pajamas; she couldn't be bothered to get dressed today. She didn't have the energy to cook either; she made a couple of sandwiches and opened another bottle of red wine.

It took her a long time to get to sleep after the conversation with her mother last night.

The scent from a bowl of white hyacinths reaches her nostrils. She doesn't really understand why the decorations irritate her so much—all the Advent candle bridges in dark wood, the red apples surrounding the chunky candles in lanterns tastefully arranged in groups on the floor. Fragrant fir branches have been scattered across the porch, and white Advent stars hang in virtually every window, spreading their warm glow.

It's typical of Lydia to decorate the entire house for Christmas, even though the family has spent only one weekend here in December and will be away on their cruise until well after New Year.

To be fair, she probably didn't do it herself. Last year she'd employed a company to both buy and decorate the tree. Everything was done by the time the family flew up from Stockholm on December 22.

Hanna sighs. She shouldn't be so negative—Lydia means well. It's just that she can be a little . . . suffocating. Her sister's enormous energy makes Hanna feel small and inadequate, even though Lydia has often been her only refuge and support. Without Lydia as a buffer between Hanna and her mother, life would have been unbearable when they were growing up.

I'm fine, she texts back. She always makes a point of answering her sister's messages; otherwise three more will arrive in quick succession. Lydia isn't the kind of person to give up at the first hurdle.

She reaches for the remote to see what's available on Netflix. The last thing she wants to watch is a feel-good movie where the girl falls into the boy's arms at the end, to the sound of slushy music. Nor is she interested in crime thrillers—too close to reality. She can't cope with being reminded of her profession right now.

It's the only thing she's ever wanted to be. A police officer.

Before she realized that, the future was unclear, incomprehensible. After she graduated from high school, she drifted around doing casual jobs, mostly in bars in Europe. She partied a lot more than she should have done, demonstrating precisely the lack of character that her mother accused her of.

While Lydia sailed through law school and secured a post as an associate attorney with a prestigious law firm, Hanna perfected the role of the useless kid sister, the one who was incapable of pulling herself together and training for a career.

She tightens her grip on the wineglass. She knows exactly what it was that gave her a new direction in life.

It was the rape in Barcelona.

She can still see the cramped cellar, the irregular gray stone walls, the disgusting smell of damp and mold. The earth floor shredding the skin on her back as she was roughly pressed down beneath the weight of the bar owner. She can still feel Miguel's disgusting fingers on her body, the sense of powerlessness as she tried in vain to push him off, make him stop.

He was her boss, and considerably older. She was only twenty-two, young and naive.

Afterward, when she'd made it home to Sweden and the physical scars had healed, her rage and all those other emotions needed an outlet. Joining the police gave her the opportunity to hit back, to stand up and show those bastards that they couldn't treat a woman however they wanted.

Every time she put away a pimp or an abuser, the sharp edges of the pain inside her softened slightly.

Her phone buzzes again. She glances at the display and gives a start.

What the hell?

It's Christian. Which means he must have been back to the apartment and found out what she did before she left.

Hanna blushes as she remembers pouring his expensive red wine down the sink. He'd bought it at an auction and was saving it until the day he could afford his own cellar.

At the same time, there is an underlying feeling of satisfaction. It serves him right.

She wonders if he's checked out his wardrobe.

In a way she realizes it wasn't entirely rational to cut up his ties or pour ketchup all over his designer suits, but immediately after he'd walked out, she'd searched blindly for a way of getting her revenge. She had to do something concrete. The tears had stopped flowing when she meticulously set about ruining his precious clothes.

She would never have imagined that she could do such a thing.

Hanna has no intention of responding to Christian's message. She switches her phone to silent and puts it aside. She ought to eat something, but she isn't hungry.

She glances in the direction of the kitchen, at the other end of the house. The whole of the upper floor is open plan, with the living room, library, kitchen, and dining room seamlessly flowing into one another. She's never been particularly interested in interior design; that was Christian's thing. However, even she can see that the muted shades of gray, beige, and chocolate brown create a tasteful harmony. Each little brass knob has been carefully chosen. Beautiful reindeer-horn ceiling lamps echo the surrounding mountain landscape and its fauna.

It is only Hanna herself who sticks out like a sore thumb. She is the detail that jars, an item from IKEA that has lost its way and ended up in Nordiska Galleriet.

She reaches out to touch a candlestick, feels the cool metal against her fingertips.

The house bears no resemblance to the cabin with pine furniture and bunk beds that their parents used to rent on the outskirts of Åre when Hanna was growing up. This place is designed for her sister's perfect family, for cozy dinners in front of a crackling log fire, adults enjoying a glass of wine at the table while the children hang out in the TV room downstairs. Everyone can enjoy the mountain environment while de-stressing from their demanding high-level jobs in the city.

The fact that it's also possible to spend time with other successful families from the same Stockholm suburbs, because they've also built houses in Åre, only improves the situation.

There is no danger of having to step outside their social circle.

Hanna's glass is empty. So is the bottle. She heads for the kitchen to fetch another. Lydia said she could take whatever she wanted, but she can't help feeling guilty.

She opens the wine cabinet, but closes it again. She needs to slow down.

She wonders what will happen when Christian discovers that she's put mustard in his Italian shoes. She's never done anything halfheartedly—he ought to know that by now.

20

Ebba is lying on top of the unmade bed. She ought to start cleaning up after the party. The kitchen is a mess, and the living room still stinks of smoke. Instead she stares up at the ceiling, following a barely visible crack with her gaze.

Harald was here a few minutes ago, asking questions about Amanda. He was clearly worried.

Ebba thought she'd gone home to Pilgrimsvägen, since she hadn't slept over, but it seems that no one has seen her since last night.

Harald's anxiety frightened Ebba.

What if something really has happened to her?

Why would she simply disappear?

Ebba didn't say anything about Viktor. Maybe she should have?

She knows that Amanda hasn't told her parents about him, because of his reputation. Amanda assured Ebba that Viktor has definitely changed—what happened in Umeå was an accident. He swore that the situation with that girl was nothing more than a misunderstanding.

Amanda believed him.

Ebba picks up her phone and realizes that she hasn't had a single message from Amanda in almost twenty-four hours. They're usually in touch all the time.

She checks Instagram to see if Amanda has been active since yesterday, but there's nothing. The latest post is the picture she uploaded just before the party started. They are standing side by side with their glasses raised to the camera, lips pursed in exaggerated kisses, cheeks pressed together.

Party time, Amanda has written, followed by a series of stupid emojis.

Where has she gone?

Ebba tries to swallow her fear. She shivers and pulls up the covers. She is struggling to remember what happened in the bathroom, what Amanda said before she left the party.

Everything is kind of blurred. She recalls only fragments of the last few hours before she passed out.

Amanda was kneeling beside her as she threw up into the toilet. After that everything is blank. Hang on . . . Wasn't Amanda mad at Viktor?

Could this really be something to do with him?

Ebba has no idea what time he left. But surely he would never hurt Amanda . . . ?

The guilty feelings burrow deeper in her chest. If Ebba hadn't gotten so drunk, then maybe she could have persuaded Amanda to stay and everything would be okay now.

She really wants her mom, but if she calls and tells her what's happened, she'll also have to tell her about the party, and she dare not do that.

Instead she sends yet another message to Amanda.

She is terrified of not getting a reply.

21

When Harald pulls up in front of the family's red-painted wooden house, the police car on the drive is the first thing he sees.

For a moment he doesn't want to get out of his car; it's easier just to sit here in the darkness.

He closes his eyes and rests his forehead on the steering wheel as a strong urge to drive off spreads through his body. He isn't ready to hear anything negative about Amanda. It's bad enough that she wasn't at Ebba's.

The minutes pass. In the end reason takes over and Harald straightens his back and switches off the engine. During the short walk up to the house, he tries to pull himself together. He mustn't break down. The police might be here about something else altogether.

His hands are shaking as he opens the unlocked front door. Ludde comes running, but Harald doesn't even notice him.

Lena is in the living room, sitting opposite two police officers. There is no sign of the twins.

All of Harald's worst fears are about to be confirmed.

"What's happened?" He barks the question, he can't help himself. He takes a couple of rapid steps toward the two strangers, stares at them. "Is she . . . ?" He can't finish the sentence. He stands there in his outdoor clothes, waiting for the answer. He feels hot and cold at the same time. A small puddle is forming around his boots as the snow melts. "Is Amanda . . . ?"

There isn't enough air in the room.

"It was me who called them," Lena says, getting to her feet.

It takes a few seconds before Harald is capable of answering. "So she's okay?"

Lena's face crumples. "She's still missing. I couldn't wait any longer, so I rang one-one-two."

One of the men stands up and introduces himself as Daniel Lindskog from the Åre police. His fair-haired colleague is Anton Lundgren.

Daniel suggests that Harald should take off his coat and join them so they can have a chat. He sounds perfectly in control, not worried at all.

Harald feels numb. He tries to find a sense of inner calm, but it's too much, he can't do it. When he saw the police officers in his living room, he was sure they'd come to inform him and Lena that Amanda was gone.

He notices a picture of his daughter on the coffee table. It's an old photograph, from before she dyed her hair black. She still has her natural light-brown shade, very similar to Lena's. Her expression is kind of sulky, as if she doesn't really want her photo taken, but at least she's looking straight into the camera, which has captured both her freckles and her still-rounded cheeks. Her chin juts out, suggesting a level of defiance. She's so like her mother. That's why they clash all the time.

His darling daughter.

Harald clutches the arm of the chair tightly.

Daniel Lindskog asks one question after another. He has brown hair and a short, neatly trimmed beard. He bears a resemblance to Prince Carl Philip, although he's taller.

"Has Amanda left home before?" Anton Lundgren asks. "Or given any indication that she's not happy here?"

Lena shakes her head as if the question is absurd. Her voice is shrill when she answers. "What makes you think she's run away? Don't you understand—something terrible must have happened to her! Amanda would never leave home without talking to us first!"

"That's not what we're saying," Daniel says reassuringly. "But we have to ask certain questions so that we have a clear idea of what's going on. We have to form a picture of your daughter and her normal patterns of behavior."

Lena nods, her eyes shining with unshed tears.

"How were things between you when you last spoke?" Daniel goes on. "Had you . . . quarreled before Amanda went to the party?"

Lena's cheeks flush red.

"Not . . . not really. We hadn't fallen out. My daughter and I get along well."

Harald wonders whether he ought to mention the tense atmosphere between them, but decides against it.

"Could she have slept over at a friend's without letting you know?"

"I've contacted her adviser and everyone in her class," Lena says, spreading her hands wide. "I've been on the phone for the last hour, calling everyone we know. No one has seen her."

"Okay." Daniel makes a note. "What's the name of her adviser?"

"Lasse Sandahl. He's looked after Amanda's class all the way through high school."

"I've just been to see her best friend, Ebba," Harald says, and tells them about his visit to Trollvägen.

Lena's eyes are wide with fear by the time he's finished. "You have to do something! What if she was hit by a car when she was on her way home last night? She could be lying in a snowdrift along the road!"

It is even colder than yesterday. Harald can't help glancing at the window that overlooks the garden. The blackness is impenetrable. It is impossible to see the snow-covered fir trees behind the house.

"Oh God," Lena murmurs, "why didn't she phone and ask us to pick her up? If only she'd called . . ."

Anton's expression is full of sympathy. "Does your daughter use any kind of tracking function, for example, Find My iPhone?"

Lena shakes her head. "Not that we have access to. She refused to give us the code."

Harald turns to Daniel. "Shouldn't you contact Missing People? Isn't it standard practice to involve them in situations like this? I know Bosse Lundh, who runs the local branch."

The two officers exchange a glance.

"We'll do everything we can to find Amanda," Daniel says, getting to his feet. Anton closes his notebook and follows suit.

Harald sees that Daniel is holding a pink top. Is it Amanda's? Does that mean they're going to bring in dogs to search for her?

"We'll be in touch as soon as we have any information," Daniel continues.

"You're leaving already?" Lena stares at the two men in confusion. Ludde moves forward and places his nose in her lap, as if he can tell that she's upset.

"We'll be organizing things from the station," Daniel explains. "But as I said, we'll be in touch."

He hands Lena a card bearing the police logo. "This is my number—you can call me any time." He places a consoling hand on her arm. "Most people who disappear come back within one to three days."

Harald wants to say something, but Lena gets there first.

"And what about those who don't?" she whispers.

When Amanda opens her eyes, she is lying under a thin blanket on a mattress. She looks around the room and sees untreated wooden walls and a door. There is a soapstone stove in one corner. This must be a mountain cabin.

She is on the verge of panic. She is all alone and has no idea where she is.

How did she end up here?

Vague memories of swaying, of twists and turns, come into her mind. She was tied up, lying on her back, unable to move her arms or legs.

She remembers the wind in her face, as if she were on a sled being pulled by a snowmobile, traveling at high speed.

She staggers to her feet and tries to orient herself. The cabin consists of just one room. Apart from the bunk beds attached to the wall, there is only a shabby plastic table and two plastic chairs. A few comic books are strewn across a window seat.

She shivers and realizes that her clothes are gone. She is wearing nothing but her bra and panties.

He's taken everything else, including her boots.

Amanda searches for something she can put on, but the only fabric in the room is the blanket and the stained mattresses on the beds.

She tries the door—locked. Outside the window, which is partly covered by a crossbar, it is pitch dark. She screws up her eyes and thinks she can make out huge piles of snow.

Is she up in the mountains? Where the hell is she?

There is a fire burning in the stove. She crouches down and holds out her hands to the warmth.

She has no idea where she is, or how she is going to get away. The door is locked, and even if she managed to get it or the window open, she dare not go out into the bitter cold without her clothes.

Her phone is gone too.

She can't hold back the tears. No one can hear her crying.

"Mommy," she whispers. "Help me."

22

Daniel gets into the passenger seat and lets Anton drive. He gazes out of the side window as they swing around to head back to the station.

Once again he thinks that most missing teenagers turn up within a few days. However, Amanda's mother was adamant that she would never disappear of her own accord.

Daniel's main concern is that the girl might have met with an accident. At the moment there is no evidence of a crime. However, he is well aware that Amanda could have frozen to death if she was very drunk and lay down to rest in a snowdrift.

Most people don't understand how close to death they can be, wearing unsuitable clothing in extreme cold. He has seen girls tottering home in high heels in the middle of the night, sometimes setting off in completely the wrong direction on a trek of more than six miles. Far too many travel up to Åre by train, check in to their accommodation, then take a cab straight to the bar. At the end of the night, they have no idea where they're going or how far it is.

If Amanda tried to walk home in the dark, and was drunk enough to fall asleep outdoors, things could have gone very badly.

He briefly considers the possibility that she might have taken her own life, but pushes the thought aside. Nothing the parents had said pointed in that direction.

Anton signals a right turn for Kurortsvägen, where the relatively new police station is situated. It is housed in the same building as the health center, fresh and modern, but the design hasn't really been thought through. It would be a simple matter to block every entrance and exit to sabotage an emergency police dispatch.

They tend not to mention this.

Daniel's phone beeps. It's the telecoms operator he contacted on his way to the Halvorssens'. Amanda's phone hasn't been used since one o'clock this morning.

Not a good sign.

"We need a search dog," Anton says as he parks the car. "Shall we bring in Jarmo?"

Jarmo Mäkinen, who lives in Järpen, is the only dog handler in the area. All the rest are based in Östersund, which is an hour and a quarter's drive away, and Daniel is far from sure that they can afford to wait that long.

"Good idea," he says. "Ask him to meet us on Trollvägen as soon as possible. And call the cab companies, find out if anyone's seen anything."

Åre's cab firms often help. Every year they make a huge contribution to public safety, picking up drunken skiers staggering home in the middle of the night.

Anton nods and undoes his seatbelt. They are stopping off briefly at the station in order to plan their next moves. Daniel wants to apprise his superiors in Östersund of the situation. Helicopters are sometimes required in a major search, and the Mountain Rescue teams might also be needed.

For the moment the plan is to have a patrol car check out the local area and the route between Amanda's home and Trollvägen, where the party took place. There aren't many options, and if the girl has fallen asleep in a snowdrift, they should be able to spot her.

He doesn't want to think about what state she'll be in.

He also wants to speak to Ebba, Amanda's best friend, see what she has to say.

It is almost six thirty. It's going to be a while before he can get back to Ida and Alice. He won't be able to bathe his daughter tonight—for the first time since she was born.

He takes out his phone and sends a quick message to Ida.

Have to work late, it can't be helped. Sorry.❤

23

The aftermath of the party is all too evident when Daniel and Anton enter Ebba's house. Cigarettes and booze weren't the only substances on offer; the smell of cannabis lingers in the stuffy air.

Daniel isn't surprised. Drug dealing is the latest major criminal activity in the area, and problems with drugs have increased significantly during the past few years. Not long ago alcohol was the biggest concern, but nowadays fifteen-year-olds are smoking weed while gaming.

Ebba is standing in the hallway, chewing on a strand of hair. Her mascara is smudged, and she looks tired and hungover.

When Daniel looks beyond her to the kitchen, he understands why. There are beer cans and empty bottles everywhere. He recognizes a Russian brand of vodka. Back in the day everyone bought moonshine, but that's no longer necessary now that there's cheap smuggled booze or older siblings who are prepared to make a purchase on behalf of younger teens. Kids today have a lot more money than his generation did.

"Can we have a chat?" he says, as Anton steps aside to take a call.

Ebba leads the way into the kitchen, clearing one end of the table so they can sit down. She perches on the edge of the chair, arms tightly wrapped around her upper body. Daniel feels sorry for her. Sharp words about alcohol and drug abuse can wait. Right now he needs to find out as much as possible about Amanda, what happened at the party before she disappeared.

"Are your parents home?" he begins.

"They're in Stockholm." Ebba looks guilty. "Will they have to know about the party?" she asks quietly.

"We'll see. The most important thing right now is to track down your friend."

"She just took off," Ebba mumbles.

"Why?"

"I don't know."

"Could something have happened to make her leave?"

Ebba shrugs. "I don't remember. Ask Viktor, he might know."

Anton joins them, his phone still pressed to his ear.

"One of our patrols has found a scarf by the side of the E14, just next to the rest stop before the VM8 chairlift."

He holds out his phone to Ebba, shows her a picture of a red knitted scarf lying on the snowy ground. "Do you recognize this?"

Ebba nods. "It's Amanda's. I've got one almost exactly the same." She disappears into the hallway and comes back with a bright-pink scarf with an identical pattern. "We bought them together, in a sale at H&M." Her voice is unsteady as she goes on: "What's it doing there?"

There could be countless explanations, but Daniel doesn't want to go into them now. However, the discovery is clearly a step forward. It indicates that Amanda was heading toward her home. The distance between Trollvägen and Pilgrimsvägen, where the Halvorssens live, is just over three miles—a walk that should take around forty minutes in the middle of the night. The rest stop is roughly halfway.

"Which side of the road was it on?" Daniel asks.

"They found it on the southern side."

This suggests that Amanda was walking in the same direction as the traffic—maybe she was hoping for a lift? It was a foolish decision; the main road has no sidewalks. There is no space for pedestrians, and on a dark, snowy night, it could be lethal. However, Amanda seems to have set off along the E14 and lost her scarf. Then she went up in smoke.

"Ask Jarmo to go there instead of coming here," Daniel says.

"He's already on his way."

Anton glances around the kitchen, and Daniel can see that he is drawing the same conclusions about the party. Anton is five years younger than Daniel, but pretty experienced.

He turns to Ebba. "You mentioned a guy called Viktor—why?"

Ebba looks as if she regrets giving Viktor's name.

"They are together," she mumbles reluctantly. "Well . . . nearly."

"What do you mean?"

"They hang out, but it isn't exactly . . . official."

"Why not?"

Ebba's lips tremble. "Amanda doesn't want that."

Daniel studies her closely. He has learned that it's sometimes better to keep quiet until the other person speaks, but Ebba won't meet his gaze and is clearly unwilling to elaborate.

"Was everything okay between them?" Daniel asks.

"I think they had a fight," Ebba replies, her voice fading.

"What kind of fight?"

"I think she was mad at him when she left, but I don't really remember. I was too drunk." She hides her head in her hands. "I'm so sorry," she says, and begins to cry.

SATURDAY, DECEMBER 14

24

It is only five past six when Hanna opens her eyes. It is the first time since she arrived in Åre that she has woken early by herself.

It is pitch black outside, and for a few seconds she can't work out where she is. Then it all comes flooding back. She is lying in the huge double bed in one of Lydia's guest rooms. She refrained from drinking wine last night, so she is neither hungover nor sleepy.

She switches on the bedside lamp, opens up her laptop, and surfs the net for a while. She tries to stay away from Christian's Facebook page, but without success. He's into regular updates and likes to post photos showing the good life—a glass of wine at sunset, a beer on the ski slope. Or cool pictures of all the attractive apartments he sells.

This morning Hanna can't see anything new. He hasn't posted for several days. Oh . . . yes, he has. He's changed his status. It used to say, "In a relationship with Hanna Ahlander."

Now he's in a relationship with Valérie Ohlin.

Hanna goes cold all over.

She stares at the screen for several minutes, digging her nails into the palm of her hand to prevent herself from crying. He's not worth it. Christian is no different from all the other idiots out there. He has lied and been unfaithful, gone behind her back with this Valérie.

He doesn't think about anybody but himself.

The tears are burning behind her eyelids. She forces herself to shut down his profile. Checks out the local weather, goes back to surfing aimlessly.

She finds herself on a group page called Åre Local. Someone has posted a photo of a girl in her late teens with black hair. The caption catches Hanna's attention:

Have you seen Amanda?

She reads on and learns that the girl disappeared in the early hours of Friday morning. Her scarf has been found by the side of the E14, not far from the VM8. Any information could be useful.

The post was placed by a woman—Lena Halvorssen.

When Hanna checks out Lena's own page, she sees the same picture and the same caption. Suddenly she sees the resemblance and realizes what the connection is: they are mother and daughter.

So sad. She hopes the missing girl isn't yet another young woman who has fallen victim to a brutal man.

The memory of Josefin is never far away; Hanna has brooded about her for months. Her body was found at home, with severe head injuries. Five-year-old Lisa lost her mother. Her violent father, Niklas Konradsson, worked in narcotics, three floors above Hanna in the same building.

The City Police didn't want to put a colleague behind bars, so instead everything was swept under the carpet. The official version was that Josefin had slipped in the bathroom and banged her head on the edge of the bathtub. The forensic examination wasn't worth the paper it was written on, and the verdict was accidental death.

The only person who dared to question the mishandling of the investigation was Hanna. She fought for the case to be reopened, for Josefin's death to be looked into properly. Maybe the investigating officers should report themselves for gross misconduct? The assertion that Josefin had died as a result of an accident was clearly an invention. Why had no one questioned Niklas's behavior toward his wife? Why was his version of events simply accepted?

Her boss grew tired of her complaints and accused her of being difficult to work with.

It still hurts.

Hanna returns to the group page. The request was posted only a few hours ago, but there are already lots of supportive comments.

As she reads through them, a fresh update appears, this time from Missing People. Anyone who wants to help search for Amanda is asked to gather in the town square at eight o'clock this morning—the more the better.

Hanna glances at her watch—seven o'clock. She hasn't set foot outside the house since she arrived on Tuesday. She has drunk wine, cried, and moped over Christian. Lydia told her she could use the Mitsubishi in the garage.

Hanna has some knowledge of professional searches, how to go about looking for a missing person.

She would like to help.

She didn't manage to get justice for Josefin, but maybe she can make a useful contribution to the search for Amanda?

And maybe she would feel better if she had something else to think about?

25

When Daniel arrives in the square shortly before eight, about twenty warmly dressed people have already gathered. He recognizes quite a few and nods to them but avoids getting drawn into their conversations.

It wasn't Daniel's idea to contact Missing People—Amanda's parents called them. He doesn't have anything against the organization, given their excellent volunteer base and usefulness on many occasions in the past. But since there is so little to go on, he would have liked more time for the police to get further in their investigation first.

Anyway, it's too late to change things now. The police already made the decision to issue a request for information about Amanda last night after discovering her scarf. Her photograph and description are now on the police home page.

Should he have brought in Missing People right away? Impossible to answer.

Daniel yawns; he has been awake nearly all night. He tossed and turned for a few hours while Ida and Alice slept. The adrenaline is temporarily compensating for his lack of sleep, but it's only a matter of time before his body demands rest.

Anton is approaching from the upper parking lot on Stationsvägen. He is carrying two coffees, and hands one to Daniel.

"You look like shit," he observes. Daniel doesn't bother replying; Anton doesn't look that good either. He gratefully sips the black coffee, feeling its heat spread through his body.

"Östersund sent up two more dog teams," Anton informs him. "Jarmo is here too—they're waiting in the parking lot."

A man in his fifties, wearing a wool hat and holding a blue megaphone, positions himself on the steps of the black building that houses a restaurant above the Stadium Store.

"Good morning!" he shouts. "Can I have your attention?"

Bosse Lundh is a local businessman whom Daniel knows in passing. He owns one of the smaller hotels and a few gas stations. His partner, Annika, stands beside him; she is about the same age, dressed in a dark-green padded jacket, its high collar partly covering her face. Her expression is serious.

It is immediately obvious that Lundh is used to organizing things. Quickly and efficiently, he divides the volunteers into teams. He gives them different tasks and phone numbers to call if they find anything interesting. Other helpers from Missing People distribute maps and Amanda's picture before sending the searchers on their way.

After a final reminder that everyone should return to the square to report back between eleven and twelve, Lundh walks down the steps and joins Daniel and Anton. Annika is right behind him.

"This is a sad story," he says. The pom-pom on his hat bounces up and down as he shakes his head. "I really hope we find her soon."

His partner nods in agreement. "It's difficult to imagine a worse situation than a child going missing," she says. "Even though ours are grown up now."

Lundh puts his arm around her shoulders. "How are the parents taking it?" he asks.

Daniel has specifically asked the Halvorssens not to participate in the search. It's better for them to stay at home in case Amanda gets in touch. Just then he sees Harald Halvorssen drive into the square. He parks carelessly, clambers out of the car, and looks around wildly.

Daniel can hardly blame him for showing up. He himself hasn't been a father for very long, but he knows that nothing would induce him to sit at home if anything happened to Alice.

Halvorssen breaks into a run to catch up with the last search team. His jacket is unfastened and his head is bare. The family's black Labrador retriever trots along behind.

"Poor bastard," Lundh says sympathetically. "It must be terrible for him."

Anton crumples up his empty coffee cup. "I didn't know you were involved in Missing People," he says.

Lundh shrugs, as if he doesn't want any recognition for his efforts. "You do what you can. One of the advantages of living in a small place is that you try to be there for one another. When Missing People asked for local volunteers, it was impossible to say no." He looks Anton in the eye. "When you grow up here, you know what it means to look out for your neighbors. You would have done the same thing if you weren't already a cop, wouldn't you?"

Anton nods without hesitation. He has a lot of family in the area, and is well rooted in the fells and mountains of Jämtland.

Lundh raises a hand in farewell. "Time to get searching," he says, heading off in the direction of the Åregården Hotel parking lot.

Daniel remains where he is, mentally reviewing the situation even though nothing new has come up since last night. Amanda's phone still hasn't been used, and there have been no interesting leads reported on the hotline Östersund has set up.

The most likely explanation is that the girl was picked up in a car near to where she dropped her scarf. The fact that the scarf was found at a rest stop supports that theory. Kids hitching a ride late at night isn't exactly unusual around here.

The problem is the implications of such a scenario. If Amanda had gotten a ride with someone, then she should have made it home safely. It is now thirty hours since she was last seen.

It is becoming increasingly difficult to rule out the suspicion of a crime, but the question is what crime? It could be a coverup after a car accident. If Amanda had been fatally struck by a vehicle, then the driver might have taken the body and dumped it in a spot where it wouldn't be found.

Another equally dreadful possibility is that she has been abducted by a person who wants to exploit her or do her harm.

Daniel has experience of women being kidnapped with a sexual motive, but up here it seems less likely. He would prefer to think that evil of that kind belongs in the big city, not an idyllic mountain environment—although of course that's a naive assumption. Serious crime exists everywhere.

Right now he is still hoping that his colleagues or Missing People will manage to track down Amanda.

Time is running out, but it's not too late to find her alive.

26

The pole that Hanna cautiously pushes down into the thick snow goes deep, without meeting any resistance. She pulls it out, takes a few steps, and repeats the maneuver. She knows that a lifeless body can be covered quickly during heavy snowfall, becoming invisible in a very short time.

The weather during the past few days isn't making the search any easier. It is difficult to make progress, as she repeatedly takes missteps and gets snow in her boots.

She has joined a group searching to the south of the E14, directly below the spot where Amanda's scarf was found. The area lies between the main road and the lake. Åre isn't very big, but in a situation like this, where every square inch must be examined, it's bigger than you think. There are also surprisingly few buildings; the terrain is mostly public or undeveloped land. Hanna has spent many winter breaks in Åre over the years, but has never realized how quickly the wilderness takes over outside the town center.

It is a laborious process. There are seven in the team, all different ages, slowly moving forward in a broad line.

The sun has risen, but the sky is bleak and gray. The light scarcely penetrates the thick cloud cover. Here and there the bare branches of slender mountain birch poke up through the snow, like spidery ink drawings in the ice-cold landscape. Fir trees keep them company, their lower branches brushing the ground as the snow weighs them down.

They have all been given a description of Amanda, but Hanna knows it won't help much. The girl was wearing a black jacket, a yellow top, and black jeans. A red or orange jacket would have been much better, but what teenager would wear something like that?

She stares at the ground, trying to spot anything out of the ordinary, a shape that doesn't belong, but everything disappears in the white blanket that fools the eye and distorts proportions.

"This feels kind of creepy," says the young woman closest to Hanna. Her voice is high and girlish, and she looks about the same age as Hanna. She is wearing a dark-brown padded jacket that has clearly been with her for quite some time. "Have you done this before?" she goes on.

"A few times," Hanna murmurs.

"Imagine if you push your pole down into her body . . ."

Hanna doesn't quite know how to reply to that.

"My name's Karoline, by the way, but everybody calls me Karro."

"Hanna."

She doesn't really want to chat, and turns her attention to the lake. Amanda definitely hasn't drowned. The lake must be frozen almost to the bottom in these temperatures. At this time of year, it's used mainly for snowmobiles and ice racing.

Hanna recalls one winter's evening when she was ten or eleven years old. She sat on the snowmobile behind her father, with her arms around his waist, and they went out onto the ice. The speed was intoxicating, and he laughed at her excitement. She loved it when it was just the two of them, when she escaped her mother's critical gaze.

What happened next? She doesn't remember, just the feeling of being happy. One of the few good memories from her visits to Åre.

"Are you from Stockholm?" Karro seems determined to start a conversation.

"Is it that obvious?"

Karro laughs. "Åre's not very big, and I haven't seen you before. Plus, you can't imagine how many Stockholmers are moving up here these days, wanting to get away from the big city. Where are you staying?"

"In Sadeln—in my sister's house."

"What's your job?"

Hanna hesitates. She has no desire to tell Karro about her situation, but at the same time she doesn't want to be unfriendly.

"I'm a police officer."

"So is my brother!" Karro says. "Will you be taking up a post here in Åre?"

Hanna shakes her head. "I'm not working at the moment."

Karro's expression is openly curious. "Burnout?"

"Not exactly . . ." Hanna isn't about to elaborate.

"Everyone burns out," Karro says in the same tone as if she were discussing the weather. "Nobody can cope with this crazy tempo anymore. There are cuts and reductions all over the place. I work in a preschool; the constant idiotic suggestions from politicians about how to save money drive us crazy."

"Mmm . . ."

Hanna chooses not to correct Karro. Better for her to think that Hanna has burned out rather than to discover she's been fired.

The very thought of it makes her stomach turn over.

Hanna focuses on the search, fixes her gaze a few yards in front of her feet, and tries to find a steady rhythm. She pushes the pole into the snow at the same time as she puts down her right foot. They haven't been out for very long, but Hanna is freezing cold despite the clothes she borrowed from Lydia's extensive wardrobe: thick thermal dungarees and boots.

"Do you know the Halvorssen family?" Karro asks after a while.

"No."

"In that case it's good of you to help."

Hanna mumbles something unintelligible.

"I saw the mother's post on Facebook and immediately decided to join in," Karro continues. "In a little place like this, you have to take care of one another. My oldest daughter is in elementary school with Amanda's little brother and sister. Märta knows exactly who she is."

Karro keeps chatting away, apparently undaunted by Hanna's monosyllabic responses. She's nice—sweetly disarming.

Hanna glances up toward the E14. They've been out for an hour and a half, but they haven't gotten very far. If Amanda had set off along the E14 on foot, it seems unlikely that she would have turned off here to plod through deep snow and take a different route home.

Hanna is becoming increasingly convinced that they are wasting their time, but she doesn't want to openly criticize Missing People's input. Sometimes it's better to keep quiet and follow orders; that's something she's learned from her mistakes over the past few months.

"You know he's a politician?" Karro interrupts Hanna's train of thought. "He's actually the chair of the local council."

"Who?"

"Amanda's father—Harald Halvorssen."

"Right." Hanna had no idea what the parents did.

"I suppose he does the best he can, but . . ." Karro pauses, leaving Hanna to draw her own conclusion before adding, "He hasn't made himself very popular."

Hanna is reluctant to join in the gossip about Amanda's parents, it doesn't feel right, yet she can't help asking the obvious question: "How come?"

Karro stops. She raises her right hand, rubs her thumb meaningfully against her fingers, though the gesture loses something inside the thick mitten she's wearing. "It was that business of the world championship last winter."

"The world championship?"

Hanna feels stupid—she doesn't know what Karro is talking about. Well, of course she knows the world championship in downhill skiing recently took place in Åre, but that's about it.

"The calculations were completely wrong," Karro explains. "A lot of people lost big money. There was going to be a huge festival, the hotels would be full, everyone would have the opportunity to make plenty of money from the different events. But all the fuss surrounding the world championship frightened away the ordinary tourists, and most businesses lost revenue instead. And the weather was crap."

Karro sounds upset, but she seems to want to share her feelings rather than badmouth individuals. Hanna can't think of a good answer, so she keeps quiet as they set off again, pushing their poles into the deep snow.

"I also heard the boyfriend might be involved," Karro suddenly says.

Hanna turns to look at her. "Who's that?"

"His name is Viktor Landahl. He goes to the same school as Amanda, in a parallel class. The family lives in Björnänge."

"And why would he be behind her disappearance?"

Hanna hears the sharpness in her tone, but Karro doesn't seem to notice. She lowers her voice, a conspiratorial look in her eyes. "My friend's kid brother knows him. Apparently, Viktor's a bit of a . . . bad boy, if you understand my meaning." Her cheeks are pink with the cold. "He beat up his ex-girlfriend. The family is from Umeå, so not many people around here know about it. They moved here after it happened—he was only fifteen at the time. Believe it or not, he wasn't even fined or referred to youth services. He just got some kind of warning."

"A caution," Hanna says. It just slips out. A caution is used for young offenders who haven't committed a crime in the past and who are deemed to be able to get the help and support they need from their own family. If the individual reoffends within six months, then the caution is withdrawn and the case goes to court. Otherwise, the crime is struck from the records.

"If I was a cop, I'd arrest him right away," Karro says.

Hanna doesn't comment. Karro means well—she's just making small talk.

Karro pushes down her pole with some force. "They say that once doesn't count . . ."

"Do the police know about the boyfriend and his background?" Hanna asks. "Have you mentioned him to your brother?"

Karro laughs out loud. "To Anton? There's no point."

"Why not?"

"I'm a preschool teacher. I don't know anything about police work."

"What you said sounds important to me."

Karro looks embarrassed. "It's probably just gossip."

They have reached a flat area of virgin snow, and the team spreads out. Hanna sinks up to her knees with each step. They are no more than five minutes by car from the central square in Åre, yet this place feels desolate and deserted.

So there's a boyfriend with a history of abuse. Could he be involved? Hanna wouldn't be surprised if there were a crime behind Amanda's disappearance.

In ninety percent of cases of violence against women, the perpetrator is someone close to the victim.

27

When the police car pulls up outside the Halvorssens' house, Lena's body reacts with sheer panic. A buzzing sound fills her ears, as if a swarm of bees has taken up residence inside her head. She is shivering, her skin clammy with cold sweat.

It's the same two officers as the previous day.

The one with the beard looks up at the house and shakes his head, the other says something and locks the car. Then they begin to walk toward the front door, their expressions grave.

They have come to tell Lena that Amanda is dead. She knows it—a mother's instinct is never wrong.

Dear God, what has she done to be punished like this?

The doorbell rings, but she doesn't move. Then she hears Daniel Lindskog's deep voice from the hallway.

"Hello? Anyone home?"

Lena wants to yell *Go away!* but she knows her voice will break.

"Can we come in?"

The paralysis eases, and she manages to croak, "Of course."

Lena isn't able to stand up when Daniel and his colleague Anton enter the kitchen. She grips the edge of the table to stop herself from fainting, forces out her question through lips that barely move: "Is she dead?"

Daniel's look of surprise gives her the answer.

"No. Or to be more accurate, we don't know. We've circulated her description, and we're still searching."

The relief is so great that Lena sways on her chair. Daniel quickly puts an arm around her shoulders to support her. The physical contact brings her back to reality. She buries her face in both hands and begins to cry.

"Can I get you some water?" Daniel asks. Without waiting for her to reply, he finds a glass and fills it. Lena takes tiny sips as she struggles to regain control.

Daniel sits down opposite her, gives her a minute.

"The search is ongoing," he assures her. "We've brought in additional officers from Östersund, and Missing People is looking too—I saw that your husband had joined them. We just need to talk to you, if that's okay?"

Lena nods and puts down the glass. Her hand is shaking so much that the glass rattles against the surface of the table, but at least she doesn't knock it over.

Daniel leans forward, his elbow touching a gouge in the table—the result of Amanda slamming down a cast-iron trivet when she lost her temper. She was sent to her room as a punishment. Right now Lena would give anything to have her standing here throwing a tantrum.

The tears are still flowing.

Why did they argue so much? She can't even remember. Instead she pictures Amanda in the twins' room, reading them a story with such enthusiasm that it turns into a full performance. When Lena is washing the dishes, Amanda often creeps up behind her and surprises her with a hug. She still curls up on the sofa with her head on Lena's lap to watch TV, purring like a cat and wanting her mother to rub her back, like she did when Amanda was a little girl.

"We need to understand more about your daughter and her habits," Daniel goes on. "She may have been seen on the E14 in the early hours of Friday morning. Someone called our hotline and said he saw a pedestrian on the road and a dark-colored car that stopped in the rest stop where her scarf was found."

Lena's mind is working in slow motion. "Oh?" she says, wiping her eyes with the back of her hand.

"Do you know if Amanda has any enemies? Anyone who might have followed her when she left the party?"

"I find that hard to believe." Lena turns the idea over; it seems completely bizarre. "Why would someone want to hurt her? She's only a child!"

"We're looking into every possibility." Daniel's expression is unreadable.

"Does she have many friends?" Anton asks, taking the chair next to his colleague.

"Yes. She's very popular."

Lena sees the wry smile she often wore when heading off to school, as if she'd rather go there than stay at home. All those times when Lena searched for the right words to say before Amanda left the house. Usually she only managed *Have a nice day.*

"She is happy in her class—they're a good group of kids, and she and Ebba have hung out together since they were little. Amanda is very likable; she has lots of ideas, and she's creative. She's always there for her friends."

"We're intending to speak to her adviser, the guy you mentioned yesterday," Daniel informs her. "Did she like him?"

Lena thinks for a moment. Amanda seemed very keen on Lasse during her first year at high school, but since then she's talked about him less and less.

"I think so."

Daniel nods. "Her boyfriend, Viktor—what can you tell us about him?"

Lena is confused. "Who?"

"Viktor Landahl. According to Ebba, they were together."

"I don't know anything about that," Lena admits. "He's never been here."

Daniel strokes his beard. "Could there have been anyone else involved?"

"I don't know."

"We're wondering if Amanda might have arranged to meet someone after the party without telling you or Ebba," Anton explains. "If she might have gone off with some boy and things went wrong."

Lena looks away. They have so many questions, and she has no answers. Her cheeks burn with shame; she is a bad mother, knowing so little about her eldest daughter's love life. She should have kept an eye on things, but everyday life has swallowed her up: her job, the twins, all the activities she must fit in.

The days have simply run away with her. She hasn't had time to stop, reflect.

"Is Amanda active on social media?" Daniel asks. "Could she have met someone that way?"

Amanda was always connected, always online. Whenever Lena knocked on her door and went into her room, the laptop was open, but the second she saw her mother she would slam it shut. Lena has no idea who Amanda hung out with in cyberspace. It is impossible to have that kind of control over an eighteen-year-old.

"I can't answer that."

"What about her finances?" Anton says. "Has she had more money to spend recently?"

She has, come to think of it. Over the past year Amanda has rarely begged for more money for clothes and makeup.

Suddenly Lena realizes the implications of the question. "Are you saying she's met an older man?"

"We need to explore every alternative," Daniel replies.

"It's not unusual for older men to make contact with young girls through various online forums," Anton adds.

"I can't imagine Amanda doing that," Lena whispers. She can't bring herself to wonder about the reasons behind Amanda's improved finances. She doesn't want to speculate. Her daughter has become more reticent over the past twelve months. When Lena has asked questions, Amanda has mostly snapped at her to butt out. Lena has told herself that it's just a phase, that it's going to pass.

"How would you describe your daughter?" Daniel says. "What about her ability to see the consequences of her actions? Is she mature for her age?"

Lena scratches her wrist. "I suppose she's like most teenagers," she says, even though she has often complained to Harald that Amanda doesn't take enough responsibility at home. She can't tell them that; it would be a betrayal. She settles on a compromise. "She's not irresponsible. She would never do anything stupid or illegal. She takes care of her little brother and sister."

"Do you think she would have gotten into a stranger's car if he offered her a ride?" Anton is constantly taking notes, as if every word is significant.

Lena isn't sure. There are buses, but they stop running pretty early on the weekends. Teenagers usually walk or cycle, but of course they sometimes hitch a ride. She has often picked up kids wandering along the road with their thumb in the air. They live in a safe place; she has never been afraid of giving a hitchhiker a ride.

"It's possible," she says.

Daniel signals to Anton and stands up.

"We'd like to see Amanda's room," he says. "We also need to take her computer, if that's okay."

"Of course."

Lena gets to her feet, feeling as if she doesn't belong in her own body. Standing outside Amanda's door, she experiences the weirdest sensation; for a millisecond she is convinced that her daughter is in there, lying in bed.

That this is all just a huge misunderstanding.

Then she opens the door of the empty room and remembers that the nightmare is real.

Both police officers follow her in. Lena sees what they see: an untidy room with a bed, a desk from IKEA, and an old blue wing-back armchair by the window. There is a pile of clothes at the foot of the unmade bed.

Lena wants to go over and touch the clothes, bury her nose in them to reassure herself that she hasn't forgotten her daughter's smell.

The bulletin board above the desk is adorned with photographs of Amanda and her friends. One is of Amanda in a yellow bikini on the shore of Lake Åre, with an almost identical picture of Ebba next to it. In a photo-booth strip, Amanda is making silly faces. It is hanging a little askew.

Anton has found Amanda's laptop on the armchair under a gray woolen sweater. He opens it up, and Amanda's suntanned face beams out at them. Her screensaver is a photo of herself and the twins.

"Do you know the password?"

Lena shakes her head. Amanda would never share that information.

"Does she have an iPad too?"

"No, just the laptop and her phone."

As they leave the room, Daniel pauses in the doorway. "If you think of anyone Amanda might have been in touch with, maybe someone outside her usual circle, you need to contact us right away."

Lena nods. She really does want to help, but all she can hear is the same question, repeated over and over again inside her head:

Why can't you find her?

28

The Landahl family lives on Jämtgårdsvägen in an old wooden house that is slightly isolated, with no neighbors in sight. Festive torches are burning by the entrance when Daniel parks on the drive. He and Anton have come to see Viktor, Amanda's secret boyfriend.

He might well have been one of the last people to see her.

When the front door opens, they are met with the sound of Christmas music and the aroma of mulled wine and gingerbread cookies. A woman in her fifties wearing an apron over a sparkly top is standing there with a big smile on her face.

The smile disappears when she sees Daniel holding up his police ID.

"Oh—I was expecting someone else. We're having a party shortly."

"This won't take long. We need to speak to Viktor Landahl—I'm assuming you're his mother?"

The woman nods. "Maria Landahl." She looks worried. "Why are you looking for Viktor? What's happened?" Her hands flutter nervously over her apron.

"We just need a word with him," Anton says. "It's about his schoolmate Amanda Halvorssen—as I'm sure you're aware, she went missing in the early hours of Friday morning."

Maria Landahl inhales sharply. "Such a terrible thing! I feel so sorry for her parents."

She goes to the foot of the stairs and shouts, "Viktor, could you come down please?"

After a minute or so, a boy in a black hoodie comes shambling down the stairs. He is barefoot and makes no attempt to hurry. There is a ragged hole in one knee of his jeans.

Daniel requested a background check on him, but nothing interesting came up.

"These two police officers want to talk to you," his mother explains. She smooths down her hair and glances anxiously out of the window. If she's worried about a police car on the drive, she can rest easy; they came in an unmarked vehicle.

"Is there somewhere we can talk in private?" Daniel wonders.

Maria looks over at the front door.

"Our guests will be arriving at any minute, and I presume you don't want to be disturbed. Could you go upstairs?" She licks her lips, checks her watch. "Can I be there?"

Daniel shakes his head. "I'm afraid not—it's best if we see Viktor on his own. He is eighteen, after all."

Maria doesn't insist; she just gives them one last worried look before disappearing into the kitchen.

Daniel and Anton follow Viktor up the stairs to a spacious room with a gray corner sofa. There is a large flatscreen TV on the wall, with a movie paused in the middle of a scene where two small people are climbing a mountain. It's *The Lord of the Rings*—Daniel has seen the trilogy several times.

There is a half-empty bag of chips and a can of Fanta on the coffee table, and crumbs litter the floor and cushions.

Viktor parks himself in one corner, as far from the two officers as possible.

"What's this about?" he says, putting his feet on the coffee table.

"We have some questions about one of your classmates, Amanda Halvorssen," Daniel begins.

"She's not in my class."

"But she's in a parallel class?" Anton says.

Viktor nods, then yawns, revealing his back teeth. He seems as slow and hungover as Ebba was the previous evening.

"Amanda is missing."

"Mmm, I know."

"You were at Ebba's party when she disappeared. Did Amanda speak to you before she left?"

"I haven't done anything."

The answer comes a little too quickly.

"We're not saying you did," Anton assures him. "We just want to know what happened before she left the party."

"Right."

"Can you tell us about the evening?" Daniel prompts him.

"We kind of hung out, you know. Talked shit." He runs a hand through the dark hair hanging over his forehead. "We stood in the kitchen, drank some beer. A while later I saw her put on her jacket and leave."

"What time was this?"

"I don't remember—pretty late. Definitely after midnight. One o'clock, maybe?"

"Did she say where she was going?"

"No."

"Did she seem different in any way?"

"No."

"Do you know if she was afraid for any reason?"

"No."

Viktor answers in a monotone, with no real engagement. He sinks deeper into the cushions and digs his phone out of his back pocket, checks the screen.

"Had you had a fight?" Daniel's tone is sharper now.

Viktor glares at him. "It was just banter."

"Ebba told us the two of you are together. And that you'd quarreled during the evening."

Viktor reaches for the Fanta and takes a few slugs, leaving a sticky orange residue at the corners of his mouth.

"Had you?" Daniel pushes him.

"She was pretty pissed off at me before she left. She thought I was too drunk."

"And were you?"

Viktor gives a faint grin. He puts his phone down on the table; the case shows a picture of a coiled snake against a black background.

"I was completely out of it."

Now it is Daniel's turn to glare. "Is that all you have to say?"

At least Viktor has the grace to look embarrassed. He picks up his phone, checks the screen again. It is less than thirty seconds since he put it down; this is clearly some kind of compulsion.

"We're talking about your girlfriend here," Daniel points out.

"She's not my girlfriend. We just hook up sometimes."

The boy's lethargic attitude annoys Daniel. Why doesn't he understand the gravity of the situation? His girlfriend could die while he lies on the sofa, stuffing his face with chips. Daniel had a few messy years as a teenager, but at least he used his brain.

Then he notices Viktor's dilated pupils, and suddenly it all makes sense. He's taken something. This explains why the boy has barely reacted to the fact that Amanda is missing; he's in a world of his own.

Daniel sniffs the air but can't detect any hint of cannabis. He feels a surge of anger.

"Listen to me, you little shit!" he roars, slamming his hand down on the table with such force that Viktor jumps. "We need your help!"

Anton gives him a look. Daniel takes a couple of deep breaths to calm himself. He rarely loses his temper at work.

Viktor is staring angrily at him. "I've already told you—I don't know what happened!"

Anton steps in before Daniel can respond.

"What did you do after Amanda left the party?" His tone is considerably gentler than his colleague's.

"I fell asleep at Ebba's. I went straight to school from her house the next morning. Wille was there too."

"You didn't find it strange when Amanda didn't show up at school?"

"No." Viktor extends his arms out. "I just thought she was at home sleeping it off, like everybody else. I didn't feel too good myself; I went home straight after the Lucia procession. I couldn't handle staying for classes. Wille did the same."

"And what have you done today?"

"Nothing much. I've mostly been lying here watching movies."

Daniel is beyond frustrated. This spaced-out kid is no help at all. They ought to speak to his mother, tell her what her son is up to, but right now there are more important things to take care of.

He places his card on the table.

"If you think of anything, anything at all that might help us to find Amanda, you need to call us."

Viktor is already reaching for the remote.

"Sure," he mumbles as he presses play.

29

Briefing in the conference room at Åre police station. The room is furnished with an oval table and ten chairs. The seats are upholstered in red, while everything else is white, including the walls and the surface of the table.

The large whiteboard almost blends in with the background.

Daniel is seated at one end of the table, with Anton and Raffe beside him. They have just linked up with Östersund, where several other officers are participating via Zoom.

Chief Inspector Birgitta Grip, head of the Serious Crimes Unit and Daniel's boss, appears onscreen to open the meeting. She is due to retire in a couple of years, but her commitment is undiminished. She was responsible for Daniel's appointment. They had gotten to know each other in Gothenburg when he worked for what was then known as the narcotics squad, led by Grip. Eventually she moved north to Östersund, where she grew up. Five years later, when Daniel wanted to get away from Gothenburg, she had brought him onto her team.

She listens attentively as Daniel summarizes the situation.

Missing People has not found Amanda, nor anything that might explain her disappearance. There is nothing to indicate violence or a scuffle near the rest stop where her scarf was found, and no evidence of a traffic collision. Amanda's boyfriend, Viktor, had little to contribute.

"The scarf in the rest stop is the last clue we have to go on," he concludes. "Therefore the most likely scenario is that she either got into a car voluntarily, or was dragged into it against her will."

He mentions the caller who spotted a stationary vehicle on the E14; unfortunately this person couldn't recall either the make or the registration number, merely that the car was large and dark, possibly a black SUV.

"Why wouldn't Amanda contact her mom or dad if she'd gone with someone voluntarily?" Raffe asks.

"Maybe she was mad at her parents and wanted to punish them," Anton replies. "It wouldn't be the first time."

The fact that Amanda's phone hasn't been used since she went missing is a concern. Research shows that most teenagers access their phone roughly every five minutes.

Maybe she's lost it? But you can always borrow someone else's phone.

Every hypothesis leads to fresh, unanswered questions. Daniel suppresses a yawn; he really needs to go home, get some sleep.

Birgitta Grip clears her throat. Her gray hair is cut in a practical style that underlines her no-nonsense approach.

"Is there anything to suggest abduction?" she says. "Possibly with a financial motive?"

Daniel shakes his head. There has been no ransom demand, plus that kind of kidnapping is extremely rare in Sweden. The idea that someone is holding Amanda captive in order to extort money from Harald and Lena Halvorssen seems very far-fetched.

"The parents aren't especially well off," he replies. "Admittedly the father is the chair of the local council, but I think his capital is more political than financial. As far as I know, they have no other significant resources, and no one has asked for money."

"What about political motives?" Grip wonders.

"A lot of people were furious about the council's handling of the world championship last winter," Anton concedes. "However, I find it difficult to imagine that someone would exact revenge by abducting

Halvorssen's daughter almost a year later." He scratches the back of his neck beneath his dark-blue T-shirt, showing off his well-defined muscles. He is short but very toned; fitness is one of his main interests, alongside music.

"Okay, we'll leave that for the moment." Grip makes a note on her pad, then continues: "If the girl went voluntarily, then it's likely that she knew the driver. Let's focus on that. Start with her circle of friends and those who were at the party, see if there's anyone she hangs out with who has a record of violence or any other criminal act. Check out the school, find out if she has a part-time job. Begin with the basics."

Daniel nods. Time to get down to business. The search for a missing eighteen-year-old girl has turned into a criminal investigation.

"Assuming she was picked up by a car—are there cameras on that road?" Grip asks. If they'd been in England or Switzerland, there would have been cameras everywhere. In Sweden only speed cameras are used. The chances of a kidnapper driving fast enough to risk being snapped are minimal, but of course they ought to check it out.

"We'll contact Kiruna," Daniel assures his boss. The unit that issues fines to speeding drivers is based in Kiruna. Daniel signals to Anton, who nods and rubs his forehead. He seems hot even though he is wearing a T-shirt, his normal attire whatever the season.

"I'll check with the gas stations too," Raffe offers. "Most of them have CCTV. It's worth finding out if anyone in Amanda's circle of acquaintances has been caught on camera."

Grip agrees.

Daniel wonders how they are going to get everything done. There's no shortage of tasks, but their resources are limited. Even with Anton and Raffe, they are badly understaffed. Right now there are three unfilled posts in the Serious Crimes Unit in Östersund, and the staffing situation is equally dire in Åre. The fact that they have lost several experienced investigators in recent years because of the heavily criticized reorganization of the police service in 2015 doesn't exactly help matters.

His gaze falls on the clock on the wall. It is five to two. Amanda has been missing for approximately thirty-six hours.

Frustration makes him clench his fists under the table. Every hour is critical.

Amanda is lying on the bed, her eyes fixed on the glow as the last of the logs burns down.

Now there is nothing else to make a fire with.

She is freezing cold.

She has already used everything she could find, stained old comic books and the threadbare rug. She dare not shove the mattresses into the stove; she's afraid they are so flammable that the whole cabin would catch fire. The risk is too great.

How long has she been locked up?

It is impossible to say, she just knows that her hunger has gone away. She is thirsty, though.

Why is she here? Why hasn't anyone come to rescue her?

Soon the glow will fade and die. Then she will be alone in the darkness.

She is more afraid of the dark than the cold.

With the last of her strength, she drags herself over to the window. Everything is black and desolate; there isn't a soul in sight. Should she try to get out that way?

It is pointless—barefoot and without clothes, she will freeze to death in a few short hours. She doesn't even know if she'd be able to crawl under the bar across the pane.

She finds a rusty fork on the table and scratches her name on the window frame, right next to the glass.

She wants to write more, that she is alone and locked in, that she needs help, but she doesn't have the energy. Instead she crawls back to the bed and curls up under the thin coverlet and the mattress from the top bunk, which she pulled down for extra warmth. There is nothing else.

Mommy, *she thinks again, wondering if they are searching for her.*

Surely someone should be out there looking? It must be many hours since she disappeared.

Or is that an illusion too?

She no longer knows what is a dream and what is reality.

She doesn't want to die like this.

All alone.

30

When Hanna parks Lydia's Mitsubishi on the drive behind the house, she is still frozen stiff after the search with Missing People.

The short time in the car hasn't warmed her up, and she isn't used to the cold. Up here it gets right into your bones, freezing your body from the inside. It's dangerous if you're not wearing the right clothes.

She unlocks the door and goes straight into the kitchen, takes out cocoa, milk, and sugar. Her body longs for something sweet and comforting; a cup of hot chocolate is exactly what she needs.

As she stands at the stove, stirring the mixture, the aroma evokes a different kitchen in another house in Åre, twenty-five years ago.

The house they used to rent during the February break when she was growing up.

She sees her mother whisking cocoa, milk, and sugar in a pan. Hanna is sitting at the table, waiting. How old was she then? Eight or nine, maybe?

There is a plate of freshly baked cinnamon buns in the middle of the table. They smell amazing, but Hanna doesn't dare take one without permission. She and Daddy have been out skiing; she is happy and in a good mood. He told her she had real talent, and that she was better than Lydia had been at the same age.

The praise makes her proud; she feels grown up and clever as she sits there resting her chin on her hands.

Everything changes when she spills chocolate on her expensive new ski suit. Her stomach contracts. She is afraid of doing the wrong thing;

Mommy told her to be careful. She can't move, not even to wipe away the spot.

Mommy's face darkens as soon as she sees what has happened. She sighs in that special way, the way that kills the atmosphere in a second. Then she doesn't say a word all evening, as if everything has been ruined.

Her father didn't speak up in Hanna's defense. He let her mother's feelings destroy their special day, just as he always let her mood swings dictate family life.

Hanna pours the chocolate into a mug and drops the pan into the sink with such force that the small amount of liquid remaining splashes up and scalds her.

Her father has never gone against her mother. When Ulla finds out about the situation with Christian, she will go on and on about it until Hanna falls apart. And her father will do nothing to stop it.

She can't think about her parents anymore. At this time of day, they will probably be relaxing by the pool, enjoying the day's first glass of rosé.

Hanna forces herself to think about something else as she sips her chocolate. After the search, Karro had asked if she wanted to go for coffee. She seemed kind, the sort of person who wants everyone to be okay. Hanna remembers what Karro told her about Amanda, her father, and her boyfriend.

When they returned to the square to report back, Karro pointed out Harald Halvorssen. He was standing with his dog, talking to two men. He had a tortured expression on his face.

Hanna moves to the table and opens her laptop. She wants to know more about Harald and his family. Maybe this will dispel her own dark thoughts. She googles the name, which brings up several images. Harald is smiling in every one, his blue eyes are striking. The surname sounds Norwegian. Quite right—his father comes from Trondheim, but Harald grew up in Järpen with his Swedish mother and a younger brother.

Hanna reads everything she can find.

He has been a member of the Center Party throughout his adult life, active in the local youth federation, and he has always lived in Jämtland except for a few years when he studied economics at the University of Umeå. Married to Lena, his childhood sweetheart. Amanda is the eldest of three children. Harald has done a lot of cross-country skiing—he even competed for a while—and of course he owns a snowmobile like everyone else in this part of the country.

The chocolate has warmed Hanna up. Her fingers and toes hurt as they begin to thaw out. She grimaces in pain as her feet come back to life, and she has to massage her soles to ease the agony.

There is nothing else on Harald Halvorssen, so she decides to google the World Downhill Skiing Championships in Åre instead. The screen is immediately filled with news headlines. The event was clearly controversial, just as Karro had said. There was no shortage of criticism afterward, and some local businesses even demanded compensation from the council.

Hanna finishes her chocolate and looks out of the window. Darkness is already falling, Renfjället is barely visible now, and Åreskutan is enveloped in clouds. The sun sets at twenty past two; the five hours of daylight pass quickly.

She can't find anything interesting online about the Halvorssen family, but Karro mentioned a boyfriend—Viktor Landahl. He didn't sound like much of a catch. It's unusual for such young men to commit serious crimes like kidnapping or homicide, but it does happen.

Once again she thinks about poor Josefin.

Hanna can't help wondering whether the investigating officers know about Viktor's background; it's information they should have. If he really was given a caution, then it should be on record. It is reasonable to assume that the local police have already discovered this and questioned the boy.

Unless of course Viktor has time on his side. A caution is struck from the records after three years; if he's lucky, it might just have vanished. Karro said he was fifteen when it happened.

Hanna shakes her head. It's not her responsibility to follow it up.

She adjusts the steel-gray sheepskin over the back of the chair. The soft, curly fleece makes her feel warm and cozy; her fingers and toes are almost back to normal, but it has taken her almost an hour to reach this stage. If Amanda is outdoors, there is no chance that she is still alive.

31

Ida shakes Daniel by the shoulder.

"Wake up, darling."

He doesn't want to, his whole body aches from the lack of sleep, but finally he opens his eyes. Ida is holding his phone.

"It's work," she says, sounding worried. "They've tried to get a hold of you several times."

Daniel's brain isn't working properly. "What time is it?" he mumbles.

"Almost seven o'clock in the evening."

That means he's slept for three hours. When he got back to the apartment, he was so exhausted that he went straight to the bedroom and collapsed next to Alice, who was snoozing away contentedly.

He realizes she's not there anymore, and tries to blink away the drowsiness. He takes the phone from Ida. "Okay."

Anton answers when Daniel calls back. Anton had been allowed to go home and sleep last night, so he took over station duties when Daniel went off to get some rest.

"You need to come in," he says immediately. "We've found something interesting."

"What?"

A voice says a few words in the background.

"Just get here as soon as you can."

The call ends, and Daniel sits there with the phone in his hand. When he glances up, Ida is still there, looking anxious. She isn't used to this kind of activity; there has never been an investigation like this since Daniel moved to Åre.

Things were different in Gothenburg, of course. Sometimes everything else had to be put to one side while he worked day and night on an urgent case. He's gotten used to working in a different way up here, in a calmer environment.

He hasn't told Ida that he was in considerable danger following a serious homicide down south. During the eighteen months they've been together, he has come home and eaten dinner with her almost every evening.

"I have to go."

"You're going back to work?" Ida fingers the long braid hanging over one shoulder.

Daniel holds up his hands, palms outward.

"I'm sorry, but I really do have to go."

"But you were out all night."

"It's an emergency. An eighteen-year-old girl is missing."

She nods and takes a step closer, strokes his cheek. "I understand. It's terrible." She takes a deep breath, exhales through her nose. "I'm kind of ashamed to say this when you're under so much pressure, but it's not easy being alone with Alice all the time. It drives me crazy when she just cries and cries and you're not here. I don't know if I can do this on my own."

Ida's eyes well up with tears.

Daniel can't help feeling stressed. The last thing he wants is to upset her, but she ought to understand the seriousness of the situation.

"Listen, I promise things will get better. I'll help out more in the future. As soon as this case is over."

He really doesn't want a quarrel. He flares up easily when they fight, and he doesn't have time for that right now. He knows from bitter experience what can happen when he loses control. His damned temper has caused so many problems. The legacy of his Italian ancestors, especially his maternal grandfather, is much too near the surface.

He pulls Ida close, kisses her forehead. At first her body is rigid; then she relaxes.

"I really hope you find her," she murmurs into his chest. "Do you know she was in her first year at high school when Sara was in her final year?"

Sara is Ida's younger sister; she is training to be a hairdresser in Sundsvall, just as their mother, Elisabeth, once did. Elisabeth now owns a salon in Järpen.

A piercing yell splits the air from the living room, where Alice was sleeping in her buggy. This is the time when the colic usually kicks in, but every evening they hope it won't happen.

Ida looks at Daniel, her eyes full of gentle warmth. "I'll take care of Alice," she says. "You go."

32

The parking lot at the police station is almost full when Daniel arrives in his silver-gray Kia Sportage. The wind grabs the car door as soon as he opens it, and he fights his way to the main entrance through the swirling snow.

Anton is coming toward him along the corridor. He looks stressed and is wearing plastic gloves, as if he has just been handling evidence.

Daniel's pulse quickens.

"Come with me," Anton says without stopping.

The large conference room has been turned into a temporary hub. Pictures of Amanda are displayed on a notice board, along with the photo of the rest stop where her scarf was found. However, something else catches Daniel's attention.

Several items of clothing are laid out on the table. A black padded jacket with a hood, a pair of dark-colored jeans, white socks. Light-brown UGG boots, a bright-yellow crop top.

He immediately understands what this means. "You've found Amanda's clothes!"

Anton nods, pulls out a chair. "We were incredibly lucky," he says, bouncing slightly on his seat and brimming with excitement.

Daniel takes the chair opposite his colleague. "What happened?"

"A local guy called us an hour ago. He was out on the mountain on his snowmobile despite the bad weather. When he was on the trail north of Ullådalen, he spotted a plastic bag pushed into a crevice. He thought it might contain food scraps and didn't want animals to spread them, so he stopped and took the bag with the intention of throwing it in the trash when he got home. He happened to open it and found the clothes."

Anton is right—it's an unbelievable stroke of luck. Exactly what they need right now.

Daniel puts on a pair of plastic gloves and picks up the jeans to take a closer look. "How did he know there was a connection with Amanda's disappearance?"

"He'd seen the appeal Missing People posted on Facebook, with Amanda's description. It was the yellow top that made him call us."

Missing People.

Daniel was uneasy about their involvement, but now he's grateful. The organization has a reach that official police channels can't compete with. He's also pleased that Amanda was wearing such an easily recognizable bright-yellow top when she went missing.

He examines each item carefully. Nothing seems to have been ripped, which means the clothes probably weren't removed with force. Not even a button is missing.

"Any sign of violence?" he asks. "Any traces of blood?"

Anton shakes his head.

"How about semen?"

Even if they don't know whether a man or a woman is behind the possible abduction, statistically it is more likely to be a man. Of all crimes involving a threat to life, eighty-five percent are committed by men.

"Nothing visible to the naked eye, but we can't be sure until forensics has checked everything."

The absence of blood and semen is good; it means that in the best-case scenario, the girl hasn't been injured.

Daniel stares at the clothes. Something is missing.

"No bra or panties—weren't they there?"

"No."

The thought of a perpetrator making a young girl strip half-naked is chilling.

"What kind of bag was everything in?"

"An ordinary plastic grocery bag," Anton replies. "We're sending it off to forensics as well—there might be fingerprints or DNA."

Daniel thinks out loud. "Why did someone try to hide her clothes? What does that mean?"

Raffe has just come into the room. "At least it proves that she didn't run away. She would hardly have hidden them in such an odd place."

Daniel nods. "Any sign of her phone?"

"No."

"The location must be significant," Daniel muses. "Who hides something by a snowmobile trail?"

"A person who's out on the mountain anyway?" Anton suggests. "Traveling by snowmobile?"

"Someone who's used to the mountains, then."

Anton nods.

"Someone local," Daniel goes on. "Who else would it be?"

"If so, that's terrible!"

Anton seems to take the idea personally. He is a local patriot who would never willingly set foot in a big city.

"I'm wondering if the perp might have dropped Amanda off somewhere and disposed of the bag on his way back," Raffe says. "He—or she—maybe wanted to get rid of it before going home, in order to reduce the risk of discovery."

"Sounds reasonable," Anton says.

"In which case he or she must have a family of their own; otherwise it would be irrelevant," Daniel counters. He walks around the table to study the clothes from a different angle. They are in small sizes. Amanda isn't very tall, only five foot four. She would have no chance against an adult, especially a man.

"If we assume the kidnapper is male . . . why has he taken everything except her underwear?"

"If she's locked up in an isolated spot in only her bra and panties, she can't run away," Anton points out. "She'd freeze to death in less than an hour."

Daniel nods. He is no longer tired, his mind is sharp and clear. "Could she be held captive in a place that's accessible only by snowmobile?" he speculates. "If so, we ought to be searching for her on the mountain."

He glances over at the window. It is still snowing, and the temperature is due to plummet overnight.

If Amanda is in a cabin, they have an enormous task before them. She could be anywhere between Åre and the Norwegian border. Or even farther away. It is a vast area, impossible to search at night.

He tries to picture the scene, reluctantly acknowledges the logic behind keeping a victim in an isolated mountain cabin where no one can find her. Or hear her scream.

The perpetrator is using nature as a prison guard.

Amanda is completely at the mercy of her abductor.

33

Daniel is at his desk, trying to plan a search for the next morning. The weather is too bad to make a start during the night; they are going to have to wait until it's light and the wind has hopefully dropped.

It is eight thirty in the evening when his phone rings.

"Lindskog."

"Hi, Daniel," says Bosse Lundh, the coordinator of Missing People. "How's it going?"

"We're doing our best."

"It's a shame we didn't manage to track down Amanda this morning," Bosse goes on. "I'd really hoped that we'd at least find some clues to help you out."

"Mmm." Daniel doesn't have time for small talk. The team is due to meet again shortly, as soon as Anton has sourced a detailed map of the mountain, but he doesn't want to seem rude. Bosse is dedicated, a real powerhouse who does a great deal for the area.

"We had so many volunteers," Bosse says with warmth in his voice. "Over fifty people, out there searching in the cold. That's community spirit for you. The fact that everyone wants to help makes me so proud."

Anton sticks his head around the door and signals that he's ready.

"Did you want anything in particular?" Daniel does his best not to sound curt.

"Oh yes—I've been in touch with our sister organization in Trondheim; that's why I'm calling. They'd also like to get involved, if they can be of any use."

Daniel thinks for a moment. It is no more than one hundred miles between Åre and Trondheim. They have decided to focus on Ullådalen to begin with, but they might well need to extend the search toward the border.

"Good to know. I'll get back to you on that."

Bosse sighs. "It's hard to think about anything but Amanda right now. And her poor parents. Have you made any fresh discoveries?"

Daniel pictures Amanda's clothes, laid out on the table. "I can't go into detail, but we have found certain items of clothing."

"Really? Surely that must be a good sign? It means she's still alive!"

"Let's hope so. I'd appreciate it if you'd keep this to yourself for the time being."

"Of course. Where did you find them?"

"I'm afraid I can't tell you that."

"I understand. If you need people to search the area where you found the clothes, just let me know."

Daniel considers the idea. They haven't finished planning the search yet; there's no point in Missing People deploying its volunteers prematurely.

"Leave it for now," he says. "We need to do some work before we can decide where to continue searching. We'll keep in touch."

"Lots of people want to help," Bosse assures him. "Just say the word and we'll muster the troops!"

"Thank you," Daniel says sincerely. "We really appreciate your input, but we do need a little time."

The support is there, but he's not sure he can risk sending out civilians in bad weather and on difficult terrain.

The last thing they need right now is for more people to disappear in the mountains.

34

Anton has found a large map showing the snowmobile trails between Duved and Åre. It is pinned on the wall in the conference room, and Daniel is standing in front of it, scrutinizing the area around Ullådalen.

It is to the west of Åreskutan—around the back of the mountain, so to speak. A popular destination for cross-country skiers, especially in the spring when the weather is milder and the evenings are light.

He pictures the undulating landscape with the now-frozen lake in the middle.

The valley is softly rounded, with low ridges and huge white expanses that sparkle in the sunshine. Here and there are groves of windblown mountain birch trees; higher up, the trees disappear, leaving only black low-growing shrubs that can barely break through the snow's crust. Snow-covered hunting and fishing lodges are dotted around, painted in colors that have worn away over the decades. Sometimes only the chimney is sticking up above the deep snow. A snowmobile is essential transportation.

Ullådalen is one of the most beautiful areas in Åre, but right now it looks like a crime scene.

Raffe joins them with a large sheet of paper under one arm. His dark, shoulder-length hair is tied back in a ponytail, his shirt sleeves rolled up to the elbows.

"This is the property map from the Land Registration Authority for the region between Storlien and Järpen."

He holds it up: a motley collection of dots, lines, and tiny squares indicating various buildings.

It's like looking at a war between different colonies of ants.

Daniel sits down and rests his chin on his hands.

"Where do we start?" Anton says, as if he can read Daniel's mind.

Raffe spreads the map out on the table and places a used coffee cup on each corner to stop it from rolling up.

"So we're assuming that the perpetrator traveled by snowmobile, and we suspect that Amanda is being held in a cabin on the mountain," Anton says. "We ought to be able to match the register of snowmobile owners with property owners in this area."

"A hell of a lot of people in Åre have a snowmobile," Raffe interrupts.

Daniel holds up his hand. "Let him finish."

"Maybe, but it's still a limited number," Anton continues. "And even fewer own land outside the population centers."

He picks up a pen and draws a large circle with Ullådalen in the middle.

Daniel understands.

The search zone is more limited than it looks, because the cabin is not likely near any of the plowed roads or the perpetrator wouldn't use a snowmobile. He probably also lives within a reasonable radius of the cabin; otherwise it would be too far to travel back and forth.

They should be able to limit the search even further by concentrating on the area west of Åreskutan, since Amanda's clothes were found in Ullådalen.

Anton folds his arms. "What about the coffee kiosks in Ullådalen? We need to talk to the staff, check if they've seen anything."

Anton grew up in Åre, so he knows the place like the back of his hand.

"What are you thinking of?" Daniel asks.

"Tväråstugan Ski Lodge, to begin with. Then there's Lillåstugan's waffle café. We should also speak to the staff at Buustamon Fjällgård Hotel, just to be on the safe side."

He places a cross on the map by Tväråstugan. It is deep in the valley, just north of Ullådalen ski lift, and has no connections by road. Daniel remembers skiing past it several times back in the spring. It is in a stunning location, with its own waterfall at the foot of Åreskutan.

Anton marks Lillåstugan with another cross. It is closer to Tegefjäll and the E14, above the spot known as Ängarna. It also lacks road access but is easier to get to. Finally, he adds a cross for Buustamon, by Rödkullen.

Then he goes over to the map on the wall, the one showing the snowmobile trails. He marks the same three locations, then draws a large circle not far from Tväråstugan.

"This is where the bag of clothes was found," he says.

It's all becoming clearer now.

The trail runs through the northern section of Ullådalen. Amanda's clothes were hidden south of the trail and diagonally to the east of the Tväråstugan conference center.

Daniel can breathe more easily. There is a starting point where they can begin their search. Staff who may have vital information.

Could they be in luck?

"We need to bring in Mountain Rescue," he says. "And a helicopter with a thermal-imaging camera."

"What about Missing People?" Raffe wonders.

"They could do more harm than good," Anton comments.

Daniel thinks about his recent conversation with Bosse Lundh. "We'll leave them out of it for now."

Bosse ought to understand—at least Daniel hopes so. It's one thing to have civilians searching along the E14 and close to populated areas, but it's quite another to send them out onto the mountain in ice-cold temperatures.

He looks out of the window at the swirling snow.

"Anyone checked the weather forecast for the next twelve hours?"

Raffe nods. "It's not great. Strong winds and minus twenty, just like yesterday. And it's going to continue snowing."

Difficult conditions for the helicopter, but it can't be helped; they can't afford to wait.

"We start searching at first light."

Amanda is no longer freezing cold.

Her body is numb. Even the intermittent shivering has stopped. Now her muscles are sluggish, as if they belong to someone else.

Her heart is beating slowly; her breathing is shallow.

Amanda is lying on the mattress, dreaming.

She sees Mom and Dad in front of her, with Mimi and Kalle. She reaches out to embrace them, but like shadow figures they vanish every time.

She can't get a hold of anyone.

"Give me a hug," she murmurs, trying to put her arms around her little brother, but he slips away just like the others.

She can see Ludde, but she can't hear him barking.

Why was she so cold earlier on? She can't remember; she just knows that she isn't cold anymore.

Breathing isn't easy, but she is not afraid, just very, very sleepy.

She folds back the coverlet and the other mattress; she doesn't need them anymore.

For the first time since she woke up in the cabin, she is warm.

All she wants is to go on sleeping.

SUNDAY, DECEMBER 15

35

The sound of the front door being opened and closed with a little bang wakes Hanna. It is only seven o'clock in the morning.

She found it difficult to get to sleep again last night; she lay awake brooding over Christian's crushing betrayal for hours.

Now she is wide awake, her pulse racing. Someone else is in the house. She hears footsteps that stop for a few seconds, then continue.

Something isn't right.

Hanna holds her breath. It's unlikely that a burglar would have access to the keycode for the front door, but she still feels uneasy. She pulls on a robe and pads barefoot up the stairs to the hallway.

As she reaches the top step, she hears a crash and a scream.

A dark-haired young woman with high cheekbones and narrow eyes is standing in front of the cleaning cupboard. A vacuum cleaner is lying upside down on the floor, with the hose beside it like a writhing snake.

Hanna and the woman stare at each other. Hanna pulls herself together first. "Who are you?"

"So sorry!" The woman looks panic stricken as she sees that a couple of bottles of cleaning fluid have also fallen out of the cupboard. The top has come off one of them, and the thick liquid is seeping out onto the stone floor. The sight seems to terrify her.

Hanna gently touches her arm. "It's fine. Don't worry about it. We can wipe it up."

The woman begins to cry. Her fear is entirely disproportionate—anyone can knock over a vacuum cleaner or spill some detergent.

"It really is fine," Hanna repeats. "What's your name?" When the woman doesn't respond to the question in Swedish, she tries English instead.

"Zuhra," the woman says without looking at Hanna. Her lower lip is still trembling. "Sorry!"

Hanna fetches a roll of kitchen paper, cleans up the mess, and throws the used paper in the trash can.

Zuhra still seems terrified.

"Would you like a coffee?" Hanna asks, sticking to English.

When Zuhra doesn't answer, Hanna leads her into the kitchen and settles her down at the table. She quickly inserts a capsule in the Nespresso machine and fixes her a coffee.

"Milk?"

Zuhra shakes her head.

Hanna takes the chair opposite her. She seems very young—no more than eighteen or nineteen.

"Where are you from?"

"Uzbekistan."

"Have you been in Sweden for long?"

Zuhra makes a gesture that is impossible to interpret. She still looks scared.

"There's nothing to worry about," Hanna assures her. "It was an accident—no harm done."

Silence. Zuhra fingers her cup. Her nails are bitten very short, and her lips haven't stopped trembling. She is almost motionless, as if she's not sure whether she's allowed to move.

"No people home," she blurts out eventually. "I clean every other week, house empty."

Now it all makes sense. Hanna tries to explain that her sister has lent her the house at short notice and presumably forgot to inform Zuhra's employer that Hanna would be here for a few weeks.

Hanna isn't surprised that Lydia has a cleaner. It's typical of her to make sure the place is spotless regardless of whether the family is there. However, she can't quite see why Zuhra is so agitated. Could this be a cash-in-hand arrangement, off the books so to speak? It's hard to believe that Lydia would do such a thing. She is a well-known lawyer; her reputation is worth far more than a few thousand saved on cleaning costs.

Zuhra has finished her coffee. "I clean now?" she says, getting up a little too quickly.

"Of course. I'll keep out of your way."

The only response is a nervous nod. It's hard to tell whether Zuhra understands. She scuttles back to the cleaning cupboard, and Hanna hears her assembling the vacuum cleaner.

As Hanna heads for the shower, she can't shake off her unease. That terrified expression in Zuhra's eyes, the way she cowers as if she is afraid of being struck.

The girl's reaction makes Hanna think of other women she has met during the course of her work as a police officer.

Frightened women who are abused by their partners.

36

Afterward Daniel will always remember exactly where he was when the news came in.

The team has gathered in the conference room to plan the search. Two men from Mountain Rescue are there, along with a woman from the Local Defense Volunteers with her gray hair tied back in a high ponytail. Raffe, Anton, and Daniel are seated at the top of the table.

The map they used yesterday evening is spread out in front of them.

Östersund is linked via Zoom. Birgitta Grip is sitting to the right on the screen. There is no mistaking the concern on her lined face as she listens to the briefing.

The gravity of the situation is clear in the tone of the meeting. No one interrupts, and the sarcastic quips that are sometimes used to lighten the atmosphere are notable by their absence.

Everyone is totally focused as they discuss the best approach.

They have been working for just over an hour. The meeting is due to end shortly, at nine thirty, as soon as it is light enough outside to facilitate the search. They have two helicopters with thermal-imaging cameras, plus a significant number of snowmobiles. It has been decided that Anton and Raffe will join the search while Daniel remains at the station.

The weather forecast is marginally on their side. It is still snowing, and the wind is strong up on ***Åreskutan***, but it has died down enough to allow the helicopters to fly.

Daniel desperately hopes that they have chosen the right area. He has been up since six and has already drunk three cups of coffee. He got five hours' sleep last night; Ida and Alice were fast asleep both when he arrived home and when he left.

"Did you manage to speak to the staff at Tväråstugan?" Birgitta asks, after listening carefully to Daniel's summary.

"Dead end," Anton replies. "The place was closed over Lucia."

It was the same with Lillåstugan, which doesn't open for the season until December 26. They will talk to the staff at Buustamon later today, but they've already had a chat with the maître d', who hadn't seen anything unusual.

They have just gone through the final details when Daniel sees a woman in civilian clothing enter the conference room in ***Östersund***. She interrupts discreetly by tapping Birgitta on the shoulder, and they conduct a whispered conversation.

Birgitta's tense jawline doesn't bode well. This is bad news, Daniel can feel it.

What's going on?

Birgitta turns back to the camera. She sighs deeply, runs a hand over her forehead.

"Dispatch has just received an emergency call in your area," she informs her colleagues in ***Åre***. "A chairlift attendant has found a dead body on VM6. You need to get over there right away."

Daniel stands up with such force that he knocks his chair over.

It has to be Amanda—who else could it be?

37

It takes only a few minutes to drive from the police station on Kurortsvägen to the chairlift on Kabinebanvägen, and yet the trip seems to last an eternity. Daniel's head is buzzing with questions as Anton drives as fast as he dares on the treacherous road surface.

Why would Amanda be found in such a strange place? Could it be someone else? If so, who?

It was a boy who called it in, but he was so shaken that it was impossible to conduct a sensible conversation. He just kept repeating that there was a dead body on the lift.

The windshield wipers are laboring by the time they skid into the parking lot, followed by two squad cars. Daniel flings open the door and begins to run through the snow, up the hill toward the large red station alongside the VM6 chairlift.

He takes in the scene through a curtain of whirling snow.

The lift isn't moving, but one of the chairs has stopped at the turning point. There is some kind of bundle on the ground below.

A young man is waiting for them with his arms wrapped around his body, as if he is losing control. In spite of the cold, he is wearing neither a hat nor gloves. His cheerful red jacket with its SkiStar emblem seems inappropriate under the circumstances.

He doesn't react as they approach, looking up only when Daniel is standing right in front of him.

"Police," Daniel informs him breathlessly. "Was it you who called about a dead body on the lift?"

The boy nods. He waves a hand toward the platform, but studiously avoids looking in that direction. "Over there."

His hair is thick with snow, his lips blue with the cold.

"Go inside and get warm," Daniel says.

The boy looks hesitant, then shambles off toward the door.

At that moment Anton catches up, followed by two uniformed officers.

Out of the corner of his eye, Daniel sees a couple of skiers watching with curiosity. It won't be long before half the village knows what has happened. The media will have a field day with this, as he knows from previous experience.

"Cordon off the area," he shouts to his colleagues. "Make sure no unauthorized individuals get too close."

He ducks underneath the steel fence that surrounds the waiting area and walks over to the platform.

The sun has barely risen, the shadows are still long.

He can just make out a naked back. The body is facing the hill. It is hard to distinguish the contours, but he sees a slender waist, rounded hips. Then he registers the bra and panties. It takes a few seconds; the items of clothing are so pale that they blend in with the soft snowflakes beginning to cover the body.

He takes a few more steps so that he can see the face. Amanda is lying there, her cheek resting on the ground.

Shit.

Even though he was prepared, it is still a shock to recognize her dead face in the snow. Until now he has seen her only in photographs, smiling or laughing into the camera, making faces, radiating energy. Everything in color.

Now he is looking at a monochrome version.

Amanda has become a frozen shell of a person, an ice doll who will never smile at her parents and her little brother and sister again.

Despite all their efforts, they didn't manage to save her.

The sound of sirens shatters the silence. In the distance an officer is trying to shoo away nosy skiers. A young man takes out his phone to start filming, but receives a sharp reprimand.

Daniel crouches down beside the dead girl.

Amanda's eyes are closed, her face is peaceful. The body is slightly hunched. She must have been dead for a while—he doesn't need a forensic pathologist to tell him that.

Ice crystals shimmer on her skin.

Daniel straightens up. Half an hour ago they were planning a search, hoping to find Amanda alive before it was too late.

The evidence of their failure lies before them.

Now it's time to start searching for something else entirely.

A murderer.

38

Daniel parks outside the Halvorssen family's white brick house, Anton beside him. He has spent the drive over trying to work out the best way of delivering the tragic news, but it probably doesn't matter. The parents will be devastated anyway.

He undoes his seatbelt, wishing it were all over. He never gets used to these situations; this is absolutely the worst aspect of his job.

He will end up lying awake tonight, wondering if he could have handled things differently, if they could have done more to find Amanda in time.

Only half an hour has passed since they established that the victim was her. The forensic pathologist and CSIs are on their way, and the whole area around VM6 has been cordoned off. Daniel wanted to inform the family as soon as possible; he can't risk them hearing the news via the media.

At least he can spare them from that shock.

"Let's do this," Anton says. "No point in drawing it out."

Neither of them speaks during the short walk to the front door. Anton also looks as if he'd rather be anywhere else. He has pushed both hands deep into his pockets, as if he doesn't know what to do with them.

Daniel rings the bell. He is freezing. Why does it have to be so damned cold all the time?

Eventually Harald opens the door. His face is ashen, and he is unshaven.

"May we come in?" Daniel says. "We need to speak to you and your wife."

Lena comes running down the stairs, her eyes red and swollen from crying. They sit down at the kitchen table, with Lena as close as possible to her husband. She is clutching a piece of paper towel, and she repeatedly dabs at the tears pouring down her cheeks.

Daniel searches for the right words—do they even exist?

He can't put it off any longer.

"I'm afraid we have some bad news."

Lena's eyes widen, and Harald grips the edge of the table with both hands.

"A call came through this morning. Amanda has been found over by the chairlift at VM6." Daniel takes a deep breath. "I'm very sorry, but your daughter is dead."

At first Lena remains absolutely still, as if she hasn't really heard what he said. Then she makes a strange noise, like nothing Daniel has ever heard before. It is animalistic and guttural, a despairing howl from deep inside her body.

Harald doesn't move. He sits there with his eyes closed as Lena's howl grows in volume, filling the room.

Eventually it fades away and she collapses, hiding her face in her hands.

The kitchen clock ticks loudly in the silence.

"How did it happen?" Harald asks quietly, without looking at Daniel. "How did my daughter die?"

"We can't answer that at the moment. The cause of death hasn't yet been established."

Harald clenches his fists. "What did she look like? Was she . . . injured?"

"She looked perfectly normal," Daniel assures him. He doesn't mention that Amanda was wearing only her bra and panties. That piece of information can wait.

"Can we . . . can we see her?"

"Of course, but she'll be sent straight to Umeå for the autopsy, and then we'll hopefully be able to tell you the cause of death."

"You're going to cut her open?" Lena whispers. She covers her mouth with her hands, her fingers are shaking.

"In circumstances like these, there has to be an autopsy," Anton says.

"I don't want you to cut my daughter open."

"I'm very sorry."

Daniel gathers his strength for the next question. Amanda's parents are already traumatized; the next part of the conversation isn't going to make them feel any better.

He gives himself a few extra seconds, runs his thumb over the surface of the table. It bears the scars of family life—rings from hot cups, a burn mark from a dropped match, deep lines where someone has chopped food without a cutting board.

"We have reason to suspect that a crime lies behind Amanda's death. We'd like to ask one or two questions, if that's okay with you."

Lena takes no notice; she is sobbing helplessly, shutting out everything around her.

Only Harald reacts. "What do you mean?"

"We believe that Amanda was abducted against her will, and that she may have been held captive in a cabin on the mountain during the period between her disappearance and the discovery of her body this morning."

Harald gives himself a little shake. "Why would anyone do that?"

"That's what we need to talk to you about." Daniel leans forward. "Has anyone been following your daughter recently? Has she mentioned feeling uncomfortable around anyone?"

"No. Not that I'm aware of."

"Do you know if she was afraid of anyone?" Anton wonders.

"I don't think so."

"Has she received any unpleasant messages, for example, on Instagram or other social media?"

Harald looks completely bewildered. "I don't understand why someone would do this to her." His voice breaks. "To us."

He looks at Lena, who has covered her face with her hands once more. She is totally wrapped up in grief.

"Do you have any enemies?" Daniel persists. "Maybe an old conflict that has flared up again? Sometimes we have to dig into the past, even if it seems unlikely."

Harald simply shakes his head.

"It's essential that we find out if there are people around Amanda who could be responsible for her abduction," Daniel goes on.

"She's only eighteen!" Harald exclaims. "Who would want to harm her?"

It is painful to hear Harald referring to his daughter in the present tense. Daniel can't imagine the agony of losing a child. He sees Alice in his mind's eye. If anything happened to her, he doesn't know how he would go on living. "I realize this is difficult. We won't keep you for long."

He is going to have to ask about Harald's political involvement. Threats against local politicians are a growing problem.

"This might be hard to answer right now, but I'm wondering if there are those who might want to get at you through your daughter?"

Harald is already pale, but any remaining color drains from his face. "You think Amanda was killed because someone wants revenge on me?"

"You're a politician," Daniel says gently. "There can be . . . disputes within the political arena. Do you have any enemies?"

Harald slumps on his chair. "Not that I know of."

"Have you received any threatening letters or messages in the course of your work? Any calls from an unknown number in the middle of the night?"

"No."

"What about after the world championship earlier this year?" Anton asks. "No strong reactions at the time? Things got pretty heated, as I recall."

Another shake of the head. "As a politician you get used to the fact that not everyone likes the measures that have to be taken," Harald says with tension in his voice. "Sometimes tricky choices have to be made." He falls silent for a few seconds, then continues: "The world championship was a disappointment to many, but I can't imagine that my political opponents would go after my daughter . . ."

His voice dies away as the sound of lively chatter is heard on the stairs. The twins, Mimi and Kalle, burst into the kitchen in their striped pajamas. They are astonishingly alike, with the same straight noses and slender build. They don't really look like their older sister; Amanda had inherited Lena's appearance.

The chatter stops as soon as they see their mother. They stand motionless, as if someone has cast a spell over them, and a wary expression comes into their eyes.

The fear shines through.

They look from Lena to Harald, then to the two strangers. Kalle takes a step closer to his sister, who puts her arm around him in a protective gesture.

Daniel knows from experience that their lives will never be the same again. As a police officer he has witnessed many family tragedies; there will be a *before* and *after* Amanda's death.

Lena opens her arms, and they both rush toward her.

"Amanda is dead," she forces herself to say. "Your big sister is gone."

39

There is no new information about Amanda on Missing People's Facebook page when Hanna sits down at the kitchen table and opens her laptop. There are, however, many sympathetic comments from the residents of Åre and other locals.

Karro, whom she met during the search and swapped phone numbers with, has written a few lines of support to Amanda's parents, accompanied by lots of red hearts.

Zuhra has just left, with one final anxious glance at the patch on the floor where she spilled the detergent. Hanna had assured her several times that it was fine, and she didn't need to pay any money or report it to her boss. She had whirled around the house like a tornado for five hours, and now the whole place is sparkling and smells of lemon.

It is disappointing to find that no further searches are planned. Even though yesterday's efforts were in vain, Hanna wouldn't mind taking part in a new initiative to distract her from the torment of her personal life back in Stockholm.

She would have liked to get involved in the investigation as a serving police officer. Anything would be better than sitting here with nothing to do, brooding over what has happened.

Or is it ***Åre*** that is making her feel so low?

She gets up and goes over to the patio doors. It is snowing, as it has been on and off since she got here. She ought to clear away the worst from the patio.

Through the swirling flakes she can see the neighboring houses decorated with Christmas lights, twinkling in the darkness. It is the third Sunday in Advent, but she hasn't bothered lighting any of the candles in the Advent wreath.

Deep down she knows that ***Åre*** itself was never the problem.

Just like Lydia she loved coming here, seeing the open sky and the snow-covered mountaintops. She knows her way around and has skied every ravine and slope. ***Åreskutan*** is like a second home to her.

And yet she never wanted to return.

She has managed to avoid the fells and mountains of Jämtland for fifteen years. Now she's here, and the painful childhood memories are rising to the surface, just as she feared.

Her phone rings: Lydia. It is a relief to be interrupted, to be able to push the dark thoughts aside.

"Have you heard what's happened?" Lydia sounds agitated, in contrast to her typically controlled demeanor.

"No." Hanna wanders back to the table.

"It just came out, I got a news alert on my phone."

"*What* just came out?"

"The dead girl in ***Åre***."

Hanna stiffens. "Have they found her?"

"So you know about it?"

Hanna avoids a detailed explanation about Missing People and the search. "I knew a young girl had gone missing in the area." As she talks she brings up the home page of one of the evening papers and immediately sees the banner headline:

Dead Girl Found in Åre

A blurred photograph taken from a distance, presumably on a phone, shows a body lying on the ground below a motionless chairlift. It must be VM6—Hanna recognizes it.

Her skin crawls.

"It's terrible!" Lydia says. "A young girl murdered in the middle of Åre."

"Do they know that for sure?"

Lydia pauses, taken aback. "I assume so—why else would she turn up dead, without her clothes on?"

Hanna skims the article on the screen. Apparently Amanda was wearing only a bra and panties when she was found. There are details of her disappearance and the efforts that have been made over the past few days to find her.

It is beyond belief that the newspaper has already gotten hold of so many details. Hanna can imagine what the investigating officers think of that.

"I just wanted to check that you're okay," Lydia goes on. "That you're looking after yourself."

"I am," Hanna reassures her.

Lydia still sounds concerned. "You've gone through a lot over the past few days—how are you really?"

Hanna leans back on her chair and thinks.

Actually, she's feeling a little better. It's been almost a week, and the immediate shock of the first day or two has passed. She is still bitterly disappointed in Christian, but she doesn't long for him in the same way, so that her whole body hurts.

However, the pain of being kicked out of the City Police is no less raw.

"I'm getting by," she says.

"Promise?"

"Promise."

They chat a little more and are about to end the call when Hanna remembers Zuhra.

"By the way, a girl showed up this morning to clean the house."

"Great."

"What's the name of the cleaning company you use?" Hanna asks.

"Why? Has she broken something?"

Typical of Lydia to jump to conclusions.

"No." Hanna opts for a white lie. "She left her hat behind—I just wanted to give them a call to let them know."

"Oh okay." Lydia sounds relieved. "I'll have to check. We signed a cleaning contract when the house was finished, but I don't remember the name of the firm."

Should Hanna mention how frightened and cowed Zuhra seemed to be? Then again, it was only a fleeting impression—she has nothing to go on. And yet she can't shake off the feeling that something wasn't right.

No point in bringing it up with Lydia.

"It's not important, but if you do have the chance to check, maybe you could text me the name of the company."

They hang up, and Hanna sits there holding her phone. The news about Amanda's death is dreadful. She wishes she could help.

Do the investigating officers know about the boyfriend's background by now? Should she contact Karro, ask her to speak to her brother?

Just to be on the safe side?

40

A quick hash with fried eggs and beetroot at Werséns restaurant on the square in Åre gives Daniel and Anton breathing room.

They need to refuel; it is only twelve thirty, but they are exhausted after the visit to the Halvorssen family. Daniel shovels down the food without really tasting it.

The atmosphere is strained when they return to the station. No one is unaffected; the death of a young girl is hard to take in.

Raffe and two CSIs who are just back from VM6 are already seated at the table when Daniel and Anton walk into the conference room. Daniel recognizes the CSIs, but can't remember their names.

Ylva Labba, the forensic pathologist, is also there. Her dark hair is secured at the nape of her neck by a barrette, but it looks a little tousled, as if she has just pulled off her hat. It is pure luck that Ylva is here. She is normally based in Umeå, but she happened to be in Östersund over the weekend. When the call came in, she decided to drive over to Åre.

She will soon be heading back to her hometown to carry out the autopsy on Amanda's body, but has promised a brief preliminary report before she leaves.

Daniel sits down opposite her. They have met only via video link in the past; the kind of crime that demands her expertise on-site has been rare in ***Åre***, at least during his tenure here.

She is warmly dressed in a woolen sweater, with padded pants tucked into sturdy boots. The scarf around her neck is in the colors of the Sámi flag.

"So what do you think?" Daniel begins. "When did she die?"

Ylva fishes out a pair of glasses and carefully places them on her nose, then opens the thick black notebook in front of her.

"I'm sure you're aware of what the cold does to dead bodies," she says. "It literally freezes time."

"Could you venture a guess?" Anton asks. He looks very tired, and Daniel suspects they are both thinking along the same lines. If only they'd started searching for Amanda earlier. If only they'd managed to find her while she was still alive. He knows it's pointless to go down that route, but he can't help it. Disappointment and failure are coursing through his veins.

Ylva chews her pen. "There isn't much to go on," she says after a moment. "There were no signs of livor mortis to give us any guidance, and no evidence of decomposition. Under normal circumstances the body is as stiff as a board after eight to twelve hours, but in temperatures like this, it becomes more complicated. The question is whether the body has stiffened because of the cold, or if we're looking at rigor mortis that has set in after death."

"How long do you think she would have survived, if we assume she was outside in this weather?" Raffe asks.

"That depends on a range of factors, including her general health, the amount of subcutaneous fat, and of course the clothes she was wearing."

Daniel pictures Amanda's frozen body. She was wearing next to nothing, and she was relatively slim and small.

"What actually happens?" Raffe says. "If you don't mind my asking."

"Of course not. Normal body temperature is around thirty-seven degrees Celsius, but at thirty-three the situation is already serious. The person in question becomes apathetic, the heartbeat is erratic, and breathing is shallow. If the temperature drops even further, the blood pressure is affected, causing confusion. Below thirty degrees breathing becomes increasingly difficult, and the heart beats so slowly that fluid can get into the lungs. The person is usually unconscious by this stage, and eventually the heart stops. When the body temperature reaches nineteen or twenty degrees, all brain activity ceases. The person is then clinically dead."

Ylva is very clear and matter-of-fact, but what she has told them doesn't help at all.

"Can you say anything about the time of death?" Daniel pushes her. He doesn't want her to head off to Umeå without giving them something concrete to work on.

"I'd say at least twelve hours must have passed," Ylva replies eventually. "I can't be any more specific at this point."

Amanda disappeared between one and two in the morning on Friday. Approximately fifty-five hours have passed between that time and the discovery of her body. So she must have been alive for a while.

Where was she?

Possibly on the mountain, in the cabin they had intended to start searching for this morning.

"What about the cause of death? Any ideas?"

"I hope you understand that I've carried out only a visual inspection."

"Absolutely," Anton says quickly.

"There are marks on the throat and upper arms, but no other signs of external force. No scratches, contusions, or other injuries."

"Strangulation?" Daniel says.

"It looks that way."

"But you can't say if that's the cause of death?"

"Not at this stage."

Daniel feels even worse as he digests Ylva's observations.

Given that there are so few signs of external force, Amanda may well have gone willingly with her killer, which suggests he or she was someone she wasn't afraid of.

Someone she already knew. Someone local.

41

How many conference calls have they had with Östersund over the past couple of days? Daniel has lost count as he prepares to speak to his colleagues yet again.

Ylva Labba and the two CSIs have left.

Daniel rubs his eyes before opening up the link. Modern communications technology makes life easier in so many ways, and yet he finds it strange that resources are so centralized that most meetings now take place via screens.

In the city, you take it for granted that everything will be on hand, but in rural areas it's very different. The idea of increasing efficiency by joining forces might sound good, but the reality is hard to manage when the scene of the crime is in ***Åre***, senior officers are in ***Östersund***, and the regional communication center, known as LKC, is in Umeå.

Plus there is something about personal contact that is lost when discussions are carried out over a link. It is hard to pick up the small signals, a glance showing agreement, a critical movement of the head—the silent thoughts that colleagues give away during the course of a meeting.

The door opens behind him.

"Ready?" Anton is holding yet another cup of coffee, and Raffe is right behind him.

"Give me a minute," Daniel replies. His phone pings, but he ignores the text message. Something else is occupying his mind.

"How did the body end up on the chairlift?"

Anton turns to look at him. "What?"

"How did the killer get Amanda on the chairlift?"

Anton puts down his coffee and takes a seat. "What's your theory?"

"She must have been placed there during the night."

"The lift operator said he discovered the body when he started up the machinery in the morning," Raffe interjects. He'd stayed and questioned the boy while Daniel and Anton went to inform Amanda's parents.

Sebbe had struggled to pull himself together after the shock; apparently he had been in the year above Amanda at school and had recognized her immediately. As soon as he's feeling better, they will talk to him again, but Raffe had managed to get a few details out of him.

"He said Amanda was already half-lying on the seat when the chair was on its way down."

"In which case the killer must have put her there in the turning zone up at the top," Daniel says.

There's nowhere else it could have happened. Daniel has skied in that area many times. The chairlift is high above ground level. As soon as it has turned, the chairs are several feet up in the air.

"Wait a minute . . ." The image of a small building at the top of the lift comes into his mind. "SkiStar employs staff both at the embarkation and disembarkation points, don't they? In case people can't get off without assistance. There's always an attendant keeping an eye on the chairs up at the top as well, isn't there?"

Anton nods.

"We need to get a hold of that person—as soon as possible."

Daniel turns his attention to the large monitor used for online communications. It is time to start the meeting with the newly formed task force, convened specifically for this case. According to the manual, such a group should consist of approximately twenty-five people, but there are never that many. There is no chance of their resources stretching so far.

Birgitta Grip appears onscreen, along with two detectives from Östersund.

"It's already hit the press," she begins. "With photos of the victim, the whole shebang."

Her tone reveals irritation, even though like everyone these days she knows it is virtually impossible to stop this kind of exposure. Private individuals have no qualms about filming or uploading material to social media when tragedies happen. There are stories of road traffic accidents where passersby unashamedly filmed the chaos instead of helping dying victims.

"We cordoned off the area as quickly as we could," Anton protests.

"We're holding a press conference this afternoon," Birgitta continues. "We'll come back to that."

The lack of enthusiasm is palpable. Press conferences are not a highlight of police work.

"Daniel, where are we?"

He does his best to summarize the course of events since Amanda's body was found. He hopes that Ylva Labba and the CSIs will find something vital that will lead them to the perpetrator, but he knows better than to count on it. At least Ylva has promised to make a start on the autopsy right away; they won't have to wait in line as was always the case in Gothenburg.

"We're going through Amanda's contacts before she disappeared. Her phone is still missing, but IT has her laptop and is working to gain access. Her clothes have been sent to forensics, and we're looking for potential witnesses who were in the vicinity of VM6 during the past twenty-four hours."

Forming a picture of Amanda's world is a time-consuming task. It is a jigsaw puzzle made up of tiny pieces that have to be assembled as the life of the deceased is reconstructed. They also need to work out the course of events leading up to her death, understand the whole chain from her abduction to the moment her body was found.

Daniel alters his position on his chair. They don't even have a tenable hypothesis at this point. They have no motive, no possible perpetrator. Amanda's boyfriend, Viktor, has an alibi.

Grip looks searchingly at Daniel.

He is aware that she knows the circumstances surrounding his relocation from Gothenburg to ***Åre***. He had to get away because his final homicide investigation brought him too close to a dangerous biker gang. The risk to his personal safety was extremely stressful; he had never been so close to burnout.

She also knows that he suffered from nightmares and had found it difficult to sleep when he joined her section, but since moving to Jämtland, he has regained his equilibrium. Something has healed over the past few years.

He has come home.

"Are you up to this?" she asks, getting straight to the heart of the matter.

Daniel wants to say yes; anything else would be a defeat. However, this isn't only about him. The truth is that they are short on resources. Five years ago, there were fourteen staff members at ***Åre*** police station. Today there are ten, a cut of almost thirty percent. Of those ten posts, only seven are filled at present. The situation is equally dire in the Serious Crimes Unit in ***Östersund***, where three out of ten posts are currently vacant.

At the same time, it goes against the grain to let Birgitta Grip hand the case to another member of the team in ***Östersund***. Daniel moved to ***Åre*** because he wanted to live a different life, be part of the community. When it comes to the crunch, he doesn't want to back down. He feels a sense of belonging now and understands residents' fear.

This homicide must be solved as quickly as possible, but the workload will be brutal. He has no idea how he is going to find time for Alice and Ida over the coming days.

"Of course," he assures Birgitta. "No problem."

Anton and Raffe nod in agreement. Even though they are stationed in Åre and the case is technically within the jurisdiction of Serious Crimes in Östersund, there is no doubt that they are part of the task force.

"Okay," Birgitta says. "In that case you need to get in the car and drive down here for the press conference. It starts at two."

Is she joking?

She wants him to drive over an hour each way to attend a press conference, when every minute counts? The whole day will be gone by the time he gets back.

Daniel stares at his boss. "I'm needed here."

"If you're going to lead the preliminary investigation, then you have to step up. You also need to speak to the prosecutor—Ahlqvist has taken the case."

Daniel has worked with Tobias Ahlqvist before. He's a conscientious prosecutor and not a man who makes quick decisions. However, it's better to have the prosecutor on board from the start than to have him jump in halfway through the investigation after they've identified a suspect.

Birgitta's expression makes it clear that there is no room for discussion.

Daniel sighs to himself. "I'll be there." He can't help asking sourly, "Who's going to do my work while I'm away?"

The screen has gone blank. ***Östersund*** has ended the meeting and disconnected ***Åre***.

Daniel suppresses a curse.

"Drive carefully," Anton says with a grin.

42

It takes Daniel an hour and sixteen minutes to drive on the icy roads from Åre to Östersund. Occasionally he gets stuck behind a slow truck. Every time, he itches to overtake, but he sticks to the speed limits. He can hardly claim he's on an emergency call if a speed camera catches him.

As soon as he got in the car, he called Ida. She sounded tired; she probably had Alice in her arms. Daniel could hear gentle gurgling in the background and could almost smell the baby scent of his daughter.

He's hardly seen her since Friday. All he has done is press his lips to her sleeping forehead before leaving again.

Ida couldn't hide her disappointment when he told her he'd almost certainly be late home again this evening. He doesn't know how long the press conference will go on, and then he has to meet with the prosecutor to go through the case.

"I'm so sorry about this," he said, overwhelmed with feelings of guilt as he ended the call.

When he reaches Östersund, the streets are deserted. Police HQ is on Fyrvallavägen, in a pale-yellow building east of the town center that also houses the customs service, SOS Alarm—the operator of the emergency call service—and the fire and rescue department.

The press conference will take place on the second floor. Daniel arrives fifteen minutes before it is due to begin and goes to see his boss, who is changing into her uniform. She is just about to put on her jacket when he knocks on the door.

Birgitta Grip is unimpressed by his thick sweater and jeans.

"You look as if you've come straight off the mountain."

Daniel attempts to smooth down his hair with one hand. It didn't occur to him to change his clothes. He rarely attended press conferences in Gothenburg; they were dealt with by the communications department or senior officers.

He already feels uncomfortable, and Birgitta's comment doesn't help.

"Come with me," she says, leading the way along a narrow corridor to a closed dark-brown door. The faint hum of conversation can be heard inside the room.

Tobias Ahlqvist appears with Ulrika Berge, the press officer. She is wearing a dark-purple jacket with black pants and boots, her high heels tip-tapping on the floor.

She greets Daniel and tucks her short blond hair behind her ears.

"We've had so many inquiries," she says. "Including from the overseas press. A young girl found murdered and half-naked on a chairlift—it's a juicy story. The phone is ringing off the hook, and public interest is very high."

Daniel rarely gets nervous, but he is perspiring now. He keeps his sweater on; he doesn't want to sit in front of the cameras with dark patches under his arms.

To be honest, he doesn't want to sit there at all. Speaking to the mass media isn't his thing. It's not a question of shyness; he just doesn't like being center stage. He's never enjoyed the limelight.

Tobias checks his phone. He's wearing a gray tweed jacket and looks perfectly calm.

"Shall we have a chat afterward?" he says to Daniel. It sounds like a question, but it's more of an order.

"SkiStar's head of marketing called a little while ago," Ulrika says. "She's concerned about all the pictures of VM6 that are appearing in the press. She's asking us to keep the reporters away."

Daniel nods, even though he's finding it difficult to focus.

Birgitta looks at her watch.

"Okay, let's do this." She opens the door and marches in. Daniel lets both Ulrika and Tobias go before him, out of sheer self-preservation rather than politeness.

The feeling of being thrown to the wolves is overwhelming.

Birgitta takes the middle seat at a rectangular table on the podium. Ulrika and Tobias sit down on one side of her, Daniel on the other. He keeps his eyes down for as long as possible, and when he eventually has to look up, he sees a dozen or so unfamiliar faces. Both SVT and TV4 have cameras in place. Little red flashing lights indicate that they are broadcasting live.

Birgitta outlines the situation, then introduces Tobias as the prosecutor in charge and Daniel as the leader of the preliminary investigation. Then she invites questions from the floor.

A young woman with thick eye makeup immediately puts up her hand. She is from one of the tabloids.

"Do you have any suspects?" she asks in a high, slightly shrill voice.

Birgitta has just explained why they don't have any suspects at this stage. Without changing her expression, she replies, "Not at the moment. It's too early. We will of course inform you as and when further developments occur."

"When do you think you'll have a suspect?" the journalist persists.

"We can't say at the moment, but this is a major investigation, and the case is our top priority."

The young woman doesn't look happy. She scribbles in her notebook with such force that the point of her pencil snaps off.

Birgitta nods to a man in a blue jacket, from a morning paper.

"The police have been criticized for not finding the victim earlier when they knew about her disappearance several days before her body was discovered. Do you have any comment on that?"

Birgitta looks at Daniel. He isn't ready, but he leans toward the microphone anyway. His mouth is as dry as dust. At first he can't get a single word out. He has to clear his throat, which sounds unnaturally loud over the microphone.

Someone sniggers.

"We had to search a very extensive area," he explains. "Both the heavy snowfall and the severe cold made the search particularly challenging."

It sounds as if he's making excuses. His face flushes bright red—he can't help it.

Birgitta steps in and saves him—for now.

"The search was conducted according to our normal routines. We have full confidence in the efforts that were made locally. It is essential to take particular care in weather conditions like this."

Her calm, experienced voice puts across the message much more effectively. Daniel feels the sweat trickling down his spine from the nape of his neck.

A hand is waving at the back of the room.

"Apparently it was left to the girl's parents to contact Missing People—why didn't the police turn to them right from the start?" the journalist demands indignantly.

Daniel can't understand what point he's making. The police weren't ignoring Missing People, they just needed to complete their analysis first. This guy is making it sound as if they were guilty of gross misconduct.

"Could it have made a difference?" the man goes on. "Could you have found the girl alive if Missing People had been involved from the outset?"

Daniel looks up at the ceiling and sighs. It is an impossible question; is this guy trying to blame him for Amanda's death? He leans forward again.

"Hindsight is a wonderful thing."

He tries not to sound defensive, and glances at his watch.

How much longer is this going to go on?

"Will you be closing down ***Åre***?" asks a man from a national TV channel.

"We have no plans to do so," Birgitta answers.

He's not giving up.

"Is it safe to let families travel to ***Åre*** to celebrate Christmas when there's a killer on the loose?"

Birgitta has had enough. "No comment," she snaps.

After brief concluding remarks, she gets to her feet. The press conference is finally over.

Daniel follows the others through the side door, dripping with sweat.

43

Mimi and Kalle are watching TV in the living room. They were treated to takeaway pizza for dinner, then settled in front of the new version of *The Lion King*, which is a big favorite. Lena can hear them from the kitchen, laughing at some funny lines. Children have the ability to detach from the seriousness of a situation.

They know that their big sister is gone, but right now they are absorbed in the movie.

Lena can neither eat nor watch TV. Instead she wanders from room to room, adjusting the red Christmas cloth on the kitchen table, nipping a few wilting leaves off a poinsettia, taking a glass out of the cupboard above the sink. Then she stands there wondering why she has a glass in her hand. It is several minutes before she remembers that she was going to pour herself some water.

Why? She isn't thirsty.

Fear and suppressed panic drive her on; she can't keep still. It is taking all her strength to hold it together in front of the children rather than scream uncontrollably.

Harald isn't home, he went out in the car several hours ago.

"I need some fresh air," he'd said, jangling the car keys. "I can't just sit here."

Lena has no idea whether this is a good thing or a bad thing, whether she wants him to stay with her or if it's better for him to be somewhere else. When he isn't here she feels upset and abandoned. When he is here she can't bear to see her own pain reflected in his eyes.

Ludde pads along behind her like a shadow when she leaves the kitchen. Maybe he understands that something is wrong. The sound of his claws on the wooden floor follows her up the stairs and into the bedroom. Mechanically she puffs up a pillow, straightens the pink blanket. Then she gathers it up and throws it on the floor.

What does it matter whether the blanket is neat and tidy when Amanda is never coming back?

Lena goes into her daughter's room. She curls up on the bed, buries her face in one of Amanda's tops, inhaling the scent that still lingers.

Three days have passed since she saw Amanda for the last time, though she didn't realize it then. The pain is sharp and intense. She feels as if someone has stuck a knife in her heart.

Ludde places both his front paws on the bed. Lena lets him jump up and lie down beside her. He isn't allowed on the beds, but it no longer matters. He wags his tail a few times, then rests his head on her shoulder.

She feels the warmth of his body as her tears drip onto his soft fur.

44

Ebba is lying in the double bed in her parents' room with the covers pulled up to her chin. She is desperate to see her mother. Both she and Ebba's father are on their way back from Stockholm.

Ebba has spoken to them several times since the news about Amanda's death came out, but it's not the same as having them home.

The news has spread quickly via social media during the course of the day. Messages have poured in from classmates and the rest of the school. Everyone knows that Ebba and Amanda were best friends. They assume that she will be able to fill them in on all the details.

She hasn't replied to a single one.

Her phone buzzes. The name on the display makes her feel even worse. It is Lasse, their adviser.

Will he get mad if she doesn't talk to him?

She realizes she ought to answer, but she can't do it. Instead she stares at the screen until he cancels the call.

Yucky Lasse—that's what Amanda used to call him.

Ebba pushes her phone under the pillow so she doesn't have to look at it.

The TV is on with the volume turned up high; silence is too difficult. That's when thoughts of Amanda come crowding in. She can't take in the fact that her best friend is dead, that they'll never see each other again.

The evening news has started. Suddenly she is aware that they are talking about the murder. A photo of Amanda appears on the screen, standing on a shore in the sunshine.

Ebba can't breathe. She was there that day. She was the one who took the picture on her phone when they went swimming in the lake last summer.

When Amanda was still alive.

Every sound fades away. Each breath is a struggle, becoming painful and shallow. She can't get any air.

She feels an increasing pressure on her chest, as if she can't get oxygen.

Her lungs are burning.

Ebba thumps her chest on the left side repeatedly in an effort to keep her heart beating; she is convinced she is going to die, just like Amanda.

Eventually she is able to breathe regularly again.

The panic attack is over.

When Ebba opens her eyes, she sees images from a press conference on TV. Two women and two men are sitting at a table on a podium. She recognizes one of them—it's Daniel, the detective who was here on Friday.

She stares at his face, makes it her fixed point, and concentrates hard to stop the panic from overwhelming her again.

Her hands are still shaking.

She buries her head in the pillow and wishes once again that her mom were here. She needs to hear her voice, telling Ebba that everything will be okay.

If only she had the courage to tell her mom what happened.

It seems unreal to think that it's only a few days since she and Amanda sat talking during recess.

The memory of that conversation on the bench outside school during a cigarette break still haunts her, but right now she is in the same situation as Amanda was, wondering what to do.

There is no one she can talk to.

45

Hanna is lying on the sofa in the living room with a book she can't concentrate on. It's about the #MeToo movement in New York. She chose it from the bookshelf but hasn't gotten past page fifteen, even though the topic is close to her heart and the title has been on the bestseller lists for a long time. The news of Amanda's body being found is crowding in on her thoughts.

It is six thirty. She has no desire to cook dinner. Her phone pings as she reaches for the remote to switch on the TV.

> *Thanks for the chat yesterday. A group of us are going to Supper this evening—want to join us? Karro x*

It takes Hanna a few seconds to realize this is the Karro she met during the search with Missing People.

What is Supper?

A quick google gives her the answer: it's a popular restaurant in the middle of ***Åre***, with a good score on TripAdvisor. The home page shows attractive pictures of South American food in bright colors.

Her instinctive reaction is to say no. It's nice of Karro to ask, but she can't cope with being around other people at the moment.

Then it's as if she hears her sister's voice: *You can't sit at home, grieving over Christian. He doesn't deserve it.*

No, he doesn't. For the first time since she arrived in ***Åre***, Hanna is more angry than upset.

She hasn't replied to his message about the ruined clothes, and he hasn't sent any more. She has no regrets—he deserves it after what he did. How could he be in a relationship behind her back?

She still can't get her head around the fact that he lied like that.

Her gaze is drawn to the cover of the book, the title emblazoned in red: *She Said*. Clearly there are plenty of male bastards out there.

Why did she fall for Christian in the first place?

She pulls a cushion onto her lap and settles down in the corner of the sofa. To be honest he isn't her type at all; he's too smooth and polished for her taste. The first time they met, at a party organized by one of her few childhood friends, he came across as decent and well mannered. Hanna described him to Lydia as a mother-in-law's dream.

And yet she was charmed by his persistence when he showed up with roses and champagne. She was flattered when he refused to give up, even though she usually finds that kind of behavior over the top, bordering on stalking.

She had never dated someone so good looking, someone who fit her parents' template so perfectly. Maybe that made him more interesting?

Her mother had always loathed Hanna's previous boyfriends—not that she took many of them home. She had grown tired of being told that neither she nor they were good enough.

Life with Christian became so easy Hanna simply allowed herself to be swept along. It was wonderful to see her mother's face light up for once when she introduced her new guy. His presence saved the trips to Spain and the unbearable family dinners. When she was with him, she became the successful daughter.

Until today, she had never admitted to herself that she was becoming someone else, a Hanna that she didn't really recognize.

Now she is sitting here, her heart broken by a man she probably should never have been with.

She reads Karro's message again; she is tempted. If she joins her for dinner, then maybe she can ask a few more questions about Amanda's boyfriend, Viktor; she can't stop thinking about him.

Before she can change her mind, she accepts the invitation.

Karro answers immediately:

Great. See you there at eight thirty.

46

The dark-brown council offices in Järpen are silent and deserted when Harald turns into the empty parking lot. He unlocks the main door and takes the elevator up to his office on the third floor.

He switches on the desk lamp, then takes a bottle of vodka out of the bottom drawer. It has been there for years. He would never drink at work, but it was a present, and he just left it in the drawer.

He fetches a glass from the staff kitchen. Pours himself a generous measure, and knocks it back with his eyes closed.

The alcohol is tepid and sears his throat.

Harald doesn't like neat spirits, but he feels the warmth spreading through his body. His tense muscles relax. He immediately longs for more, but resists temptation. He must stay sober enough to drive home. He can't get behind the wheel if he's drunk; after all these years in politics, it's part of his DNA.

Then again, he doesn't want to go home. He can't bring himself to pretend in front of Mimi and Kalle, can't bear to see Lena's despair.

The soft glow of the lamp lights up the family photo with Amanda in the middle. His wonderful daughter, whom he'd held and fed and sang to sleep so many times. When she was tiny he carried her in a sling on his stomach. He can still feel the weight of that little body, see the look in those dark-blue eyes as they met his, remember her first smile.

Becoming a father at the age of twenty-three was kind of unreal, but he loved Amanda from the very first second. He would have died for her sake.

Now she's the one who's dead.

His beautiful child will never smile at him again.

Tears spring to his eyes. Harald reaches for the bottle, but with a huge effort of will, he manages to pull back his hand. Instead he collapses onto his chair, his heart racing out of control.

He presses the palms of his hands together in front of his nose and mouth, presses so hard that the muscles scream.

That kind of pain is better than the one in his chest.

Only when his hands and wrists are trembling with exhaustion does he lower his arms slowly to the desk. His forehead is damp with sweat. He is breathing heavily, and takes out a handkerchief to wipe his face.

His phone pings. Yet another message offering condolences. The words are followed by a string of red hearts and "sorry" emojis.

Messages have been arriving all day, from every possible direction. Even his greatest political opponents have contacted him to show their sympathy. *Åre* isn't very big, and he is a well-known figure.

Thinking of you, they write. *Let us know if there's anything we can do. We are here for you and the family.*

Harald puts his phone in his pocket. Hearts and emojis can't help them through this.

After a few seconds he takes it out again. He is desperate to see Mira; she is the only one who can give him comfort right now. He hesitates, then writes:

I'm at the office, can you come?

He stares at the screen. The tension is unbearable. The minutes pass.

Then three dots appear; someone is replying.

Not possible.

The negative response makes him want to cry. He tries again:

Please.

When the screen remains blank, he makes one last attempt:

I need you.

The answer comes immediately.

I can't come. Don't message me at this time.

Harald's grip tightens on the phone. Then he reaches for the vodka bottle.

47

The wind snatches at Hanna as she finds her way to the restaurant where she is meeting Karro. She hopes the snowplow will do its job before she goes back to Lydia's house; it is snowing so heavily that she can barely see her hand in front of her face.

Supper is an old red-painted hunting lodge between the square and the train station. When she opens the door, she is met by a festive atmosphere and the hum of conversation. The place is packed, even though it's a Sunday.

"Hi," says a girl with a ponytail who appears to be the maître d'. She smiles warmly. "Have you booked a table?"

Hanna realizes that she doesn't know in whose name the booking was made, but then Karro appears. Gone are the cap and the shabby jacket from the search party. Her honey-blond hair has been carefully blow dried and curled, and she is wearing a leopard-print blouse with a generous décolletage.

"She's with us," Karro says, leading Hanna upstairs to a corner table where two other girls are already seated. Malin has long hair with blond streaks, and she is wearing a sparkly top. Jenny's arms are festooned with bangles, complementing her boatneck black top with trumpet sleeves.

Hanna, who is in her usual jeans teamed with a white shirt, immediately feels underdressed.

"Let's get this party started," Karro calls, beckoning over the waitress.

Hanna drove the car here. She can't afford a cab and doesn't want to spend too much on booze. However, she should be able to manage one drink if she sticks to water afterward.

"Four mojitos," Karro decides.

The dark-haired waitress takes down their order with a smile on her lips; she tends to say "Fantastic" with unnecessary frequency. Hanna counts four times before she moves on.

"Make them strong," Karro adds with a wink.

Hanna looks around.

It's a big restaurant with space for plenty of people. The upper floor is divided into two areas—a long bar with lots of room to hang out, and on the other side there is a long table with tall stools. Behind the table is the kitchen, where the cooks can be seen preparing the food.

The place is noisy and full, with South American dance music playing in the background.

Hanna manages a smile and tries to get in the party mood. Christian is not going to ruin this evening.

The waitress returns with their cocktails. Straws, ice, and bright-green mint leaves adorn the tall glasses.

"We usually let the kitchen put together the menu," Karro informs Hanna. "They know what's best on the night."

Hanna nods as if this is an excellent idea.

She just hopes it won't be too expensive.

They clink glasses, and the mojitos are every bit as delicious as they look. Hanna's shoulders relax a fraction. She'll worry about the tab tomorrow; these girls don't seem the kind to go crazy. She needs this.

Karro describes at length how she and Hanna met during the search for Amanda. She makes it sound as if they were out on some kind of adventure.

"It's just terrible," Malin says with a sigh, tossing her hair. "Hard to believe that something like this can happen in a place like *Åre*."

The waitress is back with another tray, and begins to set out the food. Prawn tacos, ceviche, and grilled corn on the cob. It looks wonderful. Hanna reaches for a couple of sweet-potato fries dusted with Parmesan. They both smell and taste amazing, and she helps herself to a few more.

Jenny leans across the table. Her lipstick is a pretty shade of dark pink, but the plumpness of her top lip seems unnatural to Hanna. She can't help wondering if Jenny has had some kind of filler. You see it all the time in Stockholm, but she'd thought it was a big-city phenomenon.

"I really hope they find the person who did it," Jenny says. "I'm almost scared to go out."

Karro gives Hanna a little nudge. "You're a cop—what's your theory?"

Hanna is embarrassed. She wishes Karro hadn't mentioned her profession; she has no desire to explain her current circumstances.

"Who do you think murdered Amanda?" Karro persists.

Hanna picks up the dish of prawn tacos and passes it around as a distraction, but to no avail.

"I'm only here for a few weeks," she says dismissively.

"What exactly do you do in Stockholm?" Malin has no idea how much this question hurts. Hanna's throat tightens; she pretends to have a coughing fit and hides her face in her napkin.

"Have some water," Karro says, handing her a glass. Hanna drinks gratefully and hopes they will change the subject, but Malin won't let it go.

"What do you work on?"

"I deal with . . . domestic abuse," Hanna replies quietly. She uses the present tense even though they don't want her there anymore. It's too hard to use the past tense.

"Wow," Jenny says. "That sounds tough."

Hanna tries to come up with a suitable response. The truth can destroy the best of atmospheres—she's been there before.

During her seven years with the City Police she has seen most things, from sexual harassment to rape or serious violence within a marriage. She can't talk about the heartrending murder of Josefin; the very thought causes her anguish.

This is not something to chat about over a minty drink in a crowded bar. She settles on a compromise.

"My department works on the abuse of women, that kind of thing," she says with a fake smile. "Far too depressing for an evening like this."

"I could never stay around if my boyfriend hit me," Karro says firmly. "I'd walk out right away."

Hanna is grateful for Karro's input, even though she probably doesn't understand how difficult it is to leave a relationship like that. Most women don't leave the first time they experience violence, although they should. Instead they stay, convince themselves that it was a one-off. When it happens again, they find new reasons to stay. They do it over and over again until they are so cowed they can no longer see clearly.

However, this is not the time for that kind of lecture.

Malin returns to the subject of Amanda's death. "Her poor parents. It must be unbearable to lose a daughter in that way."

Hanna nods. The statistics suggest that the boyfriend is guilty. She's been looking for an opportunity to mention Viktor, and here it is. Malin and Jenny are busy passing various dishes to each other, while Karro has just picked up her knife and fork. Hanna takes her chance.

"The boyfriend you told me about yesterday, the one who'd beaten up his ex-girlfriend," she says quietly to Karro. "Viktor Landahl. Did you pass the information on to your brother?"

Karro shakes her head.

"Don't you think you should? It might be important."

Suddenly Karro is very preoccupied with her food.

"I don't know . . . ," she says evasively.

The other girls aren't listening, but Karro seems uncomfortable, as if she regrets saying anything to Hanna. "I can't go poking my nose into Anton's job. I'd feel . . . dumb."

Hanna realizes she needs to drop the matter, and nods. It's none of her business anyway.

She shrugs to show that it doesn't matter. It was kind of Karro to invite her out, even though they hardly know each other. The least she can do is show a little sensitivity.

"Skål!" she says, raising her glass. "Thanks for inviting me to join you."

48

The bedroom is in darkness when Daniel creeps in at eleven o'clock. Alice must have fallen asleep long ago, and Ida has done the same; she is lying on her side in her pale-blue nightgown.

Daniel is exhausted, but pauses for a moment by Alice's crib. She is on her back, snoring softly. Her tiny eyelids are closed, her hands resting on the pink blanket, the fingers slightly curved in a grip reflex.

His heart contracts at the thought of anything happening to her.

How is he going to be able to protect his daughter when she grows up? More than most people, he is only too aware of everything that can befall a young girl. Evil makes no exceptions for the children of police officers.

With one last look at his sleeping baby, he goes around to his side of the bed. He is worn out from the tensions of the day. With a bit of luck, he might get six or seven hours, if Alice has a good night.

He gets undressed without switching on the light, and slips into bed. Ida turns to him in the darkness.

"Mom saw you on TV," she says quietly to avoid waking Alice.

"Mmm."

"Why didn't you tell me?"

"I didn't have time."

"You didn't have time?"

"I hadn't expected the TV cameras to be there," he says evasively. The press conference is the last thing he wants to talk about.

"Mom's really upset," Ida goes on. "She says such terrible things have never happened in our community."

Ida's mother, Elisabeth, calls almost every day and has opinions on most things—especially how Alice should be cared for.

"She's too scared to go out," Ida adds.

Daniel hasn't got the energy to discuss his mother-in-law at this time of night. Instead he tries to bring the conversation to an end.

"She's exaggerating," he says, deliberately yawning loudly. "Good night, sweetheart."

"She thought you seemed very tense and nervous on TV." Ida rubs his back. "Was it hard?"

Daniel doesn't need reminding of his contribution. He watched it afterward and is still embarrassed. He came across as an amateur. Why did Birgitta Grip insist on dragging him down there? Next time they can do it on their own.

"I have to sleep. I need to be up before six."

"Okay. I just wanted a chat." The silent reproach hangs in the air. "You've hardly been home since Friday."

Daniel knows it's not easy for Ida to carry the whole burden on her own, but he still wishes she had some sympathy for his situation. It's been a long day, full of frustration.

He had hoped to find Amanda alive, right up to the last minute. This morning's disappointment is eating away at him.

"I thought you might want to talk about . . . how you're feeling?" Ida says quietly, adjusting the covers.

Daniel reaches out and draws her close, nuzzling the back of her neck. "I'm sorry. I'm just tired."

She smells good, her freshly washed hair fills his nostrils with the scent of apples. Her nightgown has ridden up; he can feel her warm thighs against his.

Suddenly he is nowhere near as exhausted as he was.

He turns so they are facing each other, then gently runs his fingers over her collarbone and down to her lovely, voluptuous breasts. He has barely been allowed to touch them in recent months.

Ida wriggles slightly away from him. "Alice might wake up."

"She's fast asleep."

They haven't had sex for an eternity—not since Alice was born. He is seized by an intense longing to get close to Ida, to move inside her warmth. Make passionate love like they did in the beginning, before she got pregnant and Alice came into the world.

His yearning grows. He searches for Ida's lips, presses his body against hers. "You're so beautiful," he breathes in her ear.

Ida is still resisting, but then she softens and kisses him back.

"I thought you said you were tired?" she teases him.

Her fingers find their way to his stomach and continue their sensual journey. Daniel closes his eyes as desire fills every cell in his body.

"Not *that* tired," he replies, kissing her again.

49

Hanna finds it difficult to wind down after the evening at Supper. She is lying sleepless on her back in the darkness of Lydia's guest room, arms above her head.

The food was excellent and the evening enjoyable, but the whole thing was alarmingly expensive, even though she stuck to one cocktail. Fortunately, they didn't split the bill equally—each person paid their own.

She doesn't want to think about how little she has in the bank, or how she is going to get the money for a new apartment. From January it seems as if she will have no job and nowhere to live.

She absolutely doesn't want to borrow from Lydia, who has already been so generous. Asking her parents for help is out of the question.

The wooden walls creak occasionally; otherwise there is total silence.

In sharp contrast to the city, the quiet up here brings peace to the soul. Sadeln is more peaceful than the village center, because the gardens are large and the houses farther apart. Plus there's hardly any traffic in the evenings and at night.

You sleep well in the mountains—that's what Hanna's father always used to say as he tucked her in when she was a little girl.

She smiles at the memory and turns onto her side. She doesn't remember her mother reading bedtime stories, it was always either Lydia or her father, but surely Mom must have stepped in sometimes?

She's glad she went to Supper this evening. It was good to get out of the house, meet new people. The girls were pleasant; it was easy to join in the conversation and forget her troubles for a few hours. The only weird thing was Karro's reluctance to talk to her brother about Amanda's boyfriend. Still, maybe they have unspoken rules in their sibling relationship that Hanna doesn't know about.

What would happen if Hanna contacted the investigating officers? Just to double-check that they know about Viktor's background . . .

Karro isn't married, so she and her brother, Anton, should have the same family name. There can't be more than one detective in *Åre* called Anton Lundgren.

Karro doesn't need to know about it.

Hanna adjusts her pillow and pulls up the covers. She must get some sleep—it's very late.

Maybe it's stupid to interfere in a case that has nothing to do with her. That kind of behavior is exactly why the City Police don't want her anymore.

But what if no one involved in the investigation knows what the boyfriend has done?

MONDAY, DECEMBER 16

50

The house is silent when Lena opens her eyes. She peers groggily at the clock: ten to six in the morning.

She is lying in Amanda's bed, fully dressed. She must have fallen asleep. Ludde is gone.

Lena sits up and pushes back her tousled hair. She tiptoes along the landing to check on the twins; they are both fast asleep.

Then she goes into the kitchen, shivering as she pours herself a glass of water. All the lights are on downstairs; Harald must have forgotten to switch them off.

Suddenly Ludde starts barking loudly in the hallway. Lena hurries to see what's wrong, tries to calm him.

"Shh, what is it?"

She places a hand on his soft head, but he shakes it off and trots toward the front door.

"Quiet, Ludde!" As a well-trained hunting dog, he usually obeys her commands without blinking. Now he is rigid, barking at the door.

He is almost howling.

Lena grabs his collar. "Quiet!" she says as forcefully as she can without raising her voice. "You'll wake everyone!"

Ludde stops barking, but switches to a low growl.

Lena tries to peer through the frosted glass. "Is someone out there?"

Is it Amanda?

The thought makes her fling the door wide open, and the icy air comes rushing in. Snow whirls into the hallway, settling on the mat.

She peers out into the darkness. There is no sign of anyone. It is only the wind, blowing so hard that it is bending the tops of the trees into unnatural angles.

The realization hits her with full force.

Amanda is dead.

She sways on the spot. Her chest hurts as the pain takes over.

Ludde growls again, demanding her attention. Could there be a stranger in the garden? Someone who wishes them harm?

She pushes her bare feet into a pair of boots and pulls on a jacket, then steps out onto the porch. She narrows her eyes, stares into the blackness.

Ludde follows. He barks again, pads past her.

Lena sees footprints in the snow. Someone has walked up to the front door, then turned and gone back the same way. It can't have been long ago; otherwise the snow would have covered the prints.

Who has been here? At this time of day?

Lena holds on to the railing and makes her way down the steps. She follows the tracks all the way to the gate; they disappear on the street outside.

There are no lights on in any of the neighboring houses; everyone is sleeping.

The gate is closed, just as it should be, but it has obviously been opened; a half-moon shape is visible in the snow.

Lena can't stop staring, even though there is nothing to see. White flakes swirl around in the glow of the streetlamp, tiny sharp crystals falling steadily from the black sky.

She begins to shiver uncontrollably.

"Come, Ludde." She turns back toward the house, but the dog refuses to follow. He is still standing by the gate, ears pricked, nose pointing at the footprints.

"Please, Ludde. We must go in. It's too cold to be outside."

The dog doesn't move. Lena gives up.

Sometimes she lets him out into the garden when he needs to pee in the morning. He can scratch at the door when he wants to come back in; it shouldn't take more than ten minutes.

She makes one last attempt. "Come, Ludde."

Then she hurries back into the warmth and closes the door.

51

Harald is still sitting in his desk chair when he wakes up, feeling stiff and rough. He has spent the whole night in the council offices, it is twenty to seven and still dark outside his window.

His gaze falls on the empty bottle in front of him. He doesn't remember drinking the contents.

How could he be so stupid?

He rubs his eyes, tries to bring his body to life. It's high time he went home, but he doesn't know if he's fit to drive.

Lena will be worried. If he's lucky, he will be back before she wakes up, in which case he won't have to explain that he drove to work and drank himself into a stupor in the middle of the night.

Harald goes to the bathroom and splashes his face with cold water. The mirror is unforgiving—he looks terrible. Pale, hollow-eyed, and the gray stubble doesn't help. The nausea comes without warning. He just manages to bend over the toilet before his stomach turns itself inside out.

He vomits until there is nothing but yellowish-gray bile. When it is finally over, he rinses his mouth with ice-cold water and staggers back to his office to fetch his jacket. At the last minute he remembers the vodka bottle; he can't leave it on the desk for his colleagues to see.

His car is covered in snow when he steps outside, and the wind is howling. He manages to brush the snow off the roof and scrapes the windshield before getting in and switching on the engine. The seat is freezing cold, every breath hurts his throat.

He puts the car in reverse, but lingers with one hand on the wheel. Should he drive? Would he pass a breathalyzer test?

The road beyond the parking lot is deserted. There is no traffic at this hour of the morning. He knows the way home from Järpen so well the car almost steers itself; he's driven it virtually every day for years.

He's only twenty minutes from Pilgrimsvägen.

He promises himself that he will drive slowly and cautiously. They can't afford any more disasters in the family. Plus he is desperate for a long, hot shower and his own bed.

Against his better judgment he reverses, then heads for the E14.

52

Lena dozes off on the sofa in the living room. She lay down there so she'd be able to hear when Ludde scratched at the door, wanting to come in.

When she wakes at seven thirty, it is still dark. Over an hour has passed—why hasn't Ludde woken her?

She hurries to the front door to look for him. Where has he gone? She thought he'd be back after a few minutes; it's much too cold to stay out.

How could she fall asleep without letting him in? She's not herself; she's still in shock after Amanda's death.

"Ludde," she calls in her softest voice. "Come to Mommy. Come to Mommy, sweetheart."

She waits, calls again, but there is no sign of the dog.

Fear floods her body. Ludde always comes when she calls him.

"Ludde!" Her voice is significantly louder this time. "Ludde!"

It is just as dark and silent as it was earlier.

She pulls on her boots and jacket once more and plods through the garden. It has continued snowing, there is hardly any sign of the footsteps she discovered before, and the half-moon from the gate being opened is almost gone too.

The snow has eased slightly, but the wind is bitterly cold.

"Ludde!" The name comes out like an anxious sob. "Ludde, where are you?"

She goes out onto the road and looks around, then returns to the garden. At last she finds him.

Ludde is lying on his side next to the garage wall. His fur is covered in snow, and he isn't moving.

Lena rushes over. "Ludde!"

When he sees her he tries to raise his head, but with little success. He doesn't even bark; he simply whimpers when he sees his owner. Lena has to half carry, half drag him back into the warmth of the house. He weighs around sixty pounds; it takes a huge effort to get the limp body into the hallway. They collapse together just inside the door.

Lena sits up, sees Ludde's dull eyes. The pupils are pinpricks, and he is drooling in a way she has never seen before. White mucus drips onto the floor. His breathing is rapid and uneven, and fitful shudders pass through him.

"What's happened to you?" Lena cries.

She runs her fingers up and down his limbs, his belly, but finds nothing that can explain the state he's in. He has no injuries as far as she can tell; he's not bleeding. It's just as if all the strength has seeped out of him.

While she lay sleeping.

Self-loathing bubbles up in her breast, but she has no time to wallow in shame. She needs to wake Harald so that he can look after the twins while she takes Ludde to the vet.

She races up the stairs, flings open the door, but the bedroom is empty. The bed is untouched; the pink blanket is still on the floor where she threw it yesterday.

She was sure that Harald was still asleep. He can't be gone too . . .

Lena clutches the door handle, tries to stop herself from panicking. The most important thing right now is to get a hold of a vet.

Where's her phone?

When did she last use it? Presumably last night, but it's not in the back pocket of her jeans. Could it be in Amanda's room? She runs to her daughter's room, scrabbles around in the bed, finds it among the crumpled sheets.

They usually go to the nice vet in Undersåker. Feverishly she googles the number, calls as she hurries down the stairs and drops to her knees beside Ludde again.

Please, please let there be someone in the clinic even though it's so early!

The phone rings, but no one answers. Eventually the call is disconnected. Lena stares at the phone, tries again. This time an answering machine picks up. After some hesitation she describes Ludde's symptoms as best she can. She begs them to call her as soon as they get this message. It's hard to talk; she is in tears, and her voice is thick with emotion.

Ludde whimpers piteously. His breathing is labored now. As if he is dying.

The thought is unbearably painful.

Not Ludde too.

53

Daniel was back at the station at six thirty in the morning. Now he is sitting at his desk, trying to catch up with the reports of various interviews that were conducted yesterday.

The team has begun to work through those who were at Ebba's party. The attendant from the top station of the VM6 chairlift has been questioned, but she hadn't seen anything suspicious. Nor had she noticed Amanda on the chair when the lift started up in the morning. Forensics are still trying to get into Amanda's computer, and a colleague in *Östersund* is going through the family's finances and use of credit and debit cards.

They are also checking to see whether Amanda's phone has connected to one or more of the cell towers in the area, but it usually takes a couple of days for the information to come through.

Anton comes in and sits down. "I just had a weird call."

"Okay?"

"It was a woman who introduced herself as an investigator with Stockholm City Police. Her name is Hanna Ahlander, and she deals with domestic abuse. She said she had some information about Amanda, or rather her boyfriend, Viktor."

Daniel frowns. "Why would Stockholm be interested in our case?"

"Apparently she's up here for personal reasons and has found out something she thinks we ought to know. Since she's worked in that particular field, I asked her to come in. Better to hear whatever it is face-to-face, I thought."

Anton rubs his eyes. He must be every bit as tired as Daniel after the weekend's activities. However, he doesn't have a baby waking him up during the night. Anton is single and lives alone. During the three years they've known each other, he's never mentioned a girlfriend.

"She'll be here soon," he adds.

Daniel is still thinking about Ylva Labba's preliminary findings. She saw no signs of sexual abuse, which means there must be other reasons behind Amanda's abduction. He gets to his feet.

"Come with me to the conference room."

An overview of the material will help him to think more clearly. Virtually the entire noticeboard is covered with pictures now, new photographs taken from different angles.

Daniel studies the close-ups of Amanda's body. The pale figure is covered with a thin layer of snow. She is curled up, as if she made one last attempt to get warm before she died.

"Why were you taken?" he murmurs. That's the big question.

Anton reattaches a picture that has come loose at one corner. "Could we be looking at blackmail?" he wonders. "Some kind of revenge? Retribution?" So many possibilities. "Let's look at the MO. Why was the body found on the chairlift?"

This is the strangest aspect of the case. Why did the perpetrator place Amanda's dead body on a chairlift?

"As a warning?" Daniel suggests. He sits down, clasps his hands behind his neck, elbows sticking out.

"What do you mean?"

Daniel doesn't know. He continues to speculate, thinking aloud. "It was too cold to bury her, and he had to put her somewhere."

"He could have simply left her out on the mountain. She might not have been found until the spring, when the thaw sets in."

"Maybe he was afraid we'd trace her back to the cabin where we think he kept her hidden."

Anton shakes his head. "With a good snowmobile he could have dumped her miles away in the wrong direction."

"He was afraid of leaving tracks?"

"That's no good either. They'd have disappeared in hours, with the snowfall we've had over the past couple of days."

The two of them continue to examine various possibilities. Daniel pushes his hands deep in his pockets and paces back and forth as they talk. When he stops he is faced with a smiling, suntanned Amanda in the photo they borrowed from her bedroom.

The contrast with the images of her frozen body is brutal.

"You know, I think the perp wanted us to find her," he says at last. "Placing the body on the chairlift meant there was no chance she'd be missed."

Anton nods.

"But why?" Daniel goes on. "To show off what he'd done? To demonstrate his power over Amanda, both living and dead?"

Anton spreads his hands wide. "I'm no expert in violent crimes against women. You need to have that conversation with others."

"Like who?"

"How about this woman from Stockholm, Hanna Ahlander? It sounds as if that's her area of expertise."

After a brief silence, Anton says slowly, "What if he didn't mean to kill her and wanted to return the body? Or he hoped the police operation would be scaled down when she was found?"

Is that the explanation?

Daniel resumes his pacing.

Could it be so simple, so tragic?

The key to the mystery lies with Amanda. The killer didn't intend to take just any young girl—she was the one he was after.

54

The sense of being in deep waters accompanies Hanna as she makes her way to the police station in Åre.

The second she dialed Anton Lundgren's number, she regretted it, but he answered right away. She couldn't bring herself to end the call, so she told him her name and explained why she wanted to speak to him.

The fact that he'd asked her to come down to the station only added to her apprehension.

She waits in reception, becoming more nervous by the second.

A young man of about her own age appears. His thick blond hair is styled with gel, and his dark-blue T-shirt shows off his muscles. He looks fit and athletic, like a walking ad for a police officer in the mountains.

"Hanna?" he says.

Hanna nods, shakes the extended hand. Anton doesn't look much like Karro, but there's something about his open expression and warmth that the siblings have in common. Should she mention that she's met his sister? No, best not; it's more professional this way. Plus of course Karro didn't want to bring up the subject of Viktor with her brother.

"This way," he says, using his pass to let her in through the locked door that leads into the main part of the station. There is a staff kitchen on the left and a series of offices on the right.

"Coffee?"

Without waiting for a reply, Anton stops at a coffee machine and fills two mugs before continuing to a conference room at the end of the corridor.

Hanna walks in and stops dead.

One wall appears to be virtually covered in photographs of Amanda, everything from pictures of her smiling into the camera to close-up images of her dead body in the location where she was found.

A man in his midthirties is sitting at the table. He has symmetrical features and a neatly trimmed reddish-brown beard. His eyes are intelligent, but he looks worn out. His hair is a little untidy.

"This is Detective Inspector Daniel Lindskog from the Serious Crimes Unit in *Östersund*," Anton says. "He's leading the investigation."

Daniel's handshake is firm. He looks searchingly at Hanna, as if her credibility is yet to be proven. He has considerably more gravitas than his younger colleague, and Hanna is acutely aware of her messy ponytail and lack of makeup. This morning she had just pulled on her jeans and the sweater lying on the floor by the bed.

Will they take her seriously?

"I believe you have something to tell us," Daniel says.

Hanna clears her throat, feeling uncomfortable. She doesn't want to repeat the mistakes that led to the catastrophic outcome in Stockholm.

"On Saturday I joined one of the search parties that Missing People organized," she begins. "I heard something I think you ought to be aware of."

She summarizes the information about Viktor Landahl, the teenager who beat up his ex-girlfriend when he was fifteen. Because of his age, he got away with a caution.

"Maybe you already know this, but I wanted to make sure, because that kind of caution disappears after three years if the offender is a minor. If it's already been struck from the records, then you wouldn't find it in an official review."

She falls silent, glances down at her unpainted nails, and wishes she were somewhere else.

"It's an easy thing to miss," she adds. "Something similar happened to me in Stockholm, which is why I got in touch."

Daniel Lindskog nods in a way that Hanna would like to think is encouraging.

"It does seem as if we've missed this," he says. "We've spoken to Viktor, of course, but this is new to me. We definitely need to take a closer look at him." His expression is appreciative now. "Clearly we should have had a better handle on things. Thank you."

Hanna feels a wave of relief. She made the right decision. The problem is that she no longer has the courage to trust her instincts. Her boss in Stockholm has made her doubt herself in a way that she never did in the past.

"How's life in Stockholm?" Anton asks. "You're with the City Police, I believe?"

He opens a tin of gingerbread cookies on the table, takes two, and pops one in his mouth.

Hanna had hoped to avoid the question. Playing for time, she picks up her coffee and sips as slowly as possible. She can't tell them the truth, nor does she want to lie.

"I was based in the Stockholm City area," she says eventually. "I worked on domestic abuse, that kind of thing."

"You've left?"

Hanna opts for a white lie.

"I'm just considering my options." Which is true, from a purely technical point of view. "I needed a change," she adds quickly. "My sister has a house in Sadeln, and she's letting me stay there while I think about the next step."

Again, perfectly true.

"When do you go back to work?" Anton wonders.

"That's up in the air."

She sees a spark of interest in his eyes.

"That kind of crime takes its toll," she murmurs without going into detail. Hopefully they will draw their own conclusions. It is no secret that officers investigating violence against women and children often suffer burnout, or end up hating men.

Daniel points to the wall of pictures. "What's your view on this case? Anything you'd like to say about the perpetrator?"

His eyes are hazel and totally focused.

Hanna may have specialized in this field throughout her career, and she has also taken psychology courses to deepen her understanding, but she is neither a qualified psychologist nor a profiler.

"It's hard to come up with something off the top of my head," she says hesitantly. "I presume you're looking for a man, given the statistics."

The numbers tell their own story; there is no need for her to repeat them. Anton and Daniel must be aware that almost ninety percent of those convicted of violent crimes are men. The use of violence is strongly linked to the male sex.

She studies the photographs for a few seconds.

Amanda's half-naked body is exposed in the close-ups, and Hanna feels a surge of rage. Not letting the bastards get away with it has always been her greatest driving force. Every time a perp was sent down thanks to her efforts, she was striking a blow against Miguel, the bar owner in Barcelona, the man whose bad breath and body odor she can never forget.

Every guilty verdict was a step toward paying off the debt that still weighs her down, even though she was the innocent victim.

"It's easy to look for a sexual motive," she says. "But in fact cases of sexual violence are usually about power and dominance. When men use violence within close relationships, for example, through sexual humiliation or physical abuse, it's almost invariably because the perpetrator wants to demonstrate his position of power. He wants to show that he is in complete control of his partner. It is a damaging pattern of control and the exertion of power that has very little to do with his sex drive."

The two men are listening closely.

Hanna is beginning to feel pleased that she has captured their attention. She is not a bad police officer; she knows what she's talking about. In this context she is professional, secure.

"Because Amanda's boyfriend has a history of violence toward his girlfriends, that makes him a person of interest." She turns to Anton. "Do you know if they quarreled on the night she went missing? Could she have dumped him? That can be enough of a trigger."

Anton nods slowly. "Her girlfriend Ebba told us that Viktor and Amanda had had a fight at the party. Apparently Viktor was pretty drunk."

Daniel rests his chin on his hand. "We've been wondering whether Amanda might have died by mistake."

"Can you explain?" Hanna says.

"We're not sure the intention was for her to die. We think things might have gone wrong."

"Of course—that's why he put her on the chairlift!" Hanna exclaims. "Because he wanted to give her back."

Daniel seems surprised. He looks at Anton. "Have you already discussed this?"

Anton shakes his head.

Hanna's mind is racing.

"We mustn't underestimate the feelings of guilt and fear that follow an assault," she says. "Many perpetrators regret what they have done, and at that moment they are capable of honesty and decency. The problem is that the criminal behavior pattern is too strong. After a short while they fall back into the same pattern. The parameters of what is acceptable are gradually extended, and eventually the violence is normalized. What was initially unthinkable appears reasonable, or at least doable."

"Go on," Daniel says with interest.

"If the boyfriend is the killer, he might well have regretted his actions. When his girlfriend was dead, he could have felt shame, a need to atone for his sins. Giving back the body was a way of making everything right again. As right as it could be."

She pauses to allow for any follow-up questions, but when neither speaks she goes on: "Amanda was bound to be discovered on the lift. If he'd left her out in the open, there was a risk that her body might disappear beneath the snow, and she wouldn't be found until the spring."

Hanna goes over to a photograph that clearly shows VM6. It is taken from the south.

"VM6 is one of the most central lifts in the entire resort. It's obvious that he wanted her to be found—why else would he put her there?"

She points to the heavy metal structure, the steel cables holding the chairs.

"Presumably he dumped her before they opened up in the morning. The chairs are stacked together at the embarkation station overnight, and there's no security guard. It wouldn't have been difficult to drive up there from the back of the mountain on a snowmobile and place her in one of the chairs—one where the back of the chair concealed the view from the valley, so nobody would be able to see what he was doing."

Daniel looks at her sharply. "Say that again."

Has she said something stupid? Hanna doesn't understand why he's reacting so strongly.

"Sorry?"

"What you just said—say it again."

Hanna searches her memory. "The back of the chair concealed the view from the valley?"

"Exactly!"

Daniel leaps to his feet, the legs of his chair scraping on the floor.

"We've been speculating that the body was placed on the chair up at the top," he explains. "The attendant at the bottom said he saw Amanda when the chair came down toward the valley station. Therefore, we assumed that the body was put there at the top of the mountain—but when we spoke to the girl who works at the top station, she hadn't seen it." He runs a hand through his hair. "You're right, of course. The body must have been placed on the chair at the embarkation point, then gone round a full circuit before it came back down."

"I guess the perp was assuming she'd be found before the lift started up," Hanna says.

Anton gives her a thumbs-up. "Can we requisition you?" he says with a grin. "We could definitely use someone like you."

Is he serious? Hanna gets the feeling that he's wondering if she'd fit in with the team.

Daniel checks his watch.

"Thanks for your time," he says. "You've been very helpful."

Hanna nods. "You're welcome."

"I'll show you out," Anton says. Daniel disappears down the corridor before Hanna can say anything else.

55

Hanna is sitting in the car with the engine idling. She's slightly overwhelmed after the meeting with Anton and Daniel, but also . . . happy.

At last she felt like a real cop again. Both Anton and Daniel had looked at her with respect; they'd had a proper discussion. She had made a valuable contribution, and they were interested in her views.

She has longed for that kind of affirmation. Only now does she realize how much she has missed it. How much it has hurt to know that she doesn't count.

Something else happened after the meeting.

On the way out Anton asked whether she'd consider working in *Åre*, if she really wasn't intending to go back to Stockholm. How would she feel about a temporary post up here?

Åre? The idea had never crossed her mind. She has been totally preoccupied with the knowledge that Manfred Lidwall never wants to set eyes on her again. That she is no longer needed as far as the City Police are concerned.

She heard her own voice say "Yes" much too quickly.

Anton explained that the decision wasn't up to him, but that he would have a serious talk with Daniel.

"It's not as if I have anything else going on at the moment," she managed to say, lightening the atmosphere.

It is still hard to take in the good news, the fact that someone might want her.

Hanna puts the car in gear and drives out of the parking lot toward the E14 and home to Sadeln.

Toward the end, her working life in Stockholm was torture. Assignments disappeared, one after another, until eventually she felt like a pariah, an unwanted outsider. She might as well have walked around with *unclean* written on her forehead.

A few of her colleagues offered support, but no one was really prepared to stand up for Hanna or show that they were on her side. Instead they told her to let it go, move on. There was no point in being difficult, the bosses always came out on top anyway. The case was closed, and there were new challenges to tackle.

That made things even worse.

Hanna doesn't want to think about it anymore. She hates the fact that Josefin's husband, Niklas Konradsson, escaped justice, but there's nothing she can do about that now. Her fight for Josefin has already cost her her job; there is nothing to be gained by brooding about it now.

For some reason Zuhra comes into her mind, how scared she looked when she spilled the cleaning fluid yesterday morning. The look that suggested she was afraid of being hit. However, that doesn't necessarily mean anything. Hanna is probably damaged from all those years spent dealing with domestic violence.

She stops at the supermarket to buy milk and bread. The liquor store is right next door. Maybe she should buy a bottle or two to replenish Lydia's stock of wine?

She decides against it. The final nail in the coffin at work was the day she launched an outburst of rage at her boss. From then on she consoled herself with a few glasses of wine in the evenings for several weeks.

It's time to cut down.

Lydia calls just as she turns onto the E14. As usual she gets straight to the point.

"I have good news. I've spoken to Manfred Lidwall."

The very mention of his name kills the optimism Hanna felt after this morning's meeting.

"He wasn't very accommodating." In Lydia-speak, that means she had to twist his arm. Then again, that's her specialty.

"How did it go?"

"Well . . ." She takes her time, but sounds pleased. "You're welcome to apply elsewhere within the force. While you're considering your options, you're on leave but with full pay, so you don't need to stress about making a decision. Above all, you will have excellent references."

"Thank you!" Hanna exclaims. "Thank you, thank you, thank you."

It feels as if someone has removed a heavy burden from her shoulders; in one second she is twenty pounds lighter. She doesn't need to worry about money, and her career won't be jeopardized.

"It wasn't actually that hard. I simply pointed out one or two basic principles of employment law." Lydia is almost laughing. "I might have asked how it would look if the press found out that the police would rather get rid of a young female officer than admit their own mistakes—especially when the conflict involves a colleague who has been awarded custody of a small child, despite having been suspected of murdering his wife. I also wondered what the union would think of some of the comments your boss made to you."

Hanna lets out a low whistle. "You said that? For real?"

She hadn't expected her big sister to resort to blackmail to get what she wanted. Particularly for Hanna's sake. A wave of gratitude washes over her.

"I dropped the odd hint," Lydia replies. "He seemed pretty keen that it shouldn't come out, above all the way he'd spoken to you."

"You're amazing," Hanna says, her voice thick with tears.

Lydia has saved her, and Anton's question has given her fresh hope, even though he couldn't promise anything.

Maybe there's another workplace that will want her?

Maybe she isn't finished as a cop, in spite of everything?

56

When Anton and Daniel walk into the restaurant for lunch, the smell of fried food hangs heavy in the air. Broken serves the best burgers in the village. At the long bar Daniel orders a large Coca-Cola and the biggest meal on the menu. He is starving; breakfast consisted of coffee and a few gingerbread cookies.

They choose a corner table and attack their food with relish.

"What did you think of Hanna?" Anton asks when they've finished eating and moved on to coffee.

"Why?"

"I thought she was very sharp. Interesting background. And I like the fact that she thinks outside the box."

Daniel wipes his mouth with a napkin.

"And she looks pretty good," Anton continues. "Or at least she would if she fixed herself up."

Daniel refrains from commenting on Hanna's appearance.

"We need someone like Hanna, given all the unfilled posts we have. It would be good if we could borrow her for a while."

Daniel can't contradict Anton on that point. Of the ten posts in Serious Crimes in *Östersund*, only seven are currently occupied. That's why Anton and Raffe have been co-opted to the task force investigating Amanda's murder. They are both stationed in *Åre* and are supposed to deal with what is known as volume crime—theft, criminal damage, assault, and so on.

"Plus it would be good to have a woman on board, wouldn't you say?" Anton winks. "The team is nearly all men."

Again, he's right. There are only two females, apart from Birgitta Grip. Hanna Ahlander would definitely be an interesting addition. She might also shake them up, in a good way.

Daniel finishes his coffee as a large group enters the restaurant, bringing with them a blast of cold air that reaches all the way to the corner where he and Anton are sitting.

Anton is determined not to give up. "I think we should check if it's possible to secure a temporary transfer for her—even if *Östersund* has to pay her salary. Hanna's already here, she could start right away, increase the effectiveness of the task force."

Daniel looks at him. This seems to be a sales campaign. "How do you know she could start right away?"

"When I showed her out, I asked her if she'd consider working in *Åre*. She sounded interested, said she had nothing else going on at the moment."

Bringing someone in just like that is an unconventional idea. In fact they need more than one person; Amanda's case is eating up all their resources, and they're under more pressure because of the interest from the public and the media.

"You know how long things take in this organization," Daniel says gloomily.

"If you don't ask, you don't get," Anton replies, leaning back and patting his belly contentedly. "What's the worst that can happen if you suggest it to Grip? Give her a call, ask her to speak to Hanna's boss in Stockholm. Those guys in HR must be able to find a shortcut, arrange a quick placement with us. It can't be the first time they've had to be inventive."

"I'll think about it." Daniel changes the subject. They are going to visit Amanda's school in Järpen this afternoon, talk to the staff. "We need to speak to Amanda's boyfriend again," he says. "In light of the information Hanna gave us."

"Absolutely. He should be in school at this time of day."

"Okay, let's go."

The teachers might have something to say about Viktor's relationship with Amanda, Daniel thinks on the way to the car. Viktor definitely has some explaining to do.

57

The national flag is flying at half-mast when Daniel and Anton arrive at the school.

The atmosphere is subdued as they walk in through the main doors. The foyer leads to a cafeteria, where the walls are decorated with diplomas and prizes the students have won. Small groups of children are talking quietly. One girl is sitting in a corner, crying, her face buried in her hands.

There is a photograph of Amanda on a small podium with a candle burning beside it.

A receptionist shows them to an interview room with green velvet curtains, then goes to fetch Lasse Sandahl, Amanda's adviser.

The door opens, and a man of about thirty-five in jeans and a V-neck sweater comes in. He makes a boyish impression in spite of his thinning hair.

He greets them with a firm handshake, and all three men sit down.

"We understand you were Amanda Halvorssen's adviser," Daniel begins.

"Yes." Lasse sighs loudly. "It's such a tragedy—impossible to take in. I keep expecting her to show up in the corridor."

"How long had you been her adviser?" Daniel takes out his notebook, clicks his ballpoint pen several times before it decides to cooperate.

"Since she started here."

"How well would you say you knew her?"

"Pretty well, given how many students we have to advise. I work with everyone studying economics—eighteen in total."

"How would you describe Amanda?" Anton asks.

Lasse thinks for a moment. "Amanda was a lovely girl, and a loyal friend. She was clever, with a good head on her shoulders. She also had a well-developed sense of right and wrong; she often argued in class, and wasn't afraid of a heated discussion. She was into sociology." He falls silent. He seems genuinely moved by Amanda's fate, and his voice is subdued when he continues. "I can't believe she's gone. She was a person you noticed, and she had a mind of her own. A lot of girls her age don't want to stand out, but Amanda spoke up for what she believed in."

"Did she have any problems in school that you're aware of?" Anton asks. "Any enemies?"

Lasse shakes his head. "I've always regarded Amanda as a popular girl. She had plenty of friends, she and Ebba used to hang out with a bigger group, and the class as a whole got along well. I hear they had a Lucia party at Ebba's on Thursday."

There is a noise from the corridor as a group of students passes by. Even from a distance the sorrowful tone of their conversation is unmistakable.

"What about Viktor, her boyfriend?" Daniel says. "Are you his adviser too?"

"No, he's in the automotive technology program."

"But you know who he is?"

"Yes."

"What's he like as a person?"

"What do you mean?"

"He seems to have a bad reputation," Anton clarifies.

Lasse hesitates. "I can't comment on that."

"But you must have an opinion?"

Lasse changes position on his chair, his gaze slides away toward the window. "He can be a little . . . volatile," he admits.

"Go on," Daniel prompts.

"I don't know if I should speak about a student if I'm not his adviser . . ."

Daniel gives him a reassuring smile. "This will stay between us."

Lasse nods, moistens his lips. "There was an incident last year. Viktor got into a fight with another student. He lost his temper and kicked in the door of a toilet stall. It should have been reported, of course, but his parents paid for the damage and persuaded the principal to let it go." Lasse Sandahl doesn't sound as if he shares his boss's view on that topic.

"It appears that Viktor was the last person to see Amanda before she disappeared," Daniel says.

"So I heard."

"Any thoughts?"

"It's difficult. I mean . . . I don't want to suspect one of our students of a serious crime . . ." Lasse runs a hand through his hair, breaks off as if he's already said too much. "I guess I'm kind of in shock, like everyone else in the school. What's happened is incomprehensible." He closes his eyes, inhales deeply through his nose. "I can't get my head around the fact that Amanda has been murdered."

58

The lactic acid is burning in her thighs. Hanna is nearing the end of the well-lit cross-country ski track in Björnen, not far from Lydia's house.

She is enjoying the peace and quiet, the sense of being in sole charge of the snow-covered landscape. The track follows an elegant course through the forest in a wide circle, with a frozen marsh at its center. She glides silently through a cathedral of tall firs. The snow has stopped falling, and the area is sheltered from the mountain winds.

She isn't unfit, but over the last few years, she has mostly concentrated on downhill skiing. However, her muscle memory has kicked in, even if her thighs are protesting after almost ten miles. The rhythm is dictated by her regular breathing and the steady beating of her heart.

Her brain can rest while her body works.

The last stretch is downhill. She normally loves the speed, but tonight she holds back. This is where people often injure themselves. Cross-country skis are thin and unstable and can be difficult to control.

She snowplows down to make sure she doesn't fall. When she reaches the end of the track, she is completely exhausted.

Far away a dog barks briefly.

Something within her has eased. The visit to the police station gave her fresh energy. For the first time since she arrived here, she wanted to get out and exercise.

Sweat is pouring down her back as she plods home with the skis over her shoulder. It's a fifteen-minute walk, and for once the cold is welcome. Her breath emerges from her mouth like dense smoke.

Back at the house she takes a long, hot shower, letting the water run, making the most of Lydia's expensive shower gel, then generously applying Lydia's even more expensive body lotion, which she herself could never afford. Then she pulls on her velour sweatpants and top, goes into the kitchen, and opens her computer.

Lydia has sent the name and address of the cleaning company. Hanna had almost forgotten her concerns about the incident with Zuhra yesterday, but now it all comes back to her.

She has seen frightened eyes like that before; she recognizes the cowed posture.

She googles the name, "Fjäll-städ AB," to find out more about Zuhra's employer. The firm seems to be one of the largest in *Åre*. She checks out a website that gives details of companies' financial positions and annual accounts, including profits, turnover, and taxes paid, for the last five years.

Fjäll-städ AB has twenty employees and an overall turnover of twenty-two million. The previous year they made a profit of almost three million kronor. Hanna does a quick calculation. That's a profit margin of just over thirteen percent. Not bad.

She moves on to information about the chair and board. The names mean nothing to her. All five members are white men, as is the chair. They are all between forty and sixty, except for the chair, who is almost seventy. The fact that the cleaning seems to be mainly carried out by women, as are the administrative roles, doesn't appear to have impacted the composition of the board.

Hanna finds the age and gender profile annoying, but it's no different from many Swedish businesses. The women do the work and the men sit in positions of power and make the decisions.

Hanna is familiar with the pattern.

She sees Zuhra's anxious face in her mind's eye. Hanna has found nothing to suggest that the fault lies with her employer. Could she be afraid of a violent boyfriend or a married man? She would like to meet

Zuhra again, ask her straight out. There is help available for vulnerable women.

She sits back, clasps her hands behind her neck.

This morning's meeting at the police station is the first glimmer of light in a long time. Anton's question about whether she might consider working in *Åre* came like a bolt from the blue.

The more she thinks about it, the more interested she is.

Anton made it clear that Daniel is the one who will decide. He is leading the investigation, which falls under the authority of the Serious Crimes Unit in *Östersund*. If there's anyone who can pull the right strings, it's him. Anton is stationed in *Åre* and usually works on other types of crime. He has no influence over employment matters.

On an impulse she googles "Daniel Lindskog," suddenly curious about the man who might, just might, be able to set her life on the right course once more.

She can't find anyone who resembles the man she met earlier today. He doesn't even seem to be on Facebook.

She tries again, types in "Daniel Lindskog + police officer," and this time there are several hits, mainly newspaper articles from *Göteborgs-Posten*, where he is mentioned by name in connection with various investigations.

In one of them he talks about a serious homicide case with links to a biker gang in one of Gothenburg's socially deprived suburbs. A man was found brutally beaten to death in the forest. Hanna remembers the case; it attracted a significant amount of attention three or four years ago.

Judging by the articles, Daniel spent quite some time in Gothenburg; he is clearly an experienced detective.

Hanna can't help wondering what an officer with his background is doing in *Åre*. Drunk driving or drunk Norwegians getting into a fight are a lot more common in the mountains—crimes that don't exactly match Daniel's level of competence. But maybe he wanted a different kind of life? Lots of people move up here because they've grown tired of the city.

She reads a little while longer, then exits the page and stretches.

A few days ago she was convinced she was worthless, certain that her career was over. No one would ever want to employ her again, not when Manfred Lidwall so clearly wanted her out of the City Police. The unplanned meeting with Daniel and Anton could mean a new future, one she hadn't dared to dream of.

She would give her soul for a second chance.

59

Ludde is lying in a black plastic sack in the garage. Lydia has been sitting at the kitchen table for a long time, simply staring at a point on the wall. The last few hours are like a fog. The house is empty. Harald has taken Mimi and Kalle to the supermarket to buy food.

The grief and pain are so intense that she feels like a stranger in her own body, as if it belongs to someone else.

Darling Ludde, with his big brown eyes. He has been with them since he was nine weeks old, the sweetest puppy you could imagine. A tiny, furry bundle of pure love that the whole family adored.

Amanda worshipped Ludde.

Now they are both gone, within just a few days.

Lena doesn't understand what happened; Ludde was only four years old. How can a healthy, lively dog die in a couple of hours?

He was here, warm and alive, sitting close by her side, seeming to offer comfort as she fell apart inside. Last night she wept into his silky fur and warmed her ice-cold hands on his soft paws.

Now he is lying in the garage, as stiff as Amanda when she was found on the chairlift.

The thought is so painful that Lena is incapable of holding herself upright. She slides down onto the kitchen floor and curls up in the fetal position, groaning and rocking back and forth. With her cheek resting on the cold wooden boards, her breathing becomes rapid and shallow, she pants with her mouth open just like Ludde sometimes used to do.

Harald didn't even make it home in time.

When he walked in through the door, it was already too late. She was sitting on the floor with Ludde's head resting on her knee, begging him not to give up even though he was already dead.

She could have sat there for hours if Harald hadn't persuaded her to get up and go into the kitchen. He was the one who fetched the plastic sack and carried Ludde into the garage so that the twins wouldn't see him when they woke up.

They don't know he's dead yet. Harald told them that Ludde is in the animal hospital.

It is impossible to tell them the truth; Mimi and Kalle can't suffer another loss so close to Amanda's death.

Amanda.

Lena moans. Her daughter is still in the hospital morgue in Umeå, where the forensic pathologist is slicing open her dead body.

They haven't been allowed to see her yet.

She would do anything to turn back the clock, speak to Amanda one last time. Tell her how much she loves her, explain that all the recent bickering meant nothing at all.

She regrets it so much—all the unnecessary irritation she vented without thinking.

If only she'd realized that time was running out. There are so many things she would have done differently.

Lena sobs. The wooden floor beneath her cheek is wet, but she can't stop.

"Amanda," she whispers to herself. "Darling Amanda. Come back to us."

60

The table in the conference room is covered in documents.

Daniel is standing with a cup of coffee in his hand, trying to get a mental overview. He is tired and dispirited. They haven't found anything noteworthy in the family's finances, and the bank has informed them that Amanda's debit card hasn't been used since Thursday. Her phone is still missing, even after an additional search along the E14. They are still waiting for the phone company to get back to them and for the results of forensic IT specialists' efforts to get into Amanda's computer. Some members of staff in that department are at home, looking after sick children, so it could take a few more days.

Daniel sighs and sips his cold coffee.

They haven't managed to get a hold of Viktor Landahl either. They had intended to speak to him after the conversation with Amanda's adviser, but Viktor wasn't in school, and no one in the family was home when they went over to his house. They will try again tomorrow. Meanwhile they have contacted colleagues in Umeå for more details on the events that led to Viktor receiving a caution, which was struck from the records only a few months ago. He was indeed guilty of assault.

In Daniel's opinion, it was only luck that allowed Viktor to avoid consequences he probably deserved. If he'd been just a few years older, he would have been given a much harsher punishment.

They have also double-checked his alibi and concluded that none of his friends can swear that Viktor was still at Ebba's after Amanda left the party.

Wille, the friend Viktor specifically mentioned, was so drunk that he can't confirm anything at all. Ebba says the same thing—she can't remember. They have interviewed everyone who was at the party, and nobody is one hundred percent certain where Viktor was between midnight and three o'clock on Friday morning. Maybe Amanda wasn't persuaded to get in someone's car after all. Maybe Viktor caught up with her on the E14 and things got out of hand.

Daniel scratches the back of his neck.

He is waiting for Anton. They are going to spend the next hour trying to identify the cabin owners in Ullådalen who also own a snowmobile. The plan is to pin down individuals who would have been able to transport Amanda's body to VM6. The theory that she was held captive in a mountain cabin is still their strongest card. He also wants to check if Viktor has any links to Ullådalen.

He sits down, finds the lists from the land registry and the vehicle licensing authority. The number of property owners is nothing compared with the list of registered snowmobile owners in *Åre*. As of the beginning of the year, there were slightly over 5,000, of which 3,600 were in regular use.

This is going to take a while.

By the time Anton arrives, Daniel has made a note of those who have a cabin, but no snowmobile. Six men and two women, in alphabetical order.

Bergstrand, Göran
Björk, Stefan
Grönvall, Arne
Mäkinen, Pentti
Nilsson, Carl-Johan
Pettersson, Torgils
Pihl, Anna-Britta
Risberg, Annika

"Is she some kind of property magnate in Ullådalen?" Daniel asks, pointing to the last name, which has come up several times.

Anton shakes his head. "The family has lived in the area for years. She probably inherited the cabin from her father; he died some time ago."

Daniel puts the sheet of paper to one side and concentrates on the printouts Anton has brought with him—the names and home addresses of those who have a place in Ullådalen *and* are registered owners of a snowmobile. There are lots of them, presumably because it's not possible to get to a cabin in Ullådalen without a snowmobile. Eighty percent are men, most but not all live in the local community. They need to go and visit these men. They're ruling out the women because they believe they're looking for a male perpetrator.

Hanna was thinking along the same lines, Daniel remembers. The statistics support the view that it is a man.

Daniel scans the home addresses and groans to himself. They'll start with those who live close by; property owners farther afield will have to wait. They also need to run the names through their own system, see if anyone has a criminal record.

He decides to pass that task to Östersund. They're already doing background checks on everyone in Amanda's circle of friends.

His phone rings as Anton goes off to collect more printouts. It's Bosse Lundh.

"How's it going?" Bosse asks in a friendly tone of voice.

Daniel takes the opportunity to stand up and stretch his spine. "We're pressing on. There's a lot to do in the beginning."

"I can understand that."

They chat for a few minutes; then Bosse clears his throat. "So . . . the reason I called is the press conference that was on TV yesterday."

Daniel grimaces; he'd prefer to forget the whole thing.

"I heard some journalists were asking if the police should have worked more closely with Missing People," Bosse goes on. "I don't understand the question. We were contacted by the family and started searching on Saturday morning. I thought we worked very well together." He pauses. "I wasn't the one who spoke to the press—I just wanted you to know that."

Daniel appreciates Bosse's comments. He had felt under pressure when the reporter questioned him.

"I didn't think it was you, but thanks for the information."

"Anything we can do, just let me know," Bosse says, ending the call.

Daniel goes back to the lists. "Do you recognize any of these names?" he asks when Anton returns.

His colleague studies the documents, picks out familiar names, but nothing sets off alarm bells. This is exactly what Daniel doesn't want to hear. He continues reading.

"It would help if there were more of us," Anton says with a sigh after a while. "Have you given any more thought to Hanna Ahlander? Why don't you ask Grip to see if the City Police will allow her to take up a temporary placement with us?"

Daniel looks up. Hanna Ahlander again. She certainly seems to have made an impression on Anton, and he has to admit that she came across as both competent and experienced. She also seemed comfortable in herself; he would enjoy working with her.

No harm in asking, as Anton quite rightly pointed out over lunch. Daniel takes out his phone, weighs it in his hand. Should he give it a go?

Why not?

He calls Birgitta Grip's number before he can change his mind.

61

Hanna is idly surfing the net in semidarkness at the big kitchen table. The tab with the information about the cleaning company is still open, but she's reading about Amanda's murder at the moment. The tabloids have devoted many pages to the case; speculation is rife, and there are dozens of comments.

It's a juicy story—ideal click bait.

Eventually she decides she's had enough and pushes her laptop away. She can't face reading any more about that poor girl.

It is almost six thirty. She glances toward the tall windows. The wind has died down. She pushes back her chair and walks over to the patio doors.

The valley is resting in the shadow of Renfjället. The clouds have finally dispersed, revealing a star-studded sky, millions of tiny white dots sparkling at the earth.

She has so many memories from this place, both happy and sad. Mostly from the time after Lydia had left home, when only she and her parents came to Åre for the winter break.

The best times were when she went skiing with her father, when it was just the two of them on the ski lift or in the café. She pictures him now. He always wanted to keep the peace at home; he couldn't bear conflict in the family. His dislike of raised voices and dramatic scenes meant that her mother always got her own way.

He was as stylish as a Hollywood star, but lacked the moral strength to put his child before his wife.

Strangely enough, she is less angry with him than with her mother—maybe because he's so old? He's eighty-six now, eleven years older than Ulla, and he has become a silent shadow of his former self. He never had much to say, but these days he hardly speaks at all. He merely nods and agrees when Ulla talks.

It's possible that he is in the early stages of dementia, but it doesn't matter. The father who hurt Hanna so deeply is gone. She can't be angry with someone who no longer exists.

Hanna stares out into the darkness.

The house they always used to rent isn't far from VM6. She hasn't wanted to go and look; she has enough to deal with right now.

A little snow slides down from the roof. It lands with a thud on the drive, a tiny white pile beside the much bigger one left behind by the snowplow.

Until now Hanna has never been back to Åre as an adult. Over the years Lydia has asked her many times to come with them, but Hanna has always said no. And yet she has never stopped loving the mountains; the ties of nature have held her close. Despite the long absence she still feels at home here.

She rests her forehead on the cool glass, closes her eyes. Could the place where she skied as a child give her a new future?

She's not sure if she dares to believe in the chance of a placement in Åre. Is it just another castle in the air that will collapse?

62

Daniel can't explain why he's on his way to see Hanna Ahlander at this time of the evening.

Birgitta Grip thought he was joking when he suggested they should offer Hanna a temporary placement effective immediately.

"That's not how it works," she had snapped. There were procedures, she'd gone on to explain, that must be followed, protocols that must be observed. Plus hurdles in the hiring process always arose when they were transferring personnel between different regions of the police force.

Daniel stuck to his guns, surprising himself with the strength of his reasoning. He insisted it almost amounted to a dereliction of duty if they didn't make use of a highly competent officer who happened to be in the area, especially as she was prepared to step in right away, and resources, as Birgitta was well aware, were badly stretched.

The task force needed all the help it could get.

He had checked out Hanna's background as best he could and highlighted her work with domestic abuse cases in Stockholm City as particularly useful.

Eventually Birgitta gave in and promised to look into the possibility, provided Daniel vouched for Hanna and took personal responsibility for her involvement in the investigation into Amanda Halvorssen's murder.

"This is urgent," Daniel said as he ended the call. "I want to bring her in as soon as possible."

They agreed to speak the following day.

Daniel has met Hanna only once, but he recognizes a good police officer. It is a concern that there are so few women on the team. He has learned that many women have a different way of looking at things; they focus on different issues. Mixed groups work better, that's the simple truth—and Hanna's background makes her perfect for this case.

He drives through the center of Björnen and turns into Sadeln from Fröåvägen. The car rolls down the hill, past a row of wood-paneled three-story buildings that weren't there last year. Another result of the construction boom.

He takes Västra Sadelviksvägen, looking out for Hanna's address, and realizes that the huge house at the end of the road must be the right place.

Wow! It's hard to suppress a whistle.

Three seconds later he parks on the drive. He doesn't bother locking the car. When Hanna opens the front door, he can see the surprise in her eyes. She is wearing velour sweatpants and a faded college sweater.

"Hi?"

Daniel almost wishes he hadn't come. Maybe this was a terrible idea.

He shivers in the biting cold. "Have you got time for a chat?"

"Er . . . of course. Come on in." She steps back, opens the door wide. "You just took me by surprise."

Daniel walks into the hallway, which leads to the open-plan living room, library, and dining space. The oval shape of the great room offers a panoramic view of the lake.

The ground floor alone must measure 1,600 square feet.

"Shit, what a place!" he exclaims. "How many people live here?"

"Just my sister and her family." Hanna looks a little embarrassed. She goes over to the kitchen, with its gray wooden cupboards and a marble island.

"Would you like a drink? Coffee, wine—a beer?"

"Coffee would be good."

While Hanna fixes two cups from a Nespresso machine, Daniel takes a look around. The house could easily grace the pages of any interior-design magazine.

“I’d be scared to touch anything,” he says. “Are you allowed to sit on the sofa?”

Hanna rolls her eyes. “You just have to be careful. It’s not exactly my style, to be honest.”

They sit down at the table. Daniel pours a drop of milk into his cup. Best to get straight to the point, as he did in his conversation with Birgitta Grip.

“Anton said you were interested in working up here.”

Hanna nods enthusiastically. “I wasn’t sure he was serious when he mentioned it.”

Daniel rests his arm on the back of the chair beside him. “I’ve spoken to my boss, Birgitta Grip, who runs the Serious Crimes Unit in Östersund. We have three unfilled posts in the team, and we really need help—especially with the investigation into Amanda’s death.”

“I can start right away.”

Daniel gets the feeling that Hanna doesn’t want to seem pushy, but her eagerness spills over anyway. Her eyes are shining in the light of the deer-horn lamp on the ceiling.

“I mean . . . ,” she goes on. “I’m not doing anything at the moment, and just hanging out is getting kind of boring. If you’re a cop, you’re a cop.” She turns her head away for a second, and when she looks at him again, her gaze is steady and confident. “A case like Amanda’s has to be solved as quickly as possible. It must be a terrible strain on her family. I’d be happy to help.”

“We’ve discussed the possibility of a temporary placement effective immediately.”

“Seriously?” Hanna is so thrilled that she spills her coffee. She quickly gets up and grabs a cloth to wipe the table. “Sorry,” she mumbles as she sits down again.

"It's fine," Daniel assures her. "I'm hoping to hear within a couple of days, but can I take it you're interested if we can persuade the City Police to agree?"

"Absolutely."

There is a brief silence. Hanna draws a little circle on the table with her index finger. Just as Daniel is about to get up and leave, she takes a deep breath.

"Before you go, can I ask you about something completely different? It's a company in Åre. Since you're here anyway."

"Of course."

She fetches her laptop, opens it up, and brings up a business analysis on a finance site. At the top of the page it says Fjäll-städ AB.

"Are you familiar with this company?"

"It's a cleaning firm in Åre. There are quite a few."

"Do you know anything about their clients?"

"I presume they include some of your neighbors. These new holiday homes have created a significant demand for cleaning services. The houses are often rented out when the owners aren't using them, so there's a lot of activity in the winter season."

"I understand."

Hanna opens another tab with pictures of five middle-aged men. Daniel realizes they must make up the board of Fjäll-städ AB.

"Do you recognize any of these men?"

Daniel peers at the screen. Most of the names are familiar, but not all. Anton would have a better idea.

"What about the chair?" Hanna points to the top name, Arvid Gustafsson.

The name means nothing to Daniel. "That guy lives in Duved," he says, indicating the next line down. "Anders Matsson. He runs an ICA grocery store. Fredrik Bergfors owns a construction company; he's built houses for many of your neighbors here in Sadeln." The second name from the bottom is familiar too. "That's Bosse Lundh. He's the local organizer for Missing People—they helped with the search for Amanda over the weekend."

"That's why I recognized him," Hanna says with a nod.

"He's a local entrepreneur," Daniel explains. He can't place the last name on the list. "Why do you ask?"

Hanna smiles. "My sister uses the company. She asked me to check something out, that's all. Thanks for your help." She closes the laptop, then makes a sweeping gesture toward the kitchen.

"Would you like another coffee? Or something to eat? I haven't had dinner yet."

It's tempting. Daniel would have liked to stay, toss ideas back and forth, but it could be misinterpreted.

This evening's meeting has reinforced the impression he got this morning: she is a committed police officer who knows what she's talking about. There's a lot he'd like to discuss with her, but it will have to wait until later. At the station.

"I have to go," he says. "Thanks anyway. I'll be in touch as soon as I know what's happening. My boss is going to contact your boss in Stockholm."

Hanna's face closes down for a second; then she looks normal again.

"Of course."

"If you could send me your references, that would be great," he says, getting to his feet.

TUESDAY, DECEMBER 17

63

The soft sound of gurgling wakes Daniel.

He is alert in a second; his sleep was superficial, even though he fell into bed as soon as he got home last night.

Ida doesn't stir as he slips out of bed and gently picks up his daughter. He prepares a bottle and carries her into the living room. Ida is still breastfeeding, but Alice often has formula when Daniel feeds her.

He settles down on the sofa with her head resting in the crook of his arm. Her downy hair barely covers her scalp, where the fontanelles are just visible.

Every time he sees his child, it feels like a miracle. He still can't quite believe that she exists, that he and Ida have created this new little person.

He hears smacking noises as Alice's mouth closes around the teat of the bottle. She is intent on one thing and one thing only.

His thoughts drift away to Harald and Lena's gaunt faces, the anguish that has hollowed out their cheeks in a matter of days. Daniel doesn't know what it's like to lose a child, but he is familiar with the pain of loss.

Once again he feels brokenhearted that his mother, Francesca, never had the opportunity to meet Alice before she passed away. He constantly searches his daughter's face for any sign of a resemblance between them, but Alice has blue eyes, not hazel. At least he and Ida gave Alice Francesca as a middle name.

Daniel often wonders how his mother would have reacted to Alice. Presumably she would have adored her granddaughter, loved being a grandma. He knows that she secretly mourned the fact that he was an only child.

What would she have thought of Ida?

It is almost five o'clock when he puts Alice down again. She falls asleep immediately. Her eyelids flutter; then she is snuffling contentedly.

He really ought to go back to bed, but instead he pulls up a chair and sits for a while with Alice's tiny hand in his.

64

What do you do about school when your children have just lost their big sister?

Harald has no idea. Nothing in his life has prepared him for this moment. Yesterday they were allowed to stay home, but somehow a kind of normality must resume.

He is grasping desperately for routine. He has managed to get up, get the kids dressed, and go down to the kitchen on autopilot. Now he is standing by the counter with a cup of coffee while Mimi and Kalle push their breakfast around their plates.

Neither of them says a word, and their usual bickering has stopped, as if someone has flicked an invisible switch.

Harald remembers how irritated he used to get by the noise that constantly filled the house. The never-ending squabbles, the constant pinging from tablets and phones. Now the silence is eating him up. Even the sound of Ludde's claws tip-tapping across the floor can no longer be heard. Harald still doesn't understand what happened. Ludde was a young dog. On Sunday he was perfectly fit and healthy.

He hardly sees Lena. She has completely collapsed. When their family doctor came by yesterday evening with some sleeping tablets, she practically fell on them. Since then she has remained in a deep slumber, allowing her to escape reality, at least temporarily.

Harald would like to escape too, but he doesn't know where to go. He longs for Mira; he wants to weep in her arms, shut out the horror for a while.

The coffee aroma is making him feel sick; he empties the cup into the sink.

Kalle takes a small sip of his chocolate milk, then puts down the glass very carefully, as if he is afraid of disturbing the atmosphere.

The kitchen clock shows seven thirty, the time when the twins usually set off for school.

Routines, Harald thinks. *It's best to stick to routines.*

"I'll drive you to school today," he offers.

Mimi looks up at him anxiously. She hasn't finished her cheese sandwich. "Isn't Mommy having breakfast?" she asks in a small voice.

"Mommy's asleep." Harald almost manages to sound normal. "I expect she'll have something when she wakes up."

"I can make her a sandwich," Kalle says.

"It's better to let her rest for as long as she needs to. Go and get your things."

"Do we have to go to school?" Mimi says. Her lower lip is trembling, and the skin beneath her eyes is almost transparent from a lack of sleep. She too cried herself to sleep last night.

Harald sits down on the chair beside her and pulls her close. He wants to cry and shut himself in the bedroom like Lena has done, but if he does that, who will hold the family together?

Deep down he wants someone else to take charge, establish what is right and wrong. Spell things out so that he doesn't have to make all the decisions.

He isn't religious, but if he were, he would ask God, *How can you be so cruel? How can you allow our daughter to be murdered, then take our dog away from us?*

"Let's forget about school," he whispers into Mimi's hair, which still has a sweet, babyish scent. "Would you like to stay home and watch a movie instead? We can make popcorn, eat candy?"

Mimi nods, and so does Kalle.

"Can we really?" Mimi asks.

"Of course you can."

Harald clenches his fists to avoid losing control. He must be strong in front of the children. He must get through this.

He hardly slept last night; he just lay awake with a thousand questions swirling around in his head.

His phone vibrates in his pocket. He hopes it's Mira—she's the only person he wants to see right now. He texted her a while ago, asked if they could meet up outside the office. He can't go into work. If he has to face the sympathy of his colleagues, he will break down.

"Daddy might need to go out for a few hours," he says. "Will you be okay, or should I call Grandma?"

Mimi shakes her head. "We'll be fine."

Harald takes out his phone, glances at the display. Mira has replied.

Eleven o'clock at the usual place?

For a moment the weight lifts from his shoulders. She *is* there for him.

65

Hanna is sitting at the table with a cup of coffee and a marmalade sandwich for breakfast. She woke early, and it is still dark outside.

It would be fantastic if she could get a new post up here. Daniel probably doesn't understand how happy it would make her; she hardly slept with excitement. The very fact that he came to the house means so much.

She is teetering between optimism and the fear that it will come to nothing, but if he wasn't serious, then surely he wouldn't have stopped by?

She takes a bite of her sandwich. The worrying thing is that Daniel's boss might speak to Hanna's boss, Manfred Lidwall, who hates her.

Lydia said he'd promised to give her a good reference, but can she trust him? If Manfred reneges on the agreement he made with Lydia, it's all over. Now that Daniel has asked her to send him her references, she has to find someone who's on her side.

She goes through her colleagues in the department. Only one person tried to support her when the shit hit the fan: Astrid Ståhl, an experienced inspector who is approaching retirement.

Astrid isn't afraid of Lidwall. Would she be prepared to put herself on the line for Hanna?

Lie to Daniel?

Not lie, Hanna corrects herself. *Just give him a different version of events.*

She massages the back of her neck with one hand while thinking it over.

All Astrid needs to do is take Daniel's call and say positive things about Hanna's service in Stockholm. Explain that Hanna left because she was burned out, exhausted by the kind of crime she had worked with for so long.

Which isn't too far from the truth.

She has been worn down by the endless stream of abused women and violent men, the children who suffer in destructive family relationships. Surely this contributed to how strongly she reacted to Josefin's case. But the exact role that particular case played in her departure from the department need not be mentioned at this time.

Hanna checks her watch—eight thirty. Astrid should be at work by now.

Dare she make the call?

She doesn't have any choice; she needs to protect herself.

She tries Astrid's number and takes a deep breath when Astrid answers right away. Hanna gathers her courage and explains the situation.

"Of course you can tell him to contact me," Astrid says. "I'll sing your praises—you have nothing to worry about. You're a good cop—never forget that."

Hanna doesn't know how to thank her. "This is so kind of you, Astrid."

"It's the least I can do. The way Manfred has treated you is an absolute disgrace. Tell Daniel he can call me anytime."

Astrid's unreserved backing restores Hanna's faith in humanity. She ends the call with a warm feeling in her tummy. There are people who care about her, who value her competence. Even her dark thoughts about Christian have lightened a little.

66

Daniel's phone beeps in his back pocket just as he's about to fetch his third coffee of the day at the police station. He's just ended a conversation with Astrid Ståhl, Hanna's referee with the City Police in Stockholm. Hanna texted him Astrid's contact details this morning, and her colleague had nothing but positive things to say about her.

He takes out his phone again; he has a text from Ylva Labba, the forensic pathologist.

Autopsy completed. Call me.

He alerts the others and heads for the conference room. Raffe and Anton join him at the oval table. Daniel enters the link code, and Ylva's face appears on the screen. She is still wearing her protective clothing, as if she has just left the autopsy room. However, she has taken off her latex gloves and is sitting at a desk.

"That was quick," she says.

"What can you tell us?"

"I worked until late last night; then I double-checked a few things this morning. I haven't gotten around to writing my report yet, but I think I have a clear picture of what happened."

Daniel is so eager that he is almost drumming his fingers.

"It's as I suspected from the start: the girl froze to death. The body is largely intact, apart from a certain amount of damage due to frostbite, which is perfectly normal under the circumstances. My observations of the heart and lungs support this hypothesis. I have of course sent away samples for toxicology analysis, but I'm pretty sure they'll come back negative."

She pauses as if to allow for any questions, and picks up a pencil in her right hand.

"However, I have found a number of other interesting things, including minute particles of skin under a couple of fingernails, which hopefully will give us the perpetrator's DNA. There are also marks on the girl's throat, contusions indicating that pressure has been applied. Her upper arms are also bruised."

The strength of the wind has increased again outside the window. The night was fairly calm, but now the slender birches are swaying around and bending so far they seem close to snapping. In Åre a storm can arrive and grow to full force in less than an hour.

"So what are your conclusions?" Daniel asks.

"I think the perpetrator held her tightly. If she struggled at first, that would explain the bruises on her arms. At some point he switched to a stranglehold, hence the marks on her throat. He was probably wearing gloves, because I can't find any impressions left by fingernails on her skin."

"Which means we're looking at a person with sufficient physical strength to subdue her for some time?" Anton says.

Ylva nods.

Daniel thinks about Viktor in his black hoodie. Medium height, broad shoulders. Amanda would have been no match for him.

"There wasn't enough violence to cause death," Ylva goes on. "For example, there are no clear signs of stasis—a blockage preventing blood flow. Nor is the larynx badly damaged. It is possible that she might have lost consciousness for a period."

"Any idea how long?" Daniel says. "Can you tell if she was unconscious when she froze to death?"

"You mean did she come around and realize she'd been abducted before she actually died?"

"Something like that."

Daniel hopes the answer will be no. He hates the thought of Amanda coming around, groggy and half-naked, in an unfamiliar location on the mountain before she passed away. Of her being sufficiently compos mentis to realize what would happen as the cold increased and she couldn't escape.

The fear of death must have been horrific.

"I can't tell you that," Ylva replies. Daniel can see in her eyes that she knows exactly why he's asking.

They end the video call, and the screen goes black. Daniel takes out his phone; he has received a new text message, which he reads with growing interest.

One of the drivers of a SkiStar snow groomer has contacted the police. He was working late on Saturday night, just a few hours before Amanda's body was found on the chairlift.

He thinks he saw someone driving a snowmobile on the piste around that time.

"We need to leave right now," Daniel says to Anton.

67

Harald is driving toward Undersåker. He is meeting Mira at Vällistegården campsite—a place where no one is likely to see them.

Everyone knows everyone else in a small community like Åre; he has to be careful.

There isn't a soul in sight when he pulls into the parking lot and switches off the engine. He's early, which is perhaps a good thing. It is such a relief to get away from home; he could use a few minutes alone.

Everything back there reminds him of Amanda. The air is so heavy with grief that he feels the pressure on his shoulders. It is paralyzing.

Harald leans back in the driver's seat.

He wishes he had the moral strength to stay away from Mira, but right now there is no one he needs more. She is the only one whose presence he craves, the only one who can give him solace.

He fell in love with her when he first interviewed her for the job. She was a fantastic PA and quickly slipped into her role as his right-hand woman. They became close, as people do in that kind of working relationship.

He couldn't help hoping for more, but he was careful not to show it. Instead he did his best to win her empathy and trust. He tried to be an understanding and supportive boss and always allowed her to set her own hours. If she had to leave early because of her daughter, he never objected.

The more they got to know each other, the more Harald realized how alone she felt within her marriage.

Mira's husband, Fredrik, put his heart and soul into his company, which took its toll. Their relationship suffered because he was never home, and it seemed to Mira that she always came second.

One evening at the office, when she and Harald were alone, she broke down. Harald comforted her, listened for hours as she wept on his shoulder.

Then he kissed her, and life was transformed.

She turned him into a new person, ten years younger and full of energy. He was ecstatically happy, even though he had to lie to Lena and come up with excuses to carve out time together with Mira. She was the last thing he thought about before he went to sleep, and the first thing when he woke.

But Mira got cold feet.

She started talking about her marriage vows and Fredrik's jealousy. She was terrified that he would find out what she was up to.

She ended it.

Harald has made a number of futile attempts to change her mind in the month that's passed since she broke off their relationship. He never felt so alive as during the six months they were together.

Wonderful, bewitching Mira, with her shiny black hair and the faint dimple in one cheek.

He and Lena were so young when they met; he'd hardly been with anyone else before they married and their beloved Amanda was born. The years passed, the twins came along, life went on. Their relationship has become a partnership, a friendship, with shared responsibility for the home and children. They're not unhappy, they haven't fallen out, they're just not . . . in love.

Harald had forgotten the heady excitement of falling in love when Mira came into his life. He was forty years old by the time he understood what passion between a man and a woman could be like.

He hears the sound of an approaching engine, and her white Toyota appears. That alone is enough to fill him with desire.

For a moment, reality disappears. Excitement is coursing through his veins, his mouth goes dry.

Nothing exists but Mira.

68

Daniel and Anton are on their way to Rödkullen, where SkiStar keeps its snow groomers in a huge garage.

Preparing the slopes is a constant, ongoing task. As soon as the lifts close, the groomers start work. They are often out until two in the morning, particularly when it snows as heavily as in recent weeks. Sometimes they have to go out again at six, before the lifts start up.

The guy who contacted the police is Tor Marklund.

"He must be from Skellefteå," Anton says as they head west. "Everyone from Skellefteå has the surname Marklund."

Daniel raises his eyebrows. "You wouldn't be prejudiced, would you?"

"It's true," Anton insists. "Everyone who's born up here knows that."

Daniel has no counterargument.

Tor is waiting for them in the parking lot at Rödkullen. Daniel spots him as soon as he turns off the road—a tall, slightly stooped man wearing a woolly hat and a red jacket with the SkiStar logo. He is standing with his legs wide apart in the area between the vehicles and the skiing area.

"Are you Tor?" Daniel asks.

"Yes."

Tor's Skellefteå accent is unmistakable, even from that one word. Anton pokes Daniel meaningfully in the side.

"We can go into the cabin," Tor says, pointing to a low, brown-painted wooden building next to Rautjoxa, the local restaurant. The cabin consists of one room with a square table and a few chairs. Along one wall there is a counter with several shelves and a Melitta coffee machine. A pot is standing on the hotplate, its contents pitch black.

"Coffee?" Tor says, pouring himself a cup.

"I just had some, thanks," Anton replies quickly.

Daniel accepts a cup that smells worryingly bitter.

"So," Tor begins. "I don't know if I was right to contact you, but my partner said I should."

"Please tell us what you saw—we're grateful for any information," Daniel reassures him.

"I was out on the machine in the early hours of Sunday morning. It was late, and I was about to finish my shift. It was after two—I'd been out all evening because of the heavy snow."

Tor takes out a tin of snuff and tucks a plug under his top lip.

"I'd just finished the top of Stjärnbacken when I saw a snowmobile zooming along down below me. I couldn't hear anything because my engine is pretty loud, but I saw the beam of the headlights as it got closer."

"Where did it come from?" Anton asks. "What direction?"

Tor adjusts the plug of snuff, frowns as if he's trying hard to remember. "It came from the west. It was on the transportation route for number forty-seven, the one that starts at Rödkullen and ends at the Hummel lift."

Daniel tries to remember what the piste map looks like. Åre has something like a hundred runs, if you count Duved and Björnen.

"Can you tell us exactly where you were?" he says. "Be as precise as possible."

"Let me think." Tor is in no hurry. He adjusts his hat, scratches above one ear. "I was just below the top station on VM6, maybe a hundred yards from the transportation route. My snow groomer was at an angle facing toward the mountain, so my headlights were pointing upward."

"So whoever was on the snowmobile wouldn't have seen you."

"I shouldn't think so."

"Then what happened?"

"The snowmobile turned off and drove down Stjärnbacken. It looked as if it was heading for the VM6 embarkation station, but it disappeared behind the trees, so I couldn't see."

"Was there anything in particular that struck you as strange?" Daniel asks.

"It was very late, like I said. At that time of night, it's usually only us and the snowmakers who are out and about."

"Snowmakers?" Daniel is unfamiliar with the term.

"They look after the cannons that produce artificial snow. Some cannons are automatic, but some have to be switched on and off manually. They also need a certain amount of maintenance—cleaning and so on." Tor makes it sound like the most obvious explanation in the world. "Between November and February we produce artificial snow so that there's enough to last the season," he adds. "The snow must always be at least twenty inches deep on the pistes."

"I understand," Daniel says, keeping quiet about the fact that he knows nothing about artificial snow. "So it was the snowmobile that made you react?"

"The thing is, the snowmakers always work in pairs. They're not allowed to go out on their own, for health and safety reasons. That's why I suspected it was a private snowmobile, and there was no reason for it to be there." Tor takes a sip of his coffee and makes a face. "Pure fox poison," he says.

"Do you remember what the snowmobile looked like?" Daniel wonders.

"That was the odd part. It was way too dark to belong to SkiStar. I can't tell you the exact color, but I'm guessing it was black, because it was hard to make out."

"What do your snowmobiles look like?"

"They have orange stripes on a white background. The idea is that they should be clearly visible, even in bad weather. The drivers also wear high-vis clothing—their jackets are neon yellow. Plus all our snowmobiles have extra equipment—for example, there's a flag on the handlebars."

Daniel is impressed—there's nothing wrong with Tor's powers of observation.

"With hindsight, maybe I should have reacted more quickly," Tor continues, "but I thought maybe some kids were messing around, or on their way home after a late party. Teenagers do take a shortcut across the slopes sometimes, and there's not much we can do about it." He looks down at his big hands. A small amount of snuff has attached itself to his index finger, staining the tip brown. "When I saw the news on TV about that poor girl, I started to wonder. I told my partner, and she said I ought to contact you."

"I'm very pleased you did," Daniel replies. "Any idea what make the snowmobile was?"

Tor frowns. "SkiStar mostly uses Lynx, although there are a few Ski-Doos. This was a different make—possibly Yamaha, but I can't be sure. As I said, it was a very dark color, and it was moving pretty fast. I just got the feeling something wasn't right. I can't really explain why."

Daniel is unexpectedly grateful that Tor has turned out to be a real Skellefteå guy, or at least someone who intuitively knows the difference between snowmobiles. Personally, he wouldn't be able to tell one from another.

"It might have been a Polaris," Tor adds. "But that's just a guess."

Lynx is one of the leading snowmobile brands, as is Ski-Doo. Yamaha is a smaller manufacturer, but very popular. There must be hundreds of these models in the area, but it's still useful information.

Anton has another question. "You didn't happen to see the registration number?"

Tor shakes his head. "Sorry. It was too far away."

"But you're sure it was heading toward VM6?"

"Yes. I could see the beam of the headlights moving through the darkness across the snow as it turned off for the valley. You couldn't miss it."

"Do you remember anything else?" Daniel asks. "Even the smallest detail could be important."

Tor glances out of the window at the T-bar lifts moving up to the Rödkullen mountain station. The sight is almost hypnotic as the bars regularly slide forward, swing around, then disappear with a steady rhythm.

"Actually, there was one more thing. I'm almost sure the driver was pulling a sled. I thought I saw it by the rear lights when he turned down the slope; something seemed to be sliding along behind him."

Daniel and Anton exchange a look.

"Thank you so much," Daniel says. "If you think of anything else, please don't hesitate to contact us."

It can't possibly be a coincidence that a snowmobile was out so late in the vicinity of VM6, just hours before Amanda was found on the chairlift. And moving a dead body would be no problem with a sled.

Plus the snowmobile came from the west.

Ullådalen lies to the west.

69

Harald notices that Mira looks around carefully before leaving her car. She has pulled her hat all the way down and is wearing dark glasses, even though it's December.

When she sits down beside him, Harald can no longer control himself. He pulls her close, kisses her with such passion that he doesn't realize she's resisting.

He comes to his senses only when she shouts "Stop!" and pushes him away.

Harald's shoulders slump. "I'm sorry," he mumbles. "I just had to . . ." He can't explain himself; he has no idea what to say, so he simply opens his hands in a wordless gesture of apology.

Mira's eyes are full of sympathy. She takes his hand, caresses the back with a featherlight touch. The warmth of her fingertips spreads through his body.

"I'm so sorry about Amanda," Mira says, her voice breaking. "It's terrible."

Harald can't talk about his dead daughter. All he wants right now is to touch Mira, feel her soft body against his. Forget everything, if only for a few minutes. He tries to kiss her again, but she pulls away.

"Don't do that."

"Please, Mira . . ."

She edges a little closer to the door, and a shadow passes across her face. "It's over between us. You know that."

"I need you." Harald can't suppress a low groan. "I can't do this on my own. I'm drowning." He presses his fist to his mouth to avoid losing control completely.

"It's over," Mira says again.

How can she be like this after what's happened? Harald is devastated, he needs her—surely she must understand that?

But Mira's voice is flat and neutral when she continues: "What we did wasn't fair on your family or mine. We agreed on that."

She falls silent, looks down at her wedding ring and her engagement ring, with its sparkling solitaire diamond.

"Especially not now. You have to think about Lena and the twins—they're going to need you more than ever."

Harald is on the verge of tears. Lena was still asleep when he left the house. He has already realized that they are incapable of supporting each other through this. He takes Mira's hand and squeezes it. He doesn't want to beg, but he can't stop himself when she's sitting so close to him.

"Just one last time," he pleads.

She snatches her hand away and puts on her gloves.

"Sorry," he mutters.

Mira takes a pink lip gloss out of her purse, as if she wants to give him the chance to pull himself together.

"Don't text me late on a Sunday night again," she says. Her tone is gentle, her message crystal clear.

Harald had forgotten that he'd sent her a text when the vodka rush took over. He is even more ashamed now.

"I had to come up with a story about urgent council business, but I don't think Fredrik believed me." Mira drops the lip gloss back in her purse. Her dark eyes are filled with worry. "I think he knows what we've been doing, Harald. You should have seen the way he looked at me. He knows we've been seeing each other outside work."

"That's impossible—we've been so careful."

"Fredrik has a lot of friends and acquaintances around here. Anyone could have seen us and told him . . ." Mira bites her lip. "You know what he's like. Fredrik isn't the kind of man who finds it easy to forgive."

Harald has met him on a number of occasions, both socially and through his job. Fredrik is a tall man with a serious nature and a perpetually grim expression, the complete opposite of his petite, witty wife. He is an entrepreneur who has successfully built up his own construction company through hard work. The property boom in Åre created great opportunities for businesspeople; SkiStar's investment gave the whole place a boost. Many people were tempted to buy a luxurious second home, and Mira's husband was one of those involved in the project at Sadeln.

"Don't contact me outside working hours again." There is fear in her soft voice. "Promise."

Harald gazes at her lovely profile, the straight nose that defines her face, the long, dark eyelashes. Her eyes are fixed on some distant point, as if she is already wondering what Fredrik would do if the truth came out.

Harald is prepared to go to any lengths to be with her.

"I love you," he says hoarsely.

When Mira turns to face him, her expression is one of pity, not desire. "You're still in shock. You don't know what you're talking about."

Harald stares through the windshield. It has stopped snowing. Everything around them is white, except for the jagged black branches of the trees against the overcast sky. The campsite is empty and desolate, with no hint of the summer's lively buzz of activity.

There aren't even footprints in the snow.

Mira presses her lips together and seems to reach a decision. She opens the passenger door, and the ice-cold air rushes in. She pats Harald's knee gently with her left hand. "Go home to Lena. That's the best thing you can do."

Then she gets out of the car and slams the door.

Harald closes his eyes. He is finding it difficult to take in what she has said. His daughter has been murdered, he is in the worst situation of his entire life, and Mira has dismissed him, just like that.

When he looks up she is already reversing her car. She doesn't even glance at him as she swings around. Within seconds the Toyota has disappeared.

Harald wraps his arms tightly around his upper body. He rocks back and forth in his seat, oblivious to the world around him.

Everything hurts.

70

Harald has spent hours in the car.

After Mira left, he simply sat there until eventually the cold made him start the engine and leave the campsite. He drove toward the Norwegian border without any real idea of where he was going. He ended up in Storlien, almost fifty miles from home.

Storlien is a construction site this winter; a huge border shopping mall is being built. As chair of the council, Harald supported the project. It is an important investment for the area, plus it's better if the Norwegians shop here rather than causing traffic problems in Åre with their Teslas.

Today he merely glances in passing at the half-finished buildings and the noisy machinery. Then he turns the car around and heads back. Thoughts of Amanda's death and Mira's departure pulsate through his body like bleeding wounds.

It is dark by the time he reaches the outskirts of Åre. Soon he will be passing Ängarna, an area only five minutes to the west of the village center.

The area where Mira lives.

He feels a stabbing pain in his chest. He has stopped by a few times to drop off papers or a document he has signed. It is on the opposite side of the village, but not far from his home.

He ought to go home to the children; he's already been gone for far too long.

Instead he leaves the E14 and heads for Mira's house. It is on a slight hill, with a beautiful view of the lake. A substantial red wooden house with white eaves and window frames.

A real master builder's house.

He turns into Mira's street, crawls past the property, looking for signs of life. No one seems to be home. There are no cars on the drive, and Mira's white Toyota isn't there.

She'll be at work, of course. While he sat there at the campsite, completely floored, she went into the office as if nothing had happened.

When he reaches the end of the street, he pauses, then drives back again. He stops by Mira's mailbox and stares stupidly at the impressive house on the hill. That's where she spends every night, lying by her husband's side.

Fredrik, the man she doesn't want to leave. Dare not leave.

Harald has lost her, and his life is in ruins.

His breathing is labored. He can see tire tracks in the snow on the drive, presumably from Fredrik's SUV. He has seen it on many occasions, when Fredrik has picked up Mira from work.

A fresh thought strikes him. If Fredrik found out about Harald and Mira's affair . . . if he knows she's cheated on him . . .

The police asked if Harald had any enemies and Harald said no, not that he was aware of. Fredrik is the only person who actually has a motive to harm him and his family.

His mouth goes dry.

Would Fredrik do something so terrible as to kill Amanda? In order to punish Harald?

Controlled, taciturn Fredrik, who loves Jämtland and frequently goes off to the mountain on his snowmobile to find peace and quiet.

Whichever way Harald looks at it, he keeps reaching the same conclusion. There is no one else who would wish him so much harm.

71

Restlessness drives Hanna out of the house. She can't stay indoors with all those thoughts whirling around in her head.

All she is doing is waiting for a call from Daniel.

The minutes had crept by all day as she'd sat there worrying about Manfred Lidwall badmouthing her.

She takes Lydia's car and drives down to the village. She needs to be around people, do something; otherwise she'll go crazy. Should she check out the cleaning company Zuhra works for? When she opened her laptop this morning, the page she'd shown Daniel yesterday evening was still on the screen. The office is on Årevägen—it can't be far.

She has decided to trust her instincts. After all those years with the City Police and the extensive contact she has had with vulnerable women, she can feel that something is wrong.

It is surprisingly easy to find a parking space. She leaves the car opposite the Åregården Hotel and looks around in the fading afternoon light.

The Advent atmosphere is irresistible. The stores around the square all have beautiful festive displays in their windows, glowing invitingly. Every tree is decorated with strings of tiny white lights that catch the rime frost in the treetops, making it sparkle.

The shimmering snow crystals create an over-the-top Christmassy feeling, as if Walt Disney himself had passed through, sprinkling the entire village with glitter.

It has stopped snowing, but it is still so cold that the dry snow crunches audibly beneath Hanna's feet.

She makes her way to Årevägen 100B, which turns out to be a brown-painted three-story building a short distance up the hill. She finds the entrance around the back. The name of the company, Fjäll-städ AB, is printed on a slim metal sign above the door.

It isn't locked. Hanna steps into a dark hallway with linoleum flooring and a shabby doormat. There is a coat stand with a lone jacket on it in one corner.

"Hello?" she calls out tentatively.

She moves forward and sees that the hallway leads into a larger, sparsely furnished room. A desk and computer are positioned by the window. Several prints with mountain-landscape motifs are displayed on the walls. Buckets containing cleaning equipment are lined up along one side of the room, with a row of mop handles standing to attention.

Piles of papers are spread out across the desk.

A door opens behind Hanna, and a brown-haired woman wearing glasses emerges from a bathroom. She is wearing a knitted sweater and jeans and is holding a phone. A name badge reveals that she is called Linda.

She looks at Hanna in surprise as Hanna quickly searches for something to say.

"Oh hi, great, I was just wondering where everyone was" is the best she can come up with.

"Do you have an appointment?" Linda sounds a little suspicious.

Hanna takes a couple of steps back.

"Not exactly." She needs a credible explanation for her visit. "My name is Hanna Ahlander. Is this Fjäll-städ's office?"

"Yes." Linda sits down behind the desk, takes off her round glasses. "What can I do for you?"

"One of your cleaners was at my place yesterday, and she left something behind. Could you give me her number so I can call and let her know?"

Linda shakes her head. "I'm afraid we can't give out our employees' contact details."

"I understand."

Hanna runs a finger around the inside of her collar. The room is warm, and she is already sweating in her thick padded jacket. She doesn't know Zuhra's surname, so she can't look up the number for herself. However, she can't shake off the feeling that it's important to get a hold of her.

"I can leave her a message if you like?" Linda offers.

Hanna hesitates. Obviously, Zuhra hasn't left anything behind, so what reason can she give for contacting her?

"It doesn't matter. She can pick it up next time she comes."

"Up to you."

Linda puts her glasses back on and points apologetically at the computer. "I really need to . . ."

She couldn't make it any clearer that it's time Hanna left.

"Thanks anyway," Hanna says. *Thanks for nothing.* She pauses in the doorway. "Give Zuhra my best—she's very good."

Linda looks up. "Who?"

"Zuhra. My cleaner."

"We don't employ anyone by that name."

"Sorry?"

"We're a small company. I know everyone."

"But she was at my house yesterday."

"You must have the wrong company."

Lydia is rarely wrong, but Linda has no reason to lie to Hanna.

"Are there other cleaning companies in the area with a similar name?" Hanna asks, just to be on the safe side.

"There are several firms in Åre—I'm sure you can find them online."

Hanna has no choice but to leave. Something isn't right, but she doesn't quite know what to do. She decides to forget it for the time being, speak to Zuhra next time she comes to the house.

She crosses the square and is heading back to her car when she hears a woman's voice shouting her name.

"Hanna! Hi!"

When she turns around she sees Karro coming down the hill from the train station.

"Thanks for the other night," she says, giving Hanna a hug. "I'm really glad you came—it must be kind of lonely up there in Sadeln."

"No, thank you," Hanna replies. "It was good to get out for a while."

"What brings you into the village today?"

Hanna can't tell her the truth; she still feels as if she's prying.

"I was just going to go for a coffee." She points to the nearby coffee shop. "Have you got time to join me?"

"Great—I've just finished for the day."

They are in luck—one of the few tables is free. The wonderful aroma of freshly ground coffee beans fills the air. Hanna orders and pays for them both, as a small thank-you for Karro inviting her to Supper.

It doesn't take long before the conversation turns to Amanda. Hanna decides not to mention the fact that she spoke to Karro's brother about Viktor. She also keeps quiet about the possibility of a temporary placement in Åre; she doesn't want to jinx her chances.

The coffee is as delicious as the aroma promised.

Karro leans across the table, wide eyed.

"I need to tell you something, seeing that you're a cop. Guess what I heard yesterday?" Her tone is full of excitement, as if she is sitting on some really good gossip. "Amanda had an affair with her adviser in school. And he's twice her age!"

"Sorry?" Hanna isn't sure she's heard correctly.

"Can you imagine? I heard it from my neighbor Pia—she's a teaching assistant at Amanda's school."

Hanna doesn't know what to think.

"How creepy is that?" Karro goes on. "A teacher messing around with young girls! Disgusting. But then maybe it explains a few things . . ." She lowers her voice so that the people at the next table won't hear. "What if he had something to do with Amanda's death?" She shudders. "Have you come across anything like this before, when you were working in Stockholm?"

Hanna shakes her head. "Do you happen to know the name of this adviser?"

"No, but it can't be that difficult to find out."

Hanna hesitates. How reliable is this information? As recently as Sunday it seemed likely that Amanda's boyfriend was behind her disappearance; apparently now the gossip has moved on to a teacher. Karro seems to know everything about everything, but without proof this is nothing more than speculation.

Although if it's true, it's an important lead to follow up.

"Have you passed this on to your brother? It might be worth mentioning it."

"Anton?" Karro spreads her hands and smiles. "He'd never listen to me."

Hanna thinks for a moment. She would like to discuss this with Anton or Daniel, but she can't really contact them again until they've been in touch about the job—particularly not with a piece of gossip she's picked up in the village. The last thing she wants is for them to regard her as unprofessional.

At the same time, Karro's assertion needs to be looked into.

She knows exactly how she would tackle an interview with Amanda's adviser, if she got the chance.

She reaches into her pocket, runs her finger over the cold metal of her phone, desperately wishing that Daniel would call.

There is nothing she wants more than to be offered the placement in Åre and start working as a police officer again.

72

There is no sign of Lena when Harald arrives home much later than usual.

Mimi and Kalle are sitting in front of the TV, exactly as they were when he left them. The kitchen bears witness to the fact that they have made sandwiches: a sweaty piece of cheese has been left out on the counter next to a packet of warm butter and a half-empty carton of milk. There are crumbs everywhere.

The twins barely register his presence.

"Where's Mommy?" he calls out.

"She's asleep," Mimi replies without taking her eyes off the screen.

Harald is about to start tidying up the kitchen when the landline rings. At first he doesn't want to answer—what if it's a journalist? On the third ring the instinct to pick up is too strong to resist.

"Hello?"

"Hello—my name is Alina Nilsson. I'm a vet in Undersåker."

"Yes?"

"I think your wife left a message for me yesterday about your dog."

Harald tries to think. Lena did say she'd called the veterinary clinic when she found Ludde.

"I've gone through the symptoms she mentioned," the vet continues. "It sounds a lot like severe nicotine poisoning to me."

"What?"

Harald isn't sure if he's heard correctly. He gently closes the living room door to reduce the noise from the TV.

"Do you know if he could have eaten any cigarette stubs, snuff, or tobacco?" The vet pauses. "I don't want to worry you, but if he hasn't already vomited and improved, then you need to bring him in. Nicotine in large doses is very dangerous for animals. If he's consumed nicotine gum, he could also be suffering from xylitol poisoning."

"Ludde is dead," Harald says in a flat voice.

"Dead?"

"He died yesterday."

"I'm so sorry to hear that." There is genuine compassion in the woman's voice. "In that case he must have consumed a significant amount all at once."

Harald stands there with the phone in his hand.

"What about e-cigarettes?" the vet goes on. "There's so much liquid nicotine in each cartridge that it's the equivalent of at least two ordinary cigarettes. If Ludde got a hold of a pack of cartridges, that could explain what's happened. Unfortunately I've seen it before."

It doesn't matter anymore, Harald thinks. *Ludde is dead. Amanda is dead.*

When he doesn't say anything, the vet continues: "Would you like us to perform an autopsy on your dog to find out what he died of? It might be useful to know, for the insurance if nothing else."

Ludde's body is still in the garage. Harald has hardly given him a thought over the past twenty-four hours. Wait a minute—what did the vet say about the cause of death?

"What do you mean by poisoned?" he asks.

There is a brief silence.

"The symptoms your wife described on the phone indicate severe nicotine poisoning," Alina Nilsson reiterates.

She doesn't seem to realize that she's talking to the father of the murdered girl who's been in all the papers. Her voice lacks the note of pity that has been so evident in everyone else who has spoken to him.

Harald tries to digest this new information. "How could that have happened?"

"It's not that unusual."

"We don't smoke. No one in the family smokes, or takes snuff."

"Oh!" The vet is clearly surprised. "That is strange. Given how quickly he died, he must have ingested a large amount of nicotine. Chewing the odd cigarette stub out in the street would be nowhere near enough." She breaks off, thinks for a moment. "In which case you have to wonder if it was accidental."

Harald remembers arriving home in the morning and seeing Ludde lying helpless on the floor, with whitish drool around his mouth.

He feels unsteady and leans on the kitchen counter for support when he realizes what the vet means.

"Are you saying that someone deliberately poisoned our dog?"

"I can't say for sure, but it's hard to rule out the possibility."

Harald ends the call and remains frozen to the spot. It never occurred to him that Ludde didn't die of natural causes. He simply took it for granted and cursed the twist of fate that had allowed it to happen on the day after his daughter was found dead.

Now it sounds as though someone deliberately killed his dog too.

The thought horrifies him.

He can't help glancing out of the window, as if a murderer is lurking in the darkness.

He goes into the hallway and locks the front door, even though they don't usually bother during the day.

Then he sinks down at the kitchen table, thinking the same thoughts as when he was outside Mira's house earlier on. There is only one person who would wish him so much harm.

73

There are no burning torches outside the Landahl family house when Daniel arrives late in the afternoon. However, there are lights in several windows, so it looks as if someone is home this time.

On the other side of the lake, Renfjället is barely visible through the snow mist. The clouds are wrapped around the silent mountain.

The doors of the double garage are closed. There should be a Yamaha snowmobile inside, registered to Viktor's father. Daniel checked the list of snowmobile owners again after his conversation with Tor Marklund. As soon as he confirmed the make and model, he decided to come straight over.

It is safe to assume that Viktor has access to the vehicle, even if he doesn't have a snowmobile license. He passed his driving test a week after his eighteenth birthday.

The information Hanna provided about Viktor's past was very helpful. The more Daniel finds out about the kid, the more suspicious he becomes.

According to the school, Viktor hasn't shown up at all this week.

Daniel locks the car and makes his way up the drive, which has been cleared of snow. His breath looks like a plume of white smoke in the ice-cold air. The temperature is minus seventeen, and white, lacy frost covers the green mailbox.

Viktor opens the door, wearing the same hoodie as before.

Daniel studies his pupils; he appears to be sober.

"You again," Viktor mutters.

"May I come in? I have a few more questions."

Viktor steps back and lets him into the hallway, which is noticeably less tidy than on Saturday, when his parents were expecting guests. There are boots and shoes on the floor, and jackets and coats piled messily on a row of hooks on one wall.

The Landahls are a big family. Viktor has two younger siblings and an older sister who still lives at home. They moved here when Viktor started high school, presumably to avoid the gossip and questioning looks from other parents and neighbors who might know about the alleged assault that led to Viktor being issued a caution.

"Are you home alone?"

"Yes."

That's what Daniel had been hoping for, and it's the main reason why he drove over rather than calling Viktor into the station. A situation like this is much easier without the presence of the parents. Not that he is doing anything wrong; Viktor is eighteen and can be questioned alone.

The other reason is that he didn't want to give Viktor the opportunity to prepare himself.

"Shall we go into the kitchen?" Daniel suggests.

"Okay."

They sit down at an oval table in front of a large window with a view of the lake. A small amount of snow has settled on the mullions, and the ceiling light is reflected in the glass.

The draining board is littered with dirty cups and plates, a packet of bacon, and a greasy frying pan.

"Late lunch?" Daniel says.

Viktor shrugs. "I'll clean up before Mom gets home." He starts chewing the cuticle of his thumb; the skin looks red and sore.

"You know your girlfriend was murdered?"

There is no point in sugarcoating the truth. This time Viktor doesn't object to the word *girlfriend*.

"Mmm."

"How do you feel about that?"

Viktor peers at him from under his bangs. His face is slightly angular, with strong eyebrows. His medium-length hair hangs forward, giving him an air of nonchalance. No doubt he is a cool guy among his peers.

"It's . . . hard."

He rocks back and forth on his chair; he can't keep still. One knee jiggles up and down as his foot drums on the floor.

"The most common scenario in cases like this is that the perpetrator is someone the victim knew well," Daniel explains. "Someone who was in her immediate circle. It's extremely rare for a young girl to be murdered by a stranger." He lets the words sink in, hoping for a reaction. He waits until Viktor looks up. "You've been violent toward young girls in the past. You were guilty of assault."

Technically this is an exaggeration, but it has precisely the effect Daniel wants.

Viktor inhales sharply. "How do you know that?"

"Did you really think we wouldn't find out that you assaulted a girl in Umeå?"

"It was a misunderstanding! I never meant to hurt her."

"Seriously? She was only fifteen. You beat her up so badly that she ended up in the hospital with a fractured jaw. She had to live on liquids and drink through a straw for weeks."

"That's not what happened!" Viktor shouts.

"According to the case notes, you were so angry that you completely lost control."

Viktor tries to protest, but Daniel refuses to let him interrupt. He has studied every detail of the investigation, and he clearly remembers the description of an outing that went very wrong on a beautiful late-summer's evening. The result: a serious injury and a young man who would have been punished far more severely if it hadn't been for his age—and a good lawyer.

Daniel is surprised that he got away with a caution. He holds up a hand to silence Viktor.

"You lost your temper, you yelled and swore at everyone who was there. Your girlfriend was terrified. Your friends tried to calm you down, but you took no notice of them when you started hitting her."

"Listen to me!" Viktor stands up, slams his fist down on the table. "I was fucking drunk, I admit that—but I never meant to hurt Frida. I hit her in the face by accident when I threw away a full bottle of beer because I was so mad. She got in the way—it wasn't deliberate."

His face is bright red, he is breathing with his mouth half-open, and a blob of saliva is caught at the corner of his mouth.

Daniel meets Viktor's furious gaze. Is this his true personality? The lethargic boy he met on Saturday is gone.

If so, then the explanation for Amanda's disappearance is right here in front of him.

"I hit Frida by mistake," Viktor hisses grimly. "I don't know how many times I've apologized for that."

Daniel stands up so that they are face-to-face. "Did you do the same to Amanda?"

"What are you talking about?"

"Did you lose your temper and attack her, just like you did with Frida? Except that your girlfriend died this time . . ."

"Don't say that."

Daniel leans closer. "Let me tell you what I believe happened on Thursday night. You followed Amanda when she left Ebba's party. I think you got into a fight, which ended with you hiding her somewhere in Ullådalen, because you didn't know what to do. Then you changed your mind and left her body on the VM6 chairlift so that she'd be found. You used your father's snowmobile to transport her. We have a witness who saw you driving the snowmobile in the middle of the night."

This is something of an embellishment, of course. Tor Marklund has not identified Viktor as the driver, but Daniel is happy to take the risk. He is determined to put the boy under pressure, even if he gets into hot water for it later.

Viktor looks panic stricken.

"It's not true!" he stammers. "I didn't kill her!"

Daniel keeps going. "Do you know what we've found out from your friends who were at the party?" He folds his arms, mentally ticks off the statements they've gathered over the past few days. "There are witnesses who saw you quarreling with Amanda late in the evening—just as she was about to leave. You tried to stop her by grabbing her arm; she pushed you to the floor. You were yelling and swearing at her as she ran out of the door. After that, no one can confirm where you were. You mentioned your friend Wille, but he'd passed out—he doesn't know whether you were there or not."

"It wasn't me."

"No one backs up your story. No one."

Viktor's face has lost all its color. "I didn't do anything!"

Daniel registers the sound of a car pulling into the drive. He changes his tone. So far he's been playing bad cop, going in as hard as he can. Now he tries out a softer approach. He wants Viktor to feel secure, so secure that he can summon up the courage to confess.

"Admit that you got angry when Amanda wouldn't do as you said. When she left the party even though you wanted her to stay."

"It wasn't me."

"We know it was you who murdered Amanda." Daniel moves around the table, stands right next to Viktor. "You have no alibi, and you've already been convicted of assaulting your ex-girlfriend." Through the window he sees a shadow walking toward the front door. "Tell me what happened that night," he says encouragingly. "I promise it'll make you feel so much better."

"It wasn't me," Viktor whispers. "I didn't do it."

74

Daniel can't shake off the feeling of failure when he arrives back at the police station. It is almost seven o'clock, the corridors are in darkness, and everyone else has gone home. He sits down at his desk and switches on the lamp.

He was so close to getting a confession out of Viktor, and yet he didn't manage to break him. Next time he will bring him in, conduct a formal interview—but the element of surprise will be lost.

The problem is insufficient evidence. Daniel is well aware that there are holes in his argument. The family's snowmobile, Viktor's criminal record, his unsatisfactory alibi—all circumstantial.

There might not be enough to have Viktor remanded in custody. He can almost hear Tobias Ahlqvist's voice demanding solid proof, particularly when the boy is so young. It's always difficult when it comes to depriving someone under twenty of their freedom.

His chair creaks as he leans back. He interlaces his fingers behind his neck and tries to think.

The first rule in a criminal investigation is not to get hooked into a particular hypothesis or a suspect too early. All doors must be left open.

Easier said than done when so much points to one person—a young man who was also close to the victim.

If Viktor isn't the guilty party, then who is?

The team is busy checking out the people who own property in Ullådalen, all the registered snowmobiles in the area, the perpetrator's DNA from the skin particles under Amanda's fingernails, any possible traces on her clothing.

If they're lucky, the forensic evidence will contradict Viktor's statement so convincingly that he will break down and confess.

They're not there yet—not by a long shot.

His stomach rumbles. He ought to go home, but he needs to get his head straight first.

In the staff room he finds a speckled banana in a bowl and a half-empty carton of milk in the refrigerator—just enough for a glass.

Leaning against the counter, he eats the fruit and gulps the milk.

Viktor has a temper—another factor that speaks to his guilt. This is little more than Daniel's opinion, but he should know something about volatility given his own problems sometimes keeping a cool head.

Daniel has never really been able to control his temperament. When his heart is racing and the rage builds up, he can't hold back. It's as if the anger has to find an outlet, whatever the cost. The furious words come pouring out with one purpose and one purpose only—to hurt others. Those he loves the most are often in the firing line, as his mother discovered on far too many occasions.

He is still deeply ashamed of his outburst the night before his school-leaving exam. It had something to do with his suit—he doesn't even remember what the problem was, but it ended with him ripping his student cap to shreds in front of a terrified Francesca. The following day he was the only one who showed up bare headed, after she'd sat up half the night trying in vain to mend it.

Maybe that's why he suspects Viktor. An ordinary kid can lose it to the point where he does the unthinkable.

At those moments, he is explosive and unpredictable.

Daniel has no difficulty in seeing Viktor as the perpetrator. He recognizes all the signs. It didn't take him long to provoke the boy into an angry outburst; with too much booze in his system, who knows what Viktor is capable of.

If he fought with Amanda at the party, anything could have happened.

75

Lena is lying in bed, curled up under the pink blanket. It is dark and the curtains are closed.

Tears are pouring down her face and onto the pillow. She doesn't bother wiping them away, even though they are making the pillowcase cold and damp.

She doesn't fit into her own body. Everything aches, her skin is prickling and hurting as if the shock has made it shrink. Her muscles are so tense that she is trembling, making it impossible for her to relax.

If only she could escape into sleep forever, hide away in merciful oblivion.

Never wake up again.

Why did Amanda have to die? Why couldn't it have been her instead?

Amanda was only eighteen; she had her whole life ahead of her.

It's not fair.

Lena doesn't know where Harald and the twins are. She has no idea how much time has passed since she staggered up the stairs and collapsed into bed.

The world has turned black.

How can she possibly face all her relatives and friends? Many of them got in touch when Amanda was missing, wanting to talk about the situation, share her anxiety.

Now, when it's too late, she is incapable of accepting their grief and sympathy. It is impossible to share the loss of a child.

She is cold, in spite of the woolen blanket.

Harald has been into the bedroom several times, told her to get up and have a shower, come down for something to eat. The twins need her. He needs her. She can't simply shut herself off like this.

He doesn't understand.

It's not that she doesn't want to show herself—it's just that she has no idea how to do it. She no longer remembers how to make her body move, how to formulate sentences with her mouth.

Amanda is dead.

Ludde is dead.

How is it possible to function as a human being after that?

Lena has no answer.

76

It is time to go home. Daniel yawns, but the tension in his body does not ease; once again the hour is too late to give Alice her bath or even see her awake.

He pictures her little face, thinks of the treasured time he normally spends with her, and feels immense love fill his heart.

Then he thinks of Amanda's frozen body and knows why he's still at work.

How can he go home to be with his own daughter when Harald and Lena will never see theirs again?

He promises himself that he will be far more considerate toward Ida and Alice as soon as the case is over. Maybe he'll surprise Ida with a romantic dinner, if he can persuade her mom to watch Alice for a few hours.

As he's about to log out, his phone rings. It's Birgitta Grip—hopefully with good news. He needs a boost after his unsuccessful encounter with Viktor. He hasn't spoken to his boss since he went to see Hanna last night, although he did send off a quick email summarizing this morning's conversation with Astrid Ståhl, Hanna's referee.

"Lindskog."

Birgitta is not the kind of person who wastes time on small talk. She always sounds slightly out of breath on the phone, as if she is on her way to somewhere else.

"I've been in touch with the City Police in Stockholm and arranged a temporary post for Hanna Ahlander. They're lending her to us for three months initially, on our budget."

Birgitta has delivered! A big smile spreads across Daniel's face.

"That's brilliant! I think she'll be an excellent addition to the team."

"I saw your email—she certainly had a glowing reference."

There was no doubt that Astrid Ståhl valued Hanna highly, both as a police officer and a colleague.

"Yes—Ståhl is in the section where Hanna worked, and she really did sing her praises."

"Great. Contact HR with all the details so they can sort out the paperwork." Birgitta pauses. "This is on you, Daniel—don't forget."

They end the call, and Daniel immediately rings Hanna.

"We're in business! I've just been given the go-ahead from Östersund for a placement with us—at least three months. HR just has to deal with the formalities."

"Seriously?" Hanna exclaims. "I hardly dared believe it would happen!"

"We're ready to go."

"I'm very much looking forward to working with you."

Hanna's enthusiasm is infectious. The sooner she comes on board, the better. Surely it doesn't matter if the paperwork isn't done yet?

"You can start tomorrow, if you like. I assume you have your data card so that you can access all our systems and databases?"

"I have. What time shall I be there?"

"Eight o'clock would be good. We have a briefing with Östersund at seven fifteen; after that I can introduce you to the gang and bring you up to speed."

Daniel knows he ought to hang up, but he hesitates. His head is full of contradictory thoughts after his conversation with Viktor. He'd like to share his impressions with Hanna while he's got her on the line.

"Do you have time to discuss an aspect of the investigation now?"

"Of course—what's it about?"

He tells her about the two meetings he has had with Viktor and what his schoolmates said about the party. How Viktor protested his innocence, no matter how hard Daniel pressed him. Daniel understands he overstepped the mark in his determination to get a confession, but he is interested in Hanna's opinion. Could they be on the wrong track, focusing on Viktor as their prime suspect?

"There's a lot to suggest he's guilty," he concludes. "But shouldn't he have confessed if that's the case?"

"Hmm." Hanna doesn't say anything for a few seconds. "One thing that strikes me: didn't you say he was very drunk at the party?"

"I did."

He can almost hear her frowning.

"That's what bothers me. It takes considerable presence of mind to carry out the series of events you just described. Applying a stranglehold that will make the victim lose consciousness, then dealing with the consequences—transporting Amanda while she was unconscious, then hiding her away." Hanna falls silent again. "Could Viktor have done all that in the state he was apparently in?" It almost sounds like a rhetorical question. "I agree, there's a lot to suggest he's guilty," she continues, "but it also sounds as if he was too drunk to work out exactly what to do."

Daniel hadn't thought of it from that angle. Quite the reverse—he'd seen alcohol as the trigger for Viktor's behavior. That and a hot temper he couldn't control.

Hanna has made him realize that the quantity of alcohol Viktor consumed at the party could, paradoxically, be regarded as a kind of alibi.

He was too drunk to attack and abduct Amanda.

Once again Daniel is impressed by Hanna's ability to analyze a situation.

"I think it would require a certain level of sobriety to be so cold blooded," she adds.

"So we're back to square one," Daniel says gloomily.

"Not necessarily, but I wouldn't get hung up on Viktor until we have more forensic evidence." Hanna stops, then makes a little noise as if something else is on her mind.

"Any other thoughts?" Daniel prompts her.

"Amanda's adviser . . . Have you interviewed him?"

She must mean Lasse Sandahl, the teacher they met yesterday.

"Why?"

"I was having coffee with a friend this afternoon . . ." She hesitates, as if she's not sure whether to continue. "This might be nothing more than gossip, but she mentioned that there are rumors about this guy, that he's . . . interested in young girls. She even claimed he'd had an affair with Amanda."

Daniel doesn't recall anything untoward about Sandahl, but the information is definitely worth following up.

"Sounds as if we ought to check him out," Hanna adds.

"We'll take a look at him tomorrow," Daniel assures her.

He ends the call and finds his notes on the conversation with Lasse Sandahl. He reads through them carefully, in case there's anything to support what Hanna has just told him.

His email alert pings: an anonymous tip-off has come in. Daniel skims through the message and lets out a low whistle.

"Jesus," he says quietly to himself. It seems that Harald Halvorssen has been having an extramarital affair with his PA, Mira Bergfors.

The anonymous source claims that Mira's husband might have wanted to get his revenge on Harald.

WEDNESDAY, DECEMBER 18

77

The parking lot at the police station is barely half-full when Hanna arrives at eight o'clock on Wednesday morning. Her stomach is a solid lump of nerves. Everything has happened so fast she can't quite believe that she's on her way to her new job.

That they actually want her.

She sends a silent thank-you to Lydia, who made Manfred Lidwall give her a good reference so that the relocation went through.

Lydia has saved her. Yesterday evening, in the midst of her happiness, she messaged her sister and told her what had happened.

Astrid Ståhl stepped up to the plate too, Hanna reminds herself. There are people who care about her—she must remember that when she's having a bad day.

Daniel is already waiting in reception, and his warm smile makes her feel better. He swipes his key card and shows her into the area she visited on Monday.

"This is your office," he says, leading her to a room farther down the corridor. There is a key card waiting for her.

The office is small, but the beautiful view over the lake immediately lifts her mood. *This time nothing is going to go wrong,* she promises herself. The catastrophe that happened in Stockholm will not be repeated. She will keep a low profile, listen, and fit in with the team.

Daniel introduces her to a new colleague, Rafael.

"Call me Raffe," says the dark-haired bearded guy with an appealing smile. "It's great that you were able to start so soon."

"This way," Daniel says, heading for the conference room where the photographs of Amanda are pinned up.

Hanna hears a voice behind her. "Hi—welcome!"

She turns and sees Anton. "Thanks—it's good to be here."

"We're pleased to have you," he says with a wink. "Just so you know, now it's too late to change your mind."

All four of them sit down in the conference room. Daniel fills her in on the morning's briefing with Östersund.

"Things are a bit different out here in the sticks," he begins with a wry smile. "Distances are much greater, so we often use video links. We're spread out all over the place, and traveling to meet in person would take up too much time."

As soon as the discussion is underway, Hanna feels at home. She notices that Daniel sets the tone, and the others listen attentively when he speaks. There is no doubt who is leading the investigation.

He reports back on the current situation and the latest information that has come in. The IT technicians are still working on Amanda's computer. A number of property owners in Ullådalen have been contacted, but a long list still remains. Nothing useful has emerged so far. Amanda's clothing and the skin particles found beneath her nails have been sent to the National Forensic Center for analysis.

Hanna isn't surprised to hear that it will take weeks before they have the results; the waiting time at the NFC is hopelessly long.

Daniel changes the subject. "Hanna told me there are rumors that Amanda had an affair with her adviser, Lasse Sandahl—the teacher we met Monday."

Anton strokes his chin. "We need to follow that up. Well done, Hanna."

Hanna is embarrassed by his praise—it's his sister who should get the credit. However, she is glad that the others are taking it seriously.

"Speaking of affairs," Daniel continues, "we received an interesting message last night: an anonymous tip-off suggesting that we should check out Harald Halvorssen's PA, Mira Bergfors. Or rather her husband, Fredrik. It seems that Mira and Harald have been involved in a relationship." Daniel gathers up his papers. "I was thinking of going to have a chat with Bergfors." He looks at Hanna. "Want to come along? We could drop in on Lasse Sandahl too."

Hanna glances uncertainly from Daniel to Anton. If the two of them usually work together, she doesn't want to push in. Fortunately Anton seems perfectly happy with the suggestion.

"Great—Raffe and I can carry on with the list of property owners in Ullådalen."

The meeting is over. Hanna grabs her jacket and follows Daniel to the underground garage. She is buzzing with anticipation but promises herself that she will keep a low profile during the interviews.

This time she is not going to tread on anyone's toes.

78

Should he call the police, tell them about Ludde?

Harald is sitting in the dark kitchen with his elbows on the table. It is an hour before sunrise. He got up unusually early, after tossing and turning all night. Sleep came in short bursts; he woke repeatedly to find his throat thick with tears, his grief over Amanda like a stone on his chest.

He has been brooding over Ludde's death ever since his conversation with the vet. Was he really poisoned? And if so, what could the police do? They asked if Harald had any enemies, if he could think of anyone who had a grudge against him or his family.

The only person who comes to mind is Fredrik Bergfors.

Harald considers the idea yet again.

He already fears that Fredrik was responsible for Amanda's death. Could he also have poisoned their dog, to punish Harald for his affair with Mira?

She was terrified that he would find out about their relationship; Harald heard the fear in her voice yesterday.

He gets up, paces back and forth. Crumbs from the children's sandwich-making crunch beneath his feet.

There is no one he can talk to. Lena is still hiding in bed; he has hardly seen her for days. He slept in the spare room last night, couldn't face going into their bedroom, where the stuffy air is thick with despair.

The red poinsettias on the windowsills are wilting, but Harald can't be bothered to water them. Instead he leans over the sink and tries to think, his forehead resting on the cool cupboard door.

Fredrik is strong and fit. If Harald remembers correctly, he is a former mountain ranger. That means he was an elite soldier, trained to use violence.

Harald takes out a glass, lets the cold faucet run. Fills the glass with ice-cold water and drinks slowly. He remembers Mira saying that Fredrik loves his family more than anything, that he would do whatever was necessary for their sake.

Does that also mean that he is ready to take his revenge, at any price?

Harald doesn't want to believe that, but Amanda has been murdered, Ludde poisoned. It takes a special kind of rage to carry out actions like that.

Who else could it be?

However many times Harald turns it all over in his mind, he keeps coming back to the same conclusion. There is no one else who would want to harm him, not in that way.

The trust Harald has had in his fellow human beings throughout his life lies in ruins. He has read about people who have done terrible things. He just never imagined he would be a victim himself.

79

Shortly after nine Hanna and Daniel arrive in Sadeln, where Fredrik Bergfors is visiting one of his construction sites.

The sky is turning red in the east as they park by a house nearing completion on Björnhyllan. It is in a prime location, with an unimpeded view over the lake. It is no more than a stone's throw from the slope known as Hermelinbacken and has a genuine ski-in/ski-out facility.

The road is lined with vans and trucks. When Hanna and Daniel step inside, they can see why. The place is buzzing with feverish activity as a swarm of tradesmen carry out planks of wood and throw rubbish into a huge dumpster in the yard. It still looks like a construction site, but presumably not for much longer.

Fredrik Bergfors is standing by the balcony doors, having a discussion in English with a guy who appears to be the foreman.

He frowns when he sees Daniel, who holds up his police ID.

"We have a couple of questions for you—is there somewhere we can speak privately?"

Bergfors points to one of the bedrooms, which contains a small plastic table and four chairs. "In here."

"Busy?" Daniel says, tilting his head in the direction of the workmen.

Bergfors nods without cracking a smile. "Council representatives are coming to do their final inspection tomorrow. Everyone wants to be finished for Christmas, so December is always tight."

They sit down in what looks as if it will be the master bedroom. Another door leads to a luxurious en suite.

Hanna wonders how Daniel is going to begin. She knows how she would handle the interview but doesn't want to take over; she is terrified of coming across as pushy on her first day.

"As I said, we have a couple of questions—relating to the murder of Amanda Halvorssen."

Bergfors's expression doesn't change.

"How well do you know the Halvorssen family?"

"My wife works with Harald—she's his PA. I can't say I know the family at all."

"How long has she worked for him?"

"Just over three years."

"Would you say they get along well?"

"I assume so."

Daniel nods, jots something down in his notebook.

"Where were you during the night of December 12 and the early hours of December 13?"

"I was at home, asleep."

"Is there anyone who can confirm that?"

"My wife, Mira. She was lying next to me."

"What time did you go to bed?"

Bergfors looks wary now. "Pretty late, I think. There's a lot to do at this time of year." He waves a hand at the rest of the house.

A male voice shouts something in Polish, followed by a thud.

"How late?" Hanna says. She can't help herself, even though she had intended to let Daniel ask all the questions.

Bergfors shrugs. "I don't remember."

"Before or after midnight?"

"It might have been after twelve."

"Was your wife awake when you went to bed?"

"No, she was asleep."

"So she can't confirm what time you came into the bedroom."

Bergfors pushes his chair back a little way, the legs scraping loudly on the wooden floor. He is a big man, and the folding chair looks much too small for him. He only just fits on the grubby plastic seat.

"What's this about?" he demands, taking out an e-cigarette. "I have nothing to say about Harald. He's my wife's boss." His tone reveals more than he realizes. It is ice cold.

"We've heard that's not all he is," Daniel says calmly.

"What do you mean?"

"We have a source that claims your wife is in a relationship with Harald."

Daniel certainly believes in getting straight to the point. Hanna has noticed that he doesn't seem to worry about hurting someone's feelings. At the same time, she is familiar with the tactic. Sometimes it's better to go in hard right from the beginning. By shocking the interviewee, you can make him drop his guard. It's harder to lie if you've been taken by surprise.

Bergfors's jawline is rigid when he answers: "I'm not aware of that."

"No?"

Silence. Daniel seems completely at ease.

"If your wife is in a relationship with Harald Halvorssen, then I presume you're not too fond of him . . ."

Not a word passes Bergfors's lips.

"It's easy to lose perspective in these situations," Daniel continues. "Start thinking about revenge . . ."

Hanna leans forward. "How did you get that scratch on your chin?"

Bergfors touches his face. "I was playing with my daughter the other evening and she accidentally scratched me."

"Can a three-year-old inflict that kind of damage?" Daniel asks with perfect timing; it's as if he and Hanna have rehearsed their questions in advance.

Another shrug. Irritation is evident in every line of Bergfors's body.

Daniel takes a different tack. "Did you use your snowmobile over the weekend?" He told Hanna on the way that Bergfors is the registered owner of a snowmobile. "During the night between Saturday and Sunday, for example?" he adds.

Bergfors leaps to his feet, knocking the chair over. "I don't know why you're here, but I really don't have time for this!"

"If you'd like to accompany us to the station to continue this interview, that's fine by me," Daniel says.

"In that case you can call me in—along with my lawyer," Bergfors snaps.

Hanna catches Daniel's eyes as Bergfors marches out the door. She has a lot more questions.

She isn't done with Fredrik Bergfors—not by a long way.

80

It is recess when Hanna pushes open the main door of the high school in Järpen. Daniel is right behind her, with his phone pressed to his ear.

After speaking to Fredrik Bergfors, they decided to head straight for the school to speak to Lasse Sandahl. Hanna understands that Bergfors will have to wait until they have more to go on. There was no mistaking his antipathy toward Harald Halvorssen.

If his wife and Harald are having an affair, then he has a strong motive. On the other hand, there isn't much else to link him to the murder, even if he does own a snowmobile and the kind of SUV the witness thought they saw in the rest stop where Amanda disappeared.

She looks around the entrance hall. There are groups of teenagers everywhere, seemingly divided into the same cliques as when Hanna was in school. The in-crowd is sitting at a table, cool guys and pretty, carefully made-up girls. The nerds are slightly farther away, their clothing and glasses identifying them as part of this tribe. A girl is sitting in a window seat by herself, with her nose in a book. She is dressed in black, and her aura makes it clear that she wants to be alone.

She reminds Hanna of herself.

They are shown to an empty classroom by a janitor while someone goes to find Lasse Sandahl. The room is depressing, with gray wooden paneling halfway up the walls and gray chairs. Even the floor is gray.

Hanna goes over to the window and gazes out at the snow-covered yard. It looks like a parking lot—too many cars and not enough greenery.

It is as gray outside as inside.

Sandahl appears after a few minutes. He is broad shouldered but has the beginnings of a potbelly. This often happens with someone who trained a lot when they were young, but resigned themselves to a more sedentary life as they grew older.

Daniel introduces Hanna, and they sit down at one of the rectangular tables where the students usually sit.

"Thank you for finding the time to talk to us again," Daniel says. "We have one or two more questions about Amanda."

Sandahl nods while Hanna studies him closely. He looks very pleasant and seems to be the kind of person who finds it easy to communicate with students and parents. Daniel has already told her that Amanda's mother thought he was nice.

Are their suspicions misplaced? All they have to go on is gossip, but at the same time, anything untoward must be followed up.

They discussed procedure on the way, and Daniel suggested that Hanna should lead. To her relief he praised her contribution to the conversation with Bergfors, the pointed follow-up questions when his answers were inadequate.

"Can you tell us a little more about your relationship with Amanda?" she begins.

Sandahl nods. He gives the impression of a man who wants to be liked.

"We communicated well—we were very open with each other. I hope she felt the same way."

"What did you talk about the last time you saw her?"

"We had an advising session last week, a couple of days before she went missing. We went through her various subjects, discussed her grades. The usual." He shrugs.

"Was there anything out of the ordinary?" Daniel asks.

"Not really. Not that I recall."

"Amanda didn't seem worried at all?" Hanna says.

Sandahl scratches his throat, leaving a red mark. "Actually, she did seem to be having trouble concentrating over the past few weeks," he admits.

"What about absences? Everything okay on that front?"

"Now you come to mention it . . . I did bring that up at the session, the fact that she'd been missing school more than usual. She said she'd try to do better."

"Did she explain why she'd been absent?"

Sandahl pulls down his sleeve. The elbows of his gray V-neck sweater are worn and pilly.

"Something to do with her job, as I recall."

"Her job?"

Hanna gets the feeling that this information is new to Daniel as well.

"What did she do?" she asks.

"I don't know. We didn't talk about that." Sandahl scratches his temple. His blond hair is carefully arranged to hide a receding hairline. "It's not even a week since we met." His voice is strained. "It was last Tuesday." He manages a sad smile, which somehow seems to get stuck at the corners of his mouth.

"Tell us about your own family relationships," Hanna says, changing the subject.

Sandahl frowns. "Why?"

Hanna smiles reassuringly. "We just need some background information. Are you married, or living with someone?"

"No."

"Do you have a girlfriend?"

"Not at the moment."

"But you do date?"

"Yes. Yes, I do."

Sandahl mumbles his responses, as if he isn't sure where this is going.

"How old was your last girlfriend?"

"Sorry?"

Hanna tries to sound completely matter-of-fact. "We heard that you like young girls. Including schoolgirls."

Sandahl rubs his earlobe. "I would never . . ."

"Never what? Never get together with one of your students?"

His eyes are darting all over the place, which tells her all she needs to know. He has tried it on with Amanda. Maybe he didn't go all the way, but far enough to feel uncomfortable.

The old contempt comes flooding back. These fucking men who exploit their positions of power over younger women—they're everywhere.

"Did you make a pass at Amanda?" She deliberately sharpens her tone. "Did you take advantage of her?"

"What? No, absolutely not!"

"If you're lying to us, we will find out," Daniel warns him.

"I swear I had nothing to do with her death! I haven't done anything to her!"

Lasse Sandahl licks his lips.

"Did you touch her?"

Hanna is going in hard, but that is her intention. She and Daniel agreed that she should push Sandahl as far as possible.

"That's not what happened." He looks down at the floor. "You make it sound so dirty."

It *is* dirty.

"You've got one chance to tell us what happened between you. One chance."

Sandahl stares at a point on the wall. "I didn't sleep with her."

Hanna waits for him to go on.

"I just wanted to offer my support. In case she needed an adult to turn to."

"Did you try to kiss her?"

"Yes." His voice is almost inaudible.

"When?" Daniel's question is like the crack of a whip.

"At the Walpurgis Night party in the spring. I'd drunk way too much."

As if that's an excuse.

"How did Amanda react?"

"She wasn't interested. She left. That's all, I swear. I regretted it right away."

Hanna fixes him with her gaze. "Where were you on the night between December 12 and 13, when Amanda disappeared?"

"At home in my apartment."

"Is there anyone who can confirm that?"

"No, I live alone—I already told you that."

"Do you have a car?" Daniel asks.

"Yes."

"What make?"

"Volvo."

"Color?"

"Dark blue."

Daniel nods, an exaggerated gesture that is meant to be seen by Sandahl, who looks as if he is on the verge of tears.

"I didn't harm Amanda," he whispers.

81

As long as Lena stays in the darkened bedroom, it is like being inside a cocoon where no one can get to her.

She doesn't want to be awake; she just wants to lie under the covers and never get up again, but eventually her bodily needs drive her from her bed.

She slips like a shadow into the bathroom, sits down on the toilet, and does what she has to do.

The acrid smell of dried sweat reaches her nostrils. She knows that she ought to take a shower and wash her hair, but she remains seated, not moving.

It can wait. It's too much trouble; she doesn't have the energy.

She barely manages to flush the toilet.

The sound of the TV in the living room and the low murmur of the twins' voices penetrates through the bathroom door. It is like a different world, one that no longer concerns her.

Harald's voice is missing. She doesn't care. He must have slept in the spare room last night; she hasn't seen him since yesterday evening.

It doesn't matter.

On some level she knows that Mimi and Kalle need her, that she should pull herself together, but she has no idea how to do that.

Where is she going to find the strength to go on being their mom?

Everything she took for granted, the life that had been hers for so many years, no longer exists. Life with a noisy family, the kids and their friends, a constant round of activity and chat. Laundry, cooking, giving them rides all over the place.

All gone.

She has always regarded herself as a capable person, someone who could handle both success and adversity. Now she has been tested, and what she believed has turned out to be an illusion. She is weak and feeble, a pathetic, inadequate creature.

Lena sits down again, rocks silently back and forth on the toilet seat.

All that remains of her is an empty shell, a cardboard figure so flattened by grief that it contains nothing.

After a while she runs her tongue over her teeth, feels the gritty deposit, reaches for her toothbrush.

Then she lets her hand drop.

Why bother brushing her teeth when her very existence has no meaning?

She hears the twins laughing in the living room.

They are young; they will get over their grief, build a new life where the memory of Amanda fades away as they grow up.

They haven't shattered into a million pieces like Lena has done.

She knows she can never be whole again.

She stands up, grabs a hold of the washbasin to stop herself from falling. Then she sneaks back to the bedroom and closes the door so she doesn't have to listen to the children downstairs.

82

On the way back to Åre, Daniel and Hanna stop for lunch at Hållandsgården. He is so pleased to have her on board; the interview with Sandahl clearly demonstrated how experienced she is.

It feels as if they're going to work well together.

As they dig into homemade meatballs served with lingonberry preserve, mashed potatoes, and gravy, Daniel tells her what he knows about the place. It is a Christian center located right by Saint Olav's pilgrim trail, which follows the rapids of the Indal River. Saint Birgitta allegedly passed this way in the fourteenth century.

He feels the tension of the morning begin to ease as he rattles off his tourist spiel.

"It's lovely," Hanna says, nodding at the surroundings. "We all need a spiritual retreat now and again."

They'd chosen a table by the window, and now they're chatting sporadically while they eat. Only when their plates are empty and they've settled down with coffee does the conversation return to the case.

"We ought to take swabs from both Bergfors and Sandahl," Hanna says. "Test their DNA against the skin particles found under Amanda's fingernails."

"Do you think Bergfors would go along with that?"

Hanna spreads her hands. Daniel has already noticed that her body language is pretty animated. "Probably not," she concedes.

"He certainly has a credible motive. He looked furious when we mentioned his wife's affair."

"Sandahl could also have a motive," Hanna points out. "Amanda might have threatened to report him to the school principal."

"Over six months after he made a pass?"

"We only have Sandahl's word for that. Something could have happened during the last advising session. What if he did something else that upset her? What if she said she was going to tell the principal, or her parents?" Hanna turns her coffee cup around and around. "He must have known about Ebba's party, because the whole class was invited. Maybe he was waiting outside, hoping he'd get the chance to sort things out with Amanda."

"You mean he sat outside all evening, hoping she'd show up—by herself?"

It sounds like a long shot to Daniel.

The witness who called the hotline saw a dark-colored car pull up in the rest stop where Amanda's scarf was found. The assumption is that she got into the car willingly, presumably because she knew the driver.

They can't rule out the possibility that Sandahl was that driver.

The same applies to Fredrik Bergfors. And Viktor could also have had access to a car—his father is the registered owner of a dark SUV.

"Do you think Sandahl fits the profile of a typical murderer?" Daniel asks.

"What does a typical murderer look like?" Hanna wonders rhetorically.

"Anyway, I'd like to go through both Bergfors's and Sandahl's cars to check for Amanda's DNA," Daniel says, knowing perfectly well that the prosecutor, Tobias Ahlqvist, will never allow that without stronger evidence. He already sounded skeptical at the latest briefing.

A white charter bus pulls up outside and disgorges a couple of dozen visitors. They disappear in the direction of the nearby stave church.

Hanna finishes her coffee and puts the cup on the tray. "We need to speak to both Mira Bergfors and Harald Halvorssen. How about we do that on the way back to the station? I'd really like to hear what Harald has to say about Fredrik Bergfors."

83

The Halvorssen house is in darkness when Hanna and Daniel arrive—apart from one window. Hanna can almost feel the grief weighing down the family home when she rings the bell.

Harald opens the door. He looks at Daniel in bewilderment and clutches the door frame. It is only two o'clock in the afternoon, but there is no mistaking the smell of booze on his breath.

Daniel introduces Hanna as his new colleague. "May we come in?"

He turns to Hanna. "They have a dog—you're not allergic, are you?"

"Ludde is dead." Harald's voice breaks and his eyes fill with tears. "He died the day before yesterday."

Hanna places a hand on his arm. "I'm so sorry."

Harald looks as if he is about to say something, then changes his mind. He leads the way into the kitchen; there are dirty dishes everywhere.

"Are the children at school?" Hanna asks.

Harald shakes his head. "My mom has taken them for a few hours. We're letting them off school this week."

Hanna leans forward. She's been thinking about Lasse Sandahl's comments concerning Amanda's job. There was no information about a job in the case notes, and Daniel clearly didn't know about it either. She also thinks it might be better to start with something other than the alleged affair with Mira Bergfors.

"Can I ask you where Amanda worked? We'd like to have a word with her boss."

Harald looks surprised. "She didn't have a job. We didn't want her to work during the school semester; we thought it was better for her to focus on her studies." He wipes his nose with the back of his hand. "We let her spend her student allowance however she liked. We thought that was enough, along with the money she earned from her summer job in the ice-cream kiosk."

Hanna doesn't understand. Sandahl said Amanda had blamed her lack of concentration on her job. Now her father insists she didn't have a job. What's going on? Maybe her mother knows?

"Is Lena home?" Daniel is right on cue.

Harald points to the upper floor. "She's not feeling too good. She's . . . resting."

"Okay." Hanna and Daniel exchange a glance, a silent agreement to move on to the real reason for their visit.

"It's probably best if we discuss this next matter with you on your own," Daniel says.

Harald doesn't react.

"We've had an anonymous tip-off about you and your PA."

"Mira?" Harald is suddenly wary.

"Our source claims that the two of you were in a relationship."

Hanna notices that Daniel sounds much more friendly than when they spoke to Sandahl and Bergfors; he isn't out to provoke a confrontation now.

Harald blinks several times.

"We're wondering if her husband could have found out," Daniel continues. "When we spoke the other day, you said you didn't have any enemies, but if this is true, it changes things."

Harald rests his forehead on one hand.

"It's true," he says quietly. "But it ended a while ago. Lena doesn't know anything about it. You can't tell her—she wouldn't be able to cope right now."

Hanna decides to come straight out with their hypothesis. "Could Fredrik Bergfors have been out for revenge? Attacked your family?"

Harald's face loses its color. "I've asked myself the same question. I found out yesterday that our dog died of nicotine poisoning. The vet called. It seems he was killed deliberately."

"And you think it was Fredrik?"

"I don't know. Who else could it be?"

Hanna tries to catch Harald's eye, but without success. He clenches both fists on his lap.

"You have to do something," he begs. "He can't be allowed to get away with this."

84

A few hours later, Hanna is on the way home. She is tired from everything that has happened, but also relieved. She feels as if the day went well, and Daniel seemed pleased with her input.

The lump in her throat that has been there for so long has gone.

Lydia calls while she's still driving.

"Congratulations on the new job!" her sister says. "It's brilliant news—and you deserve it after everything that's happened."

Hanna tells her about the first day and her new boss, Daniel Lindskog, who made a real effort to fix up a temporary placement for her. The first meeting on Monday, when Anton asked if she'd consider working in Åre.

"It's all happened so fast," she concludes; she can hear the happiness bubbling in her voice. "But it feels fantastic."

It's so wonderful to be working in an environment where they have confidence in her.

Lydia clears her throat. "The thing is . . ." She sounds serious. "We have to talk about something else. I've spoken to Christian about the apartment, told him he can't just take it."

Hanna's heart sinks. She doesn't want to think about Christian—not today, when everything is going so well.

"You do realize he's fucking furious?"

Hanna is fucking furious too, but there's no point in bringing that up.

"Yes."

"He claims you've deliberately destroyed his suits and shoes—clothes that are worth thousands."

Hanna bites the inside of her cheek. Is it really only a week ago? It feels like a different life. She wishes Lydia hadn't found out.

"Did you do it, Hanna?"

"Do what?"

"Don't even start. Did you cut up Christian's Italian suits?"

"Maybe."

In the cold light of day, with the benefit of hindsight, it seems incomprehensible that she could have done such a thing. Hanna would never have believed herself capable of it, and yet she'd stood there wielding the scissors.

She doesn't regret it, but she knows it was a crazy, misguided act of revenge.

"He also said you'd put mustard in his shoes. From what I gather they're completely ruined. Is that true?"

"Yes," Hanna mumbles.

"For God's sake—what were you thinking?"

"I don't know. I was just so angry and upset."

She feels a surge of rage once again, remembering how Christian dumped her—just like that.

"He says he's going to report you to the police."

"What?"

Hanna can't believe her ears. Christian has cheated on her, betrayed her—and now he's threatening her with the police? What kind of person is he?

"I tried to reason with him," Lydia goes on. "Apparently he's already spoken to a lawyer, and they're intending to go for criminal damage. You could get probation or a fine. Do you understand how serious this is?"

"I'm aware of the punishment for criminal damage, thank you."

Fucking Christian.

"What did you say?"

"Nothing."

Lydia sighs in her ear. She sounds exactly like their mother. "As I see it, your only chance is to call him and offer a heartfelt apology. He might relent."

Hanna simply cannot humiliate herself in that way. Her skin crawls at the very thought of it. She never wants to see Christian again, nor does she want to speak to him.

Asking him for forgiveness is absolutely out of the question.

"I can't do it," she informs her sister through stiff lips.

"I know who his lawyer is. Experienced and slick when it comes to criminal law. You're no match for him."

Lydia sounds weary, and Hanna can't blame her. Who can cope with cleaning up their kid sister's crap all the time?

She has just left the E14 and is heading for Sadeln, driving uphill along the narrow road with its sharp bends. It reminds her of the Alps.

"You have to fix the situation with Christian." There is a sharpness to Lydia's tone. "If he goes through with his threat, the City Police might back out of the agreement with Östersund. Then what will happen to your new job?"

Hanna is going a little too fast when she reaches the center of Björnen. She passes SkiStar's reception and the drag lifts that will open at the weekend. Her back wheels skid as she turns into Sadeln.

She thinks about calling Christian.

Every fiber of her being screams *no*.

"I just can't apologize to him," she whispers. "Don't make me do that."

Lydia sighs again. "I know how you feel, but you have no choice. The sooner the better, before he contacts the police."

85

By seven thirty Hanna has been sitting in the kitchen for a long time, trying to steel herself to make the call to Christian. She can't put it off, even though the thought makes her feel sick.

Why should she say sorry to him when he's the one who's behaved like a complete shit?

The urge to pour herself a glass of wine is almost irresistible. She *needs* a drink, something to wrap her mind in cotton wool, protect her from the humiliation.

Only her self-preservation instinct stops her; she settles for a glass of Coca-Cola instead. Drinking alcohol now would be a big mistake. If she is going to get through a conversation with Christian, she needs to be sober—he would hear it in her voice if she'd been drinking.

Plus she can't show up at work with a hangover in the morning.

The two wall lamps above the kitchen counter spread a soft, golden glow. The ceiling light is off. She scrolls through pictures of Christian on her phone. Knows she ought to delete them, but doesn't have the strength.

She reminds herself of all the occasions when he criticized her behavior after they'd had dinner together. When he demanded to know why she couldn't make an effort to be more sociable, "more fun," as he put it. Did she have to be so serious all the time?

After a long day at work, when she'd encountered yet another bruised-and-battered woman trying to protect her violent partner, it wasn't easy to switch to party mood.

She has never been good at sparkling to order.

It was impossible to explain any of this to Christian. Instead she kept quiet, promised to try harder next time. In the end she didn't know what was right and wrong.

With hindsight she is ashamed of being so compliant, even though it was never enough as far as Christian was concerned.

Hanna thinks about Daniel and how well they worked together during today's interviews. Would he criticize his partner in that way? Probably not—no doubt he would be supportive. She hardly knows him, but he seems like that kind of person.

She can't help wondering if he's in a relationship. Of course he is—all the nice guys of his age have already found their soulmate.

Her phone pings.

Have you called Christian? How did it go?

Lydia has given Hanna more help than she could possibly have asked for, but she can also be unbelievably tone deaf. In Lydia's world, you make a decision, carry it through, and move on.

If only it were that easy.

Hanna sends a quick reply saying she's about to make the call; then she tucks her feet beneath her. The white upholstered dining chairs are almost like armchairs, spacious and comfortable, with generous armrests.

She brings up Christian's number on her phone and stares at the screen.

He should still be at the realtor's office, finishing up the day's work. It's Wednesday, so he's unlikely to have a viewing this evening; Mondays and Tuesdays are always the busiest.

Could she apologize by text?

She can cope with a text message, that would be nowhere near as painful as a phone call. But Lydia said Hanna had to speak to him if she was going to persuade him not to go to the police. He's already contacted a well-known lawyer, so he must be furious.

Hanna still feels no regret for her actions. She knew exactly how much he loved his Italian suits and shoes, and that's why she did it. She wanted him to be as upset and devastated as she was.

She can't admit that—it would only make matters worse.

She turns to her laptop instead; she can afford to surf the web for a few minutes to settle her thoughts.

As she puts down her phone, she knocks over the glass of Coke. It runs over the table and onto the floor, forming a big puddle, just like the other day when Zuhra accidentally spilled detergent in the hallway.

With everything that has happened, Hanna hasn't had the chance to process yesterday's visit to the cleaning company. It was strange that the woman who worked there didn't know Zuhra. That must mean she works somewhere else, but where?

She wipes up the mess, then googles cleaning companies in Åre. It should be possible to find Zuhra.

She promises herself that she will call Christian in half an hour at the latest.

She knows she has to contact him, but it really goes against the grain.

86

Daniel is at his desk, reading the printouts of the conversations with cabin owners in Ullådalen, conducted by Raffe, Anton, and one of the investigators in Östersund.

The same questions, the same nondescript answers are repeated over and over again. Few were out on their snowmobiles over the weekend because the weather was so bad. Even fewer have noticed anything unusual in the area over the past few days. No one saw a dark-colored snowmobile driving around in the middle of the night.

Daniel turns his head side to side several times. It's late and his neck is stiff. He ought to go home, but he hasn't finished yet. What if he's missed a key detail?

A little while ago he spoke to the prosecutor about Fredrik Bergfors. He wants a search warrant, but Ahlqvist is insisting on more evidence.

This isn't the first time Daniel has argued with a prosecutor, but this evening his patience was at the breaking point. He'd almost hurled his phone at the wall when the call ended.

His phone rings—Ida, no doubt wondering if he's on his way home.

"Hi, darling," he says, injecting a cheerful note into his voice.

"Where are you?" She sounds stressed. Alice is crying in the background.

"At work, of course."

"Do you know what time it is? Almost eight thirty!"

Is it that late?

"Sorry. I didn't realize."

"Couldn't you have texted to tell me you were going to be late? I've made dinner for us."

He should have let her know. He doesn't mean to disappear into his work like this.

"Sorry, sweetheart. I really don't know where the time went."

"Seriously, Daniel."

There is no mistaking the displeasure in Ida's voice.

"You've missed Alice's bath time again. And she won't go to sleep; she just keeps on screaming."

"I'll be home as soon as I can," Daniel assures her. "I just need to finish reading these reports."

THURSDAY, DECEMBER 19

87

They say the hour of the wolf falls precisely between night and dawn. When Hanna opens her eyes, night is just coming to an end.

She has slept badly, slipping in and out of superficial slumber. Her body is still clammy with sweat from the latest nightmare.

She is relieved to be awake, but the sense of disaster still lingers.

In her dream she went to see Christian and was met with scorn when she tried to apologize. Then Daniel appeared with disappointment on his face, asking why she hadn't said anything about being fired from the City Police.

She hadn't been able to face calling Christian last night. She can't shake off her anxiety over the situation. How could she have imagined that it was possible to be given a fresh opportunity?

He's going to go to the police; then everything will be ruined. She won't be allowed to stay in her new job—no one wants a colleague who's been reported for criminal damage.

She draws up the covers and closes her eyes. Just then the wind howls around the corners of the house, as if nature concurs with how dire her situation is. She looks over at the window—the roller blinds are pulled only halfway down—and realizes that a storm is in full swing out there. Gusts of wind are hurling snow at the glass, leaving icy trails across the pane.

What is she going to do?

She sinks back onto the pillow, pictures Daniel, knows that she would love to work with him long term, if she got the chance. He takes her seriously. He listens to her. He makes her feel like a real police officer again.

And there is something about him that enables her to relax. Sitting quietly in his presence doesn't stress her out.

Hanna dare not risk losing this job because she can't face contacting Christian. She *must* do it today.

The house creaks ominously in the storm.

In spite of all the stress, she must have fallen asleep again, because the next time Hanna looks at the clock, it is almost seven. The storm has abated slightly. Although it is still windy, the tall fir trees outside the bedroom are no longer swaying like tortured souls.

The sound of an approaching car makes her peer out at the road. A dark-gray Golf has stopped outside one of the houses with an old-fashioned turf roof. A figure in a bulky padded jacket gets out of the passenger seat and opens the trunk. It's hard to see clearly through the darkness and the whirling snow, but it looks as if they are gathering up cleaning equipment. The driver also gets out, walks toward the house, and unlocks the door.

Hanna presses her face to the glass. Isn't that Zuhra carrying everything up the path?

She disappears indoors, and the Golf drives away.

Hanna reacts instinctively. She pulls on jeans and a sweater, hurries into the hallway and grabs her boots and jacket.

Then she opens the door and steps out into the storm.

88

The cold is like an icy wall as Hanna crosses the street. The snowplow hasn't been up here yet, so she has to plod through thick snow. The other house is a short distance below Lydia's, with the ground floor built into the hillside.

Hanna slithers down the slippery slope leading to the front door.

She knocks, but no one answers. She tries again, but there is only silence.

Strange—she saw Zuhra go in a couple of minutes ago, plus there are lights on. After a moment she tries pushing down the handle and discovers that the door is unlocked. She hesitates, then steps into a hallway with slate flooring. There is a row of hooks for ski clothing on the wall opposite, with a bench covered in pale sheepskins underneath.

"Hello?"

No response.

Hanna really wants to speak to Zuhra. The girl's frightened reaction on Sunday evokes a particular kind of memory. Hanna has seen that look before, on the faces of the abused women she has encountered so often in Stockholm. The constant fear of being punished seeps through, the uncertainty of not knowing what is right or wrong, whatever you do, because it is impossible to predict the whim of the abuser. When that kind of insecurity has gained a foothold, it is impossible to hide.

She tries again. "Hello?"

Where has the girl gone? She can't have disappeared in such a short time—plus the door wasn't locked.

Hanna slips off her boots and peers around the corner into a large living room with a moleskin-colored sofa and armchairs. The adjoining dining area has space for ten people. The place seems to be a rental property; Hanna can't see any personal items such as photographs or ornaments.

She hears a scraping noise from the lower floor—is that where Zuhra is?

Hanna suddenly realizes that she has entered a stranger's house without permission. If someone other than Zuhra is downstairs, she is going to find it difficult to explain herself. She could even be accused of trespass.

She can't afford to get into any more trouble.

And yet she keeps going.

No one should have to be as scared as Zuhra was the other day.

Hanna sets off down the stairs, shouts "Hello" yet again, to no avail. She finds herself in a large TV room. There is a bedroom at each end of the lower story, and she can hear the hum of a vacuum cleaner from one of them. That must be where Zuhra is.

Hanna follows the noise. Zuhra has her head down and is vacuuming the skirting board with an expression of deep concentration.

"Excuse me," Hanna says loudly. When Zuhra doesn't react, she taps her gently on the shoulder. Zuhra spins around with her mouth half-open and terror in her eyes.

It takes her a couple of seconds to recognize Hanna. Her shoulders drop, and she takes a deep breath. The fear is replaced with an inquiring look.

"Hi," Hanna says, trying to sound reassuring. "Do you remember me? We met last Sunday when you cleaned my sister's house."

Zuhra nods. She is clearly still on her guard; she is clutching the metal tube of the vacuum cleaner tightly. It's hard to talk over the noise.

"Can we switch that off?" Hanna asks.

Without speaking, Zuhra reaches down and presses the button.

They stare at each other in the sudden silence. Hanna hasn't worked out what she is going to say, but knows that she will have to choose her words carefully. She wants to persuade Zuhra to open up. If the girl is in a dangerous situation, she needs help.

"Have you got time for a chat?"

Zuhra shakes her head, her dark hair falling forward. "Must work," she murmurs, eyes downcast.

"Just five minutes. Please."

When Zuhra glances at the door, Hanna sees her face in profile. A dark bruise covers her right cheek. She has seen bruises like that enough times to know what it means. Someone has slapped Zuhra across the face—hard. Hanna can almost see the impression left by the open palm.

The warning bells are ringing.

Hanna sits down on the double bed, which is waiting to be made. She pats the mattress beside her, encouraging Zuhra to join her.

"It won't take long. I only want to ask you a couple of questions."

Reluctantly Zuhra perches on the very edge of the bed.

"Are you okay?" Hanna asks tentatively, nodding at the dark shadow on the girl's cheek. At close quarters it's obvious that the injury is relatively recent; the contusion hasn't yet begun to turn purple and yellow.

"Did someone hit you?"

Zuhra touches her cheek. "It's nothing."

"Are you being ill-treated? You can tell me," Hanna says softly. Should she add that she's a police officer?

The problem is that police involvement might seem even more frightening. In many countries the police are not a safe haven for abused women, and if Zuhra's residence permit is not in order, a detective is the last person she's going to want to talk to. It could make her shut down completely.

Zuhra doesn't answer, but her eyes fill with tears.

Hanna glances at her hands. She isn't wearing a wedding ring, so presumably it wasn't a husband who hit her.

"Was it your boyfriend?"

Zuhra shakes her head.

"Can you talk to your boss about what happened?"

Zuhra looks even more terrified. "Don't talk to boss," she whispers. "Please. Boss will be very angry."

She leaps to her feet, grabs the vacuum cleaner, and switches it on, turning her back on Hanna. It is clear that she wants Hanna to leave.

"Must work," she mumbles.

All of Hanna's instincts are telling her that something is seriously wrong. The problem is that Zuhra is clearly too scared to confide in her.

Hanna has conducted many interviews with victims of domestic violence over the years. She knows it is important to show understanding and empathy, because most women feel deeply ashamed of having been abused. At the same time you have to be straight, to make it clear that the abuser's behavior is unacceptable. Through clear, direct questioning it is sometimes possible to remove the barriers that make women keep quiet about the truth.

She tries again.

"Who hit you?" she asks solicitously. "You can tell me—I'm on your side."

It can often be a relief for a victim to talk about the abuse, but Zuhra doesn't appear to fall into that category. She carries on cleaning without looking at Hanna.

"Do you have a cell phone?"

Zuhra shakes her head. "You go now. Boss very angry when I speak to . . . other girl."

What other girl?

"Who was that?"

Zuhra doesn't reply.

"Who did you speak to?"

Nothing.

Hanna doesn't want to give up. She looks around the room, searching for something to write on. In the drawer of the nightstand, she finds a pen and an old grocery-store receipt. She jots down her phone number.

"Here," she says. "You can call me anytime if you need help. In the middle of the night, if necessary."

Zuhra takes the piece of paper and tucks it into the pocket of her jeans. Her eyes are shining with unshed tears. "You go," she pleads. "Please."

89

Daniel is on his way to the conference room for a briefing with Östersund. He is tired and in a bad mood. Ida was far from happy when he finally got home yesterday evening. Alice woke up crying several times during the night. His inbox is already full, even though he worked late yesterday and came in early today.

He is failing on all fronts.

Anton and Raffe are already seated, but there is no sign of Hanna. She comes rushing in with a big bundle of papers under her arm just as he activates the link.

"Sorry I'm late," she says, her cheeks flushed red. "My alarm clock didn't go off." Her hair is tousled and her expression apologetic as she pulls out the chair next to Anton.

Birgitta Grip and two colleagues appear on the screen. The prosecutor isn't there, but Daniel hadn't expected him to be.

"Welcome to the team," Birgitta says warmly to Hanna before handing over to Daniel.

He summarizes the interviews with Lasse Sandahl and Fredrik Bergfors, as well as Harald Halvorssen's thoughts about the poisoned dog. Anton reports back on the cabin owners they spoke to yesterday—nothing new there. A number of calls have come in following the appeal for information, but none that are deemed important. A couple of people in Amanda's circle of friends have a criminal record, but not for offenses that would make them suspects in this case; it's mostly illegal snowmobile driving and the theft of a moped.

The discussion goes back and forth.

Fredrik Bergfors is considered a possible perpetrator. There is no ignoring the fact that he has an obvious motive. He owns both an SUV and a snowmobile and is an experienced snowmobile driver who often travels around in the mountains. A former business partner who got into a legal tussle with Bergfors has expressed the view that "he knows how to hold a grudge."

He also has the physique to handle Amanda's dead body.

Amanda's boyfriend is also still in the picture. Viktor is certainly strong enough to have overpowered Amanda and carried her when she was unconscious. His violent background counts against him, as do the statistics. Daniel has seen him lose his temper, and there are witnesses from the party who described the argument with Amanda just before she left Ebba's house.

Daniel is doing his best to keep an open mind. It's essential not to become fixated on one theory too early in the investigation.

"What else do we know about Sandahl?" Birgitta asks. "Now he's admitted making a pass at Amanda, we have to regard him as a suspect too."

Daniel turns to Anton. "Check if he has a record and see if he or Bergfors has a link to Ullådalen."

Anton nods and makes a note.

They divide up the day's tasks. Mira Bergfors must be interviewed as soon as possible, since her husband gave her as his alibi for the night Amanda disappeared. They also need to hear what she has to say about her relationship with Harald.

"Shouldn't we follow up this business of Amanda's job?" Hanna says. "It's strange that her adviser says one thing and her father another."

Daniel had almost forgotten about that anomaly. "Maybe she lied to Sandahl, made something up to explain her poor grades?" he suggests.

Hanna nods. "Possibly. We could speak to her best friend again. She might know things that Amanda kept from her parents. I can take care of that."

"Okay, good idea," Daniel says, then changes his mind. It seems sensible to work with Hanna during the first few days in her new post, but he has a couple of things to do first. "Actually, let's do it together. We'll leave in an hour—start with Ebba, then move on to Mira Bergfors after lunch."

90

Ebba is home alone when the doorbell rings. Her parents are at work, and her kid brother is in school. She is lying in bed, surfing the net, which she has been doing almost constantly for the last few days.

She has no energy.

She hasn't been to school since the day Amanda went missing and has no idea how she will ever be able to go back there again. She can't face the others' inquiring looks; everyone knows that she and Amanda have been best friends since they were little. They have adjoining lockers. How many times have they stood there messing around, gossiping about boys and complaining about teachers?

How can she open her own locker, knowing that Amanda will never again open hers?

The doorbell rings again. Ebba drags herself down the stairs. It's that policeman—Daniel something or other—along with a woman wearing a moss-green woolen hat.

Her pulse rate immediately shoots up.

Viktor texted and told her that Daniel had been there on Tuesday, hassling him and accusing him in a totally crazy way.

"Hi, Ebba." Daniel sounds pleasanter this time, but Ebba doesn't trust him. "May we come in?"

She can't find a good reason to say no, and hovers in the hallway while they take off their coats.

"Can we sit down somewhere?" Daniel asks.

Ebba leads the way into the kitchen. The woman introduces herself as Hanna. "How are you doing?" she says. Her voice is much warmer than Daniel's, and Ebba's eyes fill with tears.

"Not great," she mumbles.

"I can understand that. It's not easy, losing your best friend."

Hanna gets up and fetches a piece of paper towel from the roll above the sink. Ebba blows her nose, tries to force back the tears, regain control.

"Do you feel up to a little chat?"

Ebba nods.

"So we've heard that Amanda had a job and it was affecting her schoolwork. Do you know anything about that?"

The question is completely unexpected. Ebba doesn't know what to say.

The fact that she and Amanda worked a few hours now and again and were paid in cash was their secret. Nobody knew about it, and they were well paid—a hundred kronor an hour for each shift, which enabled them to buy clothes and makeup. The kind of things their student allowance couldn't quite cover.

"Sorry?"

Daniel steps in. "Apparently Amanda had a part-time job. We need to know more about it, and we're hoping you can help us."

His eyes are fixed on her. What is she going to say?

Ebba isn't stupid. Admitting to the police that she and Amanda were working for cash in hand isn't the smartest thing to do, but she has no idea how much they already know. They must know something, or why would they have come to see her?

She gnaws at her thumbnail, remembering how agitated Amanda was the last time they talked about it all.

They've worked for Linda for two seasons. It was perfect, and easy to keep secret. When they needed money, they simply contacted her via Messenger. As soon as the job was done, they were paid via Swish.

"Ebba." There is a hard edge to Daniel's voice now. "If you know about Amanda's job, then you have to tell us. It's important."

Ebba starts crying again. She wants to help, she really does.

But she's too scared.

91

Zuhra should soon be finished cleaning the neighboring house, if Hanna's calculations are correct.

She is sitting in the car on her own drive, half-hidden behind the huge pile of snow the plow has left behind. Immediately after the visit to Ebba, she told Daniel she had a workman coming around and had to go home for a little while.

Hopefully the dark-gray Golf will come to collect Zuhra, the same one that dropped her off. She can't possibly walk in this weather, not to mention carry all the cleaning equipment on her own. If Hanna can get the Golf's registration plate, she can do a little more digging.

That's why she's sneaked away for an hour, even though her full focus ought to be on Amanda.

There's just too much that feels wrong. She recognizes all the signs of a woman under coercive control. The fact that Zuhra doesn't have a cell phone is also suspicious.

Hanna is becoming increasingly convinced that what she's observed is mixed up with trafficking. According to the latest report from the UN, it is one of Europe's most lucrative criminal activities, with a turnover of billions of kronor. Most people think that vulnerable women who come to Sweden are forced into prostitution or begging on the streets, but a third end up in different forms of modern slavery, in situations where they have to work without pay or rights. Both men and women are lured to the country with promises of well-paid jobs that will enable them to send money home to their families. When they arrive it turns out that the work involves long days for little or no remuneration. They are also told that they owe the traffickers for their travel costs. The result is a vicious circle, with no escape. If threats and violence are also involved, then they are in dire straits.

Hanna glances at the instrument panel: minus nineteen degrees. Her fingers and toes are frozen, and she shuffles in her seat to improve her circulation.

It is almost midday; soon she will have to go back to the station to meet Daniel before their visit to Mira Bergfors.

She thinks back to the conversation with Ebba. She was obviously lying about Amanda's part-time job. She knew a lot more than she was prepared to share, but something was holding her back.

There must be a way of gaining Ebba's trust, persuading her to tell them everything she knows.

The dull roar of an engine brings Hanna back to the moment. The beam of twin headlights slices through the whirling snow. Hanna peers out of the windshield and sees the dark-gray Golf driving down the hill to the house where Zuhra is cleaning.

The car stops and the driver sounds the horn a couple of times. Hanna can't tell if it's a man or a woman at the wheel; it's too far away, and he or she is wearing a jacket with a hood.

The front door opens, and Zuhra emerges with a mop and bucket in one hand and the vacuum cleaner in the other. She opens the trunk, stows her equipment, and gets into the passenger seat.

Meanwhile the driver gets out and locks the front door. Clearly Zuhra is not entrusted with the keys, which says even more about her precarious situation. She is nothing more than a marionette, transported from place to place to clean the second homes of rich folk.

The Golf reverses, turns around, and sets off toward the east.

The registration plate is clearly visible before it disappears.

92

It is almost one o'clock when Hanna and Daniel arrive at the Bergfors family home. It turned out that Mira was taking the day off to look after a sick child, which saved them a trip to the council offices in Järpen.

Daniel is driving. Hanna has pushed her concerns about Zuhra to one side for the moment. She made a note of the Golf's license-plate number and will run it through the registration database as soon as she can. Right now she needs to concentrate on Amanda.

Mira opens the door, wearing jeans, a sweater, and no makeup. Her eyes are red and swollen, but she is still very beautiful, with her thick, dark hair hanging loose over her shoulders. No doubt she looks even more petite next to her tall, broad-shouldered husband.

A small child who doesn't appear to be in any way unwell comes running along. Daniel explains why they're here, and they sit down in the living room, tastefully decorated for Christmas. There is a picture of a saint on the wall and pots of white amaryllis in the windows.

The house reminds Hanna of Lydia's, with its open-plan layout and large windows overlooking the lake. However, the decor isn't quite as trendy. There are toys everywhere, and Hanna is pretty sure the sofas are from IKEA.

Suddenly an elegant blue Burmese cat strolls into the room. Mira gives a wan smile as it rubs itself around her legs. It purrs loudly and jumps up onto her lap.

"We need to talk to you about your relationship with Harald Halvorssen," Daniel begins.

Mira goes very still. "Harald is my boss."

"We have reason to believe he's rather more than that."

Mira glances at her daughter, who is absorbed in building a tower of red and blue Lego bricks.

"Can you tell us about your relationship?" Daniel continues. "It's very important that you're honest with us."

"We had a relationship, but it's over," Mira replies quietly.

"When did it end?"

"Just over a month ago. I finished it." She swallows. "It wasn't fair to Fredrik."

"Does he know about your affair?" Hanna asks.

"Yes."

"And how did he take it?"

Mira looks down, strokes the cat with her slender fingers. "Not very well."

"What did Fredrik do when he found out you'd been having an affair with Harald Halvorssen?"

Mira keeps shifting in her seat. At first the cat looks affronted; then it jumps down and stalks off in the direction of the kitchen.

"He . . . he was very angry."

"Did he hit you?"

Mira straightens her shoulders. "Fredrik has never hit me. He's not that kind of person." There is passion in Mira's voice as she defends her husband, but Hanna has a strong feeling that she is hiding something.

There are many men who would never resort to violence—until the day they do. Under certain circumstances, especially if alcohol is involved, the barriers can break. Even a controlled person like Fredrik Bergfors can cross the line if he feels sufficiently provoked.

But maybe he didn't hit his wife. Maybe he took it out on someone else.

Daniel clears his throat.

"Your husband says he was at home on the night between December 12 and 13. Can you confirm that?"

Mira seems confused; then she realizes why they're asking. Her hand flies to her mouth. "Absolutely," she says, nodding. "He was here all night."

"Did you go to bed at the same time?" Hanna says.

"I don't remember."

"Why not?"

"I usually go to bed about ten; Fredrik often stays up and works for a while."

"Is that what he did on December 12?"

"I don't think so."

"Can you really confirm that he was in bed all night?" Daniel pushes her.

Mira's cheeks are flushed. "Yes."

"How?"

"I would have noticed if he hadn't come up."

Hanna stares at her, but Mira won't allow herself to be intimidated. She stares right back and gives her husband his alibi. "He was there," she says firmly.

Hanna decides to change the subject. "Would you describe Fredrik as hotheaded?"

Mira shakes her head. "He's a calm person."

"What happens when he loses his temper?"

The question leaves Mira at a loss. She swallows several times, searches for the right words. "I don't really know."

"Surely we all get mad sometimes? Does he yell, throw things?"

"No . . ."

Hanna waits for her to go on, but Mira says nothing.

"It appears that someone has poisoned the Halvorssen family's dog," Daniel informs her. "Were you aware of that?"

Mira pushes her hands into the pockets of her sweater. "Ludde's dead?"

Daniel nods. "Could your husband be behind the poisoning?"

"Fredrik would never do such a thing!" Mira is very pale, with bright-red spots on her cheeks. "He's not like that."

"You do realize that your husband has a motive to harm Harald Halvorssen and his family?" Hanna says. "It's essential that you tell us the truth."

Mira lifts her chin and looks Hanna right in the eye. "Fredrik would never do anything to Amanda. He was with me that night."

93

When Lena wakes up, the box of sleeping pills on the nightstand is the first thing she sees. The bottle of tranquilizers is beside it.

She contemplates the drugs with eyes so swollen from crying that her eyelids are throbbing—but the pain is nothing compared to the agony of losing Amanda.

It is tearing her apart from the inside.

She reaches for the box, weighs it in her hand. The word *Imovane* on the label doesn't mean much to her.

The family doctor gave her the pills the other day. They are supposed to last for the next couple of weeks. One taken at bedtime should enable her to sleep. During the day she can take tranquilizers to help her get through.

We'll start off with these, he said, gently patting her hand.

And then?

If you're still having trouble sleeping, I can prescribe more, but these are pretty strong. I don't want to give you too many—they can be addictive.

As if that matters.

Amanda is dead, what could be worse?

The doctor said she would need the medication during the difficult period leading up to the funeral.

The thought that her beautiful daughter will lie in the cold, damp earth is unbearable.

Lena squeezes the box hard, trying to dispel the image of Amanda in a dark coffin.

After a while she opens the box and takes out a blister pack containing eleven pills. They are supposed to help her sleep for eleven more nights.

She reaches for the bottle of tranquilizers and tips out the contents: seventeen pills.

She puts the box and the bottle back on the nightstand, next to the glass of tepid water.

She pulls up the covers. Eleven plus seventeen makes twenty-eight. She thinks she can get them down all at once in a few swallows.

That should be enough to send her to sleep forever.

The thought brings her some solace.

94

Hanna is tired when she gets home in the evening. She has spent hours reading up on the investigation, making sure she is on top of everything. She, Daniel, and Anton have discussed Mira and Fredrik Bergfors at length. By seven o'clock she'd had enough.

She ought to make dinner, but instead she simply puts the kettle on for tea. Then she opens her computer, brings up the vehicle licensing authority's website and enters the number of the Golf. She has been wondering all afternoon who drove Zuhra to the house and picked her up, but she didn't want to use the police computer to carry out a search.

The information is on the screen in seconds. The registered owner is Kristina Risberg, and her address is Albins väg 11 in Undersåker.

Hanna goes into Google Maps and clicks on "street view." The house is semidetached. All she needs to do is go over there and see if the Golf is parked outside; then she can move forward, find out what Zuhra is involved in.

The kettle switches itself off, and she makes herself a big cup of tea with milk and sugar before going back to the computer and trying to summarize what she knows so far.

Zuhra reacted strongly when Hanna asked if she could speak to her boss. The woman in Fjäll-städ's office denied having anyone with Zuhra's name among their employees. But Lydia has confirmed that she uses Fjäll-städ; all the invoices come from them.

It doesn't make sense.

Once again Hanna enters "Fjäll-städ" in the search box and opens up the page that shows the company's financial position. Profits have been increasing steadily since 2016. She didn't think about that the last time she looked.

It strikes her now that the previous year, 2015, was the year a large number of immigrants came into the country because of the civil war in Syria. Sweden took more immigrants than anywhere else in Europe. Every municipal district was required to accommodate a percentage, and she knows that many came to Åre. One of the hotels, the Continental Inn, was converted into a refugee center when the situation became critical.

Could it be pure chance that the influx of immigrants and Fjäll-städ's soaring profits coincided?

Maybe that was how it started. The cleaning company recruited new arrivals, because the state subsidized their employment in order to create entry-level jobs for those who spoke little or no Swedish, and lacked education. Gradually the immigrants became more established, moved to different areas or found other, better-paid posts. By that stage Fjäll-städ had no doubt realized how lucrative a cheap workforce could be.

From there it was only a small step to exploit the system by employing trafficked individuals without permits.

Hanna searches for information about Sweden's many paperless refugees. They fall into two main categories: those whose applications for residence permits have been rejected, and who have therefore gone underground, and those who are due to be deported but can't be, because the receiving country's legal system does not fulfill the criteria for repatriation. She discovers that almost fifty thousand of the refugees who came to Sweden in 2015 have had their applications for asylum turned down. Less than half have left the country voluntarily.

Which means there must be over twenty-five thousand individuals from the refugee crisis alone who are living under the radar. On top of that, every year more desperate people arrive seeking a new homeland, but are refused. The Swedish Migration Agency's website provides a list of the ten most common countries of origin among immigrants into Sweden. Zuhra comes from Uzbekistan, which is in fourth place.

Hanna looks at her watch: seven thirty. Not too late to drive to the address in Undersåker. She picks up her car keys and pulls on her jacket. She is still tired after her long day, but the image of the bruise on Zuhra's cheek gives her no peace.

It takes less than ten minutes for Hanna to reach the exit for Undersåker off the E14. She follows the road and allows the GPS on her phone to show her the way. It kind of works; she is passing Stamgärde school when she realizes she has gone too far and has to retrace her route a short distance.

There, on the right, is Albins väg. After three hundred yards she sees number eleven; she recognizes it from Google Street View. It is a red wood-frame house overlooking the water, like so many other properties in the area. It looks spacious; the facade is freshly painted, with white eaves.

She spots a swing in the garden, suggesting that small children live here.

She parks farther down the road and gets out of the car, not wanting to draw too much attention to herself. As she gets closer she sees only a red car on the drive. There is a garage, but the doors are shut, so she has no way of knowing if there is a dark-gray Golf inside.

She keeps walking until she reaches two mailboxes on a post at the end of the drive. She reaches into the first one: empty. In the second she finds several window envelopes addressed to Kristina Risberg, which indicates that she probably isn't home yet. Maybe she's driving Zuhra somewhere?

Hanna peers at the houses. The lights are on downstairs in one, and she can see a kitchen with drawings on the wall. That must be where the family with children lives, and they have already emptied their mailbox. She assumes they own the red car.

She looks around; there is no one in sight.

Crouching slightly, she runs toward the adjoining house, which is in darkness. The two front doors are not side by side, but at opposite ends. She can't be seen from here.

She feels a surge of adrenaline as she sneaks up the steps and tries the door handle. It is locked, of course, but she doesn't have to search for long to find a spare key under an empty flower pot. In the country you always have an easily accessible spare key—she remembers that from her childhood.

It would be complete madness to enter another person's house without permission, but she's here anyway . . .

The temptation is too great.

She unlocks the door and slips inside, with a final glance in the direction of the street.

95

It takes a few seconds for Hanna's eyes to grow accustomed to the darkness in the hallway, but then she is able to orient herself and make her way into a large living room, next door to a more compact kitchen. It is easier to see in here; several Advent candle bridges give off a soft glow.

The kitchen itself is neat and tidy, with no dirty dishes lying around. Kristina Risberg seems to be someone who takes pride in a well-kept home.

Judging by the outdoor clothes in the hallway, she lives alone; there are no shoes that look as if they belong to a husband or children.

Hanna doesn't really know what she's searching for, but she picks up a pile of magazines and papers that have been left out. If only she could locate some documentation confirming a link to the cleaning company.

Or illegal employment.

Nothing on the ground floor. She glances up the stairs and decides to take the risk. She moves silently up to a small landing, with an open bedroom door. The bed is made, and the room is just as neat and tidy as the kitchen.

Hanna cautiously opens the nightstand drawers, but they contain only sundries like pens and dental floss.

Back to the landing. There are two more doors; one leads to the bathroom; the other is closed.

When she pushes it open, she finds herself in a home office. There is a desk and computer by the window. She goes over and immediately sees documents bearing the Fjäll-städ logo.

Bingo.

She moves the mouse, and the screen lights up, but the computer asks for a password that she doesn't have. There is no point in guessing; it could be anything. She flips through the documents, which show long columns of figures, then takes out her phone and photographs everything.

Suddenly Hanna hears the sound of an engine. She freezes, then peers out of the small window. Twin headlights turn into the drive. She can't tell if they belong to the dark-gray Golf.

She presses herself against the wall, her brain working overtime. If the front door opens, she will have to hide until she can sneak out. She can't be caught, not under any circumstances. How could she be so stupid, entering a house without permission?

Her heart pounds harder and harder as the car stops. Maybe she's in luck and it belongs to the family next door? Maybe they have two cars?

She holds her breath.

A car door slams shut, and she sees a tall man in dungarees walking toward the other door. A child's voice calls out: "Daddy!"

The relief makes her go weak at the knees, and her ears are buzzing with stress. She has to get out of here—right now.

She races down the stairs and out through the door, her pulse still racing. Crouching down once more she runs back to her car under cover of darkness. Just as she is leaving the garden, another pair of headlights appears farther down the street. Hanna slips behind a tree as the Golf appears. It slows down and turns onto the drive.

A woman gets out and heads for the front door. Kristina Risberg? Hanna watches her go inside.

Only when she is sitting in her own car does she dare to breathe again.

96

The bottle of cognac on the kitchen table in front of Harald is half-empty when he opens his eyes. He must have fallen asleep after putting the children to bed.

His arm is numb where his head was resting.

Lena is still hiding away in the bedroom with her sleeping pills. The last time Harald checked on her, she was curled up in the fetal position with her eyes closed.

The room smelled stale and musty.

His phone rings; that must have been what woke him.

He answers, and a pang shoots through his body when he realizes who it is. Mira's soft voice immediately releases a hurricane of emotions that he simply can't deal with.

"What do you want?"

"I just wanted to . . . see how you are?"

"Why?"

He can hear her shallow breathing on the other end of the line. He knows her well enough to understand that she is upset.

"Harald, please. You must realize that I still care about you."

Harald has no intention of going along with Mira's attempt to pretend he is important to her. "That's not what you said the other day."

"Things are complicated right now."

She is wrong. Things are not complicated at all. She doesn't want him, and her husband might have murdered Amanda.

"There's something I have to tell you," Mira goes on. She sounds as if her voice is on the point of breaking. "It's Fredrik. The police have been here, asking questions . . ."

"And?" Mira is in the shit. What has that got to do with him? "I'm afraid I don't have time for this." He is about to end the call when Mira yells, "You have to listen!"

"Why?"

The kitchen is unnaturally quiet. Harald stares at the Advent star in the window; Lena always had to stand on a stool to hang it up.

In another life.

"Fredrik told me he went over to your house on Monday morning when he was really angry. He found your dog outdoors." Her voice is muffled now. "He wanted revenge, so he went for Ludde. The dog struggled and scratched him, but Fredrik is strong, and he was mad with rage . . . Harald, he poisoned Ludde."

Mira's words bounce off Harald's eardrums; then they land in his brain, and their full significance hits him.

Before Mira can continue, Harald hangs up. He doesn't need to hear any more.

He puts down his phone, clenches and unclenches his fists several times. There is so little left of his old life, only loss and ineradicable pain.

If Fredrik is responsible for Amanda's death, then he will have to pay.

97

The apartment is dark and silent when Daniel unlocks the front door.

It is almost ten o'clock; Ida is probably asleep. He didn't mean to be so late, but he got stuck at the station, plowing through reports and emails. He tries to keep up with everything, and yet progress is far too slow. It's like treading water—they're getting nowhere.

The frustration makes his skin crawl.

Life with a baby is much harder than he'd imagined. He knows that Ida is carrying the heaviest load right now and he should try to do more, but he also feels as if everyone is constantly pulling at him.

He hasn't eaten and moves quietly into the kitchen. Maybe there are some leftovers? But the refrigerator is almost empty, apart from a box of eggs next to a can of low-alcohol beer. Eggs on toast, then.

A sound behind him makes him turn around.

Ida is standing in the doorway. She has put on her robe over her nightdress, her hair is tousled, and there are faint lines on her cheek from the pillow.

"Sorry if I woke you," Daniel says, taking out a frying pan and pouring in a spoonful of rapeseed oil. When it is hot enough, he cracks a couple of eggs into the pan.

"How's the case going?" Ida asks. To Daniel's relief she seems neither angry nor disappointed, just tired.

"Okay."

He's tired too. Amanda is occupying all his thoughts and all his waking hours.

"I hope you're taking care of yourself," Ida says gently.

Daniel flips the eggs over. "I'm fine. You don't need to worry about me."

When the eggs are done, he slides them onto two slices of toast, then adds ketchup and black pepper before sitting down at the table. He opens the can of beer and starts eating his supper.

Ida sits down opposite him.

"You can't keep working around the clock like this. What if you burn out?"

"I don't think there's any danger of that," he mumbles with his mouth full. "I told you—I'm fine."

"I'm afraid of something happening to you."

"Don't be."

Ida leans across the table and places her hand on his.

"Isn't there anyone else who can take over for you?"

The last thing Daniel wants is for a colleague to step into his shoes. He has assured Birgitta Grip that he can handle the investigation, especially now he has additional resources in the form of Hanna.

"This is my job, darling."

Ida's eyes fill with tears. "Think about Alice! If something happened to you, she'd only have me!"

That hits home. Daniel isn't sure whether his reaction is due to guilt or irritation. Does she have to be so dramatic?

"For God's sake, Ida—I'm a cop!"

His tone is too sharp. He regrets it the second the words are out, but the flash of anger in Ida's eyes tells him it is too late.

"How can you be so selfish? Don't you care about us anymore?"

"Of course I do. I'm sorry—I didn't mean to sound insensitive."

He hopes that she will accept his apology so they can stop bickering and go to bed. He longs to lie down, close his eyes. He is exhausted and knows he can't provide the kind of nuanced support that Ida needs. She is still full of hormones—Alice is only three months old.

They have had this kind of quarrel before, and it never ends well. He almost wishes Ida had stayed asleep. He doesn't want to have this conversation tonight. He concentrates on his food, hoping she will calm down.

Unfortunately, Ida misinterprets his silence.

"Listen to me!" she snaps. "You have a family now. A baby daughter. You can't live the way you used to!"

That's the last thing he's doing, and she ought to know that, but her words hurt.

Which is no doubt the intention.

The years in Gothenburg shaped him; for a long time, work was his number-one priority. His savior too, after Francesca's death. He sometimes misses those days when he only had himself to think about, when he didn't have to take anyone else into account. Nonetheless Ida and Alice mean the world to him.

"Mom said you'd react this way," Ida adds. "She said you wouldn't listen to me."

"Have you been discussing me with your mother?" The thought of Ida complaining to her mom makes him even more frustrated.

"Who else would I talk to? It's not as if you're ever around."

He really doesn't want to lose his temper; that will do no good at all. He can't afford a huge fight tonight.

He carefully places his knife and fork on his plate and finishes off his beer. He takes a few deep breaths, trying to regain his inner calm.

"The only thing you think about is your job."

The sharp tone is too much for him.

"A young girl has been murdered, Ida. Do you really think this is the right time to argue about this?"

"How can that take precedence over me and Alice?"

"It doesn't."

Tears of anger trickle down Ida's cheeks. She quickly wipes them away. "You never have time for us. It's as if we don't count anymore."

Daniel is so tired of feeling guilty. He does his best; he never stops trying. Why can't she see that?

"Let's go to bed. Please, Ida."

"So when are we going to talk? You're never home."

"Tomorrow. I'll try to get back early, I promise." He stands up to clear the table. "I really must get some sleep. I have to be up very early," he adds.

"How do you think I feel, all alone here with Alice, knowing you don't care about us?" Bitterness is etched on Ida's face. "Mom was right about you all along. You're completely self-obsessed. I should have realized you'd never make a good father."

That's the tipping point. There is no stopping the anger; it simply floods his body and takes over completely.

"Shut the fuck up!" he yells, picking up the plate and hurling it at the wall with all his strength.

The crash echoes around the kitchen. As if in slow motion, the plate shatters into a thousand pieces, white porcelain raining down onto the floor. There are shards everywhere.

Ida stares at him, openmouthed. "Have you lost your mind?"

Daniel can't explain what happened. Everything went black.

Inevitably Alice wakes and starts screaming.

He goes out into the hallway, grabs his jacket, and disappears into the night.

FRIDAY, DECEMBER 20

98

At dawn Harald gives up. Sleep is impossible. Thinking about Fredrik is keeping him awake.

He must be the guilty party.

Harald should have realized earlier. Mira has always said that Fredrik can be jealous and vengeful; he's not the kind of man you want as an enemy. She told him how furious Fredrik was when he found out about their relationship.

Harald remembers one morning a few months ago, when they were lying in bed after a night together in a mountain cabin he'd borrowed. It was a rare treat to wake with her beside him. They had made love slowly and gently in the early light. She rested her head on his arm, and the warmth of her body spread to his.

Somehow they started talking about Fredrik. Mira was afraid he would find out what was going on.

Fredrik never forgives an injustice, she said with a shudder that hinted at something darker than the usual ability to bear a grudge. *And he never forgets.*

Harald sits up in the guest bed. His body feels heavy, and his joints are aching. The combination of too little sleep and the booze he turned to yesterday has produced a horrible pounding in his skull.

He makes the effort to get dressed, but his shirt smells. He goes to the bedroom to fetch a clean one; the room is in darkness, and he can just make out Lena's silent figure beneath the covers. After a few seconds his eyes grow accustomed to the gloom, and he sees that she is lying on her side with her eyes closed.

She has totally checked out from everyday life.

He ought to wake her, make her have a shower and eat something, but he doesn't have the energy. Instead he gathers up his clean clothes and heads for the bathroom.

He is standing in the shower when the emotional reaction catches up with him. His daughter is dead, and it is his fault. If he hadn't started the affair with Mira, then Fredrik wouldn't have taken his revenge.

Tears pour down his cheeks, mixing with the hot water.

He sobs silently, his body shaking. In the end he must grab a hold of the shower rail to stay upright.

It doesn't help. He sinks down into a crouching position, letting the sobs take over.

Eventually they die away. He stands up, increases the water temperature, and allows it to sluice his face. It scalds his skin, and the bathroom fills with steam.

Fredrik cannot get away with this.

Harald clings to that thought.

Whatever happens, Fredrik must be punished.

99

Daniel is in the changing room at the police station, brushing his teeth. He grabbed a few hours' sleep under a blanket in the restroom, and he has just tried to shake off the tiredness by splashing his face with ice-cold water.

Shame is not so easy to wash away.

He deeply regrets his outburst but has no idea how to explain himself or how to fix things. He has texted Ida, asking her to forgive him, but it feels both pathetic and inadequate. He can't face the thought of calling her—it's too soon.

Maybe he should just stay away for a while, give her some time to get over what happened?

He gargles and spits, prepares to start the day. His heart is heavy; it's a whole day since he saw Alice, and that is entirely his fault.

If only he could control his temper. The eruptions of rage when he was young were one thing, but now he's an adult and ought to get a grip.

Alice will never need to be afraid of arguments at home.

That's what Daniel promised himself when she was born, and yet last night happened. His daughter is only three months old, and he has already had a complete meltdown.

He wonders if his grandfather felt the same deep shame whenever he lost control?

Daniel has heard people say that it must be nice to let your anger take over, to release all your emotions so that you can move on.

They have no idea.

It is terrifying to be so furious that you can't remember what you've said to someone else—especially when it's someone you love.

He is normally a calm person—restrained, even. It isn't possible to work as a police officer if you can't control your temper. Months can go by without his anger spilling over, but when it happens everything goes black. He becomes a different person, one he neither recognizes nor likes.

He turns off the faucet and wipes his mouth with a couple of paper towels, rubbing so hard that his top lip hurts.

He barely recalls what he yelled at Ida. He just remembers the overwhelming feeling that he couldn't bear to be in the same room as her. Not for one more second.

And the realization that he had to get out of there before he did something even worse.

He leans over the washbasin and stares with distaste at his reflection in the mirror.

He is not going to be like his grandfather.

Or his father.

The door opens, and Anton comes in carrying his sports bag in one hand and his saxophone case in the other. He is an hour early and immediately grasps what is going on. Yesterday's clothes in a crumpled heap on the bench, the toothbrush on the edge of the basin. He is tactful enough not to comment on Daniel's disheveled appearance.

"Everything okay at home?" he asks.

Daniel gets on well with Anton; sometimes they go for a beer together. But the situation with Ida is too personal. He can hardly explain last night's outburst to himself, let alone a colleague.

He shrugs, summons up a smile.

"See you at the briefing," he says, disappearing into the toilet.

100

Kalle is at the kitchen table, chewing listlessly on his sandwich. Mimi has an untouched glass of milk in front of her. “When is Ludde coming home?” she asks.

Harald swallows. He still hasn’t been able to bring himself to tell them that the dog is dead.

“Soon,” he says, pouring himself a cup of coffee.

“Why doesn’t Mommy have breakfast with us anymore?” Kalle wants to know. He moves his chair, the legs scraping across the floor, then tilts back at a dangerous angle so that the chair almost falls over.

“Don’t do that!” Harald bellows.

Kalle’s face crumples. “Sorry,” he mumbles, on the verge of tears.

“No, I’m sorry,” Harald says. “I didn’t mean to shout—I was afraid you’d fall and hurt yourself.” He puts down his cup and crouches beside his son. “Mommy’s sleeping,” he says in a gentler tone.

“She’s always sleeping,” Mimi points out.

The children are right. Lena hasn’t shown her face for several days. She has abdicated all her duties. Harald feels a spurt of irritation; he can’t carry the family alone.

“You know what—why don’t the two of you go upstairs and wake her?”

Maybe Lena can be persuaded to get up if the twins give her a hug—a reminder that she still has two children who need her?

He waves in the direction of the stairs. “Go and ask Mommy if she’d like some breakfast.”

The twins race out of the kitchen. He hears their footsteps on the stairs, the squeak of the hinge as the bedroom door opens. He finishes off his coffee, starts loading the dishwasher.

Kalle reappears in the doorway. "Mommy won't wake up."

Harald pauses with a plate in his hand. "What do you mean?"

"She's just lying there."

It is less than an hour since Harald checked on Lena; presumably the sleeping pills are still working. "Try again—give her a little shake," he tells his son. He doesn't mention the medication; the children don't need to know about that.

Kalle heads back upstairs, and Harald carries on cleaning up.

Something makes him stop. A suspicion he doesn't really want to acknowledge.

He leaves the kitchen, strides up the stairs. Goes into the bedroom, sees Mimi and Kalle standing by the head of the bed, tugging at Lena.

Shaking her lifeless body.

She doesn't react at all, her muscles are completely limp.

Her face is so pale.

Mimi stares at her father with frightened eyes. "Is Mommy dead too?"

101

It feels as if it has been snowing and blowing a gale forever.

Daniel longs for a sunny day, a few hours up on Åreskutan, the snow sparkling with life and the mountain landscape spreading in all directions like sugar loaves. Instead he is sitting in the conference room with the frost clinging to the windowpanes. Twilight has begun to fall; the morning vanished in a fog of interviews and video meetings.

In addition, Birgitta Grip has arranged another press conference this afternoon and is insisting that Daniel take part. She refused to listen to his objections, even though he came close to swearing at her.

The pictures of Amanda's body on the walls stare accusingly at him.

He rests his head in his hands.

How are they going to find out who killed her? Over five days have passed since she was found dead. It feels as if they are chasing a thousand balls, with no idea which is the right one.

Raffe and Anton have identified a dozen property owners in Ullådalen who might be of interest. Daniel would like to search each of their cabins, but they can't get a warrant for any of them without reasonable suspicion that a crime has been committed. For that to happen, the investigation must point to a single individual. It's a catch-22 situation.

They have continued to check out Fredrik Bergfors but haven't managed to establish a link between him and Ullådalen. He also has an alibi, because Mira still claims that her husband was lying beside her on the night in question.

Daniel interviewed Amanda's boyfriend again this morning, but nothing new emerged. This time Viktor had a lawyer with him. Daniel wasn't surprised.

Anton has looked into Lasse Sandahl's background. He has no criminal record and doesn't own a snowmobile. He swears that he never touched Amanda after the incident on Walpurgis Night. They have spoken to the principal, who was taken aback by the information that Sandahl had made a pass at a student. There have never been any complaints about him in the past.

Daniel wishes they had better forensic evidence. He has just emailed the National Forensic Center and asked them to prioritize the examination of the skin particles found under Amanda's fingernails. It would be much easier to move forward if the DNA analysis were completed.

Hanna walks in with a cup of coffee in her hand. They have been working separately since this morning. Hanna has been trying to get a hold of Ebba, hoping to persuade her to drop her guard and tell them about Amanda's part-time job, while Daniel has been tied up with interviews and video calls.

"Tough morning?" she says.

"Is it that obvious?"

"You look a little the worse for wear."

"I'm just frustrated that things are going so slowly. Plus Grip wants me to drive down to Östersund this afternoon for another press conference." Daniel sighs. Just saying those two words makes his heart sink. He doesn't mention the difficulties at home. After all, he and Hanna hardly know each other. He is doing his best to focus on the job.

"Let's go through the course of events one more time," Hanna suggests, sitting down opposite him. "Sometimes it's good to say it out loud."

Once again Daniel goes over their hypothesis.

Amanda leaves the party and walks along the E14, where someone picks her up in a dark-colored car. This is probably a person known to her; otherwise it seems unlikely that she would have gotten into the vehicle.

Some kind of quarrel erupts, the man grabs Amanda in a stranglehold, and she loses consciousness. He takes her to a cabin in Ullådalen, presumably still unconscious, and hides her there. She remains there for two days, during which time she freezes to death. The perpetrator panics and decides to return her body. He places it on the chairlift at VM6, where it is found by the lift attendant on Sunday morning.

"Did she know Fredrik Bergfors?" Hanna asks. "If we assume he's the guilty party, and not Viktor or Sandahl."

"I don't know, but maybe she recognized him and felt safe."

Hanna drinks the last of her coffee. "I really wish we had access to her phone. It would be a big help if we could read her text messages. Kids text one another all the time; maybe she had time to send something before she was abducted?"

A thought occurs to Daniel. They don't have Amanda's phone, but perhaps there's another way of accessing her texts. They took a Mac from her room; he has the same one at home and it's linked to his phone. All his personal messages come through on the computer as well as on his phone. If Amanda has done the same, they should be able to see who she has contacted.

The forensic technicians should be finished with the computer very soon; if he's going to Östersund anyway, he can check it out. He also intends to have a chat with the prosecutor, face-to-face. He is desperate to search the Bergforses' house.

He looks at his watch and realizes it's time to go.

"I need to take off," he says, getting to his feet. "Speak later."

102

As Daniel turns into the parking lot at police HQ in Östersund, he receives an unexpected text informing him that the press conference has been postponed. Birgitta Grip has to attend an urgent meeting in Stockholm, which takes precedence.

The relief is immense. He remains sitting in the car as the tension leaves his body. He really needed something to go his way today.

Everything else feels like shit right now.

He heads for the forensic technicians' department to check on Amanda's computer before going to see the prosecutor.

Markus Larsson, the technician who is working on the case, is one floor above the office Daniel uses on the days when he is based in Östersund. He has his headphones on and doesn't notice that he has company until Daniel taps him on the shoulder. He is facing three large screens, his fingers moving ceaselessly across the keyboard. There is a tangle of black cables on the floor.

"Hi, Daniel—good to see you."

"How's it going with Amanda Halvorssen's computer?"

Markus nods toward a Mac in a silver case on the desk beside him. "I'm pretty much done—I was going to call you this afternoon. Sorry about the delay."

Daniel pulls up a chair. "Can we take a look?"

Markus reaches for the Mac and opens the screen. He certainly doesn't meet Daniel's expectations of a computer geek; he isn't an introvert, or overweight, and he doesn't wear black hoodies. In fact he looks perfectly normal; he is a slim guy aged about thirty, with black-rimmed glasses and a white shirt.

"What would you like to see first?"

"I'm wondering if she'd linked her phone and her computer, which would give us access to her text messages."

Markus opens the messaging program. "Yes—there you go."

Daniel contemplates the list; nothing strikes him as suspicious.

"What about her emails?"

Markus brings up Amanda's emails, but they don't provide much more information.

"Can you access other forms of communication through the computer?" Daniel asks. "Facebook, Instagram, Snapchat?"

Markus logs in to Facebook with the help of a saved password. Amanda wasn't exactly an avid user; her posts are few, with weeks or even months in between. The latest activity was when she changed her profile picture to a selfie taken at sunset by the lake. She looks happy, her eyes are fixed on the horizon, and the soft August light gives her a golden shimmer.

It is heartrending to think that she no longer exists, that she will never be older than eighteen.

Daniel can't help seeing Alice in his mind's eye.

"Shall we try Messenger?" Markus suggests. "A lot of educational establishments use it to enable students to communicate with one another. Some employers do the same, because kids don't always keep up with email."

Judging by the plethora of unopened messages in Amanda's inbox, she belonged to that category.

"Good idea."

Markus opens a new window containing several messages. One of the senders catches Daniel's attention: a woman called Linda has been in touch with Amanda.

He doesn't remember a Linda among Amanda's friends and acquaintances.

"Can we take a look at that one?" he says, pointing.

Markus brings up the conversation.

It seems that Amanda has been working for a cleaning company. Linda has sent her addresses, times, and instructions. Ebba's name is also mentioned more than once.

Daniel scratches the back of his neck. Harald insisted that his daughter didn't have a part-time job, and Ebba said she didn't know anything about it.

Something isn't right.

"What can we find out about this Linda?"

Markus clicks on the sender and is taken to a profile page that is remarkably anonymous. The photograph is backlit; it is impossible to see the subject's face. There are no personal details or pictures.

"Suspicious," Markus says. He frowns, clicks a few more times, then shrugs. "That's not a normal profile. It's been created purely to access Messenger."

"Is that usual?"

"It does happen, but it tells us something about Linda. She doesn't want to be seen or traced."

"Do you think Linda is her real name?"

"I've no idea."

Why would an employer not want to post their image? Possibly because the work is all cash in hand. Whatever the reason, it needs to be checked out.

If there's one person who knows about Amanda's job, it's Ebba.

Time to get the truth out of her.

103

Hanna is in her new office, trying to catch up with various reports.

Her thoughts keep returning to Zuhra, even though she is trying to concentrate on Amanda.

She now has proof that the cleaning company is involved in something shady. Why would the woman in the office have denied all knowledge of Zuhra, while Kristina Risberg is driving her to different houses to do the cleaning?

There were documents in Kristina's home with the Fjäll-städ logo, so there is definitely a connection.

Hanna doesn't regret entering the house, but she is uncomfortably aware of the risks. If it came out, she would lose her job in Åre.

It is almost four o'clock when Daniel calls. The station is deserted; it is Friday afternoon, and Anton has just left.

"How's it going in Östersund?"

"I think we might have found out something interesting."

"Go on."

"There was some correspondence about Amanda's job on Messenger. She *was* working part-time for a cleaning company—but off the books, I suspect."

Hanna sits up a little straighter. "Do you know the name of the cleaning company?"

"No, but Amanda's contact calls herself Linda, although of course that could be made up."

The woman in Fjäll-städ's office was called Linda. Is it a coincidence? Could there be a link to Zuhra's precarious situation?

Before she can mention it, Daniel continues.

"Could you have a chat with Ebba, find out what she knows?"

Hanna has called Ebba several times during the course of the day and left messages, but there has been no response.

"No problem—I'll go over there right away."

While she is talking she googles "Linda" and "Fjäll-städ," but there are no matches.

"Great," Daniel says. "I'm not sure when I'll be back. I have to see Tobias Ahlqvist, the prosecutor, but he's been delayed in court, so I'm sitting around waiting for him."

Hanna isn't sure what to do; should she tell him about her own research? The problem is that she has so little that is concrete. All she can say is that a young immigrant is showing signs of both abuse and exploitation.

Gut feeling and a police officer's instinct are no substitute for solid evidence.

She has examined the documents she photographed in Kristina Risberg's office, but of course she can't reveal how she obtained them. She doesn't want to risk losing Daniel's trust and confidence in her, when everything seems to be going so well.

"Speak to you later," she says, ending the call.

She grabs her jacket and sets off to see Ebba. As she leaves the station, she realizes it has been far too long since she made any attempt to contact Christian. She has promised to call Lydia at seven this evening for a proper chat. Lydia's first question is bound to be about how things are with Christian.

Hanna decides that she will call him immediately after her visit to Ebba.

Her broken heart is no longer quite so painful, but the mere thought of apologizing still makes her feel sick.

"Fucking Christian," she mutters, heading for her car.

104

This time it is Ebba's mother, Sanna Nyrén, who answers the door. She is very much like her daughter, small and slim with short light-brown hair. Her expression is troubled as she lets Hanna in.

"Such terrible news about Lena," she says.

"Sorry?"

"Haven't you heard what's happened?"

When Hanna shakes her head, Sanna lowers her voice as if the tragic reality is too much for her.

"She's in intensive care. She tried to take her own life last night. I feel so sorry for Harald and the twins."

Hanna swallows hard. She had no idea. Yet another blow for the family in the wake of Amanda's death. Harald and those poor children must be devastated.

She accompanies Sanna into the living room. Ebba is curled up on the sofa with a gray blanket over her. She looks small and desperately unhappy. Sanna sits down beside her, offering Hanna the armchair.

"Hi, Ebba," Hanna begins. "I've been trying to get a hold of you all day. I have a few more questions about Amanda's job, which we talked about yesterday." She does her best to sound gentle and approachable. "It would be very helpful if you could tell us everything you know."

Ebba looks as if she wishes she were somewhere else, a long way away.

"We've found out that Amanda was working for a woman called Linda," Hanna continues. "Were you aware of that? Did you work for her too?"

Sanna strokes her daughter's hair. "If you know anything, you have to speak up," she says encouragingly. "The most important thing is for the police to find the person who killed Amanda."

Ebba intertwines her fingers. When she eventually speaks, her voice is shaky. "We both worked for Linda."

"And what did that involve?"

"We cleaned houses up in Björnen and Sadeln. It was a secret, that's why I didn't dare tell you before." Ebba glances at her mother. "I'm sorry I didn't say anything. I knew if I told the police, you and Dad would find out, and you'd be mad."

Sanna takes Ebba's hand. "It's fine. It's good that you're being honest now." She turns to Hanna. "We didn't want Ebba to work during the semester. We thought it was better for her to concentrate on her studies and her grades."

Hanna appreciates Sanna's support; this is not the time to chastise her daughter.

"Plus it was . . . off the books," Ebba adds. "We couldn't say anything—Amanda's dad is a politician, he always insisted that everything had to be perfect. He kept telling her mom they couldn't afford to be in the papers for cheating on their taxes or anything else that might damage his career."

"I understand," Hanna says. She isn't surprised to find that both Ebba and Amanda are involved, nor that it happened without their parents' knowledge.

"Could you tell me how it worked?"

"We just did a few jobs every other week to earn some extra money."

"This Linda—what's her surname?"

"I've never met her. We only communicated on Messenger." Ebba wipes away a drop of snot from under her nose.

"So what about the practicalities? Payment, addresses, house keys?"

Surely they must have met the mysterious Linda a couple of times at least.

"Amanda used to collect the keys and the cleaning stuff because she has . . . had . . . a driver's license." The involuntary error makes Ebba's voice break. It takes a few seconds before she is able to go on. "I haven't taken my test yet, but Amanda would borrow her mom's car, because Lena walks to work. Linda's office was in the village, so Amanda stopped there before she came to pick me up."

"Do you know the name of the cleaning company?"

Ebba shakes her head, which is disappointing. However, the fact that Linda's office is in the village points to Fjäll-städ.

"So how did the two of you start working for Linda?" Hanna asks, crossing her legs to sit more comfortably in the low armchair.

"We have a friend who did it before us—Alva." There is a little more color in Ebba's face, as if it is a relief to get all this off her chest at long last. "She left school last year and went to university in Umeå. She asked us if we wanted to take over. It was a really good way of earning money." She glances at Sanna, as if to reassure herself that her mother isn't annoyed.

"Would you be able to show us some of the houses you've cleaned?" Hanna says. "Then we could speak to the owners, find out the name of the company."

"I think so. A lot of them were in Sadeln."

It *has* to be Fjäll-städ.

Sanna gently pats her daughter's cheek. "Is that everything?"

Ebba clamps her lips together. She has the beginnings of a cold sore at one corner of her mouth, a whitish blister that is spreading.

"Not quite," she whispers.

Hanna waits patiently. She doesn't want the girl to shut down again.

"Something happened a week before Amanda . . . disappeared." Ebba tugs at the sleeve of her pale-pink sweatshirt, which covers her knuckles.

"Take your time," Hanna says. "Try to remember as much as you can."

Ebba pushes her light-brown hair back from her forehead. "Amanda was going to clean a house in Sadeln. I was supposed to be there too, but I had really bad period pains, so I stayed home." She moves a fraction closer to her mother. "When Amanda arrived, another girl was already there. A foreigner—Amanda thought she was from Uzbekistan. She spoke English, but very badly. There had been a misunderstanding about who was supposed to be working where on that day."

Hanna is holding her breath.

"Amanda realized something was wrong. This girl was really unhappy and she had lots of bruises, as if she'd been beaten. Eventually Amanda persuaded her to talk." Ebba pulls the blanket more tightly around her shoulders, as if she is freezing. "Amanda was that kind of person—people trusted her. You felt you could tell her anything."

"What was the name of this other girl?"

"I'm not sure—it sounded kind of like Zara."

It must have been Zuhra.

"What did she say to Amanda?" Hanna tries to hide her excitement.

"That she was like . . . a slave. She worked all the time, but hardly got paid any money. Apparently there were three girls of our age who were in the same situation. They just wanted to go back home, but they couldn't because they owed so much for their journey to Sweden."

"Who did they owe this money to?"

"I don't know."

"Was it Linda who was forcing the girl to work so hard?"

Ebba nods, then suddenly looks unsure. "There was someone else involved—a man. Amanda spoke to Linda, told her she couldn't treat the girl like that, but then Linda said it wasn't her idea. She claimed that her boss called all the shots, and he got really mad if anyone complained."

Hanna's brain is buzzing. This is really serious—a full-blown trafficking operation in Åre. Amanda could have gotten herself mixed up in dangerous criminal activity.

"Do you know if this young woman was also forced into prostitution?" she asks.

Both Ebba and her mother look horrified.

"I don't know," Ebba says. "Amanda was the only one who met her."

"Did she have any idea who the boss was? Someone local?"

"I don't think so."

Hanna feverishly makes notes. "Did she say anything else? I'm very grateful for anything you can remember, even the smallest detail."

Ebba chews on her thumbnail, her lips trembling.

"Amanda . . ." She hesitates. "Amanda said she had to help the girl and her friends. She couldn't let it go, she kept talking about it. At one point she said she was going to make an anonymous call to the police, tip them off." She spreads her hands helplessly. "But I don't think she got a chance . . ."

105

The corridor in the hospital at Östersund where Harald is sitting on a bench is painted an odd shade of pinkish brown. He has been waiting for hours while the doctors and nurses take care of Lena.

She is still unconscious.

The light from the fluorescent tubes on the ceiling is reflected in the linoleum flooring. A beeping noise is coming from one of the rooms, while the red lamp over the door flashes, demanding attention.

People are constantly coming and going in Lena's room. He has watched as machines are wheeled in, drip stands brought out, but no one has sat down beside him to explain what is going on.

The children are still in Åre. Harald's mother picked them up at about the same time as the ambulance took Lena. He drove to the hospital in his own car.

He stares at the wall opposite, not really seeing the picture of colorful flowers. His phone rings, but he doesn't answer. He is still so shocked that he can't even turn the pages of a newspaper, let alone conduct a conversation.

He buries his face in his hands.

If only he had made more of an effort to check on Lena, ask how she was feeling. Why didn't he go into the bedroom, try and talk to her? Why did he leave her lying there, hour after hour, without at least speaking to the doctor who had prescribed the sleeping pills?

What will happen to Mimi and Kalle if they lose their mother too?

The door opens and a woman emerges. She glances around, spots Harald, and comes over. Her name badge informs him that she is a senior doctor.

"How are you doing?" she asks.

Harald has no idea what to say. The whole situation is unreal.

"Your wife hasn't woken up yet. We've irrigated her stomach and given her charcoal to try to neutralize the medication she'd taken. The problem is that we don't know exactly when she took the pills, so I can't be sure how she's going to respond." She pushes her hands into the pockets of her scrubs. "It's good that you brought the packaging with you," she continues. "That's very helpful."

"How is she?" Harald doesn't recognize his own voice. It sounds cracked and strained; his vocal cords refuse to cooperate. He clears his throat, tries again. "Can I see her?"

"You can, but you need to be prepared for the fact that it could be . . . alarming. She has several electrodes attached to her body so that we can monitor her breathing. She's on oxygen, and we've set up a drip." She pauses. "But her condition is stable."

Harald tries to translate the medical terminology. What does that actually mean? Can you be stable even if you're dying?

"Is she going to get better?" he somehow manages to ask.

"It's too early to say."

"Is there a risk of brain damage?" He stumbles over the last two words.

"I'm sorry, but again I can't really answer that until she wakes up."

Harald is overwhelmed by a great weariness. He rests the back of his head against the wall, closes his eyes for a few seconds. His eyelids are impossibly heavy.

"Maybe you should go home for a while, try to get some rest."

"I live in Åre."

"I understand. It's a long drive." The doctor checks her watch; no doubt she needs to move on to her next patient. The lower part of her green coat is marked with patches of rusty red. "I'm sure we can find you somewhere to rest if you want to stay at the hospital overnight. I think it could be a while before your wife wakes up."

Harald reads between the lines, hears the words she doesn't want to say out loud.

If your wife wakes up.

He sees Mimi and Kalle in his mind's eye. They have just lost their beloved big sister; are they going to lose their mom too?

Lena is lying unconscious in that room, and he has let her down in the worst way imaginable. Lena, the mother of his children, the woman who has been by his side ever since they left school.

If only he had realized what the consequences of his affair with Mira would be . . .

He feels a burning sensation right behind his brow bone, a single point of distilled hatred for the man who has caused his family so much pain. He loathes himself for what he has done, but he hates Fredrik even more.

If it weren't for Fredrik's destructive actions, Lena would never have attempted suicide.

The thought that the man is wandering around out there enjoying life makes Harald want to vomit.

The doctor's expression is sympathetic. Harald notices tiny lines around her eyes in the harsh fluorescent light.

"Would you like me to help you find somewhere to rest?" she asks, gently placing a hand on his shoulder.

Harald shrugs it off and gets to his feet so abruptly that the doctor takes a couple of steps back. "I have to go home," he mumbles.

He knows he sounds rude, but he hasn't got the energy to apologize. Instead he makes for the elevator and goes straight down to the parking lot.

He is clutching the car keys so tightly that they are cutting into his skin, but the pain helps him to focus.

The twins can stay over with his mother tonight.

Fredrik has not only murdered Harald's eldest daughter and the family's beloved dog; he has also driven Lena to the brink of death.

How many more must be sacrificed before Fredrik is stopped?

106

There are lights showing in the windows when Hanna parks her car a few hundred yards from Albins väg 11. It is five thirty. She was on her way home after speaking to Ebba when she changed her mind. Instead of turning off for Björnen, she continued toward Undersåker and Kristina Risberg's home.

It might be madness to act on her own yet again, but she is sure she is onto something.

On the way she called Daniel and reported back on the conversation with Ebba. She mentioned that there is a woman called Linda in Fjäll-städs's office; it is clear that the company needs to be investigated further. She and Daniel have arranged to meet at the station first thing in the morning.

She still hasn't told him about Kristina Risberg and Zuhra but is hoping to find something in the next few hours that might link them to the investigation.

A firm piece of evidence that does not rest on her illegal entry into Risberg's house.

She takes a bite of her apple. Her thoughts turn briefly to Christian; she's supposed to be calling him now. She can't face it. She will do it later, before she talks to Lydia as arranged.

She starts to go through her notes on Fjäll-städ. On the surface it looks like a legitimate company. The annual accounts wouldn't be available online if they hadn't been submitted according to the legal requirements. However, Ebba confirmed that some of the cleaners are being paid cash in hand, and Hanna has seen Zuhra being ferried around between different houses. The fear Hanna saw in her eyes was real—she was terrified.

Ebba said that Amanda had complained to Linda, but Linda had blamed her male boss. Which means there is a man higher up in the organization who knows that Zuhra has revealed her vulnerable position to Amanda.

This increases Hanna's determination. All these fucking men, exploiting vulnerable women.

Presumably Zuhra was punished for talking to Amanda. That was why she didn't dare to tell the truth when Hanna offered to help her.

Hanna stares out at the whirling snow as she puts the pieces of the puzzle together. It is already so cold inside the car that her breath is visible. She starts the engine, directs the heater at her feet, and turns it up to maximum. She mustn't get too cold, or she won't be able to stay put.

The risk of Fjäll-städ's illegal activity being revealed is probably pretty low. The plethora of second homes and rental properties creates an excellent market for anyone with access to illicit workers. No one is going to react when there is a constant flow of new tenants, or owners who use their homes in the resort for only a few weeks in each season.

If anyone does show up while the cleaner is working, there is no real danger. Hanna has seen for herself that Zuhra was too scared to talk to her. Refugees or immigrants with no papers can neither protest nor turn to the authorities.

The whole thing is cynical but refined.

The legal part of the company is open to the tax authorities and also acts as a front for the clients. Meanwhile there is a parallel operation going on, where an underpaid workforce is exploited to earn more money. Plus they have used teenage girls, no doubt at peak times when the usual staff can't keep up.

Hanna can't help wondering whether the entire management team is in on the deal, or whether it's shadowy figures in the background who are responsible. Many board members in small companies don't really have a finger on the pulse; friends and acquaintances are often recruited in exchange for a decent fee—so why would they scrutinize the finances?

It's watertight.

Until someone like Hanna shows up and starts asking the wrong questions.

107

It is six thirty-five by the time Kristina Risberg comes out and starts up the dark-gray Golf. Hanna had almost given up hope and was about to go home and call Lydia as arranged.

Now the adrenaline is coursing through her veins.

If she's lucky, maybe Risberg will lead her further into the tangled web, possibly even to the boss? She really wants to help Zuhra and put those bastards behind bars. According to Ebba, there were two more girls from Uzbekistan who were in the same situation.

This has to stop.

She follows Risberg, keeping her distance so that the other woman won't realize she's being tailed. The Golf drives through the center of Björnen and turns off for the Copperhill district.

Risberg stops outside a dark-brown house. The lights are on inside, and suddenly Zuhra appears at the huge panoramic window.

Even from this distance Hanna can see how tired she is. Her back is bent; her movements are slow. If she started as early as she did yesterday, then she has worked since seven o'clock this morning—that's almost twelve hours.

Hanna would really like to rush in and take Zuhra away, but she can't do that, because it would mean losing the chance of finding out who's in charge. She forces herself to stay where she is and picks up her phone to get ready to take photographs.

Zuhra carries out her cleaning equipment and gets in the car, which immediately sets off. Hanna follows. The Golf signals left as they approach the E14, and enters the highway.

Is Risberg on her way back home to Undersåker? No, she continues past the exit and carries on toward Järpen.

Hanna is grateful for the darkness, which makes it more difficult for Risberg to tell if the same car is behind her the whole time.

After twenty minutes they reach Järpen—is that the final destination?

The Golf slows down and turns left onto Skansvägen, then right onto Skogsvägen. Hanna is finding it increasingly tricky to keep her distance.

The stress makes her sweat in her warm padded jacket.

They pass a row of small single-story wooden houses, and eventually the Golf turns into Hjortronstigen. It is a cul-de-sac; Hanna notices the sign at the last minute and manages to brake before the corner.

She quickly kills the engine so that the headlights won't be seen, then wriggles across to the passenger seat to try and see what's going on.

The Golf has stopped outside a four-story apartment building. It looks run down; there is graffiti on the walls, and the light over the door is broken. The curtains are drawn at several windows, as if no one lives there anymore.

Zuhra gets out of the car, this time without any cleaning equipment. Hanna glances at the clock: seven fifteen. Zuhra disappears into the building, and the door closes behind her.

The Golf reverses and passes Hanna's car, just as it did earlier in the day. She hopes Risberg won't notice her.

After a few minutes, when she is sure that Risberg has gone, she gets out of the car, scurries over to the apartment building, and tries the door.

It isn't locked.

She finds herself in a gray-painted entrance hall that is just as shabby as the outside. Once again there is graffiti on the walls, and several cigarette stubs on the floor. She looks in vain for a board listing residents' names.

There are two apartments on the ground floor, so it is reasonable to assume that the same applies to each story. Zuhra could live in any one of them. How is she going to find her?

Hanna peers at the nameplates on the two doors. Neither seems to belong to a person from Uzbekistan, but then whoever is behind the operation would hardly have allowed Zuhra to rent the apartment in her own name.

She presses her ear to the first door, listens for sounds that might provide a clue. The television is on; it sounds like the news. There is only silence behind the second door; maybe no one lives there.

Hanna tries the next floor. She hears a child crying behind one door and a loud argument in the other apartment.

She goes up the stairs and thinks she can hear a man's voice speaking to someone who answers quietly in English. She tiptoes forward, puts her ear to the door.

Is that a woman crying?

The man's voice grows louder and comes closer.

Hanna backs away and moves up the next staircase. Suddenly the door opens, and Hanna just manages to keep out of sight. She catches a glimpse of a middle-aged white man. He hurries down the stairs as the apartment door slams shut behind him.

The sobs from inside are clearly audible now.

Hanna is almost certain that she recognizes Zuhra's voice. Should she attempt to make contact now, or follow the man who stormed out?

She knows where to find Zuhra.

The man's footsteps are still echoing in the stairwell.

Hanna races after him.

108

It was quite some time before Daniel was able to return to Åre. The discussion with the prosecutor took forever, without leading to a concrete decision. Tobias Ahlqvist is insisting on more convincing evidence before he is prepared to sanction a search of Fredrik Bergfors's house.

The information from Hanna about Amanda and Ebba's part-time work is interesting. It points in a new direction and must be followed up. Hanna did a good job in getting Ebba to confide in her.

He has just passed the chocolate factory and is on his way to see Amanda's parents, even though it is almost seven thirty. Maybe they will come up with something fresh about the mysterious Linda when they hear about Amanda's secret job.

Daniel parks on the street. The house is in darkness, apart from a large Advent star glowing in the kitchen window. He rings the bell and waits. Rings again.

As he is about to leave, Harald opens the door. Daniel hardly recognizes him. It has only been a few days, but Harald looks years older. His face is gray, his cheeks sunken and unshaven.

"What do you want?" he mumbles.

"I need to speak to you—may I come in?"

Harald looks utterly exhausted, but nods and steps aside.

The younger children don't appear to be home. When Daniel glances into the kitchen, he sees a bottle of vodka on the table, along with a half-full glass.

"Is Lena home? I'd really like to talk to both of you."

Harald shakes his head. "She's in the hospital in Östersund. She . . . took an overdose last night. Sleeping pills."

That explains why Harald is such a mess.

"How is she?"

"She's in a coma. The doctors can't say whether she'll wake up again . . ." His voice falters, he closes his eyes briefly. "Or if she'll have brain damage." He can barely finish the sentence.

"I'm so sorry. It must be incredibly difficult for you. I really hope Lena recovers." Daniel hesitates; will Harald be able to cope with questions in his current state? "This won't take long. I want you to know that we're doing everything we can to find Amanda's murderer."

He quickly tells Harald about what they found on Messenger, the fact that she has been cleaning for a woman called Linda and being paid cash in hand.

Does Harald know who this Linda might be?

Harald shakes his head. "Why would Amanda do that? She knows exactly how I feel about this kind of thing. I'm a full-time politician—it's unthinkable in our family."

And with those words he makes it clear exactly why Amanda kept her job a secret. Daniel refrains from pointing this out. Instead he thanks Harald and is about to leave when Harald blocks his path.

"How's it going with Bergfors?"

Daniel is taken aback by the vicious tone.

"Has he been arrested?" Harald adds.

"The investigation is ongoing," Daniel replies evasively. "We have a lot of things to check out before we reach that stage."

"It must be him!"

"It's far too early to draw that conclusion."

"It was Fredrik who poisoned Ludde!" Harald is shouting now.

Daniel hesitates, not knowing what to believe. "Are you sure?"

"Mira told me yesterday."

Strange—they asked her about the dog, and she insisted that her husband would never do such a thing. If she was lying about that, then maybe she was lying about Fredrik's alibi too?

He doesn't want to mention this possibility to Harald, who is already highly agitated.

"Let us do our job," he says reassuringly. "We'll look into it, and as soon as we know more, we'll be in touch."

He is about to place a calming hand on Harald's arm but thinks better of it when he looks the other man in the eye. He is both drunk and furious; the gesture could be misinterpreted.

"Is there someone you can call?" he says. "So you don't have to be alone?"

Harald's expression hardens, and he turns his back on Daniel. "Get out and leave me in peace," he mutters over his shoulder.

109

Through the glass in the main door, Hanna sees two taillights disappearing down Hjortronstigen. She runs to her own car, starts the engine, and does a U-turn that almost sends her skidding off the road. She drives down Skogsvägen as fast as she dares.

Where has he gone?

She looks in all directions, trying to spot the other vehicle. She can just make out a dark-colored car in the distance—is that him?

She speeds along the snowy roadway, her thoughts whirling. She only caught a glimpse of the man leaving the apartment, but there was something familiar about him. She searches her memory but realizes she needs to concentrate on her driving. The snow is falling more heavily now; the weather has deteriorated significantly over the past hour. The windshield wipers are operating at full speed, but visibility is still poor.

She reaches the intersection of Skogsvägen and Skansvägen and peers around desperately.

Did he take Skansvägen? If so, does that mean he's on his way back to Åre? She swears out loud, knowing that she has only a few seconds. She must make a decision before he disappears and she loses the chance to catch up with him.

Skansvägen. The lights on the bridge over the river reveal a lone car, heading in the direction of Åre.

It must be him.

Hanna drives onto the bridge, hoping she's made the right choice.

Visibility is appalling now. The snow is swirling in front of the headlights, creating a mist that hides the blacktop. As the road curves she loses the other car completely, but then she spots two taillights up ahead in the darkness.

She sends up a silent prayer that it's the same car.

He is driving much too fast; she is having trouble keeping up. The tension is making her skin crawl.

The streetlights come to an end.

Now she has only her own headlights to rely on, and they are already providing insufficient visibility in the snow.

The road curves again, and a truck appears in a cloud of snow mist. Its lights dazzle her; she can barely see where the roadway ends and the ditch begins.

She ought to slow down, but dare not for fear of losing the other car.

As the truck sweeps past, her entire vehicle is shaken by its slipstream. For a brief moment the back wheels slide and she lets out a scream.

Then the tires grip the surface once more, and Hanna regains control.

Her hands are shaking now; sweat is gathering on her forehead and trickling down her temples. She can hear herself gasping for breath.

She can still see the other driver's taillights, two faint dots in the distance. She must not, cannot lose sight of him.

They are on a straight stretch of road now.

Hanna is doing fifty miles an hour, which is the speed limit, but the lights ahead are fading; he is pulling away from her. She is clutching the wheel so tightly that it hurts. She tries to speed up but is terrified of losing control again.

They have passed Hålland; the road is anything but straight from now on. Suddenly she becomes aware of a bright light in her rearview mirror.

It is much too close.

She is totally focused on not losing the car up ahead, but the one behind her seems to be accelerating.

It is getting nearer, even though conditions are so bad that the driver ought to keep his distance.

Hanna has no choice but to speed up.

The lights in her mirror are blinding her—what the fuck is he doing? It is lethal to get so close in weather like this; if he doesn't slow down, he is going to hit her from behind.

Once again, she puts her foot down.

The speedometer climbs to fifty-five, sixty, sixty-five. The car sways alarmingly from side to side as the gusts of wind whip up the snow in front of her windshield.

She screws up her eyes, switching her focus from the mirror to the road ahead and back again.

Her pulse is racing, the stress is unbearable.

A bend appears out of nowhere.

At the same time the whole car shudders as something smashes into the back fender.

The lights in the mirror have gone.

What the fuck is that idiot doing? Hanna thinks a microsecond before her car jolts violently. As if in slow motion, she sees the hood plowing forward in a completely different direction from the roadway.

Then a tree comes rushing toward her, and she tries to wrench the steering wheel to one side in a panic.

110

Fredrik must pay for what he has done.

Harald remains sitting in the dark kitchen after Daniel has left.

The bitterness he feels toward Fredrik obliterates everything else. How can he be walking around as if nothing has happened? Is he going to carry on living his life as usual, while Harald's life is in ruins? The police won't do anything—Daniel confirmed that.

Harald pictures Mira and Fredrik's home. The large, impressive, red timber house that they have put their heart and soul into. The place where they sleep soundly and securely at night with little Leah.

Their daughter is alive, while his is dead. He hates Mira now as much as Fredrik.

Fredrik ought to burn in hell for his crimes.

Harald blinks; suddenly he knows what he must do.

All at once everything is perfectly clear.

Wood burns fast; with a couple of gallons of gasoline, their house would be in flames in seconds. Particularly at this time of year, when the cold makes the fire more difficult to put out and the snow causes problems for the fire engines.

Harald begins to work out how much gasoline it would take. The calculations make him feel better; he can already see the chaotic scene, hear the crackle of the hungry flames.

All the emotions he has tried to suppress come bursting through.

Why should he be the only one to suffer?

After a few minutes he gets to his feet and puts on his boots. He doesn't bother with a jacket as he goes outside and opens the garage door. On the workbench in the corner, he finds the spare can that he usually keeps topped up with gasoline.

He picks it up, feels the weight. It is full, just as it should be. To be on the safe side, he unscrews the green cap and checks the contents. When he replaces the cap, he happens to spill a few drops on his pants.

The smell brings him a strange sense of calm. It gives him fresh strength and makes him see dancing sparks, tongues of flame licking the walls of Fredrik and Mira's home until nothing remains but charred wood and ashes.

Harald carefully tightens the cap and places the can in the trunk of his car.

It is almost eight thirty. He decides to wait a few hours, until everyone is asleep. He can park down by the E14 and walk the last part. No one will notice him. It is almost minus twenty-five degrees outside; people stay indoors when it's that cold. Plus it's snowing heavily, which will make him even more invisible.

It's going to be so easy, pouring gasoline over the dry timber walls and igniting it with his lighter.

The image of little Leah flickers through his mind, but he pushes it aside. The only thing keeping him going right now is the hope that Fredrik will pay for his crime.

He can't let the thought of Mira's child stop him.

He owes that to his own daughter.

111

It is pitch dark when Hanna comes around. The airbag has deployed, she is freezing cold, and her forehead is throbbing with pain.

It takes a few seconds for her to grasp where she is.

Then she remembers—the crazy chase along the E14, the car behind her that came too close. The impact that made her lose control of her own vehicle.

She turns her head cautiously, trying to see if her neck is injured. Her muscles cooperate; everything seems to be fine except for the pain above her eyes.

When she gently touches the skin, it hurts even more. She brings her finger to her lips and tastes blood.

Panic floods her body. She is trapped in the car, and there are no lights anywhere to be seen. No houses, not a soul in sight.

Where is she?

She was driving through the forest just before she was forced off the road. Everything happened so fast she can't remember where she was, just that the other car was way too close and bumped her from behind.

If the driver wanted to hurt her, then he or she must have followed her all the way from Zuhra's apartment building.

The thought is terrifying, although she should have known that the people exploiting Zuhra would be ruthless.

It is freezing and her teeth are chattering. The cold has penetrated her bones; her shallow breath turns to white vapor. She must have been unconscious for quite some time, because all the warmth has left her body.

She needs to get out of here.

Hanna turns the key. The engine starts—thank God—but the wheels simply spin. She tries putting the car in reverse, but it is going nowhere.

The beam of the headlights illuminates her surroundings. The tall fir trees form a dark wall in every direction; farther away she can see a large rock. The trees are close together, but somehow she has managed to steer between the trunks and stopped the car before hitting anything. Her front fender is no more than three feet away from a huge fir.

The fact that she has survived is practically a miracle.

The realization of how close to death she came makes her whole body start shaking.

If she had collided with the tree, the impact would probably have killed her. As it is, she has sustained only a cut to her forehead. She might well be suffering from concussion too; she feels dizzy and slightly nauseous and is finding it difficult to focus.

Her teeth won't stop rattling, her fingers are ice cold, and she has virtually no feeling in her feet.

She must call Daniel, send for help.

But when she fumbles in her pocket for her phone, she can't find it. Did she have it out when she got into the car? She often puts it on the passenger seat because it's illegal to hold a phone while driving.

She tries hard to remember, but everything is hazy. All she wants to do is sit back and go to sleep.

Her eyelids are heavy, but the nausea is getting worse. She feels so bad that she opens the door to throw up. Her stomach turns itself inside out as she spews onto the snow.

At least it wakes her up.

She absolutely must not fall asleep in the car. If she doesn't get out of here, she could easily freeze to death during the night.

Just like Amanda did.

Hanna forces herself to search systematically for her phone, keeping the engine running. She switches on the interior light and gropes around on the floor by the pedals in case it was thrown off the seat when she slammed on the brakes.

It must be in the car; she can't have dropped it when she ran from the apartment building. She can't be that unlucky.

She bends down as best she can, but finds nothing. If it isn't on the floor, then maybe it's slipped down the side of the driver's seat? She reaches as far as she can between the two front seats—nothing.

Tears of frustration fill her eyes. How could she be stupid enough not to tell Daniel what she was planning to do?

No one knows where she is.

If only she'd at least sent a text.

The nausea is increasing again; she is so tired; the desire to sleep is almost irresistible. She pinches the palm of her hand, forces herself to concentrate.

Could her phone have been thrown the other way, ended up under the back seat?

She doesn't want to get out into the biting cold, but scrambles into the back instead. She kneels down, feels her way slowly across the rubber mats with her fingertips, whispering, "*Please, please.*"

Suddenly she feels something solid. It must be her phone.

The relief is overwhelming. Carefully she teases it out from beneath the passenger seat.

Please don't let it be broken.

Hanna presses the screen, sees it light up.

Then it goes dark again.

She presses it once more, but nothing happens. She knows that the battery wasn't run down when she left home; she should have at least half left.

Then she understands. It's an iPhone; their batteries can't withstand extreme cold. The temperature inside the car has fallen so low that the phone has shut down. It won't work until it has warmed up.

She tucks the phone inside her sweater, inside her bra. The metal is icy, but she tells herself that's a good thing—she needs to stay awake until she can get help. She can keep the engine running for a while, but she doesn't know how long it will last before the battery dies. It is twenty to nine in the evening.

She clambers laboriously back into the driver's seat and settles down. Tries to ignore the pain wrapping itself tightly around her head, like a steel helmet with spikes on the inside.

She is about to switch off the interior light when everything goes black.

Hanna gasps for breath.

She turns the key time after time, but nothing happens. In the end she has to accept that the car is not going to start.

How far can she be from the main road?

Not too far, even though she seems to have lurched some distance into the forest. Maybe she can walk back to the E14, try to stop a car?

The thought of venturing out into the bitter night without a phone or a flashlight makes her break out in a cold sweat. How is she going to find her way to the main road in the dense darkness, even if it's only a few hundred yards? And how is she going to make herself visible to a passing driver? There is a real risk that she will be run over.

The alternative—staying put in a car with the temperature plummeting—isn't much better.

Maybe there's a flashlight in the car?

She opens the glove compartment, pokes around. When she leans forward the pain that shoots through her head is so intense that she screams out loud.

The glove compartment contains only paper and a spare ice scraper.

If she stays here, she will almost certainly fall asleep. Her arms and legs are already growing heavier, she is fighting not to let the tiredness overwhelm her. She doesn't want to freeze to death all alone in the forest.

Setting off on foot is also risking her life. She could easily head in the wrong direction, end up wandering deeper and deeper into the forest.

She retrieves her phone, tries switching it on, but is met by only a black screen.

Once again she curses herself for not letting Daniel know what she was going to do.

Why must she always tackle things on her own? She could have passed on her suspicions about Kristina Risberg, said she was thinking of keeping her under surveillance for a few hours.

Now it's too late. No one has any idea where she's gone.

She has to make a decision. Surely it's better to try and find the main road rather than sit here in the car; it could be hours before anyone finds her.

The darkness envelops her as she opens the door and sets off.

112

The waiter has just placed the freshly made pizza in front of Daniel. He has sought refuge in one of Åre's most popular Italian restaurants, Prima Pasta; he must allow himself a breathing space after the trials and tribulations of the day.

When he's eaten he will go home and fix things with Ida. He longs to see her and Alice; he has an almost physical need to feel his daughter's little warm cheek against his own.

But first he has to gather his thoughts. The news that Lena Halvorssen has tried to take her own life is difficult to deal with. From a purely logical point of view, Daniel knows it isn't his fault, but the despair in Harald's eyes torments him. There seems to be no end to the family's tragedy.

He slices into the pizza, and the aroma of tomato sauce, mozzarella, and salami provides consolation on a deeply primitive level. It makes him think about his mother. She would have understood that he sees himself as a failure right now.

His thoughts return to Amanda. He is becoming increasingly convinced that her secret cleaning job has something to do with her death. Could there be a link between the company and Fredrik Bergfors? It's possible; Bergfors is responsible for many of the newly built houses. As soon as they're finished, the owners need to hire cleaning services.

There is money to be made at every stage along the way.

According to Harald, Mira told him that Fredrik was behind the dog's death. More and more evidence points to Fredrik Bergfors, although Daniel isn't quite ready to dismiss his suspicions concerning Viktor Landahl—or Amanda's adviser.

He remembers the list of the cleaning company's board members that Hanna showed him the other night. Fredrik's name was included, wasn't it?

He is about to get out his phone to check when it buzzes in his back pocket. For a second he is tempted to finish eating before he reads the message, but then his sense of duty takes over.

The text is from an unknown number.

Sorry to bother you, but I believe you've recently started working with my younger sister, Hanna Ahlander. We were supposed to speak at about seven this evening, but I've called several times, and she's not answering. It's not like her at all—I just wanted to make sure that everything is okay.

It is signed by someone named Lydia.

Daniel looks at the time. Ten past nine.

He calls Hanna, but it goes straight to voicemail. He tries again, with the same result.

He last spoke to her at about five thirty. She had just left Ebba's house, and it sounded as if she was on her way home to Sadeln.

That was almost four hours ago.

Where is she, if she didn't go home?

Her sister would hardly have gone to the trouble of finding his number and contacting him if she wasn't concerned.

Daniel glances out of the window. The weather is still horrible. The snow is whirling in the air, and the wind has picked up. The flags in the square are standing to attention in the fierce gale.

He really wants to go home to Ida and Alice, but Lydia's message has worried him.

He sends a quick reply, telling Lydia that he will try to get a hold of Hanna. Then he gets to his feet, looking longingly at the warm pizza. He cuts himself a big piece to take with him, then heads to the counter to pay.

113

The wind is whipping Hanna's face, and it is difficult to make any progress. Snow gives way under her feet on every step as she plods along. Now she understands why the car wouldn't move; there is far too much loose snow for the wheels to get any kind of purchase.

She hunches her shoulders against the icy blast and tries to walk in the tire tracks left by her car. Logically, they should lead her to the road.

The problem is that her surroundings are bewilderingly black and she can hardly see a thing.

The fear of getting lost grows stronger with every step.

Knowing where the car is makes her feel a little better. She can always go back there if she doesn't find the road. But the Mitsubishi disappears from view alarmingly quickly. The more she peers into the darkness, the more uncertain she is of the right direction.

She has spent enough time in the mountains to know how hard it is to retain any kind of composure in darkness and a snowstorm. It is easy to take a wrong turn; that is why people get lost and die in bad weather.

Her lips are stiff, the cold is nipping at her cheeks.

Hanna draws her scarf up higher, but it doesn't help. It is already covered in a thin layer of ice as the moisture from her breath freezes.

She expects her eyes to get used to the gloom, but she still can't see properly. As she doesn't wear a wristwatch and normally relies on her phone to tell the time, she has no idea how long she has been walking.

With every minute she becomes more frightened that she is going the wrong way, heading deeper into the forest.

A car is bound to come along soon. The E14 is a major road; there must be some traffic even if it is late in the evening. She needs only one vehicle; the beam of the headlights will set her right.

She can't hold back the tears; they freeze on her lashes.

She drops to her knees, checking if she is still following the tire tracks. Her face is only a couple of feet from the ground, but it's hard to tell. She stretches out her hand to feel if the snow is flattened. She is so cold she is shaking, but it's wonderful to stop moving for a little while.

Hanna decides to lie down, settles on her side. She can afford to rest for a minute or so; then she will continue.

An attempt to get to her feet is unsuccessful. She isn't strong enough; she needs to rest for a little longer.

The pain in her head eases when she closes her eyes. The snow is soft and welcoming beneath her legs. It wraps itself around her body like lovely cushions, tempts her to snuggle down farther into its embrace.

The part of her brain that is still functioning tells her that she must resist.

She cannot stay out here in the forest, and she absolutely dare not lie down. She needs to reach the E14, get help. Soon her face and fingers will succumb to frostbite.

Either that or she will fall asleep in the snow, never to wake up again.

"I will get going again," she murmurs to herself. "Very soon. I just need a little rest first . . ."

114

The E14 is deserted as Harald drives to the Bergfors family home, his hands gripping the wheel.

By the time he is halfway there, his heart is pounding so hard that he has to pull off at a rest stop.

Air, he needs air.

He is sweating profusely, and the adrenaline is pumping as he presses the button to open the window. Ice-cold air pours in. He takes several deep breaths, and the pressure in his chest eases.

He feels a sudden desire for a cigarette, even though he hasn't smoked for more than ten years.

The headlights of an approaching truck illuminate the roadway. Harald sees his own face in the rearview mirror. The immeasurable depth of sorrow in his eyes. He has made his decision, and he knows that it is the right one. The police are not going to do anything about his daughter's killer; he realized that after Daniel's visit.

That was when he made up his mind.

He puts the car in gear and sets off.

He leaves the main road and parks a few hundred yards away from Fredrik and Mira's property. The wind hits his face as soon as he gets out of the car. The snowstorm shows no sign of abating. He is pleased about the wind; it will fan the flames and make the blaze spread more quickly.

The weather is on his side.

He glances around before opening the trunk to retrieve the gas can. There isn't a soul in sight; he is alone in the darkness.

The street leading to the house is deserted as Harald makes his way up the hill.

He is completely empty inside, he has shut down all his emotions. He was furious earlier on, but now he is calm and focused.

He has a single goal in mind, and that is to punish the man who has destroyed his life.

115

A powerful gust of wind catches Daniel as he leaves the restaurant, making the trees howl. He hurries to his car and sets off for Sadeln to check if Hanna is at home.

Presumably she is. Maybe she has fallen asleep with her phone on silent. Everything is fine.

At the same time, he can't ignore the message from her sister. Her unease is infectious.

When he turns into Hanna's street, he can see that the house is in darkness. He pulls up on the drive; the Mitsubishi he saw last time isn't there. Just to be on the safe side, he gets out of his car and knocks on the door.

The wind is even stronger up here. The halyards on the neighbors' flagpoles are flapping noisily; it sounds as if they are on the point of being ripped off. The cold freezes the back of his neck, and his facial muscles contract involuntarily.

He knocks repeatedly on the front door, but there is no answer. Then he goes around the back and tries to look in through the bedroom windows. Has Hanna gone to bed?

He uses the flashlight on his phone; the rooms are empty.

He gets back in his car. Where can she be? If she is sitting in a bar with a friend, then surely she would have called her sister, or at least answered her phone?

When his phone rings Daniel picks up immediately, hoping it is Hanna. However, it is the regional communications center.

"Yes?"

"I've just heard that one of your colleagues has been involved in a car accident," the unfamiliar voice informs him. "Her name is Hanna Ahlander—I believe she's based in Åre?"

Daniel's stomach turns over. "What's happened?"

"Apparently she came off the E14 between Järpen and Åre. Someone called it in, and when a patrol car got there, they found her in the snow a short distance from the road."

Daniel wedges the phone between his chin and shoulder as he starts the engine; he doesn't want to lose any time. He pushes thoughts of Ida and Alice out of his mind as best he can. "Is she seriously injured?"

"I can't tell you that, but an ambulance is on its way. She mumbled your name."

"Where is she now?" Anxiety makes him sound brusque.

"I'm afraid I don't know."

When Daniel reaches the E14, he ignores the red-and-white stop sign; he puts his foot down and hits the main road at such a speed that his back wheels skid.

The snowflakes in the beam of his headlights are whirling as fast as his thoughts. Hanna is a trained police officer; she knows how to drive safely.

And what was she doing on the road between Järpen and Åre so late in the evening?

The dark fir trees whizz by as he increases his speed. If it was a serious accident, she could be badly hurt.

His anxiety is growing with every passing minute.

Daniel grits his teeth and drives as fast as he can.

116

Harald can't see any lights inside the house when he reaches the fence surrounding the yard.

He puts down the gas can and looks up at the dark facade. The family must be sleeping.

His daughter's murderer is in there, and the reason for his wife's attempted suicide. Fredrik even had to take his bitterness out on their dog. Ludde's dead body is still lying in the garage, wrapped in a sack.

How low can a person sink?

His hand closes around the lighter in his pocket.

Fredrik will never get the chance to harm Harald's family again.

Everything is going to burn to the ground.

Harald looks around to make sure he is still alone, then carries the can around to the back of the house. Slowly and methodically he unscrews the cap and begins to splash the red-painted walls with gasoline. The smell is so strong that his eyes fill with tears. He blinks and blinks, and in the end he doesn't know if he is crying because of the fumes or his grief.

When he has finished, a substantial part of the facade is sodden, including the four balcony posts.

He steps back, stares at the upper floor.

A little voice says that he ought to wake Mira and little Leah, give them a chance to get out before the fire takes hold.

But then he thinks about Amanda.

His daughter wasn't given a chance. Her dead, half-naked body was dumped on a chairlift for all to see.

She was left to freeze to death, alone in the winter night.

And yet he stands there with the lighter in his pocket, unable to bring himself to take it out.

He's not like that, he's not a murderer.

Then he sees Fredrik in his mind's eye, his daughter's killer, and his grip tightens.

117

There is no missing the spot where the accident happened. Several police cars are parked on the E14, and a tow truck is also on the scene. The flashing blue lights do not bode well.

Daniel can see the tire tracks disappearing into the dark forest. The thought that Hanna might have crashed into a tree makes him feel sick.

He leaps out of the car and hurries over to a police officer he recognizes.

"I heard about the accident—what happened to the driver?"

"The ambulance has taken her to Östersund."

"How was she?"

His colleague shakes her head. "Hard to say. She was unconscious, very cold, and her face was covered in blood."

"But she's alive?"

"Well, she was."

The streets of Östersund are deserted when Daniel gets there an hour later. He speeds through the town, parks in a no-park zone outside the hospital, and races toward the emergency department entrance.

There is a line of people waiting at reception. He produces his police ID and pushes his way to the front, ignoring the curious looks.

"Hanna Ahlander," he gasps to the nurse sitting behind a glass screen. "She was brought in by ambulance after a car accident on the E14."

"Let me see . . ."

Daniel is finding it hard to stand still. "Where is she? How is she?"

The nurse raises her eyebrows. "Calm down, please," she says sharply. "You're not the only one who needs my help."

She stares at the screen for what seems like an eternity. "The doctor is with her," she informs Daniel at long last.

"What does that mean?" He has seen enough mangled bodies after serious accidents to fear the worst. "Is she going to need surgery?"

"Sit down over there and wait. Someone will be with you shortly."

He can't help raising his voice. "Can't you tell me how she is?"

"I'm afraid not."

Daniel is so frustrated. He wants to yell at the top of his lungs, but manages to control himself. "At least tell me if she's seriously hurt!"

"As I said, you need to sit down and wait." The nurse switches her attention to the person standing behind Daniel. "Next."

118

Harald is slumped in the driver's seat with his head resting on the steering wheel, his cheeks wet with tears.

He couldn't even manage to do that one simple thing—to punish his daughter's killer. When it came to the crunch, he couldn't bring himself to set fire to the house, although he'd soaked its walls with gasoline.

He is so lost in his own despair that it is a while before he realizes that his phone is vibrating in his pocket. He answers in a voice that is almost breaking.

"Is that Harald Halvorssen?" a woman asks. "I'm calling from the hospital in Östersund—I'm afraid I have some bad news."

"Bad news?"

"I'm very sorry, but your wife passed away a few minutes ago. Things were looking promising, but then she suffered a cardiac arrest. We did everything we could, but we were unable to save her. My condolences."

Harald stares at the phone for several seconds before ending the call.

As he slips it back in his pocket, his fingertips brush against the lighter. With shaking hands he takes it out and holds it up in front of his face. He flicks the wheel, allows the flame to burn for a few seconds; then he gets out of the car and slowly makes his way back up the hill to Fredrik's house.

The snow has settled, in spite of the strong wind. After many weeks the cloud cover is finally breaking up. Harald looks up at the dark vault of the sky, then drops to his knees in the snow, gathering his strength. The house still stinks of gasoline.

Then he cups one hand around the lighter and flicks the wheel again. The flame is strong, surrounded by an orange-red halo. Its glow provides a strange kind of solace; it is beautiful against the white snow in the dark night.

An eye for an eye, a tooth for a tooth.

A primitive phrase that Harald has never believed in. Well, not until this moment.

Now it is completely self-evident.

119

Daniel feels as if he has been waiting forever when a male nurse appears.

"Are you with Hanna Ahlander?"

"Yes."

"She's been transferred from emergency to the medical unit."

Is that good or bad? Daniel doesn't bother asking. He hurries along empty corridors with bare walls and bright lighting. He had never realized how big the hospital was. He gets lost, looks around in vain for someone to ask. Eventually he heads back the way he came, discovers that he should have turned left earlier instead of going straight.

At long last he reaches the medical unit and flings open the door. A gray-haired nurse in her early fifties is at the desk.

"I'm looking for Hanna Ahlander."

"Are you a close relative?"

Daniel lies and says yes. To be on the safe side, he holds up his police ID.

"She's in room seven."

"How is she?"

The nurse slips one hand into her pocket. "She's suffered a serious concussion and has a number of injuries resulting from frostbite, but the doctors don't think she will have any long-term problems. She also has a bad gash on her forehead that needed stitches. Unfortunately it might leave a scar."

Relief floods Daniel's body. "Is she awake?"

"She's been given analgesics, so she's probably asleep, but you're welcome to go in if you like."

Daniel thanks her for the information. He gently pushes open the door of Hanna's room, which is in semidarkness. There is a single lamp at the head of the bed, with a drip stand beside it.

Hanna is lying on her back with her eyes closed. She has a large white dressing on her head. She is very pale, and her cheeks bear the marks of frostbite.

Daniel sits down on the chair next to the bed. He wants to take her hand, but decides against it.

Suddenly Hanna opens her eyes and looks at him. He sees surprise, then pleasure.

"Hi," she whispers. "What are you doing here?"

It's wonderful that she feels well enough to talk.

"How are you, Hanna?"

She tries to summon up a smile, but with limited success.

"I didn't think I was going to make it . . ." Her voice dies away.

"What happened? Are you up to telling me?"

Hanna blinks a couple of times as if she is trying to recall the course of events. Fear flashes across her face. "Someone forced me off the road."

"You mean deliberately?"

She nods. "The car came up from behind. It was way too close and drove into the back of me. I lost control."

Little by little, Daniel coaxes the whole story out of her. She tells him about Kristina Risberg, and Zuhra. By the time she has finished, her face is gray with exhaustion.

"The man I glimpsed leaving Zuhra's apartment . . . I think it was . . ."

She is speaking so quietly that Daniel can hardly hear her. He leans forward, puts his ear close to her mouth.

"Bosse Lundh."

This doesn't make any sense to Daniel. Bosse Lundh from Missing People?

Hanna's eyes close.

"Get some rest," he says softly. Within a couple of minutes, she is asleep.

Daniel stays where he is, trying to digest what Hanna has told him. Zuhra and Amanda both worked for Fjäll-städ. By chance Zuhra showed up at Hanna's house, and Hanna's instinct as a cop told her that something wasn't right.

She got too close, just like Amanda.

Everything is connected.

All at once Daniel realizes how exhausted he is. It is very late; he needs to drive back to Åre. It will be after three by the time he gets home.

He glances at Hanna's sleeping form. Her black eyelashes stand out against her pale skin; her hair is spread across the pillow.

He gently strokes her arm, then silently leaves the room.

SATURDAY, DECEMBER 21

120

Daniel's body is heavy with the lack of sleep but full of adrenaline when he wakes in the restroom at the station at about eight o'clock. He has slept for only a few hours. It was after three by the time he got back to Åre; he couldn't possibly go home to Ida at that hour, even though he had planned to apologize, make things right.

His life is all over the place right now.

After a quick shower he pulls on the clothes he wore yesterday and calls the hospital.

Hanna is doing well, under the circumstances. She has had a peaceful night. They will be keeping her in for another twenty-four hours to monitor her frostbite injuries.

He asks them to tell her he called, then logs in to his computer and searches for the information about the board of the cleaning company known as Fjäll-städ AB. He stares at the list of members, and the whole picture becomes clear.

He hurries along to the conference room to find both the map of Ullådalen and the names of the property owners. Then he messages Anton, asks him to track down a few things and meet him at the station in a couple of hours.

When he has finished he goes down to the garage where the two snowmobiles are parked on their trailers. He hooks one trailer to an unmarked police car and sets off into the bitter winter morning.

It is not yet light when Daniel reaches the parking lot by the café in Ullådalen. There are no other vehicles around; the place is deserted.

He unloads the snowmobile from its trailer, puts on his helmet, and starts the engine. The beam of the headlights slices through the darkness as he speeds through the white landscape, moving easily over the frozen surface. He drives across the lake and continues in a westerly direction toward the mountain before turning off for Holmtjärn.

The only sound disturbing the inhospitable stillness is his own engine. It frightens a hare that has recently acquired its winter coat. The white animal races away and disappears down a slope.

Daniel stops to orient himself.

The air is clear, the sky cloudless. It is a relief to escape the whirling snow and icy winds that have plagued them all through December.

He takes out the land registry map and studies the placement of the properties. There are supposed to be fifteen to twenty smallish cabins, if you discount Prince Carl's hunting lodge.

The sky begins to lighten over by Rödkullen in the east.

Daniel turns his face to the glow and thinks of Hanna. She was the one who found the link with Kristina Risberg, the manager who ferried the women between the houses to be cleaned.

When they went through the list of property owners in Ullådalen, there was another person with the same surname—Annika Risberg. According to Anton, the Risberg family is one of the largest landowners in the area.

Bosse Lundh's live-in partner is Annika Risberg, who is Kristina Risberg's sister.

It can't be a coincidence.

The murderer came by snowmobile from Ullådalen, if Tor Marklund is to be believed.

Daniel finds the Risberg family cabin on the map and starts up his snowmobile once more. It will take him about ten minutes to get there.

The sun is rising above the mountain, the first rays sparkling on the snow.

The brown log cabin with its rusty corrugated metal roof is surrounded by low mountain birch. There is a slender chimney on one side and two solar panels on the roof. The place is small, no more than 120 square feet.

Daniel stops by the door. He walks around the outside, peers in through a half-shuttered window. He can just make out the contours of spartan furnishings: a bunk bed with two stained mattresses, a small table, two chairs, and a stove.

Plenty of snow has fallen since the night Amanda disappeared, but it is still possible to tell that someone has been here in the last week or so.

Just to be sure, Daniel has stopped at the other cabins along the way; they were all snowed in.

He takes his time, examines his surroundings. There is no doubt in his mind. The track leading to the door has recently been cleared; the difference in the snow levels is unmistakable. He photographs everything on his phone.

He returns to the window, peers at the stove. A small pile of ash in front of the opening suggests that it has recently been used. All the wood is gone.

No experienced cabin owner would leave the place like this.

Something is written on the windowsill, right next to the glass. He presses his nose to the pane, screws up his eyes. Eventually sees that someone has managed to scratch a single word:

Amanda

That is all Daniel needs. This must be where Amanda met her death.

The realization is both tragic and liberating.

He gets back on the snowmobile, ready to head across the shimmering white expanse of the mountain once more.

121

Anton is waiting in the conference room and raises his eyebrows when Daniel appears in his snowmobile suit with his helmet under his arm.

"How did it go?" Daniel asks, starting to remove the suit.

"I got the printouts you asked for." Anton lays out three documents on the table. "This is from the tax registry," he says, pointing to the first sheet of paper.

At the top is Annika Risberg's name, personal details, and address, followed by the name of the person who is her live-in partner: Bosse Lundh.

Anton moves on. "This is from the register of snowmobile owners. Bosse Lundh has a black Yamaha snowmobile."

The last document is from the vehicle licensing authority and shows that Bosse Lundh also owns a black Volkswagen SUV.

"I think we've got him," Daniel says slowly. He tells Anton about the cabin in Ullådalen. "If Lundh's DNA matches the particles of skin found under Amanda's fingernails, he's done for. Amanda's DNA will be in his car and in the cabin, and presumably also on the snowmobile sled he used to transport her body to the chairlift."

"Jesus," Anton says, scratching the back of his neck. "Who would have thought it? He was out there searching for her! What a bastard."

Daniel pulls out a chair and sits down. There is still a lot of work to do before they can prove beyond all reasonable doubt that Bosse Lundh murdered Hanna. They can't formally rule out the other suspects—Lasse Sandahl, Fredrik Bergfors, and Viktor Landahl—until the forensic investigation has been completed.

However, Daniel is convinced that Lundh is the perpetrator.

Presumably he was also responsible for Hanna's crash; she thought the car that drove her off the road was dark colored.

Too many people have fallen victim to Bosse Lundh.

Daniel begins to list the steps they need to take over the next twenty-four hours. Bosse Lundh and Annika Risberg will be arrested, along with Kristina Risberg and the as-yet-unidentified Linda. Lundh's car and snowmobile will be impounded, and a team of CSIs will be sent to the cabin in Ullådalen.

Hopefully there will be traces of paint from Hanna's car on the front fender of Lundh's SUV.

He works methodically, point by point.

They need to search Fjäll-städ's office, plus the apartment on Hjortronstigen, where presumably two more Uzbek women are housed. Social services must be brought in to take care of them, and the migration agency will have to be informed. Further down the line, an expert in tax fraud will look into the cleaning company's suspect bookkeeping methods.

This time Daniel has no doubt that the prosecutor will be ready to approve all the necessary measures.

"By the way, did you hear about the fire?" Anton says.

"Sorry?"

"There was a fire at Fredrik Bergfors's place last night."

Daniel stares at him. "What happened?"

"It started around midnight. Apparently it spread incredibly fast, according to the firefighters' report this morning. The whole house was destroyed. They think it was deliberate."

"Arson," Daniel says. He immediately thinks back to his conversation with Harald Halvorssen. Has he taken matters into his own hands? Daniel immediately feels guilty—he should have seen this coming. He was the one who told Harald that Bergfors was a suspect because of Harald's affair with Mira. "What about the family?"

"No one was hurt, but that was pure luck. Apparently the couple had had a massive argument earlier in the evening. Mira took their daughter and went to stay with her parents, while Fredrik slept over at his office. Otherwise they would probably all have died."

Daniel lets out a long breath.

If Harald was responsible for the fire, it's another tragedy—but at least there were no more deaths.

"Someone ought to go and see Harald Halvorssen."

Anton looks at him inquiringly.

"I went to see him yesterday. He was drunk and volatile and had some pretty nasty things to say about Fredrik Bergfors. No one has a stronger motive than Harald."

Anton nods thoughtfully. "I'm on it," he says, picking up his phone. He makes a brief call asking for Halvorssen to be brought in.

Daniel closes his eyes, tries to find fresh energy. He wants to call Ida, but that will have to wait. It's going to be yet another text message, because it's time for the video conference with Birgitta Grip and Tobias Ahlqvist. They are going to work out a plan for the rest of the day, and moving forward.

His gaze falls on Amanda's photograph on the wall. It is the first time since she was found that he can look at her without feeling as if he let her down.

He presses the button to open the meeting.

Time to get the ball rolling.

122

Daniel can see two figures in the kitchen when he arrives at Bosse Lundh and Annika Risberg's house, accompanied by Anton and a team of officers.

The couple is peacefully eating dinner. There is a bottle of wine on the table, and they each have a full glass in front of them. Three candles flicker in the Advent wreath, and the scene is framed by red Christmas curtains at the window.

They look like any other Swedish family on a Saturday evening in December.

Daniel wishes he were at home, sitting at the kitchen table with Ida and Alice.

He adjusts his bulletproof vest, which is chafing one armpit. The regulations dictate that everyone present is similarly equipped. He automatically checks that his service weapon is exactly where it should be.

It is almost six thirty.

Right now other colleagues are about to carry out the same action against Kristina Risberg and Linda Edén—the woman in the cleaning-company office.

The powdery snow gives way beneath their feet as they creep toward the house.

Daniel gives Anton a signal, then nods to the others. It is time.

While he and Anton wait outside, the door is flung open and two officers enter, guns raised.

He hears a woman scream, followed by the sound of breaking glass. Then silence.

When Daniel walks in, Bosse Lundh is on his feet staring at the men as they handcuff him. Annika Risberg is still seated, her face chalk white.

Daniel goes over to Lundh. "You are under arrest for the murder of Amanda Halvorssen, the attempted murder of Hanna Ahlander, and human exploitation," he says.

Anton deals with Annika Risberg.

Lundh blinks in confusion, as if he can't understand what is going on. His mouth opens and closes, but nothing comes out.

Daniel can't help himself. He grabs Lundh by the arm, almost spits out the words. "How the fuck could you pretend to search for Amanda when it was you all along? You let her freeze to death all alone in the cabin—she was just eighteen years old!"

Risberg inhales sharply. "What have you done?" she shouts.

"It was an accident," Lundh replies hoarsely. "I needed time to think, and when I got back it was too late to save her. I didn't think she'd use up all the logs for the stove so quickly."

Daniel looks at him with contempt as two CSIs enter the house. He steps aside and allows his uniformed colleagues to lead Lundh and Risberg out to the waiting police cars.

The flashing blue lights have already attracted the attention of the neighbors.

There is no sense of triumph. Amanda's death is a tragedy, and the consequences for all concerned are horrific. He ought to be delighted with Lundh's confession, but he is too tired. The tension of the past few days has taken its toll, the exhaustion from lack of sleep is throbbing through his body, and he has no idea what state his own relationship is in.

At the end of the day, he failed.

Amanda lost her life.

123

Daniel is standing outside his apartment, keys in hand. His brain is woolly with tiredness.

Following the arrest of Bosse Lundh and Annika Risberg, the team has started a search of their home and the cabin in Ullådalen. Social services are looking after the three girls from Uzbekistan. Kristina Risberg has already admitted that it was Lundh who drove into Hanna's vehicle. They had seen her car and suspected that someone was watching them. They managed to lead Hanna astray so that Lundh could get behind her and force her off the road.

Kristina insists that they simply wanted to frighten her.

Whether they intended to kill her is a matter for further investigation.

Daniel stares at the bunch of flowers in his hand. He stopped at a gas station and bought red roses wrapped in plastic. There is something pathetic about a guy who comes home with less-than-fresh flowers from the gas station, but he couldn't think of anything better.

He is desperate to see his girls.

He unlocks the door, steps inside. The apartment is silent—the television isn't on, and no music is playing. The kitchen is in darkness, but he can see a faint glow from the living room.

"Hello?"

He takes off his jacket and shoes and creeps into the room. Ida is sitting on the sofa, feeding Alice. Her tiny body rests against her mother, who is supporting the baby with her right arm. All Daniel can see is a downy head.

He is a total shit.

What kind of person rushes off and abandons his partner—a new mom—and their infant child for days on end?

A wave of shame floods his body.

This is his family. It's his job to take care of them.

He goes over to the sofa, drops to his knees in front of his girlfriend and daughter, and whispers, "I'm sorry."

Amanda regrets her hasty decision almost as soon as she leaves Ebba's house. It is freezing cold; she starts shivering right away as she walks toward the E14.

Fucking Viktor. Why did he have to get so drunk? She'd really been looking forward to this evening, and he ruined everything.

She reaches the main road and heads east. Walking along the E14 is not particularly smart, but there isn't much traffic at this time of night. She hopes someone will stop and offer her a ride—it's so fucking cold.

A dark SUV approaches, and Amanda sticks up her thumb to let the driver know she wants a ride. It slows down, pulls into the rest stop up ahead. Amanda breaks into a run. The window opens.

"Going my way?"

Amanda smiles gratefully and opens the door to climb in. She immediately recognizes the man behind the wheel: his name is Bosse. Her dad knows him.

He looks at her, seems surprised. "Amanda Halvorssen?"

She nods. "Thanks for stopping—it's super cold out there!" After a brief pause, she adds, "I live on Pilgrimsvägen."

She realizes she has dropped her scarf but doesn't want to ask Bosse to turn around. She will retrace her steps in the morning, see if she can find it.

"Have you been to a party?" Bosse asks.

Amanda nods. "At my friend Ebba's."

She's starting to feel sleepy. It's warm in the car, and she's had too much to drink.

Bosse keeps driving, doesn't turn off for Amanda's road.

"Sorry," she says, pointing. "I live over there."

"I know. But I need to talk to you about something."

Amanda blinks. Like what?

"It's almost as if fate has arranged this, so that you and I can have a little chat," Bosse adds.

Amanda still doesn't understand. "If you just drop me off, I can walk from here," she ventures.

Bosse leaves the E14 and takes a narrow forest track.

Amanda tells herself not to be scared. "I need to get home," she says, trying to sound calm.

Bosse doesn't seem to hear. He doesn't stop the car until they have traveled some distance into the forest. The click as he unfastens his seatbelt makes Amanda uncomfortable.

He turns to face her. The friendly expression has gone, replaced by something much darker.

"Apparently you've been talking to one of my girls," he says.

At first Amanda doesn't know what he's talking about. Then she gets it, and her chest tightens. "Do you mean Zuhra?"

"She talks a whole lot of crap, you don't want to listen to all the stuff she makes up."

The truth becomes clear to Amanda.

She had thought that the man who was exploiting Zuhra was a real pig, a gangster—she could never have imagined that he was someone like Bosse. He's an ordinary guy, a little bit older than her dad, with the same beer gut and sad clothes. She has seen him many times in the grocery store.

She remembers how terrified Zuhra was when she finally confided in Amanda about her life. She had big bruises on her arms, and tears poured down her cheeks.

Amanda promised to help her. She's spent all week trying to work out what she should do.

She stares at Bosse in shock.

"Was it you who hit her?"

Bosse's lips are compressed into a thin line. "She wouldn't keep her fucking mouth shut."

When Amanda looks into Bosse's cold eyes, she understands why Zuhra is so terrified. She glances at the car door, but Bosse is one step ahead of her.

"I've locked it. Now listen to me, and listen carefully. You don't say a word about Zuhra—not to anybody. Understand?"

Amanda tries to swallow her fear. She nods.

"If you so much as mention her existence to a single person, I will punish her. Do you hear me? You won't be the one to pay the price for your big mouth—it will be her, and it will be a lot worse than anything she's experienced so far."

Amanda nods again.

Tears spring to her eyes, but she dare not raise her hand to wipe them away. She hates the fact that he is making her feel so frightened.

She doesn't want to give in.

She doesn't want to become a victim like Zuhra.

Bosse looks calmer now.

"There you go, then," he says with a smile that makes the hairs on Amanda's arms stand on end. "It's good that we've had this chat. I'm glad I saw you walking along the road."

He turns to refasten his seatbelt, clearly pleased with himself.

Amanda hates him for that almost as much as she hates what he is doing to Zuhra.

How can Bosse use his physical strength against someone so vulnerable? Zuhra is an illegal immigrant in a foreign country where she can barely speak the language. She is eighteen years old; she should be in school like Amanda, rather than being forced to clean for twelve hours a day.

Amanda feels a sudden surge of rage that makes her forget everything else.

The alcohol she has consumed gives her extra courage.

Bosse is an asshole.

He can't tell her what to do. She has no intention of letting him have his own way. She is going to get out of this car, and he can't stop her. She starts tugging at the door handle, yelling at the top of her voice, "Let me out, you fucking idiot!" When the door doesn't open, she punches him on the shoulder as hard as she can. "I'm going to tell my dad! I'm going to tell him everything!"

Bosse reacts much faster than Amanda thought possible. She just has time to feel surprised before he hurls himself at her and grabs her upper arms. At first she can't move, but then she manages to free one hand and scratches his forehead, by the hairline.

Suddenly his hands close around her throat.

He tightens his grip, she can't breathe.

"You will do as I say!" he hisses.

Amanda tries desperately to prize his fingers away. She twists and jerks her body in an attempt to free herself, but Bosse is much too strong.

She doesn't have a chance.

He is so close that she can see his wide-open eyes, a tiny amount of saliva at one corner of his mouth.

Then she runs out of oxygen and everything goes black.

SUNDAY, DECEMBER 22

124

The sunlight is dancing across the ice on Lake Åre when Hanna's hospital transport reaches the turn-off toward Björnen. Stjärnbacken and Hummelbranten can be seen up above the village, two clear pistes following the slope of the mountain. All the lifts are open, and the tiny figures of enthusiastic skiers are swishing downhill.

Åreskutan is majestic as always, the top station highlighted against the clear blue sky.

Hanna is sitting in the back seat. She is still tired and weak, but very happy to be out of the hospital.

The car begins to climb the hill to Björnen. On the sharpest bend a frozen waterfall hangs from the rock face. The gray-green cascade has been halted by the intense cold, as if time has stopped for a moment. Layer upon layer of ice shimmers in the sun.

The fir trees, weighed down with snow, form a fairy-tale landscape as the driver continues toward Sadeln.

Hanna pulls her jacket more tightly around her body.

Did she do the right thing, investigating Kristina Risberg on her own initiative? She can't help wondering. She'd promised herself that she would keep a low profile in her new job; instead she did the exact opposite.

Will they still want her?

It had sounded that way when she spoke to Daniel. He told her about the arrests, and Lundh's confession. He called this morning to see how she was before she was discharged.

Without Hanna's research, they would never have found the connection. Daniel underlined that point several times, and she is desperate to believe him. She doesn't want to lose the chance of working with him in the future.

She remembers how safe she felt when he arrived at the hospital and sat by her bed.

Things seem to be working out with Christian too.

Lydia called earlier and said that she'd told him what had happened and why Hanna hadn't been in touch. When he heard about the accident, all his anger melted away. He won't be reporting her to the police.

She can relax.

As the car turns into Sadeln and stops in front of the house, she sees her sister in the doorway. Lydia insisted on flying up to welcome her, even though she will shortly be off on a cruise with her family. As usual, she wouldn't take no for an answer. She was adamant that Hanna shouldn't come home to an empty house after the car crash. She is staying until tomorrow and has shopped for Christmas food and everything else Hanna might need.

Hanna's eyes fill with tears at the sight of Lydia. The situation with her parents is what it is, but Lydia is there for her.

In two days it will be Christmas Eve. Hanna had almost forgotten.

ÖSTERSUNDS-POSTEN, JULY 7, 2020

Today the verdicts were delivered in the case of the human trafficking operation that was exposed in Åre during the winter. Bo Lundh, Annika Risberg, Kristina Risberg, and Linda Edén were convicted of the exploitation of three young women from Uzbekistan, who were lured to Sweden on false premises.

The situation came to light when eighteen-year-old Amanda Halvorssen disappeared under mysterious circumstances on the night before Lucia last year.

After an extensive investigation, Bo Lundh was charged with a number of serious crimes, including the attempted homicide of a female police officer after following her car at high speed and forcing her off the road.

Bo Lundh was sentenced to sixteen years' imprisonment for homicide, attempted homicide, and human exploitation. His partner, Annika Risberg, was sentenced to four years' imprisonment. Kristina Risberg was sentenced to eight years, and Linda Edén to two years and six months.

Amanda Halvorssen's father, the former chair of the council, has declined to comment. He was recently given a suspended sentence for arson in a tragic aftermath to his daughter's death.

All the defendants have signaled their intention to appeal.

ACKNOWLEDGMENTS

There is a deep connection between the mountains and the archipelago. It is something to do with the power of nature, the uninterrupted horizon, and the magnificent beauty that makes it easy to feel at home in both landscapes.

When the Coronavirus pandemic struck, I happened to be in Åre, and I remained there due to travel restrictions. Inspiration grew as time passed, and in the end I had written a crime novel set in the mountains of Jämtland, which became *Hidden in Snow*.

As an author writing the first book in a new series in a completely new environment, I relied heavily on help from kind people in the area.

Two individuals who have been invaluable during the writing process are Ulrika Baumann Edblad and Anders Edblad. Thank you so much for reading, commenting, and providing various contacts to facilitate my research. I would also like to thank Tuva Edblad, who helped me with background information about school and the lives of young people in Åre and Järpen.

Thank you to everyone in Åre who so generously shared their expertise and knowledge.

Fredrik Nyhlén, formerly with the Åre police and now with the customs authority, was able to tell me about the police service in the area over the past ten years.

Anders Aspholm, business area manager with SkiStar, helped me to understand how the company and the skiing facilities in Åre work.

Markus Kristoffersson and Andreas Lundin, investigating officers with the Åre police, described the local police station and the daily routine.

Anders Berge, a landowner in Ullådalen, took me on a long snowmobile trip to look for a good place to "hide a body."

Inger Fritzon, a teacher at Jämtland High School, told me about the school environment in Åre and Järpen.

Thanks also to Detective Inspector Rolf Hansson, who has once again answered countless questions on police work, and Judge Cecilia Klerbro, my good friend, who gave valuable opinions on prosecution and sentencing with regard to the events in this novel. My dear friends Anette Brifalk, Helen Duphorn, and Madeleine Lyrvall have all read and commented on the manuscript during the writing process. Thank you so much!

As always I have taken certain liberties—there are no roads in Åre or Järpen called Västra Sadelviksvägen or Hjortronstigen. Lydia's house is inspired by many different beautiful homes, and the chairlifts in Åre are actually tested earlier in the morning.

I also have the greatest respect for the work that Missing People does and hope no one will be offended by the fact that I have involved the organization in my story.

I take full responsibility for any errors in the narrative.

No author is an island, and *Hidden in Snow* is definitely the result of fantastic teamwork. Without the support of my committed publisher, Ebba Östberg; my good friend and developmental editor, John Häggblom; and my outstanding and tireless editor, Lisa Jonasdotter Nilsson, this would have been a very different and much worse book. A big thank-you to all of you—it is a privilege to work with you, as it is with the super-professional Sofia Heurlin and everyone else at Ester Bonnier, plus the gang at Micael Bindefeld AB.

Thanks also to my dedicated assistant, Madeleine Jonsson, who organizes my life and makes sure I can keep my head above water.

Anna Frankl, thank you for always being there!

Finally—thank you to my beloved husband, Lennart, who read the manuscript so meticulously, and my darling children, Camilla, Alexander, and Leo. Without you nothing would matter.

Åre, September 22, 2020
Viveca Sten

ABOUT THE AUTHOR

Photo © 2021 Niclas Vestefjell

Viveca Sten is the author of the #1 internationally bestselling Sandhamn Murders series, which includes *Buried in Secret*, *In Bad Company*, *In the Name of Truth*, *In the Shadow of Power*, *In Harm's Way*, *In the Heat of the Moment*, *Tonight You're Dead*, *Guiltless*, *Closed Circles*, and *Still Waters*. Since 2008, the series has sold more than seven million copies, establishing her as one of Sweden's most popular authors. Set on the island of Sandhamn, the novels have been adapted into a Swedish-language TV series shot on location and seen by ninety million viewers around the world. Viveca lives in Stockholm with her husband and three children, but she alternates between Sandhamn in the summer and Åre in the winter, where she writes and vacations with her family. For more information visit www.vivecasten.com.

ABOUT THE TRANSLATOR

Marlaine Delargy lives in Shropshire in the United Kingdom. She studied Swedish and German at the University of Wales, Aberystwyth, and she taught German for almost twenty years. She has translated novels by many authors, including Kristina Ohlsson; Helene Tursten; John Ajvide Lindqvist; Therese Bohman; Theodor Kallifatides; Johan Theorin, with whom she won the Crime Writers' Association International Dagger in 2010; and Henning Mankell, with whom she won the Crime Writers' Association International Dagger in 2018. Marlaine has also translated nine books in Viveca Sten's Sandhamn Murders series.